RANDOM HOUSE
LARGE PRINT

# THE BOOK OF LOST FRIENDS

# THE BOOK **of** LOST FRIENDS

**A Novel**

LISA WINGATE

RANDOM HOUSE
LARGE PRINT

**The Book of Lost Friends** is a work of fiction. All incidents and dialogue, and all characters with the exception of some well-known historical figures, are products of the author's imagination and are not to be construed as real. Where real-life historical persons appear, the situations, incidents, and dialogues concerning those persons are entirely fictional and are not intended to depict actual events or to change the entirely fictional nature of the work. In all other respects, any resemblance to persons living or dead is entirely coincidental.


Published in the United States of America by Random House Large Print in association with Ballantine Books, an imprint of Penguin Random House LLC.

Cover design: Ella Laytham
Cover Photographs: gift of A. H. Belo Corporation / Bridgeman Images (landscape); Pobytov/ Getty Images (tree); LiliGraphie/ Getty Images, da-kuk/ Getty Images (paper texture)

The Library of Congress has established a Cataloging-in-Publication record for this title.

ISBN: 978-0-593-28641-8

www.penguinrandomhouse.com/large-print-format-books

FIRST LARGE PRINT EDITION

Printed in the United States of America

10 9 8 7 6 5 4 3 2 1

This Large Print edition published in accord with the standards of the N.A.V.H.

**To Gloria Close, for helping today's families find safe homes.**

**To Andy and Diane, and to the dedicated keepers of the Historic New Orleans Collection. Thank you for preserving the history.**

**To the Lost Friends, wherever you might be. May your names never go unspoken and your stories forever be told.**

# THE BOOK OF LOST FRIENDS

## Prologue

A single ladybug lands featherlight on the teacher's finger, clings there, a living gemstone. A ruby with polka dots and legs. Before a slight breeze beckons the visitor away, an old children's rhyme sifts through the teacher's mind.

**Ladybug, ladybug, fly away home,**
**Your house is on fire, and your children**
**are gone.**

The words leave a murky shadow as the teacher touches a student's shoulder, feels the damp warmth beneath the girl's roughly woven calico dress. The hand-stitched neckline hangs askew over smooth amber-brown skin, the garment a little too large for the girl inside it. A single puffy scar protrudes from one loosely buttoned cuff. The teacher wonders briefly about its cause, resists allowing her mind to speculate.

**What would be the point?** she thinks.

**We all have scars.**

She glances around the makeshift gathering place under the trees, the rough slabwood benches crowded with girls on the verge of womanhood, boys seeking to step into the world of men. Leaning over crooked tables littered with nib pens, blotters, and inkwells, they read their papers, mouthing the words, intent upon the important task ahead.

All except this one girl.

"Fully prepared?" the teacher inquires, her head angling toward the girl's work. "You've practiced reading it aloud?"

"I can't do it." The girl sags, defeated in her own mind. "Not . . . not with **these** people looking on." Her young face casts miserably toward the onlookers who have gathered at the fringes of the open-air classroom—moneyed men in well-fitting suits and women in expensive dresses, petulantly waving off the afternoon heat with printed handbills and paper fans left over from the morning's fiery political speeches.

"You never know what you can do until you try,"

the teacher advises. Oh, how familiar that girlish insecurity is. Not so many years ago, the teacher **was** this girl. Uncertain of herself, overcome with fear. Paralyzed, really.

"I **can't,**" the girl moans, clutching her stomach.

Bundling cumbersome skirts and petticoats to keep them from the dust, the teacher lowers herself to catch the girl's gaze. "Where will they hear the story if not from you—the story of being stolen away from family? Of writing an advertisement seeking any word of loved ones, and hoping to save up the fifty cents to have it printed in the **Southwestern** paper, so that it might travel through all the nearby states and territories? How will they understand the desperate need to finally know, **Are my people out there, somewhere?**"

The girl's thin shoulders lift, then wilt. "These folks ain't here because they care what I've got to say. It won't change anything."

"Perhaps it will. The most important endeavors require a risk." The teacher understands this all too well. Someday, she, too, must strike off on a similar journey, one that involves a risk.

Today, however, is for her students and for the "Lost Friends" column of the **Southwestern Christian Advocate** newspaper, and for all it represents. "At the very least, we must tell our stories, mustn't we? Speak the names? You know, there is an old proverb that says, 'We die once when the last breath leaves our bodies. We die a second time when the last person speaks our name.' The first death is beyond our control, but the second one we can strive to prevent."

"If you say so," the girl acquiesces, tenuously drawing a breath. "But I best do it right off, so I don't lose my nerve. Can I go on and give my reading before the rest?"

The teacher nods. "If you start, I'm certain the others will know to follow." Stepping back, she surveys the remainder of her group. **All the stories here,** she thinks. **People separated by impossible distance, by human fallacy, by cruelty. Enduring the terrible torture of not knowing.**

And though she'd rather not—she'd give anything if not—she imagines her own scar. One hidden beneath the skin where no one else can see it. She thinks of her own lost love, out there. Somewhere. Who knows where?

A murmur of thinly veiled impatience stirs among the audience as the girl rises and proceeds along the aisle between the benches, her posture stiffening to a strangely regal bearing. The frenzied motion of paper fans ceases and fluttering handbills go silent when she turns to speak her piece, looking neither left nor right.

"I . . ." her voice falters. Rimming the crowd with her gaze, she clenches and unclenches her fingers, clutching thick folds of the blue-and-white calico dress. Time seems to hover then, like the ladybug deciding whether it will land or fly on.

Finally, the girl's chin rises with stalwart determination. Her voice carries past the students to the audience, demanding attention as she speaks a name that will not be silenced on this day. "I am Hannie Gossett."

## Lost Friends

We make no charge for publishing these letters from subscribers. All others will be charged fifty cents. Pastors will please read the requests published below from their pulpits, and report any case where friends are brought together by means of letters in the SOUTHWESTERN.

Dear Editor—I wish to inquire for my people. My mother was named Mittie. I am the middle of nine children and named Hannie Gossett. The others were named Hardy, Het, Pratt, Epheme, Addie, Easter, Ike, and Rose and were all my mother had when separated. My grandmother was Caroline and my grandfather Pap Ollie. My aunt was Jenny, who was married to Uncle Clem until he died in the war. Aunt Jenny's children were four girls, Azelle, Louisa, Martha, and Mary. Our first owner was William Gossett of Goswood Grove Plantation, where we were raised and kept until our Marse was in plans to take us from Louisiana to Texas during the war, to refugee in Texas and form a new plantation there. During plans, we encountered the difficulty of being stolen in a group from the Gossetts by Jeptha Loach, a nephew of Missus Gossett. He carried us from the Old River Road south of Baton Rouge, northward and westward across Louisiana, toward Texas. My brothers and sisters, cousins and aunt were sold and carried from us in Big Creek, Jatt, Winfield, Saline, Kimballs, Greenwood, Bethany, and finally

Powell town, Texas, where my mother was taken and never seen by me again. I am now grown, being the only one of us who was rejected by my purchaser in Marshall, Texas, and returned to the Gossetts after the facts of my true ownership became clear. I am well, but my mother is greatly missed by me, and any information of her or any of my people is dearly desired.

I pray that all pastors and friends discovering this plea will heed the desperate call of a broken heart and send word to me in care of Goswood Grove Store, Augustine, Louisiana. Any information will be acceptable and thankfully received.

# CHAPTER 1

## HANNIE GOSSETT—LOUISIANA, 1875

The dream takes me from quiet sleep, same way it's done many a time, sweeps me up like dust. Away I float, a dozen years to the past, and sift from a body that's almost a woman's into a little-girl shape only six years old. Though I don't want to, I see what my little-girl eyes saw then.

I see buyers gather in the trader's yard as I peek through the gaps in the stockade log fence. I stand in winter-cold dirt tramped by so many feet before my own two. Big feet like Mama's and small feet like mine and tiny feet like Mary Angel's. Heels and toes that's left dents in the wet ground.

**How many others been here before me?**

I wonder. **How many with hearts rattlin' and muscles knotted up, but with no place to run?**

Might be a hundred hundreds. Heels by the doubles and toes by the tens. Can't count high as that. I just turned from five years old to six a few months back. It's Feb'ary right now, a word I can't say right, ever. My mouth twists up and makes **Feb-ba-ba-ba-bary,** like a sheep. My brothers and sisters've always pestered me hard over it, all eight, even the ones that's younger. Usually, we'd tussle if Mama was off at work with the field gangs or gone to the spinnin' house, cording wool and weaving the homespun.

Our slabwood cabin would rock and rattle till finally somebody fell out the door or the window and went to howlin'. That'd bring Ol' Tati, cane switch ready, and her saying, "Gonna give you a breshin' with this switch if you don't shesh now." She'd swat butts and legs, just play-like, and we'd scamper one over top the other like baby goats scooting through the gate. We'd crawl up under them beds and try to hide, knees and elbows poking everywhere.

Can't do that no more. All my mama's children been carried off one by one and two by two. Aunt Jenny Angel and three of her four girls, gone, too. Sold away in trader yards like this one, from south Louisiana almost to Texas. My mind works hard to keep account of where all we been, our numbers dwindling by the day, as we tramp behind Jep Loach's wagon, slave chains pulling the grown folk by the wrist, and us children left with no other choice but to follow on.

But the nights been worst of all. We just hope Jep Loach falls to sleep quick from whiskey and the day's travel. It's when he don't that the bad things happen—to Mama and Aunt Jenny both, and now just to Mama, with Aunt Jenny sold off. Only Mama and me left now. Us two and Aunt Jenny's baby girl, li'l Mary Angel.

Every chance there is, Mama says them words in my ear—who's been carried away from us, and what's the names of the buyers that took them from the auction block and where're they gone to. We start with Aunt Jenny, her three oldest girls. Then come my brothers and sisters, oldest to youngest, **Hardy at Big Creek, to a man name LeBas from Woodville. Het at Jatt carried off by a man name Palmer from Big Woods. . . .**

**Prat, Epheme, Addie, Easter, Ike, and Baby Rose,** tore from my mama's arms in a place called Bethany. Baby Rose wailed and Mama fought and begged and said, "We gotta be kept as one. The baby ain't weaned! Baby ain't . . ."

It shames me now, but I clung on Mama's skirts and cried, "Mama, no! Mama, no! Don't!" My body shook and my mind ran wild circles. I was afraid they'd take my mama, too, and it'd be just me and little cousin Mary Angel left when the wagon rolled on.

Jep Loach means to put all us in his pocket before he's done, but he sells just one or two at each place, so's to get out quick. Says his uncle give him the permissions for all this, but that ain't true. Old Marse and Old Missus meant for him to do what folks all over south Louisiana been doing since the Yankee gunboats pushed on upriver from New Orleans—take their slaves west so the Federals can't set us free. Go refugee on the Gossett land in Texas till the war is over. That's why they sent us with Jep Loach, but he's stole us away, instead.

"Marse Gossett gonna come for us soon's he learns of bein' crossed by Jep Loach," Mama's promised over and over. "Won't matter about Jep bein' nephew to Old Missus then. Marse gonna send Jep off to the army for the warfaring then. Only reason Jep ain't wearin' that gray uniform a'ready is Marse been paying Jep's way out. This be the end of that, and all us be shed of Jep for good. You wait and see. And that's why we chant the names, so's we know where to gather the lost when Old Marse comes. You put it deep in your rememberings, so's you can tell it if you're the one gets found first."

But now hope comes as thin as the winter light through them East Texas piney woods, as I squat inside that log pen in the trader's yard. Just Mama and me and Mary Angel here, and one goes today. One, at least. More coins in the pocket, and whoever don't get sold tramps on with Jep Loach's wagon. He'll hit the liquor right off, happy he got away with it one more time, thieving from his own kin. All Old Missus's people—all the Loach family—just bad apples, but Jep is the rottenest, worse as Old Missus, herself. She's the devil, and he is, too.

"Come 'way from there, Hannie," Mama tells me. "Come here, close."

Of a sudden, the door's open, and a man's got Mary Angel's little arm, and Mama clings on, tears making a flood river while she whispers to the trader's man, who's big as a mountain and dark as a deer's eye, "We ain't his. We been stole away from Marse William Gossett of Goswood Grove plantation, down by the River Road south from Baton Rouge. We been carried off. We . . . been . . . we . . ."

She goes to her knees, folds over Mary Angel like she'd take that baby girl up inside of her if she could. "Please. Please! My sister, Jenny, been sold by this man already. And all her children but this li'l one, and all my children 'cept my Hannie. Fetch us last three out together. Fetch us out, all three. Tell your marse this baby girl, she sickly. Say we gotta be sold off in one lot. All three together. Have mercy. Please! Tell your marse we been stole from Marse William Gossett at Goswood Grove, down off the River Road. We stole property. We been **stole.**"

The man's groan comes old and tired. "Can't do nothin'. Can't nobody do nothin' 'bout it all. You just make it go hard on the child. You just make it go hard. Two gotta go today. In two dif'ernt lots. One at a time."

"No." Mama's eyes close hard, then open again. She looks up at the man, coughs out words and tears and spit all together. "Tell my marse William Gossett—when he comes here seeking after us—at least give word of where we gone to. Name who carries us away and where they strikes off for. Old Marse Gossett's gonna find us, take us to refugee in Texas, all us together."

The man don't answer, and Mama turns to Mary Angel, slips out a scrap of brown homespun cut from the hem of Aunt Jenny Angel's heavy winter petticoat while we camped with the wagon. By their own hands, Mama and Aunt Jenny Angel made fifteen tiny poke sacks, hung with jute strings they stole out of the wagon.

Inside each bag went three blue glass beads off the string Grandmama always kept special. Them beads was her most precious thing, come all the way from Africa. **That where my grandmama and grandpoppy's cotched from.** She'd tell that tale by the tallow candle on winter nights, all us gathered round her lap in that ring of light. Then she'd share about Africa, where our people been before here. Where they was queens and princes.

**Blue mean all us walk in the true way. The fam'ly be loyal, each to the other, always and ever,** she'd say, and then her eyes would gather at the corners and she'd take out that string of beads and let all us pass it in the circle, hold its weight in our hands. Feel a tiny piece of that far-off place . . . and the meanin' of blue.

Three beads been made ready to go with my li'l cousin, now.

Mama holds tight to Mary Angel's chin. "This a promise." Mama tucks that pouch down Mary Angel's dress and ties the strings round a skinny little baby neck that's still too small for the head on it. "You hold it close by, li'l pea. If that's the only thing you do, you keep it. This the sign of your people. We lay our eyes on each other again in this life, no matter how long it be from now, this how we, each of us, knows the other one. If long time pass, and you get up big, by the beads we still gonna know you. Listen at me. You hear Aunt Mittie, now?" She makes a motion with her hands. A needle and thread. Beads on a string. "We put this string back together someday, all us. In this world, God willing, or in the next."

Li'l Mary Angel don't nod nor blink nor speak. Used to, she'd chatter the ears off your head, but not no more. A big ol' tear spills down her brown skin as the man carries her out the door, her arms and legs stiff as a carved wood doll's.

Time jumps round then. Don't know how, but I'm back at the wall, watching betwixt the logs while Mary Angel gets brung 'cross the yard. Her little brown shoes dangle in the air, same brogans all us got in our Christmas boxes just two month ago, special made right there on Goswood by Uncle Ira, who kept the tanner shop, and mended the harness, and sewed up all them new Christmas shoes.

I think of him and home while I watch Mary Angel's little shoes up on the auction block. Cold wind snakes over her skinny legs when her dress gets pulled up and the man says she's got good, straight knees. Mama just weeps. But somebody's got to listen for who takes Mary Angel. Somebody's got to add her to the chant.

So, I do.

Seems like just a minute goes by before a big hand circles my arm, and it's me getting dragged 'cross the floor. My shoulder wrenches loose with a pop. The heels of my Christmas shoes furrow the dirt like plow blades.

"No! Mama! Help me!" My blood runs wild. I fight and scream, catch Mama's arm, and she catches mine.

**Don't let go,** my eyes tell hers. Of a sudden, I understand the big man's words and how come they broke Mama down. **Two gotta go today. In two dif'ernt lots. One at a time.**

This is the day the worse happens. Last day for me and Mama. Two gets sold here and one goes on with Jep Loach, to get sold at the next place down the road. My stomach heaves and burns in my throat, but ain't nothing there to retch up. I make water down my leg, and it fills up my shoe and soaks over to the dirt.

"Please! Please! Us two, together!" Mama begs.

The man kicks her hard, and our hands rip apart at the weave. Mama's head hits the logs, and she crumples in the little dents from all them other feet, her face quiet like she's gone asleep. A tiny brown poke dangles in her hand. Three blue beads roll loose in the dust.

"You give me any trouble, and I'll shoot her dead where she lies." The voice runs over me on spider legs. Ain't the trader's man that's got me. It's Jep Loach. I ain't being carried to the block. I'm being took to the devil wagon. I'm the one he means to sell at the someplace farther on.

I tear loose, try to run back to Mama, but my knees go soft as wet grass. I topple and stretch my fingers toward the beads, toward my mother.

"Mama! Mama!" I scream and scream and scream. . . .

It's my own voice that wakes me from the dream of that terrible day, just like always. I hear the sound of the scream, feel the raw of it in my throat. I come to, fighting off Jep Loach's big hands and crying out for the mother I ain't laid eyes on in twelve years now, since I was a six-year-old child.

"Mama! Mama! Mama!" The word spills from me three times more, travels out 'cross the night-quiet fields of Goswood Grove before I clamp my mouth closed and look back over my shoulder toward the sharecrop cabin, hoping they didn't hear me. No sense to wake everybody with my sleep-wanderings. Hard day's work ahead for me and Ol' Tati and what's left of the stray young ones she's raised these long years since the war was over and we had no mamas or papas to claim us.

Of all my brothers and sisters, of all my family stole away by Jep Loach, I was the only one Marse Gossett got back, and that was just by luck when folks at the next auction sale figured out I was stole property and called the sheriff to hold me until Marse could come. With the war on, and folks running everywhere to get away from it, and us trying to scratch a living from the wild Texas land, there wasn't any going back to look for the rest. I was a child with nobody of my own when the Federal soldiers finally made their way to our refugee place in Texas and forced the Gossetts to read the free papers out loud and say the war was over, even in Texas. Slaves could go where they pleased, now.

Old Missus warned all us we wouldn't make it five miles before we starved or got killed by road agents or scalped by Indians, and she hoped we did, if we'd be ungrateful and foolish enough to do such a thing as leave. With the war over, there wasn't no more need to refugee in Texas, and we'd best come back to Louisiana with her and Marse Gossett—who we was now to call **Mister,** not **Marse,** so's not to bring down the wrath of Federal soldiers who'd be crawling over everything like lice for a while yet. Back on the old place at Goswood Grove, we would at least have Old **Mister** and Missus to keep us safe and fed and put clothes on our miserable bodies.

"Now, you young children have no choice in the matter," she told the ones of us with no folk. "You are in our charge, and of course we will give you the benefit of transporting you away from this godforsaken Texas wilderness, back to Goswood Grove until you are of age or a parent comes to claim you."

Much as I hated Old Missus and working in the house as keeper and plaything to Little Missy Lavinia, who was a trial of her own, I rested in the promise Mama had spoke just two years before at the trader's yard. She'd come to find me, soon's she could. She'd find all us, and we'd string Grandmama's beads together again.

And so I was biddable but also restless with hope. It was the restless part that spurred me to wander at night, that conjured evil dreams of Jep Loach, and watching my people get stole away, and seeing Mama laid out on the floor of the trader's pen. Dead, for all I could know then.

For all I still **do** know.

I look down and see that I been walking in my sleep again. I'm standing out on the old cutoff pecan stump. A field of fresh soil spreads out, the season's new-planted crop still too wispy and fine to cover it. Moon ribbons fall over the row tips, so the land is a giant loom, the warp threads strung but waiting on the weaving woman to slide the shuttle back and forth, back and forth, making cloth the way the women slaves did before the war. Spinning houses sit empty now that store-bought calico comes cheap from mills in the North. But back in the old days when I was a little child, it was card the cotton, card the wool. Spin a broach of thread every night after tromping in from the field. That was Mama's life at Goswood Grove. Had to be or she'd have Old Missus to deal with.

This stump—this very one—was where the slave driver stood to watch the gangs work the field, cowhide whip dangling down like a snake ready to bite, keep everybody picking the cotton rows. Somebody lag behind, try to rest a minute, the driver would find them out. If Old Marse Gossett was home, they'd only get a little breshin' with the whip. But if Marse Gossett was off in New Orleans, where he kept his **other** family everybody knew about but didn't dare to speak of, then look out. The whipping would be bad, because Old Missus was in charge. Missus didn't like it that her husband had him a **plaçage** woman and a fawn-pale child down in New Orleans. Neighborhoods like Faubourg Marigny and Tremé—the rich planter men kept their mistresses and children there. Fancy girls, quadroons and octoroons. Women with dainty bones and olive-brown skin, living in fine houses with slaves to look after them, too.

Old ways like that been almost gone in these years since Mr. Lincoln's war ended. The slave driver and his whip, Mama and the field gangs working from see to can't see, leg irons, and auction sales like the ones that took my people—all that's a thing in the barely back of my mind.

Sometimes when I wake, I think all my people were just somethin' I pretended, never real at all. But then I touch the three glass beads on the cord at my neck, and I tell their names in the chant. **Hardy gone at Big Creek to a man from Woodville, Het at Jatt . . .**

All the way down to Baby Rose and Mary Angel. And Mama.

It was real. **We** were real. A family together.

I look off in the distant, wobble twixt a six-year-old body and one that's eighteen years growed, but not so much different. Still skinny as if I was carved out of sticks.

Mama always did say, **Hannie, you stand behind the broom handle, I can't even see you there.** Then she'd smile and touch my face and whisper, **But you a beautiful child. Always been pretty.** I hear it like she's there beside of me, a white oak basket on her arm, bound for the garden patch out behind our little cabin, last one down the end of the old quarters.

Just as quick as I feel her there, she's gone again.

"Why didn't you come?" My words hang in the night air. "Why didn't you come for your child? You never come." I sink down on the stump's edge and look out toward the trees by the road, their thick trunks hid in sifts of moon and fog.

I think I see something in it. A haint, could be.

**Too many folk buried under Goswood soil,** Ol' Tati says when she tells us tales in the cropper cabin at night. **Too much blood and sufferin' been left here. This place always gonna have ghosts.**

A horse nickers low. I see a rider on the road. A dark cloak covers the head and sweeps out, light as smoke.

That my mama, come to find me? Come to say, **You almost eighteen years old, Hannie. Why you still settin' on that same ol' stump?** I want to go to her. Go away with her.

That Old Mister, come home from fetching his wicked son out of trouble again?

That a haint, come to drag me off and drown me in the river?

I close my eyes, shake my head clear, look again. Nothing there but a drift of fog.

"Child?" Tati's whisper comes from a ways off, worried, careful-like. "Child?" Don't matter your age, if Tati raised you, you stay **child** to her. Even the strays that've growed up and moved on, they're still **child,** if they come to visit.

I cock my ear, open my mouth to answer her, but then I can't.

Somebody **is** there—a woman by the high white pillars at the Goswood gate, afoot now. The oaks whisper overhead, like it's worried their old bones to have her come to the drive. A low-hung branch grabs her hood and her long, dark hair floats free.

"M-mama?" I say.

"Child?" Tati whispers again. "You there?" I hear her hurry along, her walking stick tapping faster till she's found me.

"I see Mama coming."

"You dreamin', sugar." Tati's knobby fingers wrap my wrist, gentle-like, but she keeps a distant. Sometimes, my dreams let go with a fight. I wake kicking and clawing to get Jep Loach's hand off my arm. "Child, you all right. You just walkin' in the dream. Wake up, now. Mama ain't here, but Ol' Tati, she right here. You safe."

I glance away from the gates, then back. The woman's gone, and no matter how hard I look, I can't see her.

"Wake up, now, child." In moonglow, Tati's face is the red-brown of cypress wood pulled up from the deep water, dark against the sack-muslin cap over her silvery hair. She slides a shawl off her arm, reaches it round me. "Out here in the field in all the wetness! Get a pleurisy. Where all us be with that kind of troublement? Who Jason gonna settle in with, then?"

Tati nudges me with the cane stick, pestering. The thing she wants most is for Jason and me to marry. Once the ten years on the sharecrop contract with Old Mister is done and the land is hers, Tati needs somebody to hand it down to. Me and the twins, Jason and John, are the last of her strays. One more growing season is all that's left for the contract, but Jason and me? We been raised in Tati's house like brother and sister. Hard to see things any other way, but Jason is a good boy. Honest worker, even if both him and John did come into this world a shade slower minded than most.

"I ain't dreamin'," I say when Tati tugs me from the stump.

"Devil, you ain't. Come on back, now. We got work waitin' in the mornin'. Gonna tie your ankle to the bed, you don't stop dealing me this night misery. You been worser lately. Worser in these walkin' dreams than when you was a li'l thing."

I jerk against Tati's arm, remembering all the times as a child I wandered from my sleep pallet by Missy Lavinia's crib, and woke up to Old Missus whipping me with the kitchen spoon or a riding whip or a iron pot hook from the fireplace. Whatever was close by.

"Hesh, now. You can't help it." Tati scoops down for a pinch of dirt to throw over her shoulder. "Put it behind you. New day comin' and plenty to do. C'mon now, throw you a pinch your ownself, to be safe."

I do what she says and then make the cross over my chest, and Tati does, too. "Father, Son, Holy Ghost," we whisper together. "Guide us and protect us. Keep us ahead and behind. Ever and ever. Amen."

I hadn't ought to, then—bad business to look back for a haint once you throwed ground twixt you and it—but I do. I glance at the road.

I'm cold all over.

"What you doin'?" Tati near trips when I stop so sudden.

"I wasn't dreamin'," I whisper, and I don't just look. I point, but my hand shakes. "I was lookin' at **her.**"

## Lost Friends

We make no charge for publishing these letters from subscribers. All others will be charged fifty cents. Pastors will please read the requests published below from their pulpits, and report any case where friends are brought together by means of letters in the SOUTHWESTERN.

Dear Editor—I wish to inquire for a woman named Caroline, who belonged to a man in the Cherokee Nation, Indian Territory, named John Hawkins, or "Google-eyed" Smith, as he was commonly called. Smith took her from the Nation to Texas, and sold her again. The whole family belonged to Delanos before they were scattered and sold. Her mother's name was Letta; father's name Samuel Melton; children's names, Amerietta, Susan, Esau, Angeline, Jacob, Oliver, Emeline, and Isaac. If any of your readers hear of such a person, they will confer a favor on a dear sister, Amerietta Gibson, by addressing me at Independence, Kans., P.O. Box 94.

WM. B. AVERY, Pastor

—"Lost Friends" column of the Southwestern
August 24, 1880

## CHAPTER 2

BENEDETTA SILVA—AUGUSTINE, LOUISIANA, 1987

The truck driver lays on his horn. Brakes squeal. Tires hopscotch across asphalt. A stack of steel pipe leans in slow-motion, testing the grease-encrusted nylon binders that hold the load. One strap breaks loose and whips in the breeze as the truck skids toward the intersection.

Every muscle in my body goes stiff. I brace for impact, fleetingly imagining what might be left of my rusted-out VW Beetle after the collision.

The truck wasn't there an instant ago. I'd swear it wasn't.

**Who did I list as the emergency contact in my employee file?**

I remember the pen tip hovering over the blank line, the moment of painful, ironic indecision. Maybe I never filled in the space.

The world passes by in acute detail—the heavyset crossing guard with her blue-white hair and stooped-over body, thrusting the handheld stop sign. Wide-eyed kids motionless in the intersection. Books slip from a grade-school boy's skinny arm, tumbling, tumbling, hitting, scattering. He stumbles, hands splayed, disappears behind the pipe truck.

**No. No, no, no! Please, no.** My teeth clench. I close my eyes, turn my face away, yank the steering wheel, stomp harder on the brake, but the Bug keeps sliding.

Metal strikes metal, folds and crinkles. The car bumps over something, front wheels, then back. I feel my head collide with the window and then the roof.

**It can't be. It can't.**

**No, no, no.**

The Bug hits the curb, bounces off, then stops, the engine rumbling, rubber smoke filling the car.

**Move,** I tell myself. **Do something.**

I picture a little body in the street. Red sweatpants, too warm for the day. Faded blue T-shirt, oversized. Warm brown skin. Big dark eyes, lifeless. I noticed him yesterday in the empty schoolyard, that boy with the impossibly long eyelashes and freshly shaved head, sitting all alone by the tumbledown concrete block fence after the older kids had picked up their new class schedules and dispersed to do whatever kids do in Augustine, Louisiana, on the last day of summer.

**Is that little guy okay?** I'd asked one of the other teachers, the pasty-faced, sour-lipped one who'd repeatedly avoided me in the hall as if I were giving off a bad smell. **Is he waiting for somebody?**

**Who knows?** she'd muttered. **He'll find his way home.**

Time snaps into place. The metallic taste of blood tightens the back of my mouth. I've bitten my tongue, I guess.

There's no screaming. No siren. No outcry for somebody to call 911.

I yank the gearshift into neutral, engage the emergency brake, make sure it's going to hold before I unfasten the seatbelt, grab the handle, and ram the door with my shoulder until it finally opens. I tumble into the street, catching myself on numb feet and legs.

"What'd I tell you?" The crossing guard's voice is toneless, almost languid compared to the spiraling pulse in my neck. "What'd I tell you?" she demands again, hands on her hips as she traverses the crosswalk.

I look first at the intersection. Books, squashed lunch box, plaid thermos. That's all.

That's it.

No body. No little boy. He's standing on the curb. A girl who might be his older sister, perhaps thirteen or fourteen, has him by a fistful of clothing, so that he's stretched on tippy-toe, an incongruously distended belly hanging bare beneath the hem of his T-shirt.

"What **sign** I **gave** you just now?" The crossing guard slaps a palm hard against the four-letter word **STOP,** then thrusts the placard within inches of his face.

The little boy shrugs. He looks more bewildered than terrified. Does he know what almost happened? The teenage girl, who probably saved his life, seems annoyed as much as anything else.

"Idjut. Look out for the trucks." She shoves him forward a step onto the sidewalk, then releases her grip and wipes a palm on her jeans. Tossing back a handful of long, glossy dark braids with red beads on the ends, she glances toward the intersection, blinks at what I now realize is the Bug's bumper lying in the street, the morning's only casualty. **That's** what I ran over. Not a little boy. Only metal and nuts and bolts. A minor miracle.

The pipe-truck driver and I will exchange insurance information—I hope it won't matter that mine is out of state still—and the day will go on. He's probably as relieved as I am. More, since he's the one who ran the intersection. His insurance should take care of this. Good thing, considering that I can't even afford to cough up my deductible. Between renting one of the few houses in my price range and splitting the cost of a U-Haul with a friend who was on her way to Florida, I'm tapped out until my first paycheck comes in.

The squeal of grinding gears catches me by surprise. I turn in time to watch the pipe truck disappear down the highway.

"Hey!" I yell, and run a few yards after it. "Hey! Come back here!"

The chase proves futile. He's not stopping, the pavement is slick with the condensation of a humid south Louisiana summer morning, and I'm in sandals and a prairie skirt. The blouse I carefully ironed atop moving boxes is plastered to my skin by the time I stop.

An upscale SUV rolls by. The driver, a big-haired blonde, gapes at me, and my stomach turns over. I recognize her from the staff welcome meeting two days ago. She's a school board member, and given my last-minute employment offer and the chilly reception so far, it's no stretch to assume that I wasn't her first choice for the job . . . or anyone else's. Compounded with the fact that we all know why I'm here in this backwater little burg, it probably doesn't bode well for my surviving the probationary period of the teaching contract.

"You never know until you try." I bolster myself with the line from "Lonely People," a hit-parade anthem of my 1970s childhood, and I walk back toward the school. Oddly, life is moving along as if nothing happened. Cars roll by. The crossing guard does her job. She pointedly avoids looking my way as a school bus turns in.

The Bug's amputated limb has been moved out of the intersection—I do not know by whom—and people politely circumvent my car to reach the horseshoe-shaped drop-off lanes in front of the school.

Down the sidewalk, the teenage girl, maybe eighth or ninth grade—I'm still not very good at eyeballing kids—has resumed charge of the little crosswalk kid. The red beads on her braids swing back and forth across her color-block shirt as she drags the boy away, her demeanor indicating that she doesn't consider him worth the trouble, but she knows she'd better get him out of there. She has his books and thermos jumbled in one arm and the mangled lunch box hooked by a middle finger.

I turn a full circle beside my car, surveying the scene, befuddled by its veneer of normalcy. I tell myself to do what everyone else is doing—move on with the day. **Think of all the ways things could be worse.** I list them in my head, off and on.

This is how my teaching career officially begins.

By fourth period, the mental game of **Things could be worse** is wearing thin. I'm exhausted. I'm confused. I am effectively talking to the air. My students, who range from seventh to twelfth grade, are uninspired, unhappy, sleepy, grumpy, hungry, borderline belligerent, and, if their body language is any indication, more than ready to take me on. They've had teachers like me before—first-year suburban ninnies fresh off the college campuses, attempting to put in five years at a low-income school to have federal student loans forgiven.

This is another universe from the one I know. I did my student teaching in an upscale high school under the guidance of a master teacher who had the luxury of demanding any sort of curriculum materials she wanted. When I waltzed in halfway through the year, her freshmen were reading **Heart of Darkness** and writing neat five-paragraph essays about underlying themes and the social relevance of literature. They willingly answered discussion questions and sat up straight in their seats. They knew how to compose a topic sentence.

By contrast, the ninth graders here look at the classroom copies of **Animal Farm** with all the interest of children unwrapping a brick under the Christmas tree.

"What're we s'posed to do with **this**?" a girl in fourth period demands, her pert nose scrunching as she peers from a bird's nest of perm-damaged straw-colored hair. She's one of eight white kids in an over-stuffed class of thirty-nine. Last name **Fish.** There's another Fish, a brother or cousin of hers, in the class as well. I've already overheard whispers about the Fish family. **Swamp rats** was the reference. The white kids in this school fall into three categories: swamp rat, hick, or hood, meaning drugs are somehow involved, and that's usually a generational pattern in the family. I heard two coaches casually filing kids into those categories while sorting their class rolls during the teachers' meeting. Kids with money or real athletic talent get siphoned to the district's swanky prep academy over "on the lake," where the high-dollar houses are. Really troubled kids are shifted to some alternative school I've heard only whispers about. Everyone else ends up here.

In this school, the swamp rats and hicks sit in a cluster on the front left side of the room. It's some sort of unwritten rule. Kids from the black community take the other side of the room and most of the back. A cluster of assorted nonconformists and other-thans—Native American, Asian, punk rockers, and a nerd or two—occupy the no-man's-land in the middle.

These kids **intentionally** segregate.

Do they realize it's 1987?

"Yeah, what's **this** for?" Another girl, last name . . . **G** . . . something . . . **Gibson,** echoes the question about the book. She's of the middle-of-the-room variety—doesn't quite fit either of the other groups. Not white, not black . . . multiracial and probably part Native American?

"It's a book, Miss Gibson." I know that sounds snarky as soon as the words leave my mouth. Unprofessional, but I'm only four hours in and near the end of my chain already. "We open the pages. Take in the words."

I'm not sure how we'll make it happen, anyway. I have huge freshmen and sophomore groups, and only one classroom set of thirty copies of **Animal Farm.** They look to be ancient, the pages yellowed along the edges but the spines stiff, indicating they've never been opened. I unearthed them in my musty storage closet yesterday. They smell bad. "See what lessons the story teaches us. What it has to say about the time it was written, but also about us, here in this classroom today."

The Gibson kid drags a glittery purple fingernail across the pages, flips through a few, tosses her hair. "Why?"

My pulse upticks. At least someone has the book open and is talking . . . to me instead of to the kid at the next desk. Maybe it just takes a little while to get into the groove on the first day. This school isn't very inspiring, in truth. Cement block walls with peeling gray paint, sagging bookshelves that look like they've been here since World War II, and windows covered with some kind of streaky black paint. It feels more like a prison than a place for kids.

"Well, for one reason, because I want to know what **you** think. The great thing about literature is that it's subjective. No two readers read the same book, because we all see the words through different eyes, filter the story through different life experiences."

I'm conscious of a few more heads turning my way, mostly in the center section, nerds and outcasts and other-thans. I'll take what I can get. Every revolution starts with a spark on dry tinder.

Someone in the back row lets out a snore-snort. Someone else farts. Kids giggle. Those nearby abandon their books and flee the stench like gazelles. A half dozen boys form a jostling, poking, shoulder-butting group by the coatrack. I order them to sit down, which of course they ignore. Yelling won't help. I've tried it in other classes already.

"There are no right or wrong answers. Not when it comes to literature." My voice struggles over the racket.

"Well, this oughta be easy." I miss the source of the comment. Somewhere in the back of the room. I stretch upward and try to see.

"As long as you've **read** the **book,** there are no wrong answers," I correct. "As long as you're thinking about it."

"I'm thinkin' 'bout lunch," an oversized kid in the annoying pileup says. I cast about for his name from roll call, but all I can remember is something with an **R,** both first name and last.

"That's all you ever think about, Lil' Ray. Your brain's wired direct to your stomach."

A retaliatory shove answers. Someone jumps on someone else's back.

A sweat breaks over my skin.

Wads of paper fly. More kids get up.

Someone stumbles backward and falls across a desk, a nerd's head is grazed by a high-top tennis shoe. The victim yelps.

The swamp rat girl by the window closes the book, lets her chin bump to her palm, and stares at the blackened glass like she wishes she could pass through it by osmosis.

"That's enough!" I yell, but it's useless.

Suddenly—I'm not even sure how it happens—Lil' Ray is on the move, shoving desks aside and heading for the swamp rat section like a man on a mission. The nerds abandon ship. Chairs squeal. A desk topples over and strikes the floor like a cannon shot.

I hurdle it, land in the center of the room, slide a foot or so on the ancient speckled industrial tile, and end up right in Lil' Ray's path. "I said that is **enough,** young man!" The voice that comes out of me is three octaves lower than usual, guttural, and strangely animalistic. Never mind that it's hard to be taken seriously when you're five foot three and pixie-ish; I sound like Linda Blair in **The Exorcist.** "Get **back** in your **seat.** Right **now.**"

Lil' Ray has fire in his eye. His nostrils flare, and a fist twitches upward.

I'm aware of two things. The classroom has gone deadly silent, and Lil' Ray smells. Bad. Neither this kid nor his clothes have been washed in a while.

"Man, siddown," another boy, a skinny, good-looking kid, says. "You crazy or something? Coach Davis is gonna kill you, if he hears about this."

The rage drains from Lil' Ray's face like a fever breaking. His arms go slack. The fist loosens, and he rubs his forehead. "I'm hungry," he says. "I don't feel so good." He wobbles for a second, and I'm afraid he's going down.

"Take . . . take your seat." My hand hovers in the air, as if I might catch him. "It's seventeen . . . it's seventeen minutes until lunch." I try to collect my thoughts. **Do I let this pass? Make an example of Lil' Ray? Write him up? Send him to the principal's office? What's the demerit system at this school?**

**Did anyone hear all the noise?** I glance toward the door.

The kids take that as an excuse to depart. They grab backpacks and make a beeline for the exit, tripping over desks and chairs, bouncing off one another. They push, shove, elbow. One student attempts to escape the chaos by using the desktops as stepping-stones.

If they get out, I'm dead. The singular rule most emphasized during the teachers' meeting was **No kids in the hall during classes without adult supervision.** Period. Too much fighting, skipping, smoking, adding graffiti to the walls, and other acts of delinquency, which the weary-looking principal, Mr. Pevoto, left to our imaginations.

**If they are in your classroom, you are responsible for keeping them there.**

I join the stampede. Fortunately, I'm nimble and closer to the exit than most of my students. Only two get loose before I plant myself in the doorway, my arms stretched across the opening. It's at that point

I revisit **The Exorcist.** My head must be turning 360 degrees on my neck, because I see a pair of boys sprinting away down the hall, laughing and congratulating each other, while at the same time I observe stragglers bumping into the logjam I've created at the exit portal. Lil' Ray is at the front and fairly immovable. At least he's averse to mowing me down.

"I **said,** get back in your seats. **Now.** We still have . . ." I glance at the clock. "Fifteen minutes." Fifteen? I'll never make it that long with this bunch of miscreants. They are by far the worst of the day, and that's saying a lot.

No amount of money is worth this, and certainly not the pittance of a salary the school district has agreed to pay me for being here. I'll find some other means of repaying my student loans.

"I'm hungry," Lil' Ray complains again.

"Back to your seat."

"But I'm **hungry.**"

"You should eat before you come to school."

"Ain't got nothing in the pintry." A sheen of sweat covers his coppery skin, and his eyes are weirdly glassy. I'm struck by the sense that I have bigger problems than the stampede. Standing in front of me is a fifteen-year-old who's desperate in some way, and he expects me to solve the problem.

"All the rest of you, get in your seats!" I bark out. "Put those desks back where they belong. Plant yourselves **in** them."

The area behind Lil' Ray slowly clears. Sneaker

soles screech. Desks clatter. Chairs scrape the tile. Backpacks drop with muffled thuds.

I hear a commotion in the science room across the hall. There's a new teacher over there, too. A girls' basketball coach, fresh out of college and only about twenty-three, as I recall. I at least have a little more age on my side, having worked my way through undergrad and then piddled along to a master's degree in literature.

"Anyone who's not in a chair in the next sixty seconds owes me a paragraph. In ink. On paper." **Owes me a paragraph** was the go-to form of intimidation of Mrs. Hardy, my mentor educator. It's the English teacher's version of **Drop and give me twenty.** Most kids will do almost anything to avoid picking up a pen and writing.

Lil' Ray blinks at me, his cherub-cheeked face sagging. "Miz?" The word comes in a hoarse, uncertain whisper.

"Miss Silva." I already hate the fact that the kids' default word for me at this school is a generic **Miz,** as if I am some random stranger, maybe married, maybe not, and with no last name worth remembering. I **have** a name. It may be my father's name and, given our relationship, I have my resentments about it, but still . . .

A man-sized hand reaches out, grasps air, stretches farther, closes over my arm. "Miss . . . I don't feel so—"

The next thing I know, Lil' Ray is slumped against the frame, and we're going down. I do my best to break the fall as a million things run through my mind. Overexcitement, drugs, an illness, theatrics . . .

Lil' Ray's eyes moisten. He gives me the terrified look of a toddler lost in the grocery store, searching for his mom.

"Lil' Ray, what's going on?" No response. I turn and shout into the classroom. "Does he have a health problem?"

No one answers.

"Are you sick?" We're nose to nose now.

"I get hun . . . gry."

"Do you carry medicine? Does the nurse have medicine for you?" **Do we even have a school nurse?** "Have you been to a doctor?"

"I don't . . . I . . . jus . . . get hungry."

"When did you eat last?"

"Lunch yesterday."

"Why didn't you have breakfast this morning?"

"Nothin' in the pintry."

"Why didn't you have supper last night?"

Deep creases line his sweat-soaked forehead. He blinks at me, blinks again. "Nothin' in the pintry."

My mind speeds full throttle into the brick wall of reality. I don't even have time to put on the brakes and soften the impact. Pintry . . . pintry . . .

**Pantry.**

**Nothing in the pantry.**

I feel sick.

Meanwhile, behind me, the noise level is rising again. A pencil takes flight and hits the wall. I hear another one clatter off the metal filing cabinet by my desk.

From my pocket, I snatch the half-eaten bag of peanut M&M's left from my morning snack, stuff it into Lil' Ray's hand, and say, "Eat this."

I stand up just in time to see a red plastic ruler shoot through the half-open door.

"That is it!" I've said this at least two dozen times today. Apparently, I don't mean it, because I'm still here, in this outer realm of Dante's inferno. Just trying to survive Day One. Either it's mere stubbornness or a desperate need to succeed at something, but I start retrieving copies of **Animal Farm** from the floor and slamming them onto desks.

"What're we s'posed to do with these?" That complaint comes from the right side of the room.

"Open it. Look it over. Get out a piece of paper. Write a sentence telling me what you think the book is about."

"We got eight minutes till the bell," a punk-rocker girl with a blue-streaked Mohawk notes.

"Then hurry."

"You crazy?"

"There ain't time."

"That's not fair."

"I ain't writin' no sentence."

"I'm not readin' no book. This's got . . .

one-hun'erd forty-four pages! I can't read that in fiv . . . four minutes."

"I didn't **ask** you to read it. I asked you to **look** at it. Decide what you think it's about and write a sentence. With that sentence, you will buy your passage through my classroom door and the privilege of proceeding on to lunch." I move to the exit, where I'm just now noticing that Lil' Ray has disappeared, leaving the empty M&M's wrapper as a thank-you.

"Lil' Ray didn't write no sentence. He got to go to lunch."

"That's not your problem." I stare them down and remind myself that these are ninth graders. Fourteen-and-fifteen-year-olds. They can't hurt me.

Much.

Papers rattle. Pens smack desktops. Backpacks are zipped open.

"I don't have no paper," the skinny boy protests.

"Borrow some."

He reaches over and snatches a blank sheet off a nerd's desk. The victim sighs, reopens his backpack, and calmly gets out another piece. Thank God for nerds. I wish I had an entire classroom full. All day.

In the end, I win, sort of. I'm presented with rumpled papers and copious amounts of attitude when the bell rings and kids storm the door. It's not until the last group is draining the funnel I've created by combining my body and an empty desk that I recognize long, thin braids tipped with red beads, acid-washed jeans, and a color-block shirt. The girl who walked the little lunch box kid away from the intersection this morning. In all the chaos, I never even picked up on the fact that she was in my room.

For an instant, I foster the notion that she hasn't connected me with the near-miss crosswalk incident. Then I flip back through the last few papers on my stack, read sentences like:

> I think it's about a farm.
>
> i bet this book stooped.
>
> About a pig.
>
> It's about George Orwell's satire of Russian society.

Somebody actually copied the summary from the back cover. There's hope.

And then, **It's about a crazy lady who gets in a accident in the morning and hits her head. She wanders off into a school, but she's got no clue what she's doing there.**

**Next day, she wakes up and don't come back.**

# CHAPTER 3

## HANNIE GOSSETT—LOUISIANA, 1875

I mash the big field hat down hard to hide my face while I slide from shadow to shadow in the morning dark. It'll be trouble if I get seen here. Both me and Tati know that. Old Missus won't let no croppers near the Grand House till Seddie lights the morning lamp in the window. I get caught here at night, she'll say I come thieving.

It'll give her cause to tear up our land paper. She don't like the sharecrop contracts and hates ours more than most. Missus's plan was to keep all us stray children and work us for free round the Grand House till we got too old to put up with it. Only reason she let Tati take us to her sharecrop land was because Old

Mister said that Tati and us strays oughta have the chance at working our own plot, too. And because Missus never thought that one old freedwoman and seven half-growed kids could make it, farming on shares for ten years to earn our land, free and clear. It's a lean, hungry life when three of every four eggs, bushels, barrels, and beans you draw from the field go right back to pay the debt for the land and goods at the plantation store, since croppers ain't allowed to trade anyplace else. But that thirty acres is nearly ours, now. Thirty acres, a mule and outfit. Old Missus can't stand the fact of it. Our land sits too close to the Grand House, for one thing. She wants to hold the land for Young Mister Lyle and Missy Lavinia, even though they got more interest in spending their daddy's money than in farming fields.

But that don't matter. No mystery what'll happen if things get left up to Old Missus, and I hope we ain't soon to find out that's how it is. Tati wouldn't have hurried me into the boys' work clothes and sent me scurrying up here if there was any other way to discover what sort of ill wind has brought that girl in the hood cape sneaking up to Goswood Grove by the dark of midnight.

She might've meant for that cape to hide who she was, but Tati recognized it right off. Tati's old fingers had worked late by the light of the bottle lamp, sewing up two capes just alike for last year's Christmas—one to fit that high-yella woman Old Mister keeps in style down in New Orleans, and one for the fawn-pale daughter they made together, Juneau Jane. Old Mister likes to dress them the same, mother and daughter, and he knows Tati's trustable to always keep her sewing work hid from Old Missus. All us know better than to even mention the names of that woman or that child round here. Be safer calling the name of the devil.

Juneau Jane coming to Goswood Grove ain't a good sign. Old Mister hadn't been seen at this plantation since day after Christmas, when the word come that Mister's fine gentleman son had got hisself into another difficulty, this time in Texas. Been only two years since Mister sent the boy west to dodge a murder trial in Louisiana. The time spent on the Gossett lands in East Texas ain't improved Young Mister Lyle's behaviors, I guess.

Doubt anyplace could.

Four months ago that Old Mister left, and no word of him since. Either that little tawny-pale daughter of his knows what become of him or she's here to find out.

Child's a fool, coming to Goswood this way. The Ku Kluxers and White Camellias catch her on the road, they might not guess what she is just by looking, but no decent woman or girl goes about alone after dark. Too many carpetbaggers, road agents, and bushwhackers round in these years since the war. Too many young rowdies mad about the times, and the government, and the war, and the Louisiana constitution giving black folks the vote.

The kind of men that prowl these roads at night ain't likely to care that the girl's just fourteen.

Juneau Jane's got courage, or else she's desperate. Reason enough for me to sneak past the brick pillars that hold the Grand House's first floor eight foot off the ground, and shinny through the coal trap into the basement. Years past, the boys used it to come snitch food, but I'm the only one of Tati's strays still skinny enough to get in this way.

I don't want one thing to do with this mess, or with Juneau Jane, but if she knows information, I got to find out. If Old Mister is gone from this world and this left-hand child of his is here seeking after his death papers, I'm bound to get my fingers on our cropper contract at the same time. Make myself into a thief, which I never been. Don't have a choice about it, though. With no husband to stand in her way, Old Missus will burn them papers quick as she gets the news. Nothing the rich folk like better than to rid theirselves of a cropper right when the land contract's coming due.

I take a few steps, light and careful, one at a time. At corn shuckings and circle plays, I got the dancing feet of a butterfly. **Graceful, for a gangly thing,** Tati says. I hope that holds out. Old Missus has Seddie sleeping in a little space off the china room, and that old woman's got light ears, busy mouth. Seddie loves to tell tales to the Missus, cook up trouble, cast curses on folks, get somebody a swat with that riding bat Old Missus carries round. Seddie'll slip a little poison on anybody that crosses her—put it in the water dipper or top of a corn pone cake—make them sick enough to die or wish they would. The woman's a witch for sure. Even sees things when she's sleeping, I think.

She won't know me in this field hat, shirt, and britches. Not unless she gets a close look, and I'll make definite sure that don't happen. Seddie's old and fat and slow. I'm quicker than a cane-cutter rabbit. **Burn down the stubble. Stand at the edge of your field, you won't have me in your stew pot. I'm too fast.**

I tell myself them things while I cross the basement by the light of the moon through the window. Can't use the nursery stairs to go up. The bottom steps squeak, and they're too near Seddie's room.

The ladder to the butler's pantry floor hatch is the means I choose, instead. Many's the time my sister Epheme and me sneaked out and back in that way after Old Missus took us from Mama's little saddleback cabin in the quarters and said we was to sleep on the floor under Baby Lavinia's crib, and quieten her in the night if she fussed. I was just three and Epheme six, and both of us lonely for our folk and scared of Old Missus and Seddie. But a slave child ain't given a choice in the matter. The new baby needed playthings, and that was us.

Missy Lavinia was a troublesome little bird from the start. Round and fat-cheeked and pale, with straw-brown hair so fine you could see right through it. She wasn't the pretty child her mama wanted, or her daddy, either. That's why he always liked his child with that colored Creole woman the best. That one **is** a pretty little thing. He'd even bring her to the Grand House when Old Missus and Missy Lavinia went away to visit Missus's people down on cotton islands by the sea.

I always did wonder if him being so fond of Juneau Jane was the reason his children with Missus turned out so wrong.

I push up the hatch in the butler's pantry, peek round the cabinet door, and listen out. The air's so quiet I can hear Old Missus's azalea bushes scratch at the window glass, like a hundred fingernails. A whip-poor-will calls in the dark. That's a bad sign. Three times means death is bound to cross your path.

This one calls two.

Don't know what two times means. Nothin', I hope.

The window light in the dining room flickers with leaf shadow. I slip along to the ladies' parlor, where before the war Old Missus entertained neighbor women over tea and needlework, and gave out lemon cakes and chocolates all the way from France. But that was when folks had money for such. My work, or my sister's back then, was to stand with a big feather fan on a stick, swish it up and down to chase the heat off the ladies and the flies from the lemon cakes.

Sometimes we'd fan the sugar powder right onto the floor. **Don't ever taste it when you clean that up,** the kitchen women told us children. **Seddie sprinkles them lemon cakes with a poison if she feels like it.** Some say that was what caused Missus to birth two blue babies after Young Mister Lyle and Missy Lavinia, and to finally end up weak enough to be confined to a invalid's chair. Others say Old Missus's trouble goes back to a curse on her family. A punishment to the Loaches for the mean ways they treated their slave people.

A shudder slips up my back, rattles every bone in my spine, when I come past the hall where Seddie sleeps in her little room. A gas lamp flickers and spits overhead, turned down low. The house sighs and settles, and Seddie grunts and snorts loud enough I hear it through the door.

I round the corner into the salon, then cross it quick, figuring Juneau Jane will try to get to the library, where Old Mister keeps his desk and papers and such. Outdoor sounds get louder the closer I come—trees rustling, bugs with their night noises, a bullfrog. That girl must've got a door or a window opened. How'd she manage that? Missus won't allow windows raised on the first-floor gallery, no matter how miserable hot it gets. Too worried about thieving. Won't let the windows open on the second floor, either. So fearish of the mosquitos, she makes the yard boys keep tar pots burning outside the house day and night in all the warm months. Whole place wears a coat of pitch smoke, and the house ain't been aired in more years than I can remember.

Them windows been long painted shut, and Seddie minds all the door locks last thing at night, careful as a mama gator on a nest. Sleeps with the ring of keys tied on her neck. If Juneau Jane's found a way in, somebody from the house helped her. Question is, who and when and for why? And how'd they get away with it?

When I peek round the opening, she's sneaking in the window, so it must've took her a while to pry it up. One little slipper touches down on the wood folding chair Old Mister likes to take out to the gardens to sit and read to the plants and the statues.

I back myself into the shadows and watch-wait to see what this girl's about. Climbing off the chair, she stops, looks over to my hiding spot, but I don't move. I tell myself I'm a piece of the house. You ever been a slave at Goswood, you learn how to turn yourself into wood and wallpaper.

Easy to see this girl knows nothing of that. She moves through the room like the place is hers, barely reasonable quiet while helping herself to her daddy's big desk. Latches click as she opens parts of that desk I didn't even know there was. Must be her papa showed her how, or told her.

She ain't happy with what she finds, and gives that desk a cussing in French before moving on to the tall hallway doors like she plans to push them closed. The hinges complain, low and soft. She stops. Listens. Looks into the hall.

I back my way tighter to the wall and closer to the outside door. If Seddie comes from her bed, I'll hide behind the curtain, then climb out that window during the ruckus and get myself away from here.

The girl shuts the hall doors, all right, and I think to myself, **Oh Lord! Ain't no way Seddie didn't hear that.**

Every hair on my body stands up, but no one comes, and little Juneau Jane moves on with her business. This girl is either smart or the biggest fool I ever came upon, because next she takes her papa's little pocket lantern from the desk, opens the tin case, strikes up a Lucifer, and lights the candle.

I can see her face clear then, lit up in that circle of yellow light. She ain't a child anymore, but she ain't a woman, either, someplace in-between. A strange creature with long, dark curls that circle her like angel hair and hang far down her back. That hair moves with life of its own. She's still got that light skin, straight brows like Old Mister's, and wide eyes that slant up at the corners, same's my mama's, same's mine. But this girl's are silvery bright. Unnatural. Witchy.

She sets the lantern 'neath the desk, just enough to give some light, and she commences to fetching out ledger books from the drawer, turning pages by the light, her thin, pointed finger tracing a line here and there. She can read, reckon. Them sons and daughters born in **plaçage** live high, boys sent to France to get educated, and the girls to convent schools.

She checks over every ledger book and slip of paper she can find, shakes her head, hisses through her teeth, not happy one bit. She lifts up boxes of powdered ink, pens, pencils, tobacco, pipes, holds them to the light and looks underneath.

Be a sure miracle if this girl don't get caught. Child's getting noisier and braver by the minute.

Or else just more desperate.

Holding up the candle lamp, she goes to the shelves that rise floor to ceiling against the walls, higher than three men could reach if they stood on shoulders. For a minute, she's got the flame so close, I think it's in her mind to burn the books and the Grand House to the ground.

There's hired women and girls asleep at the attic. I can't let Juneau Jane set that flame, if she tries to. I shift from behind the curtain, creep three steps 'cross the room, almost to the moonlight squares on the cherry wood floors.

But she don't do it. She's trying to make out what the books are. Lifts onto her toes and holds the lantern high as she can. The candle tin tips, wax funneling over onto her wrist. She gasps and drops the lamp, and it falls on the carpet, the flame drowned in a wax pool. She don't even bother to go after it, just stands there with her hands on her waist, looking up at the high shelves. There's no ladder to get up there. The house girls probably took it to use for cleaning someplace.

Ain't two seconds before the cape is off that girl's shoulders, and she's testing the bottom shelf with one foot, and then climbing. Lucky thing she's still in child's skirts, just only halfway betwixt her knee and her silk slippers. She skitters her way up like a squirrel, the long hair trailing down her back making a big, fluffy tail.

Her toe slips near the top.

**Careful,** I want to say, but she rights herself and goes on, then grabs and sidesteps along the high shelves like the young boys traveling the rafters in the wagon shed.

The muscles in her arms and legs shake from the strain, and the shelf bows under her when she gets toward the middle. It's a single book she's after, one that's thick and heavy and tall. She pulls it loose and scoots it along the wobbling wood and gets herself back to the edge where it's stronger.

Down she comes, setting the book ahead of her, one shelf lower, one shelf lower.

The very last time she lays that book down, it pitches like somebody's shoved it from behind, and off it topples. Seems like forever, it goes end over end through shadows and light, then hits the floor with a smack that rattles the room and races out the door.

There's stirrings upstairs. "Sedd-ieeee?" Old Missus

calls through the house, that screech cutting up my spine like a kitchen knife. "Seddie! Who is there? Is it you? Answer me this instant! One of you girls come lift me from this bed! Put me in my chair!"

Feet scramble and doors open overhead. A housemaid runs down the attic steps and along the second-floor hall. Good thing Missus can't get up from that bed on her own. Seddie's a whole other matter, though. She's probably grabbing the old breechloader rifle right now, fixing to lay somebody under with it.

"Mother?" It's Missy Lavinia's voice comes then. What's **she** doing home? Ain't yet the end of spring term at the Melrose Female School in New Orleans. Ain't even close.

Juneau Jane grabs that book and she's out the window so quick, she don't even remember to get her cloak. She don't close the window, either, and that's good because I'm bound to get out of here, same way she did. Can't leave that cloak there, though. If Missus sees it, she'll know Tati's stitching and come asking **us** about it. If I can get it and close that window, kick the travel lantern under the desk, the rest might be all right. This library's the last place they'd think of a thief coming. Folks steal food or silver goods, not books. Any luck, a few days might pass before the candle wax on the carpet gets noticed. Even better luck, the house help will clean it up without saying a word.

I stuff the cloak down my shirt, nudge that candle

lamp with my foot, glance at the mess on the rug, think, **Oh Lord. Lord, Lord, cover me over. I want to live some more years before I die. Marry a good man. Have babies. Own that land.**

The house gets like a battleground. People running, voices hollering, doors slamming, commotion all over. Hadn't heard that much racket since the Yankee gunboats first come up the river, shelling everyplace and sending us scurrying to the woods to hide.

Before I can get on the folding chair and jump through the window, Missy Lavinia's right outside the library door. She's the **last** one needs to find me here. That girl purely delights in the taste of trouble, which is the reason her papa sent her off to the girls' deportment school in the first place.

I run back through the dining room, right past every door, because Missus's latest manservant is coming up the gallery outside. I get all the way to the butler's pantry, but there's no time to open the little hatch to the ladder, so I just crawl in the cabinet on my hands and knees and pull the doors and huddle there like a rabbit in the grass. Somebody's bound to root me out before long. By now, Missy Lavinia has spotted that open library window and maybe the wax on the carpet, too. They won't stop looking till they find out who's in here.

But after the noise dies down a bit, it's Missy Lavinia I hear say, "Mother, for the sake of all, may we return to bed now? And please leave old Seddie to her rest. Don't punish her for not waking. I troubled her already with my late arrival last evening. I'd left a book on the night table, and it's fallen, that's all. The noise only **sounded** to be coming from downstairs."

Can't guess how Missy don't see, or smell, or feel the air from that window left open. Can't guess how Seddie's slept through all this, but I count it as a blessing and close my eyes, rest my head on the backs of my hands and say my thanks. I might live awhile longer yet, if they'd just all go back to bed.

But Old Missus is boiling hot, still. Can't make out all the words that're said after, just that there's heavy discussing and carrying on awhile. Time it's over, my body is cramped and aching so bad, I'm chewing on my knuckles to keep from moving and pushing on the doors. A manservant gets left up to keep watch, so it's a long time before I gather together the courage to slip from my place, open the hatch under me, and go down the ladder to the basement. With the man still prowling the yard and the galleries, I don't dare try to get out till day breaks and Seddie unlocks the doors out to the lawn. I just hunker down, knowing Tati's probably in a fit of worry, and come morning, she'll wake Jason and John and tell them what we done. Jason will be bad troubled over it. He don't like anything out of place from one day to the next. All things the same, day after day, is his comfort.

Curled up in the dark, I wonder about the book Juneau Jane stole. That book got Old Mister's papers in it? No way to know, so finally I rest my head on the soft cloak and let myself sleep and wake. I dream of climbing up the bookshelves myself, and taking one of them books from up top and getting my hands on our land contract. All our troubles will be no more.

The door's getting opened when I come to. A slice of feathery light lays itself over the floor and the smell of morning seeps in. Seddie tells a yard boy, "Don' you touch nothin' but the shovel and the yard broom and the hoe. Every apple in the barrel been counted and every drop a' molasses, and Irish 'tater, and rice grain, too. Las' boy that try to dip in, he gone. Nobody ever see him no more."

"Yes'm." The boy sounds young. Old Missus's got such a reputation, she's running slim on choices. Has to take on babies nobody else will hire yet.

I lay up awhile before I stuff Juneau Jane's cloak back down the front of my borrowed shirt and pull John's field hat so low it bends my ears, and I work my way toward fresh air and freedom. Nobody's near when I poke my head out, and so off I go. Takes a heap of **won't-not** to walk calm 'cross the yard, just in case somebody's looking out from the house. They won't think a thing about a little colored boy moving about, slow and easy. But what I really want to do is run, go from cropper cabin to cropper cabin with the word that Missy Lavinia's showed up from school. Must be a ill wind to bring her home, news of Old Mister. Bad news.

We croppers got to coop up together, have a

meeting off in the woods, and figure our next move. All us got contracts and all us been depending on Old Mister to keep the promises that's been given.

Time to put our heads to the problem.

No sooner does my mind start on it, than I make my way round the garden hedges, and hear voices. Two of them, down under the old brick bridge that was a fine thing long ago, before the Yankees toppled the statues and the rose trellises and butchered the Goswood hogs, then threw what was left of the carcasses in the reflecting ponds. The garden was too far gone after that. Hard times don't leave money for fine things anyhow. Gate's been shut ever since the war, the footpaths left for the wisteria and brambles and climbing roses to eat up. Poison ivy drapes the old trees, and hanging moss strings down thick as silk fringes on a ladies' fan.

Who'd be **under** that bridge, except maybe boys gigging frogs or men hunting possum or squirrel for the supper pot? But it's white-sounding voices. Girls' voices, whispering.

I make my way through the brush and sidle closer till I can hear for sure. Missy Lavinia is clear as a smith's hammer on metal and just about as pleasurable: ". . . haven't kept your end of the bargain, so pray tell why should I?"

What in saint's name would Missy come **here** for? Who's she talking to? I settle real quiet near the bridge rail, point my ear.

"Our goal is selfsame." The words are Frenchy-like,

hard to make out at first. They run up and down quick as a bird whistle. "Perhaps our fate is in common, as well, if we are unsuccessful in our quest."

"You will **not** assume we hold any similarities," Missy snaps. I can picture them fat cheeks of hers puffing like the hog bladders the butcher men blow up with air and tie off for the children to play with. "You are no daughter of this house. **You** are the whelp of my father's . . . my father's . . . **concubine.** Nothing more."

"And yet, it is you who have arranged that I come here. Who have provided for me an entry to Goswood Grove House."

**They been . . . Missy did . . .**

**What in the name a' mercy? Missy was the one helped Juneau Jane get in?**

I tell Tati this news, and she'll say I'm storying.

**That's** why Missy Lavinia didn't raise a fuss last night. Might even be why Seddie didn't come out of her room, in all the ruckus. Maybe Missy Lavinia had a hand in that, too.

"And, for all my effort in assuring your passage here, Juneau Jane, I have gained nothing. You do not know where his papers are hidden any more than I do. Or perhaps you were lying when you said you could find them . . . or perhaps the fact is that **my** father lied to **you.**" Missy's low giggle follows on, them words savored like sugar crust in her mouth.

"He would not." The girl's voice rises high, takes on the sound of a child's, then trembles and thickens when she says, "He would not fail to provide for me. Always it was his promise that he—"

"You are **nothing** to this family!" Missy shrieks, sending a blackbird to flight overhead. I start looking round for where I'll go if somebody comes to see what's the trouble. "You are **nothing,** and if Father is gone, you are as penniless as you deserve to be. You and that wretched yellow woman who bore you. I almost feel **sorry** for you, Juneau Jane. A mother who fears you've grown prettier than she and a father who has tired of the burden you represent. Such a sad state of affairs."

"You will not speak of him in this manner! He does not lie. Perhaps he has only moved the papers to prevent **your** mother from throwing them to the flames. She would then claim all the holdings derived of Papa's family. With no inheritance left directly to you, you would be forced to forever do your mother's bidding. Is **that** not what you fear? Why you have brought me here?"

"I didn't **want** to bring you here." Missy's soft and amiable again, like she's coaxing a little piglet from the corner, so's to string it up and cut its throat. "If you'd only been willing to **tell** me where Father hid the papers, rather than insisting on being personally involved in looking for them . . ."

"**Ffff!** As if you could be trusted! You would steal the portion that is to be mine as quickly as your mother would steal what is to be yours."

"The portion that is to be **yours**? Really, Juneau

Jane, you belong back in Tremé with the rest of the fancy girls, waiting for your mother to sell you off to a gentleman caller, so as to pay the notes coming due. Perhaps **your** mother should have better anticipated the day when my father would no longer be here to provide for her financing."

"He is not . . . Papa is not—"

"Gone? Forever?" Missy Lavinia hadn't got a note of sadness. Not for her own daddy. Only thing she's hoping for is that what's left of the plantation farms here and in Texas don't go straight into Old Missus's hands. Juneau Jane's right, Little Missy would be under her mama's thumb forever if that happened.

"You will not say these things!" Juneau Jane chokes out.

There's a long spate of quiet then. Bad quiet that gives me the all-overs, like some evil's come stealing up on me from the shadows. Can't see it, but it's there, waiting to pounce.

"Regardless, last night's little exercise was a waste of time and considerable trouble on my part, bringing you here and ensuring your access to the library. Solving the matter will require a bit more travel for us, it seems. Just for the day, and after it's done I'll see that you're provided passage on the fastest riverboat back to New Orleans. Delivered safely to your mother's home in Tremé . . . to whatever fate awaits you. At least we'll have settled the matter."

"How can this be possible, that the matter might

so easily be solved today?" Juneau Jane sounds suspicious. She oughta be.

"I know where we shall find the man who can help. In fact, he was the last person Father spoke to before departing for Texas. I have only to order a carriage for myself, and we will be off to pay him a call. It is all very simple."

**Lord,** I think, squatting low in the thorn brush and the trumpet vines. **Oh Lord, oh Lord. Ain't nothing simple about this.**

I don't want to hear anything that comes next. Don't want to know. But wherever them girls are bound, if they're after news of Old Mister or his papers, I got to get there, too.

Question is, how?

## Lost Friends

Dear Editor—I wish to find my sister through your paper, by which many thousands have been able to see each other again. Her old name was Darkens Taylor, but she afterward went by the name Maria Walker. She had, including myself, four brothers—Sam, Peter, and Jeff; and a sister—Amy. A sister and mother are dead. We belonged to to [sic] Louis Taylor, in Bell County, Texas. Two brothers live in Austin, where she left us.

—"Lost Friends" column of
the Southwestern
March 25, 1880

## CHAPTER 4

### BENNY SILVA—AUGUSTINE, LOUISIANA, 1987

Sunday morning, I wake in a head-to-toe sweat. My last-ditch rental accommodations offer only the barely there air-conditioning of an aging window unit, but the real problem isn't this sweltering 1901 farmhouse; it's the overwhelming dread squatting on my chest like a sumo wrestler. I can't breathe.

The air is wet and muddy smelling, courtesy of a weak tropical depression spinning off the coast. The sky outside the bedroom window hangs close above the live oaks, pillowy and saturated. A drip that started in the kitchen ceiling yesterday plays a tinny tune in the largest pan I own. I've been by the office of the broker who rented the house to me.

There was a notice on the door: CLOSED FOR MEDICAL EMERGENCY. I left a note in the drop box, but so far no one has come by about the roof. They can't call, as my new home is phoneless at present. That's another one of the things I can't afford until my first paycheck comes in.

The power is out. I realize that when I roll over and look at the blank clock on the nightstand. I have no idea how late I've slept.

**Doesn't matter,** I tell myself. **You can lie here all day. The neighbors won't say anything.**

That's a little joke between me and me. A thin bit of cheer.

This house is bordered on two sides by farm fields and on the third by a cemetery. I'm not superstitious, so the proximity doesn't bother me. It's nice to have a quiet place to walk, where no one casts surreptitious glances my way, silently seeming to inquire, **What are you doing here, and how soon are you leaving?** It's the general assumption that I, like most new teachers and coaches who join the staff, am in Augustine only until something better comes along.

The hollow sense of loneliness I've begun to struggle with is familiar, yet somehow it reaches deeper now than in childhood, when my mother's flight attendant job kept her away four or five days out of seven. Depending on where we were living at the time, I stayed home in the care of sitters, neighbors, daycare providers, my mother's live-in boyfriends, and a teacher or two who watched kids for extra money. Whatever worked, wherever we were. Extended family wasn't an option. My mother had been spurned by her parents when she married my father, a **foreigner.** An **Italian,** for heaven's sake. It was an unforgivable affront, and perhaps for her that was part of his appeal, because, in reality, the marriage didn't last all that long. Of course, my father was drop-dead gorgeous, so it could have just been a case of hot-blooded attraction that wore off.

All of my mother's moving and repositioning and start-stop relationships gave me an uncanny skill in building a community outside the home. I was adept at ingratiating myself with other people's moms, friendly neighbors with dogs to walk, lonely grandparents who weren't getting enough attention from their own families.

I'm **good** at friend finding. At least I thought I was.

But Augustine, Louisiana, is putting me to the test. It calls up memories of my ill-fated teenage attempt to connect with my paternal relatives after they'd moved to New York. My mother and I were confronting issues we couldn't surmount. I needed my father and his family to open their arms to me, take me in, offer support. Instead, I felt like a stranger in a strange land, and not a welcome one.

Augustine reprises that crippling feeling of rejection. I smile at people here, I get stares in return. I crack a joke, no one laughs. I say **Good morning!,** I get grunts and curt nods, and, if I'm lucky, one-word answers.

Maybe I'm trying too hard?

I've literally learned more about Augustine from the residents of the cemetery next door than I have from its ambulatory, breathing citizens. To work off the stress of the day, I've taken to studying the raised crypts and aboveground mausoleums. The markers date back to the Civil War and beyond. There are so many stories hidden in that place. Women resting next to the babies they birthed, dead on the same day. Children granted tragically short lives. Whole broods gone within weeks of one another. Confederate soldiers with **CSA** emblazoned on their tombstones. Veterans from two world wars, Korea, Vietnam. It looks like no one has been buried there in a while, though. The newest grave belongs to Hazel Annie Burrell. Beloved wife, mother, grandmother, laid to rest twelve years ago, in 1975.

**Plink, clink, plink.** The leak in the kitchen moves from soprano to alto as I lie there thinking that, with all this rain, I can't even go walking. I am stuck here alone in this scatter-furnished house with only the basics—roughly half of the contents of a graduate-student apartment. The other half remained with Christopher, who at the last minute decided against our planned elopement and cross-country move from Berkeley to Louisiana. The breakup wasn't all his fault. I was the one who'd kept secrets, who hadn't told him everything until after the engagement. Maybe the fact that I'd held out so long spoke for itself.

Still, I miss being part of a duo in this plan for a new adventure. At the same time, there's no denying that, after four years together as a couple, I don't miss Christopher as much as I probably should.

The impending breach of my drip catcher distracts me from overanalyzing and nudges me from the bed. Time to empty the pan. Then I'll get dressed and go to town, see who else I can call for help in getting the roof situation resolved. There must be somebody.

Through the haze on the kitchen window, I make out the shape of someone walking the cemetery lane nearby. I lean closer, clear a swatch with my palm, see a man and a large yellow dog. A black umbrella partially hides the man's portly frame.

Momentarily, I think of Principal Pevoto, and my stomach tenses up. I've worn out my welcome with him this week. **Your expectations are too high, Miss Silva. Your requests for supplies are outlandish. Your hopes for the students are unrealistic.** He will not help me track down the rest of my classroom set of **Animal Farm,** which have vanished one and two at a time, until we're down to only fifteen copies. The science teacher across the hall found one stuffed in a lab drawer, and I rescued another from the trash can in the hall. The kids are actually stealing them so they won't have to read them.

It'd seem oddly resourceful if it weren't book abuse, which is wrong on so many levels.

The cemetery visitor looks like a book character himself. Paddington Bear, in his long blue raincoat and yellow hat. He walks with a stiff-legged limp that tells me he's not Principal Pevoto. Stopping at a grave, he feels for the edge of the concrete crypt without looking, then slowly bends at the waist, the umbrella descending with him until he gently places a kiss on the stone.

The sweetness of his longing dives to a tender, bruised place in me. My eyes prickle, and I absently touch my bottom lip, taste rainwater and moss and damp concrete and the passage of time. Who's buried there? A sweetheart? A child? A brother or sister? A parent or grandparent long lost?

I'll find out once he's gone. I'll visit the stone.

I withdraw from his private moment and empty the drip pot, eat, dress, empty what's in the pot again, just for safety's sake. Finally I rustle up my keys, purse, and rain gear for a trip to town.

The humidity-swollen front door and I do battle when I try to close it after myself. The antique lock is especially cantankerous today. "Stupid thing. Just . . . if you would . . . just . . . go in there. . . ."

When I turn around, the man with the dog is halfway up my front walk. Umbrella tipped against the wind, he's hidden from view until he makes his way to the leaning cement steps. He feels for the porch rail hesitantly, and then I realize the golden retriever is wearing a harness and handle, not a leash. It's a service dog.

A russet-brown hand skims the rail as owner and dog navigate the steps easily.

"May I help you?" I ask over the patter of the rain on the tin roof.

Wagging its tail, the dog peers up at me. Then the man does as well.

"Thought I'd come by and look in on Miss Retta while I was in the area. Miss Retta and I both worked in the courthouse with the judge years ago, so we've had acquaintance a long time." He nods over his shoulder toward the graveyard. "That's my grandmother, over there, Maria Walker. I'm Councilman Walker . . . well, former councilman, these days. Still a little hard to get used to that." He offers a handshake, and, leaning in, I see cloud-rimmed eyes behind his thick glasses. He cranes to one side, trying to make me out. "How is Miss Retta getting on these days? You one of her helpers?"

"I . . . just moved in last week." I glance past him, looking for a car in the driveway, someone he's with. "I'm new in town."

"You buy the place?" He chuckles. "Because you know what they say about Augustine, Louisiana. 'You purchase a house here, you'll be the last one who ever owns it.' "

I laugh at the joke. "I'm just renting."

"Oh . . . well, good for you, then. You're likely too smart for that kind of thing."

We chuckle again. The dog participates with a soft, happy yip.

"Miss Retta move into town?" Councilman Walker wants to know.

"I don't . . . I leased this place through a rental agent. I was just headed into Augustine in hopes of finding out how to get a roof leak repaired." I check the driveway again, lean around my visitor, and look toward the cemetery. How did this man get here?

The dog moves a step closer, seeking to make friends. I know it's against protocol to touch service animals, but I can't help myself. I succumb. Among all the other familiar things I miss about California are Raven and Poe, the tabby cats who kept me in their employ before I moved. They, along with various human helpers, maintained the new and used books store where I worked for a little extra money, which mostly went back into books, anyway.

"Can I give you a ride to town?" I ask, although I'm not sure where I'd put Mr. Walker and his rather hefty sidekick in the Bug.

"Sunshine and I'll sit here and wait for my grandson. He's gone on over to pick us up some Cluck and Oink barbecue for the drive back to Birmingham. That's where Sunshine and I make our place, these days." He pauses to ruffle the dog's ears and receives a wag of supreme adoration. "Had my grandson drop me here, so I could pay respects to my grandmother."

He nods toward the graveyard. "Thought I'd walk over here and give my regards to Miss Retta, too. She was sure a friend to me after I stumbled in my ways—the judge was, too. Told me, 'Louis, you better go be a lawyer or a preacher, because you like to argue your case.' Miss Retta was the judge's helper, you know. Many a wayward youngster, they took under wing. I spent a great deal of time on this porch, in my earlier years. Miss Retta helped me with my studies, and I helped her keep up the garden and the orchard. That garden saint still there by the steps? Nearly broke my back getting that thing in here for her. But Miss Retta said that statue needed a home after the library took it down. She never could turn her back on a need."

I cross the porch and look into the oleander bushes and, indeed, encased in overgrown ivy and leaning against the wall, rests some sort of statue. "There it is, I think." A sense of wonder strikes me, unexpectedly. My flower bed holds a sweet little secret. Garden saints are good luck. I'll trim back the oleander when I get a chance, fix things up a bit for the old fellow.

I make plans in my head as Councilman Walker tells me that if I want to know **anything** about **anything** in Augustine, including how and where to secure help with a leaky roof on a Sunday, I should proceed forthwith to the Cluck and Oink and speak with Granny T, who will be at the counter now that church has let out. My rental house, he says, is most likely owned by someone in the Gossett clan. This land was part of the original Goswood Grove plantation, which once stretched almost all the way to the Old River Road. Miss Retta sold the land back to Judge Gossett years ago to finance her retirement, but was allowed to live out her days in the house.

Now that the judge has passed away, someone will have inherited this particular parcel.

"You go on about your business," he says as he settles on my porch swing with Sunshine at his feet. "If you don't mind, we'll wait here. We're not bothered by the weather, us two. Into every life a little rain must fall."

I'm not sure if he's talking to me or Sunshine or himself, but I thank him for the information and leave him there in his coat and rain hat, his face turned toward the graveyard, his countenance undampened by the weather.

The rain does not seem to muck up the spirits at the Cluck and Oink, either. The tumbledown building, which sits on the highway at the far edge of town, looks like the result of an unholy mating between a cow barn and an old Texaco station, surrounded by their spawn of portable storage sheds of various sizes and vintages, some attached, some not.

The low-slung porch along the front is crowded with waiting customers, and the drive-through line, at 12:17 on a Sunday afternoon, stretches around the building and through the gravel parking lot, and blocks traffic on the right lane of the highway as people wait to turn in. Smoke belches from a screened area at the back of the building, where a crew scurries about like bees in a hive, tending a bevy of wood-fired cooking pits. Sausages, hunks of meat, and naked whole chickens turn on giant rotisseries. Flies dangle from the fascia boards in shifting black strings, climbing one over the other in hopes of gaining entry. I can't blame them. The place smells delicious.

I park next door at the aging Ben Franklin five-and-dime, and slog across the wet strip of grass between the buildings.

"They'll tow that car, if you leave it settin' over there!" a teenage employee warns me as he rushes back from the dumpster.

"I'm not staying long. Thanks!" It registers that the other restaurant customers have steered clear of the Ben Franklin lot. Even in my short time in Augustine, I've heard kids at school regularly kibitzing about the police harassing them for hanging out around town, gathering for parties, and so forth. The perceived heavy-handedness of the local law, and who gets the worst of it, is a favorite topic of student conversation while they're not listening to my lessons about **Animal Farm.** If they'd pay attention, they might spot parallels to the way this town operates in separate communities—black, white, haves, have-nots, backwoods kids, townies, and the landed gentry. The lines between them exist like an ancient but unseen network of walls, not to be crossed except through the necessary gates of commerce and employment.

Again, **Animal Farm** offers points for debate, lessons to teach. I plan to spend next week lobbying Principal Pevoto for some kind of classroom literature budget. I need books, resources that might have a hope of drawing in the kids. Maybe something more recent, like **Where the Red Fern Grows** or **The Education of Little Tree.** A story with hunting and fishing and outdoor motifs, since most of my students, no matter which group they hail from, can relate to putting food on the table via the forests, swamps, gardens, and backyard chicken coops. I'm searching for connecting points, anywhere I can find them.

The Cluck and Oink, I realize as soon as my eyes adjust to the murky interior, is a hub in this town. All the demographics of Augustine—black, white, male, female, young, old—seem at home here in this sea of fried-food smells and scurrying waitresses. Women in impossibly bright dresses and flamboyant Sunday hats tend smartly dressed children at tables crammed with multiple generations of family. Little girls with feet tucked into Mary Janes and legs circled by lace-cuffed socks sit like fluffy cake toppers on booster seats and in high chairs. Boys in bow ties and men in suits of various vintages dating all the way back to 1970s plaid tell stories and pass plates. Conversation, cordiality, and an air of jovial companionship mingle with grease smoke and cooks calling out "Order up!" or "Hot bread! Hot bread!"

Laughter rings the rafters like church bells, constant, musical, the sound amplified by the rusty tin roof and showered down again.

Boudin balls—whatever those might be—seem to be the order of the day. I check out the picture on the menu board, then wonder what's inside the deep-fried nuggets as platefuls move past, carried by fleet-footed girls in blue polyester uniform tops and jeans.

I'd like to try some, but I hear the teenager at the hostess stand, whom I quickly recognize as one of my students, telling a potential customer that the kitchen is thirty minutes behind on orders. I hope Councilman Walker's grandson scored some takeout before the post-church rush.

I'll have to wait until another time for a sample. Even if the kitchen weren't backed up, I shouldn't spend the money. I've burned through twelve boxes of off-brand snack cakes in my classroom since the Lil' Ray M&M's incident. My students constantly claim hunger pangs. I don't know who's lying and who's telling the truth, and I haven't asked as many questions as I probably should. Maybe I'm hoping that if they can't be won with books, chocolate sponge cake and fluffy filling might do the trick.

I make my way into the cash register line, studying the pies in the glass case while I advance, one satisfied customer at a time, toward the African American woman at the counter, whom I hear others addressing as **Granny T.** White-haired with hazel eyes and the stocky look of many of the people I've met in Augustine, she's decked out in a pink church dress and hat. She cuts up with customers as she flies through tickets, adding totals in her head, doling out lollipops to kids, and commenting on who's grown at least an inch since last week, **I do declare.**

"Benny Silva." I introduce myself and she reaches across the counter to shake my hand. Her thin, knobby fingers compress my palm. She's got a good grip.

"Benny?" she repeats. "Your daddy want a son, did he?"

I chuckle. That is the most oft-invoked reaction to the nickname my father saddled me with before deciding he didn't really want me, after all. "Short for Benedetta. I'm half Italian . . . and Portuguese."

"Mmm-hmmm. You got that pretty skin." She narrows one eye and looks me over.

I offer, "Well, I don't sunburn too much, at least."

"Watch out," she warns. "You best get you a good hat. This Louisiana sun, she is wicked as sin. You got your ticket so I can ring you up, sugar?"

"Oh, I didn't eat." I quickly explain the roof problem and why I've come. "The old white house out by the graveyard? I tried going by the real estate office yesterday, but the note says there was a medical emergency."

"You're lookin' for Joanie. She's laid up in the hospital up in Baton Rouge. Got misery of the gall bladder. Just get you a bucket of pitch tar and smear it round that pipe for the stove vent. On the roof, you know? Just smooth it on over the shingles in a good thick layer, like butterin' bread. That'll hold out the rain."

Suddenly, I don't doubt that this woman knows what she's talking about and has buttered many a shingle in her day. She probably still could. But

I've lived in apartments most of my life. I wouldn't know roof tar from chocolate pudding. "I'm told the house probably belongs to one of Judge Gossett's heirs. Do you know where I could find the owner? I'd just keep a bucket under the leak, but the thing is, I have to teach tomorrow, and I won't be there to empty it. I'm afraid of it spilling over and wrecking the floors." One thing the old house does have is beautiful cypress-plank flooring and timbers. I love old things and can't stand the idea of letting them go to ruin. "I'm the new English teacher at the school."

She blinks, blinks again, rolls her chin back in a way that makes me feel like someone has just made bunny ears over my head. "Oh, **you** are the Ding Dong Lady!"

There's a snicker behind me. I glance back to see the surly girl who rescued the little grade-schooler on my first day. Even though she's in class only about half the time, I have now connected her with a name—LaJuna. It's pronounced as **La** plus the name of the month, but with an **a** on the end. That's about all I know. I've tried to make headway with her during my fourth-period class, but the hour is dominated by football guys, which leaves girls, nerds, and assorted misfits with no hope of getting sufficient attention.

"You'd best quit feeding them boys cakes. Especially that Lil' Ray Rust. That one will eat you into the poor house." Granny T is still talking. Lecturing, actually. She's got a craggy index finger pointed at me. "Children want to eat, they can get their skinny behinds up out of the bed and down to the school cafeteria in time for breakfast. That food is **free.** Those boys are lazy. That's all."

I give a half-hearted nod. Word of me has gotten all the way to the Cluck and Oink. I've been dubbed in honor of a snack cake with a name that makes me sound like a ditz.

"You let a child be lazy, he'll grow up to be lazy. A young boy needs somebody to keep him in line, make him a hard worker. Back when I was a child, we were all working hard at the farm. Gals do the cookin' and the cleanin' and hire out sometimes, too, soon as they'd get old enough. Time comes to go sit at a school desk, eat food somebody **else** cooks up for us, we're thinking we're on a luxury vacation. That right, LaJuna? That's what your Aunt Dicey tells you, sure enough?"

LaJuna ducks her head, reluctantly mutters, "Yes'm." She shifts uncomfortably, pulling a sheet off her ticket pad.

Granny T is wound up now. "I'm her age, I'm workin' the farm, or in the orchard, or in this restaurant with my grandmama. And I'm going to school, and hired out to one of the Gossetts to watch her babies after the school day and in summers. Time I'm eleven years old, younger than this girl, even." Behind LaJuna and me, the checkout line is building. "By eighth grade, I've got to quit. Crop doesn't make that year, and there's bills to pay down to the Gossett Mercantile. No time for school. I was smart, too. But we can't go live under a tree. Home might not be fancy, but that's home and we're glad to have it. Grateful for everything we got, all the time."

I stand in stunned silence, letting that sink in. Just the concept of a kid . . . what, thirteen or fourteen years old . . . having to quit school to help earn a living for the family . . . it's horrifying.

Granny T motions LaJuna to the other side of the counter, hugs her around the shoulders. "Now, this one is a good girl. Gonna do all right. What'd you need, darlin'? How come you're standing here, not seeing to your tables?"

"I'm on break. Got my tables all taken care of." LaJuna extends a ticket and a twenty-dollar bill toward the counter. "Ms. Hannah ask me to bring this up so she didn't have to stand in line."

Granny T's mouth straightens. "Some people always got to have special privileges." She processes the ticket and hands LaJuna the change. "You go give this back and then you have a break."

"Yes'm."

LaJuna slides around the corner, and it's obvious that I need to move along, as well. Impatient noises and toe-taps have begun increasing among the customers behind me. On a whim, I spring for a piece of banana cream pie from the dessert case. I don't need it. I shouldn't spend the money, but it looks so good. **Comfort food,** I tell myself.

"That old house you live in," Granny T offers as we settle up. "It's been passed down since the judge died, like everything else. Judge's two older sons, Will and Manford, got the Gossett Industries mill, the foundry, and the gear plant north of town. Judge's youngest son died years ago, left behind a son and a daughter. Those two children inherited the big house and the land that would've gone to their daddy, but the girl, Robin, she's passed away since—sad thing, her just thirty-one years old. Your landlord is her brother, Mr. Nathan Gossett, Judge's grandson, but he won't be fixin' that roof. He lives down to the coast. Got him a shrimp boat. Leased out the Goswood land, left the rest to rot. That boy's the rambling one. Can't be bothered about none of it. Lot of history in that old place. Lot of stories. Sad thing when stories die for the lack of listenin' ears."

I nod in agreement, feel the whip-sting of my own family ties flapping in the wind. I don't know beans about my familial history and couldn't recite an ancestral story if my life depended on it. I've always tried to tell myself I don't care, but that statement from Granny T hits home. A blush creeps up my neck, and I hear myself blurt out, "Would you be willing to come talk to my classes sometime?"

**"Ffff!"** Her eyes widen. "Did you listen at me while ago when I told you I didn't make it past the eighth grade? You've got to have the banker, and the mayor, and the manager from the foundry come talk to these kids. Folks that's amounted to much."

"Well, just . . . please think about it." An idea blooms in my head, unfolding as if by fast-motion photography. "It's what you said about the stories. The kids should hear them, you know?" Maybe real stories from people around here would touch my students in a way that **Animal Farm** can't. "I'm not having much luck getting them interested in my classroom books, and there aren't enough copies anyway."

"This school ain't got nothin'," a forty-something freckle-faced redhead behind me mutters, air whistling through a cracked front tooth. "Our boys got all the way to district last year, and they gotta wear cleats somebody else's used before them. This school's crap. School board's crap, too. Them kids over at Lakeland school get everything, and ours don't get squat."

Something's about to spill from my mouth that's probably better left unsaid, so I just nod and take my to-go container. At least the football team has enough cleats for everyone. That's more than I can say for books in the English room.

When I exit, LaJuna is settling herself on an overturned trash can near the side of the building where two guys in meat-spattered aprons squat in the shade, smoking cigarettes. LaJuna flashes a covert glance my way as I move past, then turns her attention toward a kid on a rust-dotted spyder bike, wobbling across the highway. He barely makes it into the Ben Franklin parking lot before a minivan zips past. If I'm not mistaken, he's the little guy from the crosswalk incident. A city police car turns in, and I hope there's a safety scolding in the making, but the officer seems more interested in my improperly parked vehicle.

I hurry through tiny rain lakes in the gravel, back across the grassy muck border and to my car. Pointing at the Ben Franklin, I give the officer the thumbs-up. He rolls down the window, rests a meaty elbow on the frame, and warns, "No restaurant parkin' over here."

"Sorry! I was trying to figure out where to buy some roofing tar."

"No place open on Sunday for that. Blue law." His eyes scrunch into his sweat-sheened red cheeks as he studies my vehicle. "And get a bumper on that thang. I see it like that again, I'll write it up."

I make promises I can't afford to keep, and he leaves. **One day at a time,** I tell myself and hear the theme song from the TV show in my head. It was not only one of my favorites as a teenager—Valerie Bertinelli made being half-Italian look very cool, especially after she married Eddie Van Halen—that theme song has become my motto for this weird, transitional year.

The little boy splashes through the grassy strip on his too-big bike, lets it topple to one side, and skip-skids on the wet gravel until he manages a stop. Kicking a leg over the bar, he proceeds to the back of the Cluck. I watch as he talks through the screen, then gains a chicken leg from one of the workers, who quickly shoos him away. Off he trots, pushing the bike, chicken leg and handlebars all clutched together. The corner of the store building obscures my view, and he's gone.

**Maybe I should walk around there and talk to him about crossing streets.** I contemplate my new position as an authority figure. Teachers are supposed to look after kids. . . .

"Here." The voice startles me. LaJuna is standing on the other side of my car door. Three long, dark braids escape her hair band and bisect her young face. She lets them hang like the pickets of a stockade fence as she holds out a restaurant ticket, arm stretched as far as it'll go. "Here." Shaking the ticket, she glances uncomfortably over her shoulder.

She retracts instantly when I take what she's offering. One hand braces on a skinny hip. "That's my Aunt Sarge's phone number and address where she lives. She's fixing stuff at my Great-Aunt Dicey's house. Aunt Sarge knows how." She watches her muddy tennis shoes instead of me. "She could take care of your roof."

I'm stunned. "I'll call her. Thanks. Really."

LaJuna backs away. "She needs the money, that's all."

"I appreciate this. A lot."

"Uh-huh." Skirting a mud puddle, she departs. It's then I notice something small and rectangular in her back pocket. I lean forward, detecting what I'm pretty sure is one of my missing copies of **Animal Farm.**

I'm staring at it when she stops and looks at me over one shoulder. She starts to say something, then shakes her head, then takes two more steps before turning my way again. Her arms drop in resignation before she finally blurts out, "The judge's big old house is just across the field from that one you rented." A glance flicks in that general direction. "Got lots of books there. Whole walls full, floor to the ceiling. Books nobody even cares about anymore."

# CHAPTER 5

## HANNIE GOSSETT—AUGUSTINE, LOUISIANA, 1875

Sometime, trouble can be like a cut of thread, all tangled up and wrong-twisted from the spinning. Can't see the why of it or how to get it straight, but can't hide from it, either. Back in the old bad days, Missus come in the spinnin' house, find somebody's work a mess, and go at that girl or woman with a quirt, or a spindle, or broom handle.

That old barn was a good place and a fearful place. The women would bring their children, work and sing together, boil the thread in pots of indigo, hickory bark, and copperas to make the colors. Blue, butternut, red. A pretty delight. But always, there's the worry over a tangle, or a dropped thread, and the trouble it could bring. Even now that the wheels and the looms sit quiet and dust covered, someplace far up under the benches, where nobody but us and the mice know of it, there's the old ruined thread and hanks of bad cloth, hiding out of sight like trouble does.

Passing through the spinnin' house, I think of them old hideaways and I try to figure, how can I follow along on Missy's trip so's to find out her secrets? Then, I think, **Hannie, it'd be a heap easier to drive the carriage Missy ordered up, than to try to sneak along after it. You're already dressed like a boy. Who'd know any different?**

I hurry on down to the horse barn and the wagon shed, knowing there won't be a soul there. Percy hires hisself out, shoeing the stock on other places most days now. With Old Missus chairbound, Missy Lavinia away at school, and Old Mister gone to Texas, there's no work for a driver.

I wait in the barn for a yard boy to come running barefoot down the lane. Don't even know the child—house help ain't here long enough to get known these days—but he's so little, he's still in shirttails. The hem catches round his twiggy bare legs while he runs calling ahead that Missy Lavinia wants the cabriolet at the back garden gate, and be quick.

"Already been told," I bark out real deep. "Scoot on back to the house and say to her it'll be up directly."

Before I can blink, there's nothing left of the boy but a dust curtain hanging where he was.

I get to work, but my fingers shake on the halter and harness buckles. My heart makes the sound of Percy's smithing hammer, striking **Tonk! Deling-ding, tonk! Deling-ding.** I can barely tack up the stout copper sorrel mare Old Mister named Ginger the year before the war. She's fretful when I back her twixt the carriage shafts and fasten the straps. Her eye rolls backward to say, **Old Missus catches us at this, what'll happen, you think?**

I gather up my gumption and climb the three iron steps to the box seat that's high over the splashboard, front of the cab. If I can fool Missy Lavinia long enough to sit her in the coach, we ought to get along all right. I'm shaky on the reins, but the mare don't seem to mind. She's a kind old thing and obeys, except she stretches her neck in a long whinny when the stable goes out of view. A horse whinnies back, and that a sound seems ten miles long and loud enough to wake the dead that's buried under the soil behind the orchard.

A shiver rocks me head to foot. If Tati found out what I'm up to, she'd say I only got one oar in the water. I know that, by now, her and Jason and John are in the field, trying to give off the look of a normal day, but they're all watching the lane, wondering and fretting about me. They won't dare come round the Grand House, in case Old Missus and Seddie got suspicions after last night. If Missus sends her houseman out poking around, he won't see one thing out of normal at our place. Tati's too smart for that.

I hate that they'll worry, but there's no help for it. You can't trust nobody at Goswood Grove these days. Can't send a message by anyone.

I catch my breath and rub Grandmama's three blue beads on that leather cord round my neck, and I pray for luck. Then I turn from the home way, steering the mare toward the old garden. Branches bow down from the oaks, bramble vines tying them together like corset laces. They needle and grab at my hat as the old horse and me push on through the clutter. A deerfly pesters Ginger's ears, and she shakes her head and snorts, and jingles the harness.

"Sssshhh, there," I whisper. "Hush up, now."

She tosses her forelocks, rattling the carriage when I pull up just before the old bridge.

Nobody there. Not a sign.

"Missy Lavinia?" I whisper low and scratchy-like, hoping I sound like John, not quite man yet, but getting close. I lean over, try to see off the side of the bridge. "Anybody down there?"

What if Old Missus caught her making ready to sneak away?

A branch snaps and the mare turns her head, perks toward the trees. We listen, but there's not another sound except what's usual. Live oaks shiver, and birds talk, and squirrels argue in the branches.

A woodpecker hammers after grub worms. Ginger fusses at that deerfly, and I get down to shoo it off her ears and quieten her.

Missy Lavinia's almost on me before I hear her coming.

"Boy!" she says, and I jump out of my hide and back in. A whole string of bad memories clamor in my head. Happiest day of my life was when I left the Grand House to live with Tati, and I didn't have to nursemaid Missy anymore. That girl would pinch, hit, swat me with whatever she could get her hands on soon's she was big enough. Seem like she knew early on that it made her mama proud.

I duck my head down hard under the hat. I'll know in a minute if this plan of mine's workable. Missy Lavinia ain't stupid. But we ain't been close up to each other in a long time, either.

"Why haven't you brought me the chaise?" Her voice has the high shriek that sounds like her mama, but she don't look like her mama. Young Missy is stouter and rounder, even than I remember. Taller, too, almost tall as me. "I asked for the **cabriolet,** so as to drive **myself.** Why have you come with the calèche? When I get my hands on that yard boy . . . and where is Percy? Why hasn't he seen to this himself?"

I don't think it's best to say, **Percy's been hiring out to keep hisself in food enough since Missus cut back his pay.** So, instead, I tell her, "Cabriolet's broke, ain't been fixed. Nobody down to the stable, so I got the carriage up and come to drive it."

She's enough put out about the idea that she hauls herself into the carriage on her own without waiting for help. That's best, since I'm trying to keep away.

"We will proceed down the field levee lane, not past the Grand House," she snaps, settling herself into the seat. "Mother is abed. I'll not have her disturbed by our passage." She's trying to sound sharp and bossy like her mama, but even now that she's sixteen and in ladies' skirts, she still sounds like a girl playing at being big.

"Yes'm."

I climb up and chuck the old mare, and make a tight circle round the caved-in reflecting pond. The calèche's big wheels bounce over loose cobblestones and ivy gone wild. Once the way is clear, I hurry the mare on. She's still got a good trot, even though she's up in years enough to be white-frosted at the muzzle and eyes. Her forelocks bounce, keeping the flies off.

We come three miles down the farm levee, then cut over at the little white church where Old Missus made us go every Sunday back in slavery days. Dressed all us up in same white dresses, tied blue ribbons at our waists so we'd look impressible for all the neighbors. Up in the balcony we'd sit and hear the gospel of the white preacher. I ain't been in that building since the freedom. We got our own meetings now. Places where a colored man can preach. We move the spot all the time, to keep the Ku Kluxers and the Knights of the White Camellia away, but we all know where to go and when.

"Stop here," Missy says, and I pull up the mare. **We're goin' to the church house?** I can't ask it, though.

Out from behind comes Juneau Jane, sitting a ladies' saddle on a big gray horse, her skinny legs hanging from her little-girl dress in long black stockings. Now, in the light, I can see that the stockings are more darns than threads and her button boots are almost wore through at the toe. The blue flower-stripe dress is clean, but strained at the seams. She's growed some since that dress was bought.

The horse she's on looks like a handful, tall with a cresty neck that says he was left for stud awhile. The girl's most likely got a way with animals, though, devil-fired, like her mama and all the rest of her kind, with them strange silver-green eyes. That long hair of hers swirls down her waist to the saddle and into the horse's black mane, so the two seem like one creature.

Juneau Jane rides up to the calèche with her chin propped up so high her eyes go to thin slits when she looks down into the carriage. Still, they send a shiver over me. Did she see me watch her last night? Does she know? I push my shoulders up toward my hat to fend off any curse she might try to cast on me.

The air hangs so tight between her and Missy Lavinia you could fiddle a tune on it.

"Follow behind," Missy bites out, like she can't stand the words in her mouth.

**"C'est ce bon."** The girl's Frenchy talk rolls like music. Reminds me of the songs the orphan children sung when the nuns traipsed them out in chorales to perform at the white folks' parties before the war. "Indeed, my intention was thus."

"I won't have you sullying my father's carriage."

"Why should I have need of it, when he has given me this fine horse to ride?"

"Which is more than you merit. He assured me as much before he departed for Texas. You will soon see."

"Indeed." The girl ain't scared as she should be. "**We** will soon see."

The leaf springs complain and groan when Missy shifts in her seat, locking her hands together and stuffing them in the folds of a red day skirt Tati sewed up last summer for her to take off to school. Got to keep up appearances, Old Missus said. The red skirt was a remake from one of Old Missus's dresses. "I am merely being practical, Juneau Jane. Realistic. Were your mother a sensible woman, and not so terribly spoiled, she wouldn't be in a hardship after only a few months of no aid from Father. So, in a way, you and I both find ourselves victims of parental folly, don't we? My goodness! We **do** have something in common. We have both been betrayed by those whose duty it was to protect us, haven't we?"

Juneau Jane don't answer, except to mutter in

French. Maybe she's casting a spell. I don't want to know. I hunker forward over the footboard, far away as I can get, so it'll miss me. I pull my arms in close and stick my tongue to the roof of my mouth and shut my lips tight, so if that curse does pass by, it won't get inside.

"And, of course, we will follow Papa's intentions to the letter, once we know them." Missy Lavinia goes right on talking. She never minded a one-way conversation. "I do intend to hold you to your commitment. Once Papa's papers are found, and should it, indeed, be confirmed that the **worst** has befallen him in Texas, you will abide by his decrees without causing further trouble or embarrassment to my family."

I steer the mare over a pothole in the road, see if I can bounce Missy round a bit to quieten her up. That sugar-sweet voice brings back pokes and whacks, and thumps on the head, and a time in Texas when she give me a tea to drink with a pinch of Seddie's rat powder on top—just wanted to see what'd happen. I was only seven, barely one year past being rescued from Jep Loach's bad deed, and wishing I wouldn't live to be eight after I drank that poison. Missy was five mean years old.

Wish I could tell Juneau Jane that story, even if I got no friendliness toward her. Living high all these years down in Tremé, even as the Gossett money dried up. What did this girl think? That'd go on forever? If she and her mama end up out on the street,

I ain't sorry. About time they learn to work. Work or starve. That's how it is for the rest of us.

I got no reason to care about either one of these two girls, and I don't. All I am is somebody to tend their field, or wash their clothes, or cook their food. What do I get back for it, even now that the emancipation's come? Belly that's hungry more often than not and a roof that leaks over my head and no money to fix it till we can pay off the land contract. Just skin and muscle and bone. No mind. No heart. No dreams.

It's time I quit looking after what belongs to white people and start looking after what belongs to me.

"Boy," Missy snaps. "Hurry along."

"Road mighty rough, Missy," I drawl out, slow and deep. "Be smoother once we git up to the River Road. That road be smoother." Old Ginger's like Goswood Grove itself. Seen better days. This rain-rutted ground is hard on her.

"Do as I say!" Missy Lavinia snaps.

"She steps light in the left front hoof, your mare." Juneau Jane comes out of her quiet to speak for the horse. "Wise to spare her, if we have a distance to travel yet."

**A distance to travel yet,** I think. How long's this errand meant to take? Longer it goes, better chance of us getting caught.

A itch starts under my borrowed shirt. The kind of itch that warns of a knowing.

Mile after mile, crop field after crop field, settlement after settlement, river landing after river landing we pass by, that itch gets deeper, burrows right up under my skin and stays there. This is bad business, and now I'm too far in it to get out.

Feels like we come plumb almost to New Orleans by the time we get where Missy Lavinia has in mind. I smell the place and hear its sounds before seeing it. Coal stoves and woodsmoke. The chug and whistle and **slap-slap** of riverboats churning up the water. The **cough-puff, cough-puff** of cotton gins and steam-fired syrup mills. Smoke hangs low, another sky. It's a dirty place, black soot laying over brick buildings, clapboard houses, and men and horses alike. Mules and workers drag cotton bales, cordwood, hogsheads of sugar, molasses, and whiskey barrels to the paddle wheelers loading to go upriver, north to where folks have money to buy the goods.

Old Ginger's got a pretty good limp now, so I'm glad to pull her up, even if I don't like the look of things here. I weave the carriage through men and crates and wagons, mostly work rigs, tended to by colored help and a few white-trash croppers. There's no fancy outfit like ours anyplace in sight. No ladies, either. We catch notice, coming up the street. White men stop, scratch their chins, and cast glances our way. Coloreds peek from under their hats, shake their heads, and try to catch my eye with warning looks, like I ought to know better.

"Best git your missies on down the road," one

whispers when I climb off to lead Old Ginger through a space where two wagons been parked so narrow, there's almost no way past. "Ain't a place for them."

"Ain't my choice," I mutter low. "Not staying long, neither."

"Best not." The man shifts empty barrels to let us pass. "Don't let the moon find you and your missies out 'long the road, neither."

"Stop dallying!" Missy Lavinia grabs the coachman's whip from the seat and tries to reach the horse with it. "Leave my driver alone, boy. Move out of the way. We've business to attend to."

The man backs off.

"Let the darkies get within five feet of one another, and all they want to do is loll around and chat," Missy squawks. "Isn't that so, boy?"

"Yes'm," I say back. "That sure is true."

For the first time, there's a thrill in fooling her this way. She don't have one thin idea who she's talking to. Might be a sin to lie, but I take pride in it, of a sudden. I take power in it.

We come round some buildings that faces the river on one side. Missy Lavinia wants to go in the alleyway behind, so that's what I do.

"There," she says, like she's been here before, but I got a sense she's seeing all this for the first time. "The red door. Mr. Washburn's shipping office is inside. He is not only an adviser to Papa in matters of law, and the superintendent of Papa's land holdings in Texas, he is also one of Papa's **closest** associates in business, as you may or may not know. Papa took me to dinner with Mr. Washburn in New Orleans. They spoke late into the night in the lounge after I was to retire to our hotel suite. I lingered a bit, of course, to listen. They being members of the same . . . society of gentlemen . . . Mr. Washburn committed to looking after Father's intentions, should Father be unable. Papa later instructed me to seek out Mr. Washburn, if the need should ever arise. He will have copies of Father's papers. Why, he most likely drew them up for Papa personally."

I peek under my hat to gander at Juneau Jane. **She believing all this?** Her kid leather gloves finger the reins while she looks at that building. The big gray horse, he's troubled by her worry. He twists his head back and nuzzles her boot, then nickers soft.

"Come along," Missy pesters, and wants down from the carriage. I got no choice but to help her. "We can't solve our trouble sitting here, now can we? You've nothing to fear, Juneau Jane. Unless, of course, you really **are** uncertain of your position, that is?"

The trouble-itch goes all over me. Missy's rubbing that gold locket she's had almost long as I can remember. She only does that when she's fixing to hatch somethin' awful bad. Juneau Jane best turn that gray horse the other way and spur him to a gallop. Whatever Missy's got in mind to happen next, it ain't good.

I barely hear when that red door creaks open. A tall, well-made man with skin a light shade of brown answers. I'd take him for the butler, but he ain't wearing livery, just a work shirt and brown wool trousers that form over his strong thighs and dip into stovepipe boots at the knee.

He frowns and eyeballs us close, all three. "Yes'm?" he says to Missy. "I help you, Missus? Believe you must've come callin' at the wrong door."

"I'm expected," Missy snaps.

"Hadn't been told of anybody expected." He don't move, and Missy turns peevish.

"I'll see your employer, **boy.** Fetch him for me, now, I say."

"Moses!" A man's voice calls from inside, quick and ornery. "Mind the task I've put you to. Five more men to crew the **Genesee Star.** Healthy with strong backs. Have them here by midnight."

Moses gives us one last look before he steps back into the shadows and is gone.

A white man takes up the empty space. He's tall and thin, hollow in his cheeks with a straw-colored mustache and beard that rounds down and circles the bony point of his chin.

"I'm expected. We've come to see a friend," Missy says, but she's rubbing her neck and sounds like she's got cotton in her throat, so I know she ain't telling the truth.

Stepping out the door, the man chicken-jerks his head side to side, checking the alley. Scars run over the left side of his face like melted candle wax, and a patch covers one eye. The good eye turns my way.

"Our mutual friend specifically requested that only the two of you come."

I squat down, checking the horse's bad leg, getting myself small as possible.

"And we have. Why, other than my driver boy, of course." Missy Lavinia laughs, nervous-like. "The road isn't safe for a woman alone. Surely Mr. Washburn will understand." Missy pulls her hands behind her back, pushing her bosom up to show it off, only she ain't got much of one. She's just square and straight, all the way up and down, big shouldered like Old Mister. "I've a distance to return home on the road yet and barely the daylight needed. I'd prefer to conclude our business as efficiently as possible. I've brought what I was asked to, exactly as requested . . . by Mr. Washburn."

Don't know if anybody else sees it or not, but Missy cuts a quick nod toward Juneau Jane, like **that's** what she was told to bring—her little half sister.

The door opens wide, and the man disappears behind it. A sticky, pricklin' cold goes all over me.

Juneau Jane ties her horse to the wagon but stands flat-footed in the street, her blue-striped skirt and white petticoats catching the wind and molding to the calves of her skinny legs. She threads her arms and crinkles her nose like she's got a whiff of stink. "What is this that you have been requested to bring? How shall I be assured you have not offered compensation to Mr. Washburn as payment for a convenient lie?"

"Mr. Washburn needs nothing from me. Why, the man owns all of this." Missy waves toward the big building and the river landing on past it. "In partnership with Papa, of course. I'd be most pleased to speak with Mr. Washburn alone, but then you'd have to trust that I will bring to you what information I am able to gather. If Mr. Washburn holds the only remaining copy of Papa's papers, I could burn them right here in this building, and you would never know. I assume you'll want to see for yourself. I won't have you questioning me afterward. If you don't come in, you must accept my word."

Juneau Jane's arms go stiff at her sides. Her hands ball into fists. "More freely, I would trust a serpent."

"As I thought." Missy holds out a hand toward Juneau Jane, palm up. "Then let's go inside. We'll do it together."

Juneau Jane sweeps past the stretched hand, marches up the steps, and walks in the door. Last thing I see of her is that long, dark hair.

"Look after the horses, boy. Should anything happen to them, I'll take it out of your hide . . . one way or another." Then Missy Lavinia goes, too.

The red door swings closed, and I hear the bolt slide into the hasp.

I tie off the saddle horse, loosen the checkrein and the belly band a notch on Ginger, then find me a spot in the shade along the wall, wiggle into a empty sugar hogshead turned on its side, let my head fall back, and close my eyes.

The long night with not much sleep comes to catch me before I know it.

But so does the dream of the trader's yard.

That tipped-over barrel turns into the slave pen where I'm carried off from Mama one more time.

## Lost Friends

Dear Editor—I beg leave to make one more inquiry through your valuable paper as to the whereabouts of my brother, Calvin Alston. He left us in the year 1865 in company with a regiment of Federal soldiers. When last heard from he was in Shreveport, Texas. Please address me at Kosciusko, Miss.

D. D. ALSTON

—"Lost Friends" column of the Southwestern December 18, 1879

## CHAPTER 6

### BENNY SILVA—AUGUSTINE, LOUISIANA, 1987

The rain finally stops by the time I get home. Sloshing past the hidden garden saint and up the porch steps, I feel guilty for my slightly emotional phone call to LaJuna's aunt, which I had to let myself into the empty school building to make. Aunt Sarge, whose real name I now know is Donna Alston, probably thinks I am a basket case, but in my own defense, rain was sheeting the school windows in blinding torrents. I could only imagine how much might be streaming through the roof at home, and how close it could be to overwhelming the capacity of my makeshift countertop reservoir.

To her credit, Aunt Sarge is as good as her word. She arrives right behind me, and we enter the house and check my catch pot together, then haul it out to the porch for a dump, before even making introductions.

"You've got a problem." Aunt Sarge is all business. She's a stoutly built African American woman with the look of a fitness coach and a military bearing that silently says, **Don't mess with me.** "I can get out here tomorrow to fix it."

"Tomorrow?" I stammer. "I was hoping to get it taken care of today. Before the rain starts again."

"Tomorrow afternoon," she replies. "Best I can do." She goes on to tell me that she's watching a relative's children until then and has left a neighbor keeping them for a moment, so as to run down here.

I offer to sit with the children myself, even have them hang out there at my house if she will fix the roof.

"Two are down with strep throat," she counters. "Reason why they're not at the babysitter's. And their mama can't miss work. Jobs aren't easy to find around here." There's an edge behind that comment, one that makes me feel like I'm being accused of something. Taking a job that could have been filled by a local, maybe? But I was a last resort for this position. A week before the start of school, Principal Pevoto would've taken anyone with a teaching certificate and a pulse.

"Oh," I muse. "Sorry. I can't take a chance of getting sick. Just started work."

"I know." She adds a rueful smirk. "One of the new victims."

"Yeah."

"Subbed at the school a couple times right after I got out of the army last spring. Couldn't find anything else." The comment requires no further elaboration. Her facial expression says it all. For an instant, the atmosphere between us feels almost collegial. I think she's resisting a smile, but she says, straight-faced, "Just grab their heads and thump them together. Worked for me."

My mouth drops open.

"Course they didn't ask me back again after that." She climbs onto the brick column at the bottom of the porch post, grabs the decking above the rafters, and does a chin-up, then hangs there a minute, studying the roof, before swinging herself easily back onto the porch. The landing is superhero worthy.

This, I register silently, is no ordinary woman. I get the impression she could smoothly vault herself onto the roof barehanded. I want to be like her, not some namby-pamby suburban knucklehead who knows nothing of roof tar.

"All right," she says. "It's patchable."

"Will it cost much?"

"Thirty . . . forty bucks. I charge eight bucks an hour, plus materials."

"Sounds fair." I'm thrilled it's not worse, but this is definitely going to cut into my classroom snack-cake funds. Hopefully I can get the roof money out of my landlord soon.

"But that's not likely to be the last problem you have." She squints upward, points out several places where water has dripped through and inked mildew-colored stains on the beadboard porch ceiling. "Only place this roof needs to go's right over there." She nods toward the cemetery. "Thing's a better fit for a funeral than a prayer."

I chuckle appreciatively. "I like that saying." I'm a collector of creative idioms. I once wrote an entire graduate-level term paper about them. So far, Louisiana is a collector's dream.

"You can borrow it. No charge." A brow lowers and a hooded glance slides my way.

It's easy to forget, when you've been hanging around the college English department for years, that people outside those hallowed halls don't carry on conversations about idioms, or talk at length about the distinction between analogies and metaphors. They don't debate the dividing lines while strolling along, lugging weighty backpacks or sitting in tiny apartments sipping cheap wine in thrift-shop stemware.

I survey the bowed, splotched porch ceiling, wonder how long it might be before this sort of thing starts happening inside the house. "Maybe I can get the landlord to put on a new roof."

Aunt Sarge scratches the skin around her ear, smooths a few stray wisps into a short, slicked-back ponytail bun of chestnut hair. "Good luck with that. Only reason Nathan Gossett kept this house up at all was because Miss Retta was like part of the judge's family. She was hoping to get back here after her stroke. Now that she's passed and the judge's passed, I can pretty much guarantee—Nathan Gossett would be just as glad to let it all fall in. Doubt if he even knows someone like you rented this place."

My back stiffens. "Someone like me?"

"Out-of-towner. Woman moving in alone. This isn't that kind of house."

"I don't mind it." My hackles are rising. "I was moving with my boyfriend . . . fiancé . . . but, well, you can see it's just me here."

Sarge and I have another one of **those** moments. An instant in which some sort of line has been crossed, and we're standing on the same side, strangely simpatico. It's fleeting, like the sudden breeze that kicks up, carrying the scent of more rain. I cast a worried glance.

"That won't get here for a couple hours yet," Sarge assures me. "Be gone by tomorrow morning."

"I hope my drip pan can hold off the tide until then."

She checks her watch and starts down the porch steps. "Put the trash can under it. You've got one, right?"

"Thanks. Yeah. I will." I'm not about to admit the idea never even crossed my mind.

"Be back tomorrow." She lifts a hand in a manner

appropriate for either a dismissive wave or flipping someone the bird.

"Hey," I call just before she climbs into a red pickup truck with a ladder in the back. "How do I get to the judge's house from here? Someone said it's close enough to walk across the field."

"LaJuna tell you that?"

"Why?"

"She likes to go there."

"LaJuna? How does she get all the way out here?" My house is five miles from town.

"Bike, I imagine." Sarge meets my curiosity with a wary look. "She's not hurting anything. She's a good kid."

"Oh I know." In truth, I haven't a clue about who LaJuna really is, other than that she was nice to me at the restaurant. "It seems like a long bike ride, that's all."

Aunt Sarge pauses by her truck, studies me a moment. "Shorter by the old farm levee lane. Cuts across back there." She nods toward the orchard behind my house and the tilled field beyond, where the crops are knee-high and bright green. "Highway goes around all the property that was Goswood Grove. The farm levee lane cuts right through the middle of the plantation, takes you past the back of the big house. When I was a kid, farmers still came and went that way to bring crops to market and their cane to the syrup mill, especially the old folks farming with mules, yet. Couple miles makes a big difference when you're moving at two miles an hour."

My mind hiccups. Mules? This is 1987. I'd guess Sarge to be only in her thirties.

"Thanks again for coming by so quickly. I really appreciate it. I can't be home tomorrow to unlock the house until after school."

She squints again at the roof. "I shouldn't need to get in. Probably have it fixed and be gone before you get here."

I'm a little disappointed. LaJuna's aunt is perhaps a bit gruff, but she's an interesting personality. And she knows things about Augustine, yet I get an inkling that she's not exactly an insider, either. Her perspective could be helpful. Besides, I'd really like to make a friend or two here.

"Of course." I try again. "But if you end up still being around when I get home, I usually brew some coffee after work. Sit out on the screen porch in back and have a cup." It's an awkward invitation, but it's a start.

"Girl, I'd be up all night." She opens her truck door. Stops one more time and gives me the same perplexed look I got when I asked Granny T to speak to my classes. "You need to lay off that stuff in the evening. Messes with your sleep."

"You're probably right." Lately, I don't sleep, but I blame job trauma combined with financial stress. "Well, if I miss you tomorrow, you'll leave a bill for me? Or drop it by the school?"

"I'll stick it in your screen door. Got no interest in that school." She departs without further niceties.

I'm reminded that Augustine operates under some unwritten code I neither understand nor can communicate in. Trying to decipher it is like being tucked in the back bedroom of my father's New York apartment, sitting on the edge of a daybed with my suitcase between my knees, listening as my dad, his wife, and my grandparents conversed in rapid-fire Italian, and wondering if my little half sisters, lying in their beds in the adjoining room, could understand what was being said. About me.

I push that memory aside and hurry back into the house, where I trade my work treads for the duck shoes I used on rainy college campus days. They're the closest things I have to boots, and they will have to do. Hopefully, I won't be wading through anything too deep in order to find this levee lane. I want to at least give it a try before the rain starts again.

Curiosity nibbles as I slog off across the backyard toward the overgrown hedges of oleander and honeysuckle that separate the house property from a small orchard and garden patch, and then the surrounding farm fields.

My shoes are wet inside and encased in five pounds of mud by the time I find a rise of ground that snakes along an irrigation canal. The farm levee lane, I'm guessing. The ghost of a wagon trail traces the top of it, but mostly it's hidden beneath grass and autumn wildflowers.

A shaft of sunlight pushes its way through the haze overhead, as if to encourage me to follow. Live oaks shimmer in the golden glow, dripping diamond-like liquid from waxy leaves. Their gnarled branches clutch closer together, moss curtains swaying aimlessly beneath. In thick shadow, the road seems eerie, otherworldly, a passageway to another realm, like Narnia's wardrobe or Alice's rabbit hole.

I stand and peer down its length, my heart suspended in my chest. I wonder at the conversations this place has heard, the people and animals who have passed along this rise of ground. Who rode in the wagons that hollowed out the ruts? Where were those people going? What did they talk about?

Were there battles here? Did soldiers fire shots across this thoroughfare? Do bullets hide still, encased deep in the fiber and bark of these ancient trees? I know the cursory details of the Civil War, but almost nothing about Louisiana's history. Now that seems like a deficit. I want to understand this reedy, marshy corner of the world that scratches its existence equally from land, and river, and swamp, and sea. My home for the next five years if I can figure out how to survive here.

I need more pieces to the puzzle, but no one is going to hand them to me. I have to **find** them. Dig them from their hiding places, from the ground and the people.

**Listen,** the road seems to admonish. **Listen. I have stories.**

I close my eyes, and I hear voices. Thousands whispering all at once. I can't make out any single one, but I know they're here. What do they have to say?

Opening my eyes, I push my hands into the pockets of my purple raincoat and start walking. The air is quiet, but my mind is noisy. My heart speeds up as I form plans. I need tools to understand this place, to make inroads here. Ding Dongs are tools. Books are tools. But the stories that aren't in books, the ones no one has written down, like the one Granny T shared with me, like Aunt Sarge telling about farmers pulling wagons to market with mules: Those are tools, too.

**Sad thing when stories die for the lack of listenin' ears.** Granny T is right.

There must be other people around here with stories no one's listening to. Real stories that might teach the same lessons I was hoping to bring out in literature. What if I could make them part of my curriculum, somehow? Maybe they could help me understand this place and my students. Maybe they could help my students understand each other.

I'm so busy walking and thinking, scheming and planning and crafting positive visualizations of how to make next week different from last week, that when I come out of my imaginary world into the real one again, the tree tunnel around the road is gone and I'm walking past an enormous farm field. I have no idea how far I've hiked. My mind hasn't registered a thing.

On either side of the raised lane, neatly planted rows of what looks like spiky grass stand half submerged in water. The sunshine is gone, and the vibrant green seems startlingly bright against the cloudy day—as if I'm looking at it on a TV set and a two-year-old has been playing with the color knob.

I realize now what has stopped me in my tracks and awakened me. Two things, rather. One, I've apparently walked right past the judge's place without noticing, because if I continue beyond this field, I'll be in the fringes of town. Two, I can't continue on at the moment. A log is blocking the trail ahead . . . only it's **not** a log. It's an alligator. Not a huge alligator, but big enough that it's just sitting there, rather fearlessly sizing me up.

I fasten my gaze upon it, awed and horrified. It's the largest predator I've ever seen outside a TV screen.

"I move him for ya!" It's then that I notice, in the periphery, the little boy with the bicycle. His dirty shirt bears the evidence of the chicken leg spirited away from the Cluck and Oink earlier.

"No. No-no-**no**!" But my words have zero effect. The kid makes a run at the gator, pushing his bike like a ramrod.

"Stop! Get back!" I rush forward, with no idea what I plan to do.

Fortunately, the alligator is off-put by the brouhaha. It slinks down the side of the lane into the watery field below.

"You shouldn't do that!" I gasp. "Those are dangerous."

The kid blinks, murky light accentuating bewildered wrinkles in his forehead. Wide brown eyes regard me from beneath the impossibly thick lashes I noticed the first day I saw him sitting alone in the empty schoolyard.

"Him's not a very big'un," he says of the alligator.

My heart squeezes. His voice and the slight speech difficulty make him seem even younger than he probably is. Regardless, I don't think a five-or-six-year-old should be wandering all over town like this. Crossing streets and chasing alligators. "What are you **doing** out here by yourself?"

His bony shoulders rise, then fall under the lopsided straps of a faded, grease-striped Spider-Man muscle shirt. That plus the baggy shorts are really a pair of pajamas.

I shake the tension from my hands, try to get my wits about me. The leftover buzz of fear has me still prepared to do battle.

Leaning in, I go for eye contact. "What's your name? Do you live around here?"

He nods.

"Are you lost?"

He shakes his head.

"Do you need help?"

Another nonverbal no.

"All right then, I want you to look at me now." He

flutters a glance up, then away again. I do the teacher thing with two fingers to my eyeballs, then pointed toward his. We're locked in. "You know how to get home from here?"

His gaze holds fast to mine, his head moving uncertainly up and down. He's like a stray kitten in a corner, trying to figure out what he has to do to get away from me.

"Is it very far?"

He points vaguely toward the ramshackle cluster of houses on the other side of the field. "I want you to get on your bike and go right there. And stay there, because there's a storm coming, and I don't want you to get hit by lightning or anything like that, okay?"

He visibly deflates, displeased. He had other plans. I shudder to think of what they were.

"I'm a teacher and kids have to do what teachers say, right?" No answer. "What's your name?"

"Tobiashh."

"Tobias? Well, that's a great name. Good to make your acquaintance, Tobias." I offer a hand, and he's willing to shake, but he giggles and quickly withdraws, tucking the arm behind his back. "Tobias, you are a very brave, and might I add incredibly handsome, little Spider-Man, and I would hate to see you drowned in a rainstorm, or eaten by an alligator." His eyebrows rise, then fall, rise again, then sort of bounce around his little forehead. "And thank you for saving me from the alligator, but I don't want you to ever, ever, **ever** do that with any alligator, ever again, anywhere. Are we clear on that?"

He pulls his bottom lip between his eye teeth—the middle ones are missing—then he licks a smear of dirt or barbecue sauce.

"Promise me now. And remember, superheroes **always** keep their promises. Spider-Man, especially. Spider-Man never breaks a promise. And not to a teacher, for sure."

He likes this superhero thing. The rounded shoulders straighten. He nods. " 'Kay."

"All right. You go on home. Remember, you promised."

Turning the bike toward town, he drapes one knee clumsily over the too-high bar and looks back at me. "What your name?"

"Miss Silva."

He grins, and I wish for a second that I had an elementary teaching certificate.

"Miss Seeba," he says. In a flash, he is gone, the bike wiggling its way down the levee until it's moving fast enough to draw a straight path.

I do a quick alligator check before turning and striding off in the direction from whence I came. No more daydreaming for me. Out here, paying attention is a matter of survival.

Even though I'm watchful on my way back, I almost miss the path to the judge's old house a second time. A row of wildly overgrown crape myrtles shields the property from the lane. Thick with sucker shoots, marauding grapevine, and copious amounts of what looks like poison ivy, it's almost indistinguishable from the natural landscape, save for the empty hulls of the summer's blooms protruding like burned-out Christmas lights.

Between the roots, moss grows in a jigsaw puzzle of green, rectangular shapes. I scrape one with my shoe and uncover the paving stone of a long-ago footpath or driveway. Broken myrtle branches testify to the fact that someone has created a narrow passage through the bowed trunks.

My mind zips back to a six-month stint of living in Mississippi with my mom and her boyfriend at the time, who didn't much care for kids. As an escape, my stuffed animals and I made a secret fort among the crape myrtles of a beautiful, flower-laden estate nearby. Slipping through the gap now feels completely natural, but the garden on the other side, while unkempt, is on a much more epic scale.

Yawning live oaks, tumbledown benches, stately pecan trees, and the remains of winding brick walls provide unorthodox trellises for enormous runs of old-fashioned climbing roses. Here and there, mildew-speckled marble pillars lift their crowns above the sea of greenery, standing like dispossessed royalty, frozen in time. No one has tended this place for a very long while, yet it is beautiful even now, peaceful, despite the wind kicking up.

A ghostly white hand reaches toward my foot as

I turn a corner, and I do an involuntary cat-leap before realizing the severed limb belongs to a toppled one-armed cherub. It lounges nearby on a hammock of tangled trumpet vines, its stone eyes fixed toward heaven with eternal longing. I'm momentarily tempted to rescue it, and then I remember Councilman Walker's story about moving Miss Retta's garden saint to the flower bed at my house. The cherub is undoubtedly more than I can lift. **Maybe he's comfortable there,** I think. **It's a pretty nice view.**

I follow the path over an arched brick bridge, where rainbow-colored fish dart about the shallows below. I'm careful, working my way through the knee-high overgrowth on the other side. Alligators, for one thing. And poison ivy.

The house comes into view around the last bend. I pass a crumbling gateway, and I'm in a yard that's freshly mown, the grass thick and lush and waterlogged from the recent rain. The rumbling sky reminds me that there's more moisture on the way and I'd better not dally. If I had my druthers, I'd stand here and take it all in awhile, soaking up ambiance.

Though both show the unmistakable signs of neglect, the house and yard are magnificent, even from the back. Epic oaks and pecans line the drive and shield it overhead. At least a dozen magnolias stretch upward, their branches capped with thick green leaves. Crape myrtles with intertwined trunks as big around as my leg, antique roses, oleander, althea, milk-and-wine lilies, and spindly four-o'clocks scribble riotous patches of color alongside the old Grand House, pressing free from the artificial confines of flower beds and spilling onto the grass. The sweet scent of nectar wars with the salty air of the oncoming storm.

Presiding silently over its dominion, the stately house stands perched one story off the ground on a raised brick basement. A narrow wooden staircase up the back provides the closest entry to a wide, breezy wraparound gallery framed by thick white columns that lean inward and outward like crooked teeth. The decking groans underfoot as I traverse it, the sound mingling with a mystical, uneven melody of clinking metal and glass.

I find the music's source out front. Near a pair of grand staircases that circle from the ground in ram's horn fashion, a wind chime of forks and spoons clatters softly, testing the worn bit of twine that suspends it. Beside the porch, a barren tree strung with multicolored bottles adds a smattering of indiscriminate high notes.

I knock on the door, peek through the sidelight window, say "Hello?" a few times, even though it's clear that, while the yard has been mowed and the flower beds around the house kept up, no one lives here and no one has for a while. The circular patterns of rain-spattered dust cover the porch floor, disturbed only by the tracks I've made.

I know it instantly when I reach the window to

the room LaJuna told me of. I don't even lean close to the thick, wavy glass or shield the slight glare from the going sun. I just stand before the double glass doors, stare through the grid of cobweb-laced wood and glass, and take in rows upon rows upon rows of books.

A literary treasure trove, waiting to be mined.

## CHAPTER 7

### HANNIE GOSSETT—AUGUSTINE, LOUISIANA, 1875

It's dark when I come awake, not even a moon splinter or a gas lamp or a lit pine knot to see by. Can't think where I am, or how I come to be here, only that my neck's sore, and there's a numb spot on my head where it's rested on rough wood. I reach up to rub it, and half figure I'll find a bald place. Back in our refugee years on the Texas plantation, when work was hard and help had got thin after the swamp fever and the black tongue killed some and others run off, even us from the house worked the cotton patch right alongside the field hands. The job for the children was toting water. Buckets on our heads, back and to, back and to, and back again. So many buckets, the wood rubbed us bald on top long before the harvest.

But there's hair on my head when my fingers test it. Hair sheared short so I don't have to trouble with it, but I've got on a hat instead of a headscarf. John's field hat. My mind trips a step or two, then breaks to a run, comes back to where I am now. In a alley, dead asleep in a hogshead barrel that's still got the boiled sweet smell of cane syrup.

**Ain't supposed to be dark, and you ain't supposed to be still here, Hannie**—that's what hits me first.

Where's Missy?

Where's Juneau Jane?

A noise comes close by, and I know it's what woke me. Somebody's unbuckling the traces and tugs, unhooking Old Ginger from the calèche. "You want us to roll the wagon off in the river, Lieutenant? She's heavy enough, she'll sink mighty good. Nobody know any different, come mornin'."

A man clears his throat. When he talks, I try to decide if he's the same one who took Missy and Juneau Jane in the building hours ago. "Leave it. I'll have it disposed of before morning. Load the horses onto the **Genesee Star.** We'll wait until we're past the mouth of the Red and over the state line into Texas to sell them. The gray is the sort too easily recognized nearby. An ounce of care saves a kettle of trouble, Moses. Remember that, or it'll be your hide."

"Yas'ir, Lieutenant. I remember that."

"You're a good boy, Moses. I reward loyalty as verily as I punish the lack of it."

"Yas'ir."

**Somebody's light-fingering Old Ginger and the gray!** My body comes full alive so quick I can barely keep from jumping out, hollering. We need the horses to get us back home, and beside that, I was left to watch out for the stock and the carriage. If Missy Lavinia don't do me in, Old Missus will when she finds out. I might as soon be sunk in the river right alongside of that calèche, and take John and Jason and Tati with me. Dead from drowning's better than starving to death. Old Missus will make sure we can't get work nor a meal anyplace. Some way, this mess with Missy Lavinia will be all **my** doing, before it's over.

"You find her driver boy yet?" the man asks.

"Nah, sir. Reckon he run off."

"You **find** the boy, Moses. Get **rid** of him."

"Yas'ir. I do that directly, boss."

"See that you don't stop until it's done."

The door opens and closes and the Lieutenant goes into the building, but Moses stays. The alley's so quiet, I don't dare even get my legs bunched under me to run.

Can he hear me breathing?

These men ain't just some horse thieves. There's doings here that's worse by far. Something tied to that man Missy and Juneau Jane went to see, Mr. Washburn.

My leg twitches all on its own. The jingling harness buckles and chains go quiet, and I feel Moses looking my way. Heavy steps grind the stones in the alley, come closer one at a time, careful. A pistol slides from its holster. The hammer draws back.

I swallow my breath, press into the wood staves. **This how I die?** I think to myself. After all these years of toil, I don't grow more than eighteen years old. Don't have a husband. No babies. Just dead by the hand of a bad man and dumped off in the river.

Moses is right on me now, trying to see in the shadows. **Hide me,** I beg that old hogshead and the dark. **Hide me good.**

"Mmm-hmmm . . ." He makes the sound deep in his throat. His smells—tobacco, gun sulfur, wet wood, and sausage grease—dance up my nose.

Why's he waiting? Why don't he shoot? Should I bust out, try to get past him?

Old Ginger nickers and paws, nervous, like she knows this is trouble. Like she feels it the way animals do. She snorts and squeals, and dances over the shafts to take a kick at the gray. The man, Moses, must've stood them too close together. He don't know them two horses ain't familiar. Old boss mare like Ginger, she'll put a young rowdy gelding in his place, first chance she gets.

"Har!" Moses moves away to settle the horses. I weigh out my chances on running or keeping hid.

He stays with the stock, and I hold still. Seems like hours I wait for him to calm the horses, then check up and down the alley, knocking over stacks of crates and kicking up trash piles. Finally, he fires off a shot, but he's far down from me. I wrap my arms over my head and wonder if that bullet's coming my way, but it don't. No more follow after it.

A window slides up just over my head, and the Lieutenant hollers at Moses to get done with the job he's at; there's cargo to load yet. He wants Moses to see to it, personal. Especially the horses. Get them on the boat and get rid of the boy.

"Yas'ir."

The horses' iron shoes ring against the stones and echo on the walls when he leads them off.

I wait till the sounds fade before I creep from my spot and hurry to the calèche to feel around for Missy Lavinia's brown lace reticule. Without it, we ain't got money or food to get us back home. Once it's in my hand, I run like the devil's on my hind heels. Thing is, he might be.

I don't stop till I'm away from that building and down toward the water, where there's men and boys swarming a night-call boat like ants on a mound. Pushing Missy Lavinia's reticule down the front of my britches, I move off from the river landing to where farm wagons and freighter wagons sit parked in a camp lot, waiting for boats that'll come in tomorrow. Tents billow and sigh in the river breeze and wagon curtains and mosquito nets hang stretched to tree branches, sheltering bed pallets underneath.

I slip through the camps quiet as the breeze, the

voice of the river covering the little sounds of my passing. Water's up high from spring rains, the old Mississippi making a ear-filling noise like the drummers on their homemade drums did back before the freedom. When the harvest was in—corn was always last of all—the masters had big corn-shuckin' celebration parties, with platters of ham, sausage, fried chicken, bowls of gravy and peas, Irish potatoes, and barrels of corn liquor, all anybody wanted. Shuck corn and eat and drink and shuck more corn. Play the fiddle and banjo. Sing "Oh! Susanna" and "Swanee River." Have us a frolic, finally free of our labor till it all started up again.

After the white folks had long took their leave of the party and gone up to the Grand House, the fiddlers put away their fiddles and took out the drums, and the people danced in the old way, their bodies slick in the lantern light, swaying and stomping and feeling the rhythms. The old ones, weary in their chairs after the hard season of cane cutting and feeding the steam mill in the sugarhouse, threw back their heads in their chairs and sang songs in the tongues they learned from their mamas and grandmamas. The songs of long-gone places.

Tonight, the river's like they were then, wild and looking for a way free, crashing and pushing at the walls built up by men to keep it trapped.

I find a wagon with nobody near and climb up into a safe place between piles of oilcloth, a space just big enough for me to fit into. Gathering my knees to my chest, I wrap my arms tight, and try to make sense of things in my mind. Off through the wagons and tents, stevedores and roustabouts come and go from the buildings along the row, rolling barrels and wheeling loaded-down handcarts. They move in a rush under the gas lamps, loading the boat so it can take to the water by morning light. That the **Genesee Star** the Lieutenant man spoke of to Moses?

Moses comes and goes from the buildings to the boat, answers my question. He points, gives orders, pushes the workers along. He's a strong, brash man like the slave drivers of the old days. The driver was always the sort that'd use the cat-o'-nine-tails on his own kind to earn hisself good food and a better house. Type who'd kill his own color and bury them out in the field and plow and plant over their graves next season.

I scoot farther back in the canvas when Moses turns toward the camp, even though I know he can't see me here.

How'd Missy get herself tied up with men like these? I need to find the why of it, and so I open her lace bag to see what's there. Inside is a kerchief that smells like it's got corn pone wrapped inside. Missy don't go too many places without food. My stomach squeezes while I finger through the rest of what she was carrying. A coin pouch with six Liberty dollars, Missy's ivory hair combs, and, at the very bottom, something rolled up in one of Old Mister's black silk cravats. The thing inside is hard and heavy and jingles a little when I unwrap it. A shudder goes through me as a little pearl-handle two-shot pistol and a pair of loose rimfire cartridges drops in my palm. I dump the pistol back in the cloth and sit looking at it on my knee.

What's Missy doing with something like that? She's a fool for getting herself in this mess, that's what she is. A fool.

I let the pistol stay there while I open the corn pone and eat some. It's dry and hard to get down without water, so I don't eat much, just enough to settle my stomach and my head. I put the rest back in Missy's reticule with the money pouch. Then I sit looking at the little pistol again.

The smells of pipe smoke and leather, shaving soap and sipping whiskey rise up from the cloth that wrapped it, bringing to mind Old Mister. **He'll come home, and all this mess will be over,** I tell myself. **He'll be good to his word about the land papers. He won't let Old Missus stop it.**

**Old Mister don't know you're here.** The idea slips through my head, sudden as a thief. **Nobody knows it. Not Missus. Not even Missy Lavinia. She thinks some yard boy drove her carriage to this place. Make your way home, Hannie. Don't ever tell nobody what you seen tonight.**

That voice falls easy on my ear, takes me back to the last time somebody else tried to get me to bolt and run from trouble, but I didn't do it. If I had, maybe I'd still have a sister right now. One, at least.

"We oughta take our chance," my sister Epheme had whispered to me all them years ago when Jep Loach had us behind his wagon. We'd stumbled off into the woods to do our necessary, just us two little girls. Our bodies were stiff and sore from walking and whippings and nights on the froze-up ground. The morning air spit ice and the wind moaned like the devil when Epheme looked in my eye and said, "We oughta run, Hannie. You and me. We oughta, while we can."

My heart pounded from fear and cold. Just the night before, Jep Loach had held his knife in the firelight and told us what he'd do if we troubled him. "M-m-marse is comin' to f-fetch us," I'd stammered out, too nervous to work my mouth right.

"Ain't **nobody** gonna save us. We got to save ourselves."

Epheme was just nine, three years older than me, but she was brave. Her words peck at me now. She was right back then. We should've run while we could. Together. Epheme got sold off, two days farther down the road, and that's the last I ever laid eyes on her.

I oughta run now, before I get shot or worse.

Why's it my trouble, what young Missy's got herself into? Her and that girl, that Juneau Jane, who's been fetched up like a queen all these years? Why I oughta care? What'd anybody ever give me? Hard work till my body screams from it and my hands bleed raw from the cotton thorns and I fall to bed nine in the evening, then get up at four the next morning, start all over again.

**One more season. Just one more season, and you're finally gonna have something, Hannie. Something of your own. Make a life. Jason maybe ain't the quickest in the head, not as exciting as some, but he's a fine, honest worker. You know he'd be good to you.**

**Get walking. Get back into your dress and burn these clothes soon's you make it to home.** Nobody ever need know. The plan sets up in my head. I'll tell Tati I been holed up in the cellar of the Grand House, couldn't slip out because there's too many hired boys out sweeping the yard, then I fell asleep after that.

**Nobody's got to know.**

I set my teeth in that idea, and put away the pistol, cinch up Missy's reticule, hard and angry. What'd I do to deserve this mess, anyhow? Stuck here hiding in some wagon camp, dead of night, man chasing after me, wants to shoot me and dump me in the river?

Nothing. That's what. Just like the old days. Young Missy starts her mean ideas to rolling downhill, sits back and waits for somebody to get smushed. Then she stands with her fat little hands behind her back, rocking on them round little feet, proud that she's got away with it.

Not this time. Missy Lavinia can find her own way out of trouble.

I'm bound to get myself to the edge of town while it's still dark, seek a place off the road to hunker down till first light. Can't start for home till then. Colored folk traveling alone, there's still plenty of riders working the night roads, same as the patrollers did back in the old times, keep our kind from going place to place, unless they're doing business for white folk.

Peeking from the tarps, I look over the wagon camp to figure my best way out. Closer toward the landing, a flash of a man in a white shirt catches my eye. I pull back, in case he's looking at me. Then I see it ain't a man, just a set of clothes that's been hung up in a tree branch to dry out overnight. The little cook fire underneath sputters down to coals. A wagon curtain is stretched across and tied to the branch, a net slung over it to keep off the mosquitos.

A big pair of feet pushes up against the net, flopped out sidewards.

The first part of my plan comes clear. I slip from my hiding spot, step soundless on the ground, and move through the patches of shadow and moon to that camp.

I take the hat that dangles there, change it for the one on my head, and try not to think about if it's thieving when you take somebody's hat but leave your own in trade for it. In case Moses, or the scarred man, or his workers are still hunting me, I'll look different when I get on the road tomorrow.

My fingers fly up and down my shirt, undoing the bone buttons. I slip it off and reach for the stranger's white one before the mosquitos have time to get after me. The collar hangs up when I tug, and even though I'm tall, I have to jump to get it loose without tearing. The branch snaps back and pulls at the man's camp shelter, and he tosses on his pallet, snorts and coughs.

I stay still as the dead, waiting for him to settle, before I throw my old shirt on the branch and run off half-naked, carrying his. I hunker down in a stubble field just off from the camps to get dressed. A dog barks in the woods, and then another with it. Then a third. They sing the long, wavering song of a hunt. I hark to the days when the overseers and the patrollers rode the night with their tracking hounds, chasing after the runners that tried to hide in the swamps or head north. Sometimes, the runaways got caught quick. Sometimes, they'd stay out there for months. A few never came back, and we hoped they'd made their way to the free states we'd all heard of.

Mostly, the runners got hungry, or sick with fever, or lonesome for their people, and they wandered home on their own. What happened then depended on their marse or missus. But if a runner got caught in the field, the patrollers would let their dogs chew flesh from bone before dragging whatever was left back to the home plantation. Then everybody, the field hands and the house girls and all the little children on that place, would be stood out to see the poor, tore-up soul and watch the lashing that was to come.

Old Gossett never kept a runner. Always said if a slave wasn't grateful to be fed good and not worked on Sunday except during sugar season, and kept in clothes and shoes, and not sold off from their family, he wasn't worth having. Nearly all of the Gossett help had been raised on the place, but the slaves that'd come from the Loach family as wedding gifts to Old Missus, they had different stories to tell. Their bodies spoke in scars, and the nubs of cutoff fingers and toes, and twisted arms and legs healed crooked after being broke. Was from them and others on plantations near Goswood Grove that we learned how other folks had it. Our worst worry day by day was to watch out for Old Missus's bad temper. A life could be meaner than that, and many were.

I don't want them dogs in the woods to get after me, and since I can't tell what they're chasing tonight, I figure I better hide up closer to town, maybe try to find myself a ride out on a wagon come morning. I could pay for it with the money in Missy's reticule, but I don't dare.

I ponder that, squatting there in the stubble while I button up the shirt placket. Tucking the hem over Missy's reticule in my britches waist, I cinch John's leather belt tight to hold it. Makes me shaped like a fat-bellied boy, which is good. Fat boy in a white shirt and a gray hat. The more different I look from before, the better. Now I just need to find a likely wagon and hide before morning, when that man sees the clothes he left to dry been traded out instead.

The dogs work closer and closer up the woods, so I cross the camp yard again, move near the river landing and listen at the men talking. I watch for just the right kind of wagon—one where the driver's alone and the horses hadn't been rubbed down and picketed, which means they're headed for home at daybreak.

Light warms the sky by the time I find what I need. A old colored man guides his mules to the front of the line. The load in his wagon is covered over and tied down tight. Driver's so crippled, he can't hardly get down off the seat, and I hear him say he's from a place upriver. When the workers untie the ropes, underneath the canvas is a fancy piano like the one Old Missus had before the war. It sings lopsided notes as the men take it down, and the driver limps after it up the boardwalk to the boat, bossing every step.

I start on my way toward that wagon, listening as voices mix with the noise of ropes whining and chains jangling and pulleys squealing. Mules and cows and horses kick and fret while the men make ready to load livestock. Right after that will come passengers, last of all.

**Don't run,** I tell myself, though every inch of muscle and bone inside me wants to. **Move like you hadn't got a worry at all. Like you're just here working the docks with all the rest. Easy-like.**

I pass by a stack of empty crates, grab two and heft them on my shoulders, keeping my head down between. The hat slips low, so's all I can see is the strip of ground in front of my feet. I hear Moses's deep voice someplace nearby hollering out orders.

A pair of stovepipe boots stop in my path. I pull up short, squeezing the crates hard against my head. **Don't look up.**

The boots half turn my way. I tooth my bottom lip, bite hard.

"These'uns get took straight where you been told," the man says. I catch my breath that it ain't Moses's voice and he don't seem to be talking to me, then I check and see it's a big white man, telling a couple stevedores where to haul some trunks. "Best be quick at it, or you'll get you a ride on that boat. Wind up in Texas."

Past the man, farther on toward the river, is Moses. He stands ramrod-straight under a hanging lantern, one tall boot braced on the boardwalk and one in the mud. His palm rests over the pistol holstered to his thigh while he points and yells and tells workers where to put the goods. Every minute or two, he steps up on the boardwalk and takes a wide look around, like he's watching for something. I hope it ain't me.

I move back as the two big trunks get pushed by, strapped on handcarts. A wheel slips off the cypress planks that've been laid over the mud, and the lift handle snaps in two, sending a trunk and the worker sidewards. Something thumps inside the box, hollow like a melon. A whimper comes, low, soft.

The big white man steps forward, holds the trunk from falling on its side. "Best take care," he says while the stevedore gets to his feet. "Bruise up Boss's new dogs, he'd be mighty displeased. Watch them wheels." He puts a knee and shoulder under the trunk to help get it upright on the planks again. Just as he does, something shiny gold falls through a crack along the trunk slats. It snakes down silent and lands in the mud next to the man's foot. I know what it is, even before the workers and the man move on, and I set down one of my crates and scoop up what's been left on the ground.

I open my hand and, there in my palm, glittering in the gas lamp's flickery light, sits the little gold locket Missy Lavinia's been wearing since she got it for Christmas Day when she was six years old.

She'd be dead in her grave before she'd give that up.

## Lost Friends

Mr. Editor—My brother, Israel D. Rust, left his home and parents in New Brighton, Pa., in 1847 I think, started for New Orleans, but we heard that he went up the Arkansas river on a boat. This was the story told us by the young man who accompanied him to the South and who himself returned to Pennsylvania within a few months after they went away. We have never heard from brother since the young man returned. Brother was about 16 years old when he left, rather under size, blue eyes, and the finger next little finger (on the left hand, I think) was cut off. He has a mother, five brothers, and one sister who are extremely desirous to learn his fate, for we hardly expect him to be alive now. Address me at Ennis, Texas.

ALBERT D. RUST

—"Lost Friends" column of the Southwestern February 3, 1881

# CHAPTER 8

BENNY SILVA—AUGUSTINE, LOUISIANA, 1987

The books keep me going. I dream of those books hidden away at Goswood Grove, of tall mahogany shelves with volumes upon volumes of literary treasures, and ladders reaching to the sky. For several days in a row, when I come home from school feeling discouraged by my lack of progress with the kids, I put on my duck shoes and make the trek down the farm levee lane, slip through the crape myrtles, and follow the moss-carpeted paths of the old garden. I stand on the porch like a kid before the Macy's display window at Christmas, and fantasize about what might be possible if I could get my hands on those books.

Loren Eiseley, who was the subject of one of my favorite term papers, wrote, **If there is magic in this world, it is contained in water,** but I have always known that if there is magic in this world, it is contained in books.

I **need** magic. I need a miracle, a superpower. In almost two weeks, I have taught these kids nothing but how to bum cheap snack cakes and sleep in class . . . and that I will physically bar the door if they try to leave before the bell rings, so don't try it. Now they skip my class altogether. I don't know where they are, just that they're not in my room. My unexcused absence reports sit unbothered on a massive stack of similar pink slips in the office. Principal Pevoto's grand plan to turn this school around is in danger of falling victim to **the way things have always been**. He is like the overburdened character in Eiseley's often printed story, throwing beached starfish back into the ocean one by one, while the tide continually deposits more along an endless and merciless shore.

With most of the classroom books now missing, I have resorted to reading aloud from **Animal Farm** daily. This, to high school kids who should be reading for themselves. They don't mind. A few even listen, peeking surreptitiously from the battery of folded arms, drooped heads, and closed eyes.

LaJuna is not among my audience. After our hopeful encounter at the Cluck and Oink, she's been absent

Monday, Tuesday, Wednesday, and now Thursday. I'm disappointed in a soul-crushing sort of way.

Across the hall, a substitute teacher screams incessantly during my readings as she attempts to control science room chaos. The science teacher who started the year with me has already given up and claimed she had to move home because of a flare-up in her mother's lupus. She's gone. Just like that.

I keep telling myself I will not quit. Period. I will gain access to that library at Goswood Grove. Maybe I'm expecting too much, but I can't help believing that, for kids who are given so few choices on a daily basis, just having some could be huge. Beyond that, I want them to see that there is no faster way to change your circumstance than to open a great book.

Books were the escape hatch that carried me away during long, lonely times when my mother was gone. During the years I grew up wondering why my father didn't want much to do with me, and the times I landed in schools where, with my wild black curls and olive-toned skin, I looked different from everyone else, and kids curiously inquired, **What are you, anyway?** Books made me believe that smart girls who didn't necessarily fit in with the popular crowd could be the ones to solve mysteries, rescue people in distress, ferret out international criminals, fly spaceships to distant planets, take up arms and fight battles. Books showed me that not all fathers understand their daughters or even seek to, but that people can turn out okay despite that. Books made me feel beautiful when I wasn't. Capable when I couldn't be.

Books built my identity.

I want that for my students. For those lonely, hollow faces and unsmiling mouths and dulled, discouraged eyes that stare at me from the desks day after day.

The school library will not be a suitable source, even temporarily. The kids are not allowed to take books out because **they can't be trusted with them.** The city library, housed two blocks from the school in an old Carnegie building, is slowly fading into oblivion. The good, fully modern, and well-equipped library is, of course, situated out by the lake, far beyond our reach.

I need to know what help can be found in the hoard at Goswood Grove. To that end, I have asked Coach Davis if I might borrow a pair of the binoculars they use in the announcer's stand during games. He shrugged and muttered that he'd have one of the students bring them over after last period, but this being Thursday, he'd need them back by Friday for the football game.

Following the last-period bell, I diddle around my empty classroom until Lil' Ray and the skinny kid with the always perfectly coiffed hair finally show up at my door. Michael, the other boy, is one of Lil' Ray's favorite toadies.

"Mister Rust. Mister Daigre. I'm assuming Coach Davis sent you with something for me?"

"Mmm-hmmm."

"Yes, ma'am." Because Coach has sent the boys, they are as meek as lambs and display good manners, to boot. Lil' Ray apologizes for not getting here sooner. Michael nods.

"It's all right. I appreciate the delivery." They eyeball the snack-cake drawer, but I don't offer. After dealing with these two knuckleheads desk wrestling and mouthing off daily in class, I'm shocked and almost peeved by all this politeness. "Tell Coach Davis thanks."

"Yes, ma'am," skinny Michael says when Lil' Ray hands over the binoculars.

They start out the door, then Lil' Ray snaps his head up like he hates to ask, but somehow he **must** know, "What'd you want them spyglasses for?"

"What do you want **those** spyglasses for?" I correct. "Remember, you're in the English room, which means English class rules apply."

Michael looks down at his feet, smirks my way. "Lil' Ray and me are in the hall, though."

Good gravy, this kid is quite clever. He's been hiding that fact from me for two weeks. "I claim proximity," I say with a smile. "Technically my territory goes to the middle of the hall all along this stretch in **front** of my classroom. The other side of the hall, now that is science room territory."

Lil' Ray grins and backs up two giant steps into the safe zone. "What'd you want them spyglasses for?"

"Answer a question in my class tomorrow—any

one of the questions I ask about the reading from **Animal Farm**—and I'll tell you after class . . . about the field glasses, I mean." It's worth a try. If I could gain sway with Lil' Ray, I might start turning the tide. He carries a lot of clout in the high school social structure. "**Any** question, but you have to give a good answer. Not just nonsense to make people laugh."

I dream of the day when an actual classroom discussion takes root. Maybe tomorrow will be the day.

Lil' Ray cranes his head away, giving me the fish eye. "Never mind."

"Let me know if you decide otherwise."

They tromp off, jostling and laughing with the abandon of a couple of puppies turned loose in the hall.

I pack up my loaner binoculars and wait for four P.M., the official teacher release time. The binoculars, my notepad, and I have a mission to accomplish, and aside from that, after several days of weather that remained too wet, Aunt Sarge is due at my house at four-fifteen to finally fix the leak around the stovepipe.

I have my keys in hand and I'm grabbing my loaded backpack when I turn from my desk, and, of all people, Granny T from the Cluck and Oink is standing in my doorway with what looks like a case of Mountain Dew on her hip. I suspect that's not what is in the box, though, because her stooped-over frame supports the weight easily as she hobbles to the desk to deposit the load. She pulls out a note card with something written on it. A stern nod indicates that I should peruse the contents of the box.

I dare not refuse, and when I check, the interior is filled with what look like lumpy cocoa cookies, stacked in layer-cake fashion with sheets of waxed paper in-between.

"Quit buying Ding Dongs from the store," she commands. "These're Granny T's 'nanner oatmeal raisin pooperoos. Easy to fix up. Don't cost much. Not too sweet. Child is hungry, he'll eat them. He's not bad hungry, he'll turn up the nose. Long as you don't add more sugar. Keep them just a little sweet. **No** using chocolate chips in place of the raisins unless you're doing it for a party. Never in the classroom, you listenin' at me now? You **want** pooperoos that're just good enough for a hungry child to eat. No better. That's the secret, mmm-hmm?"

She extends the note card. "This here is the recipe. Easy. Cheap. Oatmeal. Butter. Flour. Bit a sugar. Raisin. Old, brown bananas. Ones so ripe, they're squishy like mud and smell up the kitchen. Get them almost free, end of the fresh aisle in the Piggly Wiggly. Anythin' else you need to know?"

I peer into the box, dumbfounded. After a full day at school my head is, as usual, pulsating and my body feels as if it's been run over by a tour bus. My brain is sluggish in coming up with a response. "Oh . . . I . . . oh . . . okay."

**Did I just agree to bake cookies for these little hooligans?**

Granny T wags a craggy finger at me and purses her lips like she's tasted vinegar. "Now, this here . . ." She circles her lecture finger toward the cookies. "This's **your** job, next batch. I can't be helpin' you all the time. I'm a old woman. Got the trouble in my knees. Arthritis in my back. Bad feet. Still have my mind, but I forget it sometimes. I'm old. A crippled-up old woman."

"Oh . . . okay. This was really a kind thing to do." A lump rises in my throat and tears needle my eyes in a completely unexpected assault of emotion. I am not usually the crying sort. In truth, practically never. When you grow up staying mostly in other people's houses, you learn to keep a polite lid on things, not be any bother.

I swallow hard. Think, **What is wrong with you, Benny? Stop it.** "Thanks for going to so much trouble."

"**Ffff!** Wasn't any trouble," Granny T spits out.

I pretend to be busy closing the box. "Well, I do appreciate it. A lot. And I know the kids will."

"All right, then." She points herself toward the door, her exit as self-directed as her entrance. "You stop feeding them kids Ding Dongs. They are just takin' you for a ride. Strip you clean, like locusts in a wheat field. I know. Been a Sunday school teacher longer than you been breathin' air. My departed husband led the choir sixty-nine years before traveling on to glory. Worked the restaurant in the day, practiced music at night and on Sunday. It's no favor to any child, spoilin' him. You want a cream cake from the store in a pretty little package, and you're up big enough to mow grass, pull weeds, wash somebody's windows, run the checkout at the grocery, you go get you a job, buy your **own** cream cakes. Only thing you get free, if you really **did** come hungry, is one old oat mash cookie. And that's only so the mind ain't in the belly. So it can **learn.** You get the chance to sit in a school chair all day, instead of working someplace, you are lucky. Blessed and highly favored. Children ought to appreciate it like we did in my day." She proceeds to the door, still talking. "Spoiled. Spoiled on Ding Dongs."

I wish I'd recorded every bit of that speech on cassette tape. Or better yet, VCR. I'd play it for the kids, over and over and over until something changes.

"Granny T?" I catch her before she makes her way through the door.

"Mmm-hmm?" She hesitates, lips puckered again as she cranes upward.

"Have you thought any more about coming to my class to talk to the kids? It really would be good for them to hear your story."

Once again, she fans off my idea like a giant, annoying gnat. "Oh, honey, I ain't got anything to say." She's quickly out the door, and I'm left with banana oatmeal cocoa pooperoos. Which is more than I had a few minutes ago. So, there's that.

I'm also late to meet Wonder Woman and get

my roof repaired. I put the new cookies in my Ding Dong security vault, otherwise known as the top file drawer, lock it, and hurry home.

Aunt Sarge is already on the roof by the time I pull into the driveway. There is a stepladder propped next to the porch, so I climb it and stand on the top step, my hands keeping balance on the roof, which is still at about the level of my front pants pockets.

I say hello and make my apologies for being late.

"Not a problem," Aunt Sarge mutters around a nail protruding from her mouth like a cigarette. "Didn't need you anyway. All the work's outside."

I perch there a moment, watching with no small bit of admiration as she slides the nail from between her lips and whacks it into a shingle with four efficient hammer strokes. A small package beside her appears to contain additional shingles, which worries me a little. There's more involved here than just roofing tar, clearly. This looks costly.

The ladder wobbles underfoot as I hook a knee onto the roof. Fortunately, today is laundry day, and I have on my oldest pair of work slacks, which I've decided need to go into retirement anyway. I ascend with all the grace of a performing seal trying to mount a circus pony.

A bothered look flicks my way. "You got something else you need to do, no worries. I'm fine up here." There's a sharp defensiveness, as if she's used to battling for the ground she stands on. Maybe it's a military thing. An adaptation to surviving in challenging work environments.

I wonder if that's true of the kids in my class. Could it be that their apparent disdain for me is nothing personal? The thought flutters around the edges of my mind, unexpected and appealing, a bit revolutionary. I always assume people's behaviors are a reaction to something I've done, not that they're just doing their thing.

**Hmmm . . .**

"Roof won't leak when I'm through," Sarge assures me. "I know construction work."

"Oh, I don't doubt it for a minute. And I couldn't tell one way or another, anyway. I have zero experience with roofs, other than living under one." I crawl up and sit. This thing is steep. And higher than I thought. From here, I can see the entire cemetery and across the orchard to the farm field beyond. It's quite a view. "Maybe if I watch, I'll know how to fix it next time. But I thought we were only talking about putting some tar around the pipe or something."

"Needed more than that. Unless you want it to leak again."

"Well, no. I mean, of course not, but . . ."

"You're looking to have a slipshod job done, I'm not your girl." She sits back on her heels, regards me with her head tilted away and her eyes narrowed. "If we've got some other issue, spit it out. All this"—she swirls the hammer like it's a plastic dinner fork—

"squirrel trailing around is a waste of time. Something needs to be said, just say it. That's how I operate. Other people don't like it, that's their problem." A chin wag gives weight to the words. I'm immediately reminded of LaJuna. Tough shells must run in the family.

"The money." She's right, it does feel good to just put it out there. I motion to the nails and the shingles and so forth. "I can't afford all this. I thought we were going to patch it a little until I could get in touch with the landlord," which may not be anytime soon. Finding Nathan Gossett is like chasing down a ghost. I've also tried to reach his two uncles via the offices of Gossett Industries. The Gossetts and Gossett Industries have a thinly veiled aversion to outreach from school personnel, as such communications usually involve requests for grants, donations, and sponsorship money.

Sarge nods, then goes back to work. "Already taken care of."

"I don't want you to do it without getting paid."

"Tracked down your landlord. Got the money out of him."

"What? Who? Nathan Gossett?"

"That's right."

"You **talked** to Nathan Gossett? Today? Is he here?" A hopeful pitter-patter rises in my throat. "I've been trying to contact him—or either of his uncles at Gossett Industries—all week."

"You're not rich enough for Will and Manford

Gossett to bother with, trust me." There's a chill in the summer air all of a sudden. She relents a little when she adds, "Nathan's not so much of a jerk. He's just . . . not into the whole Goswood thing."

"Do you know where I can find him?"

"Not right now. But, like I said, roof's taken care of."

"How did **you** find him?" Good news about the roof, but I want the **man.** The book hoarder.

"I caught up with him at the farmers market. Goes there first thing on Thursdays. Brings a load of shrimp from his boat. Uncle Gable sells it for him."

"**Every** Thursday?" Now we're getting somewhere. "If I went next week, I could find him there? Talk to him?"

"Possible . . . I guess." She pounds a nail, swipes another out of the box in one smooth motion, sinks it as well. **Blam, blam, blam, whack.** The sound echoes off toward the cemetery and the levee. My gaze and my train of thought follow it.

Silence draws me back. When I return to Aunt Sarge, she's squinting at me. "My advice . . . leave it be. Less he's bothered by it, less he'll be thinking about kicking you out. Enjoy the fixed-up roof. Lay low." She returns to her work. "You're welcome."

"Thank you." I mean it with all sincerity. "Although, I'm going to miss the drip bucket thing. I was getting pretty good at timing it."

A couple of nails escape the box and roll my way after her next grab. I stop them and drop them back into the box.

"He's not going to give you a donation for . . . whatever it is you're raising money for. Gossett family policy is that all requests go through public affairs at Gossett Industries." Again, that sharp edge.

"I've heard. I'm not after money, though." Just books. Books that are locked away in a closed-up house, decaying. Books nobody seems to want. Books that need a new home. And love. I'd tell that to Aunt Sarge, but I can't take the risk of anyone warning Nathan Gossett about me. The best chance for victory is a surprise attack. "I only want to talk to him."

"Suit yourself." Her tone adds, **Your funeral.** She shifts another asphalt square into place. "Need to finish this up now. Got kids to watch again tonight while their mama's gone to work."

**Blam, blam, blam, whack.**

"Still sick?"

"Seems like it goes from one to the other."

"That's terrible. And right at the beginning of the school year, too." I butt-scoot downward a bit to indicate that I really do plan to leave her to her work. I have a trek to make before dark, and with a possible line on Nathan Gossett, I'm feeling fairly psyched. "Hey, that reminds me. LaJuna's been absent from my class all week. Is she sick, too?"

"Not sure." Her tone lets me know I've strayed into uncomfortable territory. "LaJuna's mama is a cousin-in-law to me . . . well, ex-cousin-in-law. Has three little kids by two different daddies, plus LaJuna from my cousin she dated in high school. If the little kids are sick, they can't go to the sitter's. LaJuna's probably been home watching the younger ones."

I'm instantly frustrated. "LaJuna shouldn't be kept out of school so she can provide childcare." I think of seeing her with the copy of **Animal Farm** tucked in her back pocket. "She's such a smart kid. And it's the beginning of the year and she's getting further and further behind."

Aunt Sarge flicks a glance my way, jerks her head down again, hammers another nail with gusto. "You people are all the same," she murmurs with just enough volume that I can catch it. And then more loudly, "You ever notice that lots of kids don't get what they deserve? LaJuna's mama makes $3.35 an hour, sweeping floors and cleaning bathrooms down there at Gossett Industries. That's not even enough to cover food and a roof over their heads. You think LaJuna's working at the Cluck so she can get money for the movies and popcorn? She has to help her mama pay the rent. All the daddies are long gone. There's a lot of that around here. Black kids. White kids. Grow up the tough way, and then they start making it tough on themselves. Girls get pregnant young, looking for something they missed out on at home, end up left to raise babies on their own. I'm sure that's not how it is where you come from, but that's how it is for kids around here."

My cheeks flame and my stomach turns inside out. "You don't know a **thing** about where I come from. I understand a lot more than you think about what these kids are dealing with."

But as I say it, I realize it's my mother's story I'm thinking of. I hate admitting that, even to myself, because it awakens old pain and tests the long-held resentments that have kept us apart for over a decade now. But the truth is, my mother conducted our lives the way she did because she grew up in a family that was like many of the families around here. No money for college, no expectation, no encouragement; neglect, abuse, parents with substance issues and not even a source of reliable transportation most of the time. She saw an ad for flight attendant positions. She'd observed that lifestyle on TV and thought it looked like fun. She packed a backpack and hitched a ride from a dying factory town in the hills of Virginia all the way to Norfolk, where she talked her way into a job.

The world she raised me in was light-years from the one she knew. Everything that went wrong between us, my own wounds and scars, and a dull haze of pain I habitually avoid looking into has blinded me to that fact for twenty-seven years. Now I can't avoid the truth.

My mother changed her stars. And mine.

Sarge rolls a look at me. "I'm just guessing from the things you say."

"Yeah, because we've had all these heart-to-heart conversations and whatnot," I spit out. "You know all about me." I crab-crawl to the edge of the roof.

I'm done. She can take her crappy, judgmental attitude and stuff it.

I **know** stars can be changed. I've seen it.

The hammer echoes after me as I dangle one foot to test the ladder, then climb gingerly back down to the soggy grass, open the front door and ram my feet into my duck shoes, then grab the binoculars and a clipboard from the Bug and start off across the yard.

"House is unlocked," I yell in the general direction of the roof. "Go inside if you need to. Lock it when you leave."

For whatever reason, she has stopped to observe my exit, a shingle dangling between her knees. "Where're you headed with those?" She motions to the binoculars and the clipboard, as if we haven't just had words.

"Bird-watching," I snap and start walking.

"Look out for coral snakes," she calls. "That's their territory back there."

A shiver runs under my clothes, but I will not succumb to it. I'm not afraid of coral snakes. I laugh in the face of coral snakes. Besides, I've been over to Goswood Grove multiple times, and I have not seen a snake yet.

Even so, tales I've overheard at school sift through my mind. Stories of swimming holes, flooded rice fields, chicken coops, swamp boats, the dark spaces under front porches . . . and snakes. A little poem whispers as I walk. One of the country kids wrote it on a quiz paper in answer to a question about the most important lesson he'd learned from the daily reading of **Animal Farm.**

**How to tell deadly coral snakes from harmless milksnakes,** he wrote. **Red touches black, friend of Jack. Red touches yellow, kill a fellow.**

That detail was nowhere in the daily reading, but it is good information to have right now, because my borrowed field glasses and I are headed for Goswood Grove, no matter what. Even from outside the window, I'm going to be able to make out the titles gracing those rows upon glorious rows of unused books.

Coach's field glasses, Mr. Clipboard, and I are about to compose a shopping list.

## CHAPTER 9

### HANNIE GOSSETT—LOUISIANA, 1875

I stare off in the night, lay eyes on the water, deep and wide under the moon and boat lamps and shadows. Yellow and white. Light and dark. I pretend I'm back home, safe, but truth is this river's carrying me deeper into trouble by the hour and by the day. Need to go back to my hiding spot for sleep, but looking out over the rails, all I can think is, the last time I was on a packet boat like this one was when Old Marse Gossett herded up a batch of us and sent us with Jep Loach to run from the Yankees, off to Texas. Chained one to the other, and half who couldn't swim, all us knew what'd happen if that bloated-down boat hit a sandbar or a snag and went under.

My mama wept and cried out, **Take off the chains from the children. Please, take off the chains. . . .**

I feel her close to me now. I want her to make me strong. To help me know, was it right what I done when them two big trunks went up the bow ramp onto this boat, and I heard moanin' inside? There was a clatter of men nearby, wrestling the last of the livestock—two teams of fighting, kicking, biting, squealin' bay mules.

Three men, only.

Four mules.

I set down my empty crate, pushed Missy's necklace deep in my pocket, and ran to take up the line to the last mule. Onto the boat I went with that mule, and there I stayed. Hid myself in a space twixt cotton bale stacks taller than two men. Prayed not to wind up buried alive in it.

So far, I ain't.

"Mama . . ." I hear myself whisper now.

"Hush up!" Somebody grabs my wrist and pulls me hard away from the side rails. "Quieten down! Git us throwed in the river, you don't shut yer yap."

It's that boy, Gus McKlatchy, beside me, now, trying to pull me back from the deck's edge. Gus, who's twelve or fourteen years old depending on which time you ask, nothing more than a ragged little pie-eater white boy from someplace back in the bayou.

He's scrawny enough he can slip between the cotton bales and hide away like I been doing. The **Genesee Star** is loaded to the guards, hauling freight and livestock and people. She's a sad, battered old thing, and drafts low in the water, rubbing the shoals and the snags while she trudges her way upriver, slow and painful. Faster boats go by now and again and blow their whistles, passing us up like the **Genesee** is tied on at the banks.

The folk she's carrying are of the sort to barely scratch up money for deck passage. At night, they bed down in the open, with the goods and the cows and the horses. Cinders and ash swirl down from the stacks of passing boats, and we just pray it don't set fire to the cotton.

There's only a few staterooms on the boiler deck for folks that can afford cabin passage. Missy Lavinia and Juneau Jane, if they're alive yet, must be up there. Trouble is, there's no way I can know. During the day, I can mix in with the roustabouts, who are colored men, but that won't get me up in the passenger rooms.

Gus's got the opposite problem. Being a white boy, he don't pass for a roustabout, and he ain't got a ticket to show, if he was asked. He moves round the boat at night. The boy's a thief, and thievin' is a sin, but just now he's all I got to show me the way of things. We ain't friends. I had to give him one of Missy Lavinia's coins so he'd let me share the cotton bales. We help each other, though. Both know if you get caught for a stowaway, they throw you off in the river, let the paddle wheel suck you under. Gus's seen it happen before.

"Hush up," he says and tugs me back toward our hiding place. "You done gone soft in the head?"

"Come to do my necessary while it's still dark out," I say. If he decides I'm fool enough to get him caught, he'll want shed of me.

"Use the slop jar, you ain't got no more sense than to stand here a'gawkin off the edge like this," Gus hisses. "You fall off into the water, and end up gone, then I got nobody that can go about this boat durin' the day and be took for one of the workers, see? Elsewise, you ain't no concern of mine. I don't give a pig toe what you do. But I need **somebody** to sneak in the crew hall and brang me food. I's a growin' boy. Don't like goin' hongry."

"Didn't think of the slop jar," I say of the old bucket Gus stole and that we stuffed a ways down the cotton bales from our hidin' place. We got us a whole house set up under there. **The Palace,** Gus calls it.

Palace for skinny people. We tunneled it like rats. Even made myself a hiding hole for Missy's reticule. Hope Gus ain't found it while I'm gone. He knows I got secrets.

But I'm gonna have to tell him. Been on this slow-moving packet boat almost two days already and hadn't found out nothing on my own. I need Gus's thievin' skills, and the longer I wait to ask, the more it's likely something terrible comes to Missy Lavinia and Juneau Jane. More likely it is they wind up dead or wishing to be. There's things worse than death. You been in slavery days, you know there's things a heap less peaceable than being dead.

To get Gus's help, I got to tell him the truth. At least most of it.

And probably spend another dollar, too.

I wait till we're safe back in our cotton bale house. Gus squirrels into his sleeping place, still grousing about having to go get me.

I twist over on my side, then my belly, so's I can whisper to him, but I smell that he's got his feet turned my way. "Gus, I ought to tell you something."

"I'm sleepin'," he says, irritable.

"But you can't let on to another living soul about it."

"Ain't got time for yer fool talk," he snaps. "You gettin' to be more botherment then a wagonload of two-headed billy goats."

"Make a promise to me, Gus. Could be another dollar in it for you, if you can do what I'm asking. You'll need that money after you leave this boat." Gus ain't as tough as he talks. Boy's scared, just like me.

I swallow hard and tell him about Missy and Juneau Jane going into that building and never coming out, and me seeing them trunks hauled up the boardwalk to the docks, and hearing noises and the man saying it was a dog inside, and then Missy's locket falling in the mud. I don't let on that I'm a girl underneath this shirt and britches and I was Missy's lady maid when I was small. Afraid that might be more than is tolerable. Besides, he don't need to know.

He sits up then. I only know that because I hear him squeeze to his feet in the dark, turn hisself round standing, then wiggle back down twixt the bales. "Well, all that don't mean nothing. How'd you figure they wasn't just robbed or kilt and **left** in the building that one-eyed fella and that Moses fella watched over for that . . . who'd you say . . . that Washbacon man?"

"Washburn. And them trunks was heavy."

"Maybe they done stole everythin' what them girls had and put **it** in them trunks." Right now, it's clear enough, Gus knows more about bad men than I do.

"I **heard** something in that box. Thumpin'. Moanin'."

"The man said the boss had him a new dog in there, right? How you reckon that noise **weren't** a dog?"

"I **know** how a dog sounds. Been scared of dogs all my life. Got a sense when one's near. Smell it, even. Wasn't no dog in them trunks."

"How come you're feared of a dog fer?" Gus spits into the cotton. "Dogs is good to have around. Keep ya comp'ny. Fetch a shot squirrel or a duck or a goose. Tree up possum so's you can git it for supper. Nobody don't like dogs."

"It was Missy Lavinia and Juneau Jane in them trunks."

"So, wa'chew want I's supposed do about it?"

"Use your thievin' skills. Sneak up there on the boiler deck. Tonight. See can you find any sign of them in the passenger cabin or the staterooms."

"I ain't!" Gus scrabbles backward, out of reach.

"There's a dollar in it for you. A **whole** dollar."

"I don't need me a dollar that bad. This trouble of yours ain't **my** affair. I got trouble of my own. First rule a' the river. Don't get drowned. You're caught sniffin' round the first-class passengers, they shoot you, **then** drown you. You want my advisin', I say keep to yer own bid'ness. Live longer thataway. Them girls shoulda thunk what they was doin' before they done it. That's what I say. Ain't **yer** affair, neither."

I don't answer right off. This bargain with Gus needs to be worked careful, done in fine stitching a little at a time, so's he don't even feel the needle going in. "Well, you got a point. That **is** true enough about Missy Lavinia. She's a haughty sort, anyhow. Thinks she can crook a finger, make the whole world do her biddin'. Spoilt from the time she was laying in the cradle."

"Well, there you go, then. Right there."

"But that Juneau Jane, she's just a **child.**" I mutter it, like I'm trying to reason it for myself, not him. "Only a child in short skirts, yet. And Missy played a bad trick on her. Not right for something like that to happen to a child. One that's a little girl yet."

"I ain't hearin' you. I'm gone to sleep."

"Judgment Day is to come for all us sometime.

Some fine day, long away from now. Don't know what I'll say, standin' before the throne, when the good Lord asks me, 'Why'd you let something terrible happen, when you might've stopped it, Hannie?'" I've told him my name is Hannie, short for Hannibal, a boy's name.

"I ain't got religion."

"Her mama's one of them colored Creoles. A witch woman from down in New Orleans. You heard of them? Put curses on people and such."

"If that Juneau Jane gal's a witch child, why don't she fly **herself** outta that box? Come right through the keyhole?"

"Might be she can. Might be, she's hearing us right now, listening at what we say. Might be she's listening to see, **Do we mean to help her or not?** She dies, she'll be a haint, after that. A witch-haint, clinging round our necks. Witch-haints, now them are the worst kind."

"Y-you . . . now, you quit talk . . . quit talkin' like that. Crazy talk."

"**Drive** a body crazy. Them witch-haints will, sure enough. Seen it with my own eyes. Never let a body rest once they got their hackles up. Their cold hands wrap round your neck and—"

"I'm **goin'**." I hear Gus stand up so quick that the cotton trash scrapes his skin, and he lets out a string of cusses under his breath. "Quit talkin' yer crazyment at me. I'm **goin'**. And git my dollar ready."

"I'll have it when you come back." Lord, I hope

I didn't just do to him what Missy done to Juneau Jane. "Be careful, though, Gus, all right?"

"Ain't nothin' careful about this en-**tire** thang. Foolishment, that's what this is."

He's gone and I'm left there to wait. And hope.

I jerk at every little sound. It's deep into the dark of early morning before I hear rustling in the cotton bales.

"Gus?" I whisper.

"Gus's drowned." But I can tell right off, his mood is good. He's chewing on some biscuits he light-fingered up in the passenger cabin. He hands a piece over. It tastes good, but the news is bad.

"They ain't up there," he says. "Not where I can tell it, anyhow, and I done a right fine job of lookin'. Lucky somebody didn't wake up and shoot me, but I'll tell you one thang—the night before it's time for me to hop off'n this boat in Texas, I'm gonna know right where to go lift me some fine goods. Before them up-deck passengers wake and find their watches and wallets and jewelry missin', I'll be long gone."

"Best be careful about things like that. Ain't right." But Gus's habits are the least worry on me right now. "Two big trunks can't just disappear. Or two girls."

"You said that one is a half-haint child. Maybe she done disappeared herself on purpose. You ever think a' that? Maybe she disappeared herself, and while she's at it, she disappeared the **other** girl and both them boxes. A half-haint witch child wouldn't have no trouble doin' that." Bits of chewed biscuit and spit land on my arm. "That's what I think's happened. Makes passable sense, don't it?"

I brush the food off, rest my head, and try to think. "They got to be here someplace."

"Unless they's dumped off the deck, miles back downwater." Gus tries to share me another bite, but I swat it away.

"That ain't right to say." My stomach goes up my neck and burns.

"I's just postulatin'." Gus licks his fingers, carrying on, noisy about it. No telling all the places them fingers been since they last saw soap. "Reckon we best git a wink," he says, and I hear him scuttle around into his sleeping spot. "Be rested up for when we make the turn off the Mississip' onto the Red River. Point our noses toward Caddo Lake and Texas. **Texas,** now that there's the place to be. Hear tell they's so many cattle runnin' loose since the war, why a man can't help but make his fortune. And quick, too. Just gather 'em up, build a herd. That's what I aim to do. Gus McKlatchy is gonna make hisself a rich man. Just need me a horse and a outfit and I'll go round up them free . . ."

I let my muscles go slack, drift off from Gus's talking, start wondering **where** Missy and Juneau Jane might be hid on this boat. I try not to think about trunks getting pushed off in the river, filling with water a little at a time.

Gus pokes me with his toe. "You listenin'?"

"I was thinkin'."

"So, I's just sayin'," he talks drowsy and slow. "Might be a right pearly sit'ation if you come on to Texas with me. Be foreman of my herd I'm gonna gather. We rake in all that money, why then we'll—"

"I **got** me a home." I stop him before he can run on. "Got people waitin' for me down at Goswood Grove."

"**People** is overrated." He makes a strangled sound and coughs hard to cover it, and I can tell I've poked someplace tender. I don't say **sorry,** though. What I got to be sorry to a white boy for?

"Ain't no place in the world like that for me." I don't even know the words are set in my mouth till I hear them. "No place where I'm gonna get rich for just chasin' up a few cows."

"There's Texas."

"Texas won't be like that for me, either."

"Can be if you want it."

"I'm **colored,** Gus. I'm always gonna **be** colored. Ain't nobody will let me pile up a bunch of money. If I can get me part of a sharecrop farm, I'll be doing good as to be expected."

"Pays to do bigger expectin', sometimes. My pa tolt me that once't."

"You got a daddy?"

"Not really."

We're quiet awhile. I travel down my own mind like a river, try to think of, **What do I want?** Try to draw pictures of a life someplace in the wild, far off in Texas. Or maybe up north in Washington, D.C., or Canada or Ohio, with the folks who run off from their marses and missuses years ago and took the Underground Railroad to freedom, long before the soldiers bathed this land in blood and the Federals told us we didn't have to belong to nobody, not one more day forever.

But I do belong to somebody. I belong to that sharecrop farm and Jason and John and Tati. To tilling the land and hoeing the crops and bringing in the harvest. To soil and sweat and blood.

I ain't ever seen some other kind of life. Can't conjure what you never seen.

Maybe that's the reason why, every time Mama calls to me in my dreams, I wake fretful and washed in my own sweat. I'm afraid of the great big **everything** that might be out there. Afraid of all I'm blind to. All I'll never see.

"Gus?" I whisper it soft, case he's gone off to sleep.

"Yeahhh." He yawns.

"It ain't you I'm mad at. It's just things."

"I know."

"I'm grateful you went up to look for Missy and Juneau Jane. I'll fetch you that dollar."

"I don't need it. Got the biscuits for my trouble. Them's enough. I hope they ain't dead—them girls."

"I do, too."

"I don't want them hauntin' after me, is all."

"I don't think they would."

We go quiet awhile again. Then, I say, "Gus?"

"I'm sleepin'."

"All right."

"What'd you want? Might as well say, since you bothered me."

I bite my lips. Make up my mind to toss something out, like a leaf into a river, never know how far the currents might carry it, where it might wash up on shore. "You do a thing for me when you get to Texas? While you're traveling round looking for them wild cattle and such?"

"Might."

"Anywhere you go, and you talk to folks—because I know you talk a heap—you mind asking them, do they know any colored folk, name of the Gossetts or the Loaches? You find anyone like that, maybe you could ask them, have they been missing somebody by the name of Hannie? If you ever find somebody who answers yes, let them know, Hannie's still living back on the old place, Goswood Grove. Same as ever."

Hope flutters up in the hollow of my throat, clumsy like something just born and trying to find its feet. I push it down hard. Best not to let it grow too much, right off. "I got people out there, maybe. In Texas and in the north of Louisiana. All us keep three blue glass beads on a string round our necks. Beads all the way from Africa. My grandmama's beads. I'll show you once it's light enough."

"Yeah, I reckon I could ask here and there. If I think about it."

"I'd be grateful."

"Them's the saddest threesome of words I ever put my ears on, though."

"What is?"

"Them words at the tail end of your story." He smacks his lips, drowsy, while I try to remember what I said. Finally, he gives the words back to me, "**Same as ever.** Them's three mournful bad words."

We go quiet then, and sleep. First light shines above the cotton bales when we wake again. Gus and me come to at the same time, sit up and twist to see each other, worried. The **slap-slap** of the paddle wheel and the engine's rumble is gone. The cotton bale above our heads shudders side to side. We both wiggle up on our haunches at once.

Except for fire, this is the thing that's worried us most. Cotton don't get freighted all the way to Texas; it gets brought out of Texas and south Louisiana and carried north to cloth mills. Sometime before Texas, our cotton palace is bound for an offload. We just don't know when.

First night in our hiding place, we slept in shifts, so's to keep an eye out, but we've turned lazy. Water's been smooth, and the weather's clear, and the boat passes by the towns and the plantations that have their own river landings along the way. Don't even stop for folk that come out to their docks and try to wave her down to catch a berth upwater. The **Genesee Star** is loaded for the long haul. Just eats boiler wood, stops for reload here and there, and steams right on. Ain't the normal way of the river, but it's the way of the **Genesee Star.** She ain't sociable and she don't want to be troubled with new folks.

There's something peculiar about this boat, Gus says. Something wrong. Folks talk in whispers if they talk at all, and the **Genesee** creeps along like a ghost not wanting to be seen by the living.

"We ain't movin'," I whisper to Gus.

"Wooding, I bet. Must be we come in at another farm landin'. Don't hear no town sounds."

"Me neither." Ain't unusual for a boat to stop off no place particular to take on fuel. Swamp folk and farmers make their living woodcutting for the riverboats. White folk doing what used to be the work of gangs of slaves.

The cotton bales shift like something's shoved them hard. The palace sways over our heads, two bales falling together, wedged shoulder to shoulder. "What if they're taking on more than just wood, or bringing goods off the boat?" I whisper.

Gus casts a nervous look. "Hope they ain't." He wiggles to a stand, whispers, "We best git." Then he's headed down the tunnel.

I snatch up my hat, dig out Missy's reticule, shove it in my pants, and start pushing and wiggling like a burrow rabbit with a camp dog at the door. Shucks and twigs pull at my clothes and slice ribbons in my skin while I struggle toward the clear, trying to hold up the walls as I go. Dust and cotton fills the air, falls in my eyes till I can't see, clogs my nose so I can't breathe. My lungs squeeze and I keep pushing on. It's that or die.

Men outside holler and shout orders. Wood hits wood. Metal rings on metal. The floor lists sidewards underfoot. The cotton walls lean.

I hit the end of the tunnel and fall out onto the deck, half-blind and choking on the dust. I'm too turned round to even worry if anybody saw. Getting air again is all that matters.

The light outside is barely gray, the hanging lamps still burning. Men run everyplace, and passengers in deck camps scramble from their bedrolls and tents to grab buckets and carpet bags, smoking pipes and skillet pans that're sliding downhill as the **Genesee Star** leans in the water. There's too much fracas for anybody to notice me. Roustabouts and white men scurry with bundles, crates, and barrels on their backs. Bringing on a new load of cordwood, they've got the boat too overweighted on one side. On account of her shallow hull, she's started to roll. She groans as she ticks another notch sidewards. The main deck goes anthill crazy, men and women snatching up pokes and dogs and children, screaming and yelling, livestock carrying on. Chickens flap in their cages. Cows bellow loud and long and slide against the cow pens. Horses and mules dig for footing on the deck boards and thrash the stalls and whinny. Their calls carry off into blue-white fog so thick you could scoop it with a spoon.

Wood splinters. A woman screams, “My baby! Where’s my baby?”

A boatman hurries by with a load of wood. I figure I’d best get out of here before he has a good look at me.

I move toward the stock pens at the middle of the main deck, thinking I’ll slip closer by the stalls where Old Ginger and Juneau Jane’s gray still are, and pretend I been sent there to calm the horses. But there’s so much commotion, I can’t even get near. I end up pushing myself against the rails on the shoreward side, figuring if the boat goes over, at least I’ll jump. I hope Gus is where he can do the same.

Just as quick as she started leaning, the **Genesee** lets out a heavy moan and rolls back upright in the water. Goods and people slide and clatter. Horses and cattle clomp and fuss. Folks rush to set the mess right.

It’s a while before everything quietens and the crew’s back to bringing wood up from the landing. Down on the riverbank, there ain’t much more than a little cleared spot along a wide sandy stretch. It’s piled high with cut wood. Colored roustabouts and even some passengers hurry up and down the ramp, moving the load onboard. Seems like they’re putting more weight on this boat than she oughta hold. They want her loaded down with as much fuel as she can carry. The **Genesee** ain’t planning on stopping till a ways upriver.

**Might be you’d do best to get off now, Hannie,**

I tell myself. **Here, and then follow the river back home.**

Something hard and wet hits my ear so sudden, sparks bust out behind my eyes and my head rings like a church bell.

"Get to work, boy." A voice pushes through the sound. A knotted hank of rope skims down my shoulder and leg and lands on the deck. "Tote wood. You don't get paid to stand lookin'."

Pulling my hat low, I scurry down the ramp and scrabble round with the others, tying bundles and toting them up on my back. I carry all I can. I don't want to get whipped again.

The deckhand hollers, "Haul that wood! Haul that wood!"

Someplace above the ruckus, I hear Moses's deep voice. "Even out the load! Step up, now, step up!"

I keep my hat low and move in a line with all the others. Don't look at anybody. Don't talk. Make sure nobody sees me in the face.

**This's a sign to you, Hannie,** I tell myself as I work. **You got yourself a way off this boat. Right now. You got a way to leave, go back home. Just duck into them trees.**

Every trip down, I think, **Do it, now.**

Every trip up, I think, **Next round. Next round, you do it.**

But I'm still there, back on the boat when all the wood's loaded. The **Genesee Star** looks like a pregnant woman overdue for the birthing, but she's level in the water, at least.

I stand at the slats near the back, watch the men finish offloading sugar, flour, crates, and barrels of whiskey to pay for the wood. Last thing they do, before swinging in the ramp, is clear folks out of the way and lead two horses down. One sorrel, one silver-white.

Old Ginger and Juneau Jane's gray.

Somebody's decided not to carry them all the way to Texas, after all.

**Go,** I tell myself. **Go now.**

I stand there, froze up with the idea. No one's round the shore that I can see. The only movement is the roustabouts, taking up the ramps. Might be, if I wait till the boat's crawled her way off the sand, I can get a bucket or something to float me, slip into the water and kick hard toward land. The paddle wheel won't be pulling so much while the **Genesee**'s building steam.

Might be I'll end up dead, chopped to bits for the gators to make a meal on.

I try to decide while the **Genesee Star** works her way toward the channel. If I do it, will they just let me go or will they shoot me?

Before I can make up my mind, a big hand clamps over my shirt collar, pulls it up tight. I feel the tall, hard body of a man against me, warm and wet with sweat.

"You swim?" The voice is a brush of river mist against my ear, deep and moist, but I know it right off. Moses.

I make a nod, just barely.

"Then get off this boat." Another hand comes up twixt my legs, and next I know, I'm sailing over the guards and through the air.

Flying free, but not for long.

## Lost Friends

Miss Salliie [sic] Crump, of Marshall, Texas, desired information of her children, Amelia Baker, Harriet and Eliza Hall, Thirza Matilda Rogers, owned and raised by John Baker, of Abingdon, Washington, Co., Virginia. Sallie Crump was taken to Mississippi fifteen or twenty years before the surrender, by David Vance, and from there was brought to Texas, and has since resided in Marshall. Any information leading to the discovery of these long-lost children will bring gladness to a worthy mother's heart.

T. W. LINCOLN

Atlanta Advocate and Virginia papers, please copy.

—"Lost Friends" column of the Southwestern
July 1, 1880

## CHAPTER 10

### BENNY SILVA—AUGUSTINE, LOUISIANA, 1987

Just as my hopes wane, I spot what I'm looking for. Mr. Crump, who runs the Thursday morning farmers market, has already informed me that he can't exactly predict what time Nathan Gossett will show up here, but that I should watch for a blue pickup truck. A blue pickup truck has finally arrived, there are ice chests in the back, and the man driving is decades younger than the average vendor at the farmers market. I can't believe my luck, and I need luck, because I am on a crunch timeline. I've begged the new science teacher across the hall to take my first-hour class in with his if I don't quite make it to school before the first bell.

It's already seven twenty-five. I have just over thirty minutes to get there. Week three of my teaching career has been slightly better than weeks one and two, and even a slim gain is progress. The pooperoos help. Hungry kids like them just enough to eat them. Kids who are not famished would rather avoid them. As Granny T promised, the cookies are cheap to produce, and the Ding Dong budget is way down, since I am once again its only consumer.

Something about baking for the kids engenders an underlying sense of goodwill. They're impressed that I care enough to do it, I think. Either that, or they are intimidated by the fact that I am in communication with Granny T. I'm guilty of splashing her name around as an occasional power play. Every kid in town knows her. She's part nurturer, part mob boss, and as the granddame of the Carter family of Cluck and Oink fame, she controls the local pipeline of smoked meat, boudin balls, and fifteen kinds of pie. She is not a person to be trifled with.

In fact, I wish she were standing here right now. She could probably accomplish this morning's mission in five minutes or less. I ponder that as I watch Nathan Gossett unload a cooler and carry it in, exchanging a greeting along the way with an elderly man wearing a VFW jacket and overalls. The vendor, perhaps?

Nathan isn't quite what I expected. Nothing about him speaks of money. I don't know if that is intentional, or if this is laundry day, but the old jeans, cowboy boots, faded restaurant T-shirt, and baseball cap make him look as if he's dressed for a morning of hard work. After a week and a half of getting the Gossett Industries runaround, I was expecting someone uptight, unfriendly. Perhaps haughty and self-absorbed. But he looks . . . approachable. Jovial, even. Why does such a person abandon a place like Goswood Grove, buy a shrimp boat, and leave the family legacy to rot?

Perhaps I'm about to find out.

I psych myself up like a wrestler ready to jump into the ring, then I lie in wait by the door of the long open-air barn, hoping he'll come out alone. Vendors pass by, carrying stock to their booths. Fresh produce. Jams, jellies, local honey. A few antiques. Handmade baskets, potholders, quilts, and fresh bread. My mouth waters as precious minutes tick away. I'm definitely coming back here when I have more time. I am a flea market ninja. Back in California, I furnished our entire apartment with secondhand finds.

I'm antsy by the time my target emerges, then I'm annoyingly tongue-tied. "Nathan Gossett?" I sound as though I'm about to serve him with legal papers, so I stick out my hand by way of being friendly. He quirks a brow, but accepts the greeting with a grip that's politely firm, yet not crushing. Calloused. I didn't expect that.

"I am so sorry to catch you when you're in the middle of something else. I'll make it quick, I promise. I'm the new English teacher at the high school here in Augustine. Benny Silva. I'm hoping my name rings a bell?" Surely, he's picked up at least **some** of my answering machine messages, or seen my name on the rental contract, or the receptionist at Gossett Industries has relayed my request?

He doesn't respond, and I rush to fill the awkward pause. "I wanted to ask you about a couple things, but mostly the library books. I'm struggling to get the kids interested in reading **at all.** Or writing, for that matter. Less than forty percent of the students in this school read at grade level, and apologies to the late, great George Orwell, but one raggedy classroom set of **Animal Farm** paperbacks isn't doing it. The school library won't **let** the kids take the books out of the room, and the city library is only open three afternoons a week. So, I thought . . . if I could **build** a library in my classroom—a really outstanding, tempting, colorful, gorgeous library, now **that** would be a game changer. There's power in allowing kids to **choose** a book, rather than having to take what's handed to them."

I pause—I have to in order to catch a breath—but I receive no input other than a slight tilt of his head, which I can't yet interpret. And so I continue the frenetic, impassioned sales pitch. "Kids need the opportunity to try different things and get interested, be drawn in by a story. **Every** success starts with reading, even the scores on those hideous new state standardized tests. If you can't **read,** you can't understand the story problems in the math section or the science section, so it doesn't matter how talented you **really** might be at math or science. You'll get held back a grade. You'll think you're stupid. And that's not even mentioning things like the PSATs and SATs and ACTs. How are kids supposed to have a chance at college or scholarships without good reading skills?"

It registers that he's ducking his head, disappearing under the ball cap. I'm coming on too strong.

I wipe sweaty palms on the straight skirt I carefully washed and ironed and combined with heels for a professional appearance and a little more height. I've raked my wavy Italian hair into a slick French twist, added my favorite jewelry . . . done everything I could think of to make a good first impression. But my nerves are getting the best of me.

I take a breath. "I didn't mean to run on. I was really hoping that, since the books are just sitting on the shelves—looking rather lonely, I might add—that you might consider donating them, some of them at least, to a great cause? I'd probably incorporate as many as possible into my classroom and perhaps exchange others with a book dealer I worked for in college. I'd be happy to do the sorting and consult you on everything as much as you'd like, either in person or over the phone. I understand that you don't live here in town?"

His shoulders stiffen. Biceps tighten under suntanned skin. "I don't."

Mental note: **Make no further mention of that.**

"I know it's not the best approach to catch you off

guard like this. I couldn't figure out another way. I did try."

"So . . . you're after a donation for the library?" He tips his head up as if he's anticipating a right cross to the chin. I am momentarily distracted. He has the most interesting eyes, sort of a seawater color that could be green or hazel or gray-blue. Right now, they reflect the Louisiana morning sky. Murky. Slightly cloudy. Gray and troubled. "Donations from the family trust are handled through community relations over at the company. Books for classrooms seem like a valid cause. That's the kind of thing my grandfather intended the trust to support."

"I'm so glad to hear you say that." I sense two things. First, despite the town's latent resentment toward the Gossetts, the youngest grandson comes across as a decent guy. Second, this conversation has darkened what was otherwise a perfectly good day for him. His demeanor has gone from cordial to cautious and somewhat broody. "But . . . I've tried to get a response from Gossett Industries. I've left messages until the receptionists know my voice. No response, other than 'Fill out a form,' which I did. But I can't wait weeks or months. I have to figure out some way to teach these kids **now.** I'd buy books out of my own pocket if I could, but I've just paid for my move here, and I'm a first-year teacher, and I . . . well . . . I don't have the extra cash."

A blush starts around my ears and travels into my cheeks, then slowly paints the rest of my body sticky and hot. This is humiliating. I shouldn't have to resort to begging in order to do my job. "And that's why I thought, since all those books are just sitting there in the library at Goswood Grove, why not put some of them to use?"

He blinks, surprised, clenches his jaw at the mention of Goswood Grove. I realize he's only now cueing in to what I'm asking. He's probably wondering why I know about those books.

How much should I confess? I **have** been trespassing, after all. "One of my students told me about your grandfather's library. Since I'm living basically next door, I did walk over and take a peek through the window. I didn't mean to be invasive, but I'm a hopeless bibliophile."

"You're living next door?"

"I'm your renter." He's more detached from his holdings than I thought. "In the little house by the graveyard? Where Miss Retta used to live? I should have said that at the outset. I assumed you'd recognize my name. I'm the one Aunt Sa . . . I mean Donna took care of the roof emergency for."

He nods, as if I'm finally starting to make sense to him, but not in a good way. "Sorry. Yes. The place sat for quite a while after Miss Retta had her stroke. Her family must've finally gotten around to cleaning it out. I'm sure the agent thought she was doing me a favor by finding a renter, but the house wasn't in any shape for someone to move in at this point."

"Oh, wait. I'm not complaining. I love it there. It's perfect for me. I like being out of town a bit, and the neighbors are so quiet I never hear them at all."

He misses the graveyard joke at first, then his cheek twitches upward. "True." But he's fairly flat about it. "I want to make sure you're aware it's a short-term thing, though. The plans aren't public knowledge yet, so I'd appreciate your not sharing the information, but you should know, since it affects you directly. The cemetery board wants to annex that piece of property. The sale won't happen before Christmas, but after that, you'll need to find a new place."

Stress hits me with tsunami force, drowning the pull of curiosity, books for the students, and everything else. Arrange for a move in the middle of the school year? Find a rental in a town that has barely anything available, especially at this price? Transfer utilities? I'm instantly overwhelmed.

"It's not possible for me to keep the house until the end of the school year?"

"Sorry. The commitment has already been made." His gaze darts off evasively.

I push a palm to my chest to calm the sort of instant panic that always hit the minute my mother announced we were moving again. Having grown up somewhat transient, I've become an adult who values the nest. The home space is sacred. It's the zone where my books and dreams and comfy reading chair live. I need the little clapboard house in the quiet field by the cemetery, where I can walk the paths or the old farm levee lane, breathe and restore and settle my head.

I bite back the sting, stiffen my neck, and say, "I understand. You have to do what you have to do . . . I guess."

He winces, but I can see his resolve solidifying, as well.

"So . . . about the books?" I can at least try to strike that bargain, and I am running out of time to make something good come of this visit.

"The books . . ." He rubs his forehead. He's tired of me, or of the situation, or of being asked for things. Probably all three. "The agent has a key to the place. I'll let her know that it's all right to give it to you. I'm not sure exactly what you'll find in there, but the judge was a reader, and aside from that, he could never resist a kid selling encyclopedias, or **Reader's Digest** subscriptions, or whatever. The last time I was in that room, stuff was stacked everywhere, and the closets were full of books still in the shipping boxes. Somebody should clean that junk out."

I am momentarily struck silent. **Clean that junk out?** What kind of a Neanderthal talks about books that way?

Then I remember. "The real estate agent had a medical issue. She's out of the office. There's been a note on the door for well over a week now."

He frowns, seemingly unaware of that fact. Then he reaches into his pocket, sifts through his key ring, and begins removing a key. He's exasperated by the time it is finally loosed, and he extends it my way.

"Take any of the books you can use, and by the way, let's just keep that between us. If you run across Ben Rideout mowing the place, tell him you're there to sort some things for me. He won't ask for details." The hardening of Nathan's demeanor is swift and definitive, gut level, like my panic over having to move. "Don't send me lists. I don't care. I don't want to know. I don't want any of it." He blows past me, and less than a minute later he's in his truck and gone.

I stand there, drop-jawed, gaping at the bit of patinated brass in my hand. It's old-fashioned, like a skeleton key, but smaller. Scrollwork adorns the edges, and with its diminutive size, the key almost looks like something that would open a trunk, or a pirate's chest, or Alice's tiny entrance to the gardens of Wonderland. Slivers of murky morning sun slide over it, casting strange reflections on my skin. For an instant, I almost make out the shape of a face.

Just as quickly, it's gone.

Fascination grabs me in an overzealous embrace, sweeps me off my feet, fills me with a greedy, ravenous hunger. It takes everything I have to keep from driving straight to Goswood Grove to see what this key might lead to.

Unfortunately, there's the matter of dozens of kids expecting me to continue with **Animal Farm** . . . and to open the pooperoo storage drawer. With a little cooperation from traffic, I can still get there in time to meet my first-period class and properly start the day.

The Bug and I beat it back across town, dodging Gossett Industries pipe trucks and farmers in pick-ups. The replacement science teacher is more than pleased to see me when I sneak in the back door. The bell rings less than three minutes later, and kids flood my classroom.

Fortunately, my first-hour students are only seventh graders, so it's a little easier to intimidate them into taking their seats. Once they can hear me over the din, I tell them that, after we finish talking about adverbs, I'll read them a bit of **Animal Farm,** which is a book the high schoolers are using, but I know they can handle anything the freshmen and sophomores can.

They gasp, straighten in their chairs, look surprised. **Miss Silva, you seem strangely less defeated today, almost giddy,** their expressions say.

If only they knew.

I pull out the supply of pooperoos. "I burned the bottoms a little on this batch. Sorry. But they're not horrible. You know the rules. No pushing. No shoving. No noise, or I close the box. If you want one, come get one."

I attempt a half-hearted lesson on adverbs, then abandon the effort and pick up **Animal Farm** to read to them. Meanwhile, the brass key weighs heavily in my pocket and on my mind. I'm distracted.

I withdraw it between classes, study it in my palm,

contemplate all the hands that held it before mine. I study it in the light at different angles, try to re-create the reflection of a face, but nothing materializes.

I finally give up in favor of checking the wall clock every few minutes, willing it to move faster. When the final bell rings, I'm filled with jubilant energy, the only cloud over my day being that LaJuna was absent in fourth hour. She'd been back for three days in the first part of the week, now poof, gone like a whiff of smoke.

I mull that as I straighten desks, listen to school buses rumble past, and impatiently wait until teacher-release time.

When it arrives, I am out the door with the speed of a cheetah on the hunt.

It's not until I've made my way home and am hiking through the gardens at Goswood Grove that this whole thing starts to seem somewhat questionable. Why would Nathan Gossett give the key over so easily? **Don't send me lists. I don't care. I don't want any of it.** None of this means anything to him? At all? Is he really so disconnected from the house's history? From **his** history?

Am I taking unfair advantage of that?

I know where the growing specter of guilt originates from. I understand family division and family issues. Irreconcilable differences. Wounds and resentments and differing viewpoints that prevent opposite sides from ever meeting in the middle. I have paternal half sisters I've barely even met, a mother

I haven't seen in ten years and intend never to see again and can't forgive for what she did. For what she made me do.

Have I taken advantage of the very ghosts that haunt me most—spotted them somehow in Nathan Gossett and used them to get what I want?

It's a valid question, and yet I find myself on the porch at Goswood Grove anyway, trying to discern which door my key fits and telling myself that I don't care if **Take what you want** is a cannonball, fired across a family battlefield. The best place these books can be is in the hands of people who need them.

Several doors have locks far too modern for the little brass key. The house has obviously been used through the generations, its various inhabitants modernizing it in puzzle-piece fashion—a window here, a door lock there, an aging set of air-conditioners laboring in the back even though the house is vacant, a kitchen that was undoubtedly added long after the home was built. Before that, a separate one probably stood in the yard, built a short distance from the main house to isolate the heat, noise, and fire danger.

A small alcove off the current kitchen offers two entry doors. Through the windows, I can see that one leads straight ahead into a storage pantry, and a second leads to the left, into the kitchen. The tumblers on the ornate brass lock turn as if they were used yesterday. Dust, paint, and a stray coil of ivy relinquish their grip when the door falls open. The ivy slides across my neck, and I shudder in an awkward little dance, tossing it off as I bolt through then stand a moment, unwilling to close the door behind myself.

The house is still and stuffy, humid despite the air-conditioners whirring. No telling what it might take to control the climate in a place this big, rife with ancient floor-to-ceiling windows and doors that list in their frames like tired old men resting against the walls.

I move through the kitchen, which, in the fifties or sixties, must have included all the latest. The red appliances sport space-aged curves, the dials and gauges worthy of the interior of a rocket ship. Black-and-white tile completes the sense that I've stepped into some odd sort of time warp. Everything is tidy, though. The glass-fronted cabinets sit mostly empty. A dish here. A stack of Melmac plates there. A soup tureen with a broken handle. In the adjacent butler's pantry, the situation is similar, though the cabinetry is much older, the crackled, bubbled shellac testifying to the fact that it's probably original to the house. Whatever fancy china or silver the shelves once held is mostly gone. Flatware drawers hang partially open, empty. An odd scattering of remnants collect dust behind leaded glass doors. The overall feel is that of a grandmother's house on the day before the estate sale, after family members have divided up the heirlooms.

I wander, feeling like a peeping Tom as I pass through a dining room with an imposing mahogany table and chairs, the seats covered in green velvet. Massive oil-on-canvas portraits of the house's generational residents look on from the walls. Women in elaborate dresses, their midsections cinched impossibly thin. Men in waistcoats, standing with gold-tipped walking sticks or hunting dogs. A little girl in turn-of-the-century white lace.

The adjoining parlor is appointed in slightly more modern fashion. Sofa, burgundy wingback chairs, console TV in a cabinet with built-in speakers. More recent eras of Gossetts watch me from hanging portraits and easel frames atop the TV cabinet. I pause at a triple-matted display of graduation photos featuring the judge's three sons. Diplomas are framed under each picture—Will and Manford, business graduates from Rice University, and Sterling, the youngest, from the LSU College of Agriculture. It would be easy to guess, just by looking, that he was Nathan's father. There's a strong resemblance.

I can't help but think, **Doesn't Nathan want any of these photos? Not even to remember the dad who died so young?** Sterling Gossett is probably not too much older than Nathan in that photo. He didn't live many more years, I guess.

It's too sad to contemplate further, and so I move on through the parlor to what I know comes next. I'm acquainted with the layout of the house, thanks to my various porch peeking trips. Even so, when I cross the threshold into the library of Goswood Grove, I'm breathless.

The room is glorious, unchanged from what it once was and has always been. Save for the addition of electric lamps, light switches, a plug here and there, and an enormous billiard table that most likely isn't quite as old as the house, nothing has been modernized. I run a hand along the billiard table's leather cover as I pass, snag one of the countless paperbacks stacked there. The judge had so many books, they've spread like the growths of ivy outside the house. The floors, the space under the massive desk, the billiard table, and every inch of every shelf is laden.

I drink in the sight, stand mesmerized, drenched in leather and paper and gold edges and ink and words.

I'm carried away. Lost.

I'm so completely transfixed that I have no idea how much time passes before I realize I am not alone in this house.

# CHAPTER 11

## HANNIE GOSSETT—LOUISIANA, 1875

The river tugs at my clothes as I drag my body up onto the sand, then lay there coughing out water and all that was in my gut. I **can** swim, and the man threw me close enough to shore that it could've been easy to get there, but this river's got its own mind. A strainer tree spun off in the boat's wake, grabbed me up as it whirled by, and dragged me down. Took all I had to get free.

I hear a gator sliding through the mud not far away, and I push to my hands and knees and cough up more water and taste blood.

It's then I touch my neck and feel the empty place. No leather string. No Grandmama's beads.

My legs wobble as I get up and stagger to the shore looking for them. I pull my shirt up and check under it. Missy's reticule slides lower in my wet britches, but the beads ain't there.

I want to scream at that river, cuss it, but I just fall on all fours and cough up the rest of the water, think to myself, **If ever I see that Moses again, I'll kill him dead.**

He's took away all that was left of my people. The last bit of them is gone in the river. Might be it's a sign. A sign to make my way home, where I never should've strayed from. Once I get there, I'll decide who to tell about what. Might be the law can go after the men that grabbed Missy Lavinia and Juneau Jane, but the news can't come from me. I have to find another way to let the sheriff know what's happened.

Looking up and downriver one more time, I wonder how far it is to a place where I can get a ferry crossing to the home side of that big, wide, rushin' water. Not so much as a hint of people hereabouts that I can see. No buildings, no road but the one where we took on wood. It must go someplace. Might be, if the divine providence is on me, nobody's come to collect them horses yet.

It's the best hope I got, so that's where I go.

Before I get there, I hear the sound of men, the jingle of harness buckles, the groan of shafts and singletree. The soft snort of a horse. I ease up my step, but hold out a hope that the woodcutters might be colored folk who'd help me. Closer I come, the more I know their talk is some other language. Not Frenchy talk—I can pick out a handful of that—but something else.

Maybe this is some of the Indians that still live back in the swamps, married in with the whites and the slaves that run off to hide in the woods years ago.

A prickle crawls over me. A warning. Colored folk got to be careful in this world. Womenfolk got to be careful, too. I'm both, so that's double, and the only thing I have to protect myself is a derringer pistol with two cartridges that's wet and probably ruined.

A dog barks, and both men quieten their chatter. I stop where I am, drop down in the brush. The dog rummages closer, and I go fear-cold. Don't even breathe.

**Go away, dog.**

I wait for that thing to flush me out. Back and forth he moves, sniffing loud and fast. He knows he's found something.

A man hollers a sharp grunt of a word.

The dog scampers off, quick as can be.

I let my forehead sag on my arm, catch a breath.

Wagon springs squeak. Wood hits wood. A mule brays. A horse nickers and snorts and paws the ground. The men grouse and mutter, loading up their pay goods.

I crawl forward to where the brush is thin as lace and I can see through in places.

Two men. Not white. Not Indian. Not colored. Something between. Their smell drifts on the wind.

Sweat and sour grease and dirt and whiskey and bodies that don't bother with washing. Long, dark hair hangs from their hats, and mud cakes their raggedy clothes.

The dog is poor and thin, with a patchy bald hide that's bloody from it scratching its mangy skin. The mule pulling the wagon ain't much better. Old and stove-up, he's got sores where the harness's been rubbing and the flies made a feast on the raw flesh.

A good man don't do a mule that way.

Or a dog.

I stay in my hiding place, listen at their strange talk, try not to move while they lead our horses over to the wagon, tie them fast, then climb up and let off the wagon brake. I watch Old Ginger's stocking feet stomp as she fusses about the buffalo gnats and no-see-ums and deerflies. I want to run out and take her back, steal her away somehow, but I know I need to sneak off while I can, get gone from here before the snakes and the panthers come out and the haints rise from the night bayou. Before the rougarou, the man-wolf, comes from the black water and prowls looking to eat.

A quick, sharp squeal of metal on metal pinches off that thought as the wagon cargo slides and shifts. Through the hole in the leaves, I catch a flash of gold. I know what it is almost before my mind can draw up the thought of the two big trunks with brass corner plates.

What was brought onto the **Genesee Star** far upriver just got loaded off here.

Might be them trunks sit empty now. Might be I oughta forget I saw them, and just look after myself. But I follow that wagon instead, staying far back enough that even the dog don't know. My head pounds, and the sweat pours off me, and the mosquitos and the deerflies land and bite. I can't slap, and I can't run. Got to stay quiet.

It's far over yon, wherever those men are headed. Seems like mile after mile we go. My legs get weak, and the tree trunks swirl round my eyes, shadows and sun, leaves and bent crooked branches. A cypress knee catches my toe, and I fall hard into the fringe of a slough. I roll onto my back and lay there looking up at the sky, watching the pieces of blue peek through like Mama's homespun cloth, fresh dyed from the indigo fields.

I lay there waiting for whatever's to come.

Far off, the wagon axle sings out its rhythm. **Squeek, click-click, squeek, click-click, squee . . .**

The men's talk drifts back, loud and rowdy now. They been in the whiskey barrel, maybe.

I curl close to the cypress tree, hide all the bare flesh I can from the mosquitos and the blood flies, close my eyes and let their sounds drift off.

I don't know if I sleep or only fade awhile, but I feel nothing. Worry over nothing.

A touch on my face pulls me from the quiet peace. My eyes burn, sticky and dry when I try to pull them open. The tree shadows have gone long and stretchy with the afternoon sun.

The touch comes again, feathery soft like a kiss. Is it Jesus come to fetch me away? Might be I drowned in the river after all. But the touch stinks of mud and rotted meat.

Something's trying to make a meal out of me! It jumps sidewards as I swat at it, and when I look, there's the old rawboned red tick dog from before. He lowers his half-bare head and watches me with careful brown eyes, ducks his tail against his butt, but wags the tip twixt his back knees like he's hoping I'll toss him some fatback to eat. We stay there, careful about each other for a while before he moves past and laps up rainwater that's caught in the scoop of the cypress knees. I pull myself to it and do the same. That dog and me drink side by side at the same dish.

The water seeps through my body, wakes my arms and feet and mind. The dog sits down and watches, careful. He don't seem in a hurry to go. Must be he's close to home.

"Where'd you come from?" I whisper. "Your place near here?"

I shift to get my legs under me, and the dog shies back. "All right," I whisper. He's about as sad and sorry a hound as I ever saw, scratches, swole-up places, and bare spots all over his body. "You go on home now. Show me where that is."

I get to my feet, and he skitters off and I trek along behind, following his weave through the woods. He don't care to use the road, so we cross it and go down a game trail. The sweet-burn smell of a smokehouse pools the back of my mouth. Dog takes me right to it, at the rear end of a homeplace that's been hollowed out of the woods on high ground. Little slabwood house and barn, smokehouse and outhouse. The chimneys are sticks and mud, like the ones in the old cabins on the Quarter, back in Goswood Grove. Everything on this place leans one way or the other, the bayou eating it up a little at a time. A pirogue sits against the wall of the cabin, with all manner of traps for animals and beaver. The leftovers of a deer carcass hang in a tree, flies gathered so thick they climb on each other to get what they're after.

Place is still as the grave. I crouch behind a wood stack high and wide as the cabin, watch and listen while the dog goes on into the yard and sniffs round and digs hisself a hole to lay down in the cool. A horse snorts and stirs a ruckus, kicking the barn's log wall and knocking loose a shower of chink and dirt. A mule brays. The sound travels so loud it sets birds to flying, but the cabin stays still.

I creep round to the barn, peek in. The wagon's parked in the aisle. Ginger and Juneau Jane's gray stand together in a stall, the old mule in the next one. Sweat and lather covers all three. They been carrying on with each other, saying who's boss. Blood drips from the gray's leg, where he's kicked the rails. I move in a little more, so's I can see the back of the wagon. A whiskey barrel and the trunks are gone.

A few steps more and I spot them big boxes with

the brass corners, dumped on the floor of the barn, but they're open, empty inside, when I creep close and check. The smell's as bad as the sight. The stink of stomachs that've wretched up their food and bodies that've soiled theirselves makes me cover my nose, but at least it ain't the smell of death. I take some comfort in that, even if it's small comfort. Don't want to think what it means if Missy and Juneau Jane been carried into that cabin. Don't know what I can do about it, if they have.

I study on the barn, wish there'd be a rifle left there, but on the walls it's just harness hanging, still wet from the morning's work, also a half dozen old Confederate bridles, the round brasses on the browband marked with **CSA**. There's Jeff Davis saddles, too, piled together over the top of empty barrels, Confederate canteens and a kerosene lantern, plus Lucifers in a brass box to strike the fire with.

I dig up a piece of oilcloth that's half-buried in the hay, lay it out on the floor, and go to gathering. Lucifers, a canteen, a tin cup, a piece of broke-off candle, and meat from the smokehouse. I fill a canteen from the rain barrel, sling it over my shoulder and find a hank of rope to tie the oilcloth into a poke. The dog comes round, and I toss him some of the meat, and we don't bother each other. He follows when I carry the poke off to the woods and put it in the branch of a tree where I can grab it if I need to get away in a hurry.

The dog and me squat together in the brush, then,

while I look at that cabin and try to think what to do next. Go for the horses, I guess. Then worry about the rest.

It's on the way back to the barn I notice the space between the stalls and the end wall. Not much more than three foot, but it's sealed up good, hid from the outside. Don't recall seeing a door to it from the aisle. I can think up only one reason for a barn like that, with a room that's made to be a secret place.

Back inside, I search round, find a hatchet hanging through a metal loop on the wall, but it ain't there to be a hatchet. It's there to keep a hasp shut, to hide it. A length of batten wood holds the other side upright. When I wiggle off the batten and lift out the hatchet, the piece of wall comes loose like the lid of a sideways crate.

The room's what I thought. A hiding place like slave poachers used back before the freedom. Even in the shadow dark, I can see pegs hung with slave chains. Men like these would hunt down runaways in the swamp. Grab folks right off the road—free coloreds with papers, mulattos and Creoles, slaves doing their master's bidding and carrying a pass. Men like these didn't bother to question. Just throw a bag over the head of a man, woman, or child, tie them under a tarp in the back of a wagon, hide them in the swamp to sell to a trader marching some sad coffle to a auction sale far off. Men like these do their business the way Jep Loach done his.

The smell comes, then sifts up out of the dark of

that room. Same as the trunks. Stomachs and bowels emptied, then the mess left to sour and rot. "You in here?" I whisper, but no answer comes. I listen hard. Do I hear breathin'?

I move by feel, find a half-warm body dumped 'cross the straw, and then another one. Missy Lavinia and Juneau Jane ain't dead, but they ain't alive, either. They're dressed in no more than their shimmies and drawers. Can't be roused with whispering and shaking and slapping. I poke my head from the room, check the house again. The red tick dog sits in the barn door, watching me, but he just scrubs his half-bare tail back and forth over the dirt, remembering the meat. He won't be no trouble.

**Do the next thing, Hannie,** I tell myself. **Do the next thing and do it quick, before somebody comes.**

I hunt up halters and leads and bridles and the best two of them old war saddles. The cinches and leathers hang rat chewed and weak, but they'll hold, I hope. Got no choice. Only way I can keep them two girls on the horses is to have something to tie them to. Push them up there and hogtie them belly-down, just like the patrollers did to the runaway slaves back in the bad times.

Juneau Jane is a easy task, even though the gelding's tall. She don't weigh much and that horse is so glad to see her, he's gentle as a toy rocky horse while I get her settled. Missy Lavinia, she's a whole other task. She ain't ladylike and airy. She's solid. Weighs way more than a hundred-pound white oak basket full of cotton, that's for definite. But I'm a strong woman, and my heart's pumping so heavy from fear, I'm good as two strong women put together. I get her in the wagon bed, pull Old Ginger up next to it and go to pulling and pushing till Missy's flopped over the saddle and I can tie her there. The stink on her drags dried meat and bile and cypress water right on up my throat, and I swallow back and swallow back and swallow back, check the house, check the house, check the house, thankful for the whiskey them men got from the boat and lots of it. They must be stone drunk asleep in there. I hope they don't know a thing till tomorrow morning, elsewise we'll all end up back in that poacher's hold together.

I tie the old, dull hatchet on one of the saddles, and then the last matter I try to figure is the mule. Less chance of them men catching up to me if I got hooves under me and they don't. If I try to take that mule with me, he's likely to carry on and fuss with the horses and make noise, though. I can turn him loose, and if the luck's on me, he'll wander off in the woods looking for fodder. If the luck ain't, he'll linger near the home barn.

Opening the stall door, I say to that half-starved old soul, "Shush now. If you're smart, you won't ever come back here. These're bad men. They done you in a terrible way." The hide of that poor mule looks like the skin of the old folks who had come as marriage dowry from the Loach plantation. The Loaches used to brand the little ones when they turned a year old. Said it made them harder to steal. Branded the runaways, and any slave they bought, too.

This poor old mule's been hot marked a dozen different times, including by both armies. He's got to carry all that with him forever. "You're a free mule now," I tell him. "You go be free."

He follows out of the barn when I lead the horses away, but I shoo him off, so he trails at a distance while we pick up our poke and wind out from that cabin and through the woods, working inland. The hound follows, too, and I let him. "Guess you're free, too," I tell him when we're well enough away. "No bad men like that oughta have a dog, either."

Missy Lavinia and Juneau Jane's heads flop loose against stirrups. I hope nobody's dead or dying, but there's no help for it. Not one thing I can do, except get us far from here, be careful, quiet, keep my ears peeled, keep off the wagon trail, stay clear of sump holes, or swamp cabins, or towns, or wagons, or folks. Hide from everybody till Missy Lavinia and Juneau Jane can talk on their own. Ain't no way of me explaining what looks like a colored boy, toting two white girls, half dressed and tied belly-down on horses.

I'll be dead before I can even try.

## Lost Friends

Dear Editor—I wish to inquire for my children. We belonged to Mr. Gabriel Smith, president of a college in Missouri. We were sold to a negro trader and brought to Vicksburg, Miss. Pat Carter and I were sold together, and left Ruben and David and Sulier, their sister, in the trader's yard. I heard that Ruben was wounded at Vicksburg, and in the hospital, and the young ones were left with Thomas Smith in Missouri. The ones left were Abraham, William, and Jane Carter. Their father was killed by a negro trader, James Chill, before he would be taken and sold from his family. Address me care of Rev. T. J. Johnson, Carrollton, La.

MINCY CARTER

—"Lost Friends" column of the Southwestern January 10, 1884

## CHAPTER 12

### BENNY SILVA—AUGUSTINE, LOUISIANA, 1987

I slip silently through the house, tracking the sound. I picture mice, squirrels, and the giant nutria rats I've seen swimming in the canals and pools of stagnant water during my walks.

Images of ghosts and ghouls and hideous insect-like aliens percolate through my thoughts. Ax murderers and vagrants. I've always been a horror movie junkie, proud of the fact that I can watch things like that and never take them seriously. Even after years of dating, Christopher hated that I was too busy trying to figure out the next scene and plot twist to actually be scared. **You're so stinking analytical,** he always complained. **It's no fun.**

**It's all just pretend. Smoke and mirrors. Don't be such a sissy,** I'd tease. Growing up as a latchkey kid, you can't panic at every little noise.

But, here in this place, with generations of history I can only guess at, I feel my own vulnerability with strange acuity. Being alone in a shadow-filled old house is different than watching one on TV.

The sounds emanating from the kitchen area are definitely not those of someone stepping casually through the door. Whatever's there, he, she, or **it** does not want to be seen. The movements are quiet, cautious, deliberately careful . . . and so am I. I want to see **it** before it sees me.

At the butler's pantry doorway, I stop and search the long rows of tall mahogany cabinets and well-worn countertops where servants must have staged elaborate meals. The mirrors on the opposing sideboards merely reflect one another and the upper cabinets. Nothing unusual or threatening . . . except . . .

Shifting to gain a better view, I watch in consternation as a skinny rear end in jeans with silver embroidery backs its way out of the lower-left corner cabinet.

**What in the world?**

I recognize the jeans and color-block T-shirt. I've seen them in my fourth-hour class. Albeit not as much as I would like to.

"LaJuna Carter!" I say before she has even straightened. She whirls about, stands at attention. "**What** are you doing?"

I don't ask if she is supposed to be here. No need. It's clear enough from the look on that face.

She effects a jaunty chin bob that reminds me of Aunt Sarge. "I ain't hurtin' nothing." Long, thin fingers circle her skinny hip bones. "How'd you think I knew about all the books? Anyway, the judge **said** I can come. Back before he died, he told me, 'Stop by whenever you want, LaJuna.' Wasn't like anybody else ever came . . . unless they want somethin'. All the judge's kids and grandkids, kept too tied up with their houses on the lake, takin' their boats out fishing. Got to go sit on the beach, because they own places there, too. Can't let **that** go to waste. You have **all** them **houses,** you are a busy person. No time to go sit in some old place with some old man stuck in a wheelchair."

"The judge doesn't own this house anymore."

"I don't steal anything if that's what you think."

"That isn't what I said, but . . . how did you get in, anyway?"

"How did **you**?"

"I have a key."

"I don't need a key. Judge showed me **all** this house's secrets."

I'm intrigued. How could I not be? "I took your suggestion about the books—thank you for that, by the way—and got permission to come here and see what might be useful in getting a classroom library together."

Her eyes widen around their pewter centers. She's surprised and . . . dare I assume . . . impressed that I've managed to breach the ramparts of the Gossett world. "You **find** anything?"

My first inclination is to gush about the book hoard. The library is an amalgamation of the generations of residents in this house. The dust of their reading lives has been left behind like sedimentary layers of sandstone, year upon year, decade upon decade. New books and old ones that probably haven't been touched in a century. Some may be first editions, or even signed. My former boss at Book Bazaar would be weeping on the floor in sheer ecstasy by now.

But the teacher in me is possessed by a completely different agenda. "I haven't been here long . . . because **I** went to school today. That makes **one** of us, doesn't it?"

"I was sick."

"Speedy recovery, huh?" I squat down and stick my head in the cabinet she seemingly just crawled out of. Something's not normal about it, but I can't figure out what. "Look, LaJuna, I know your mother works quite a bit, and that you help out with your little brothers and sisters, but you need to be in class."

"You oughta mind your own business." The sharp-edged retort hints that she may often be in the position of defending her mother. "I hand my papers in. You got plenty of kids who don't do their work. Go hassle them."

"I do . . . well, I try." **Not that it works.** "Regardless, I don't think you should be sneaking in here."

"Mr. Nathan wouldn't care, even if he did know. He's not so bad like his uncles that own the company now. All their snotty wives and all their snotty kids think they run this town. My Great-Aunt Dicey says Sterling was different. Nice to people. Aunt Dicey was right here making lunch for the harvest crew the day Sterling got sucked up in the sugarcane combine. She stayed overnight to look after Robin and Nathan while their daddy was life-flighted off. After he died, his wife packed up the kids and moved away to some mountain. Aunt Dicey knows **all** the business about the Gossetts. She kept house for the judge forever. Used to bring me out here when she took care of me. That's how I knew the judge and that's how I knew Miss Robin."

I picture the players in my mind, imagine the long-ago afternoon when everyday life went horribly wrong.

"Nobody wants this house, anyhow," LaJuna goes on. "Judge's son died out there in the field. Judge died three years ago in his own bed. Miss Robin died two years ago, just walkin' up the stairs one night. Her heart quit. Aunt Dicey says that in every generation of Gossetts there's blue babies, and they had to do surgery on Miss Robin's heart when she was born. But my mama says Miss Robin saw a ghost and it's what killed her. Mama told me there's a curse on this place, and **that's** how come nobody wants it. So you might best get what you need of the books and get out." She shrugs toward the door in a way that lets me know she'd like to limit my tenancy on her turf.

"I'm not the least bit superstitious. Especially when books are at stake." I lean farther into her point-of-entry cabinet, try to discern how she managed that.

"You oughta be. Can't read if you're dead."

"Who says?"

She snorts. "You go to church?"

Elbowing in beside me, she grumbles, "Move your head." I'm barely out of the way before she flips a lever behind the cabinet frame, causing the shelves to fold upward and reveal a hatch underneath. "I told you . . . this house has secrets."

An ancient-looking ladder descends into the raised basement below.

A huge gray rat scurries across a bit of discarded wrought iron garden furniture, and I jerk my head out of the hole. "You came in through **there**?" I catch myself nervously brushing off my hands and arms as I stand up and LaJuna lets the cabinet fall back into place.

She rolls a glance my way. "Those rats're more scared of you than you are of them."

"I doubt that."

"Rats are **always** scared. Unless maybe you're sleeping, then you gotta watch out."

I don't even ask how she has come by that knowledge.

"The judge told me, in the old-old days, they'd bring food in through the basement and pass the trays up this hatch. That way, the kitchen slaves didn't get seen by the guests in the dining room. In the war, the Gossetts could use it to sneak away to the canebrakes if the Yankee soldiers came to arrest people for helping the Confederates. The judge **loved** to tell tales to little kids. He was a nice man. Helped Aunt Dicey get me out of foster care when my mama had to go away to prison."

She says it so naturally, I'm dumbfounded. To cover that up, I change the subject. "Listen, LaJuna, I'll make a deal with you. If you promise me you won't sneak in here anymore, you can come and help me in the afternoons . . . with sorting the library books, I mean. I know you like books. I saw you with a copy of **Animal Farm** in your back pocket."

"It ain't the worst book." She scratches a sneaker along the floor. "Not the best book, either."

"But . . . **only** if you're in school when you're supposed to be. I don't want this to interfere." She's noticeably unimpressed, and so I try to sweeten the deal. "I need to get a good gauge on what's in that library as quickly as I can before . . ." I swallow the rest of **before there's trouble with the rest of the Gossetts.**

A sly look comes my way. She knows. "Now, I **might** help you. Because of the judge. He would probably like it. But I got some conditions, too."

"Fire away. We'll see what we can settle on."

"I can't always come here. I'll try. And I'll try better about school, but lots of times, I need to keep the little kids for Mama. They sure can't go stay with their daddies. Losers. It was Donnie that got Mama in trouble for the drugs. All **she** did wrong was be in the car. Next thing, there's police dragging us off to the emergency children's shelter, and Mama's got three years in the pen. I'm just lucky I had a great-auntie on my daddy's side who could keep me. The little kids don't got that. Can't let them go back in foster care again. So, if you're out to get in our business, make trouble about my school and all, then I ain't part of this book project."

**Or you,** her expression adds. "I need to know up front, though. Yes, or no."

**How can I make that promise?**

**How can I not?**

"Okay . . . all right. Deal. But you have to keep up your end." I offer a handshake, which she avoids by staying out of reach.

Instead, she adds a late-coming codicil to our agreement, "And you can't tell nobody at school that I'm helping you." She grimaces at the thought. "In the school, we ain't friends."

I take heart in the fact that this could mean that outside of school we **are** friends. "Deal," I say, and reluctantly she steps closer, and we shake on it. "You'd probably be bad for my reputation anyway."

"**Pppfff.** Miss Silva, I hate to break it to you, but your reputation can't go anyplace but up from where it is."

"That bad, huh?"

"Miss Silva, you stand there and read to us from

that book and then ask us what we think about it and then give us a quiz. Every. Single. Day. It's **boring.**"

"What do you think we should be doing?"

Lifting her palms, she turns and starts toward the library. "I dunno. You're the teacher."

I follow along as she moves confidently through the house, and we switch into project mode. Safer territory. "So, my thought about the books is to start a stack for ones we might use in a classroom library," I tell her as we enter the room. "Anything from third or fourth grade level through high school." The reality is that I've got kids who are years behind in their reading skills. "Newer books only, though. Nothing antique. Maybe we can clear off the desktop and start putting the antique ones there. Carefully. Old books are fragile. Let's stack the classroom books over by those doors to the porch."

"That's the **gallery.** The judge liked to sit out there and read, when the flies and the skeeters weren't bad," LaJuna informs me. I watch as she steps over to peer out the doors as if she expects to find him there.

She studies the yard for a moment before she continues, "Back in the old-old days, little kid slaves had to stand there with feather fans and chase flies from the rich folks. And in the house, too, but in the dining room they had this old-timey ceiling fan called a punkah. You pulled it back and forth with a rope. They didn't have any screens back then. Just sometimes you'd put cloth on the windows, but that was mostly in cabins like where the slaves lived. Those used to be right out back of the barn and the wagon shed. There was, like, a couple dozen. But folks moved the cabins away on big rollers, so they could sharecrop different patches of land on their own."

I stand openmouthed, amazed, not only that she knows so much history, but that she recites it in such a matter-of-fact fashion. "Where did you learn all those things?"

She shrugs. "Aunt Dicey. And also the judge told me tales. Miss Robin did, too, after she moved in here. She was studying up on stuff about the place. I think she was writing a book or something before she died. She'd have Aunt Dicey, Miss Retta, other folks come out here, tell her what they remembered about Goswood. What tales their relatives passed down. Stuff the old people knew."

"I asked Granny T to come to class and share those stories with us. Maybe you can talk her into it?" From the corner of my eye, I catch what looks like a spark, so I add, "Since **Animal Farm** really isn't all that interesting."

"I was just telling the truth. **Somebody's** got to help you out." Tucking her hands into her pockets, she takes a long breath and surveys the library. "Or else you'll just leave like everybody does."

A warm feeling settles into my chest. I do my best to hide it.

"Anyhow," she goes on, crossing the room, "if you're from around Augustine, and your last name is Loach, or Gossett, no matter what color you are, your way-back history goes to this place, some time or other. Your people didn't get too far from where they started. Probably won't, either."

"There's a whole big world outside Augustine," I point out. "College and all kinds of things."

"Right. Who's got the money for that?"

"There are scholarships. Financial aid."

"Augustine School's for poor folks. The kind that stay put. What're you gonna do with a college degree here anyhow? Aunt Sarge's been to the army and got a college degree, too. You see what she's doing."

I don't have a smooth answer, so I revert to library talk instead. "So, let's stack classroom books over there. But . . . nothing that's going to give us trouble with the parents. No steamy romances or hot-blooded Westerns. If there's a high skin-to-clothes ratio on the cover, set it on the pool table for now." One thing I learned in my student teaching is that trouble with the parents is the bane of a teacher's existence. It is to be avoided at all costs.

"Miss Silva, you don't gotta worry about parents. Around here, they got bigger things to care about than what their kids are doin' in school."

"I doubt that's true."

"You're stubborn, you know that?" She flicks a bemused glance my way, studies me for a minute.

"I'm an optimist."

"I guess." Hooking a toe on a bottom shelf, she starts climbing upward the way tree frogs scale my windows on their suction-cup toes.

"What are you **doing**?" I move into position to catch her if she falls. "There's a ladder over here. Let's move it."

"That ladder can't reach all the way around here. Look at it. Its little slider track stops at the door. The track's broke on this side of the room."

"Then let's work with the bottom shelves today."

"In a minute." She keeps right on going. "But you oughta see what's up here, first."

# CHAPTER 13

## HANNIE GOSSETT—LOUISIANA, 1875

It's deep in the night when I start to say the Our Father over and over and over. Scaredest night I've had since Jep Loach dragged me from the trader's yard and left Mama behind. I whisper the Our Father now, just like I did that night all alone under the wagon, trying to call down the saints.

They came when I was a child, them saints. Took the form of a old pasty-skinned widow woman that bought me at a courthouse steps sale—did it out of pity because I was poor and thin, crusty with tears and snot and dirt. She took my chin in her hand, and asked, **Child, how old are you? Who is your master and missus? Say the names and do not lie. I'll**

**allow no one to harm you, if you speak the truth.** I stuttered out the names, and she called for the sheriff, and Jep Loach run off.

The Our Father worked that time, and so I hope it'll save us now. Never been in the swamps at night. Heard folks talk about it, but I ain't ever been. Fear walks over me as I balance behind the saddle on the gray, Juneau Jane slumped like a sack in front of me, and Old Ginger dragging along behind by the reins, lagging and stubborn.

I'm scared of the snakes, I'm scared of the gators, scared Ku Kluxers might find us now that I've had to go along the road to travel by the strip of moonlight threading through the trees. I'm scared them woodcutters might be on our heels by now. I'm scared of haints and the ol' rougarou coming up from his watery hiding place, but more than anything else, I'm scared of the panthers.

It's them you need to worry about most in the swamp at night. Panther can smell you from miles off. He'll come up without a sound, stalk you quiet, so's you don't even know till he jumps on you. He's got no fear of a horse. Panthers go after folks traveling the road alone at night, and the only way anybody can live to tell about it is to outrun the devil, horse and all. Run all the way home. Panther will chase a man right to the barn door and scratch round, try to get in.

I hear one off in the black woods, the call like a

woman's scream. Cuts into me and drives through the bone, but that one's far off. It's what I hear closer, to the left, then to the right—that's what gives me the all-overs now.

The dog barks, but he don't go off after it. Seems like he's scared as I am.

I touch for Grandmama's beads, then remember they ain't there to comfort me no more.

Something rustles down the little slope below of us. I jerk at the noise.

**Sounds like two legs,** I think to myself. **Them men . . .**

**No, four. Four legs. Something heavy. Black bear?**

**Comin' closer, stalking us. Taking our measure. Coming in.**

**No . . . farther off now.**

**Ain't nothing there. It's just your mind, Hannie. Plain crazy with fear.**

The panther screams again, but he's way over yon still. A owl hoots. I shiver hard and hold the neck of my shirt closed, even though I'm sweated down underneath it. It's keeping the mosquitos from sucking me dry.

I push the horses farther, listen into the night, try to think what to do. This old road might stretch on for miles, used for hauling cypress timber out of the swamp and goods to the river, but it ain't a road that goes from one place to the other. Been on it for a long way, and I hadn't seen or heard a sign of people yet. Not even a lamp burning in a cabin or a settlement off through the trees, or a whiff of smoke from a cook fire. Just old wagon camps and the tracks of iron tires and horseshoes. That's all there is showing that folks come and go this way.

Ginger stumbles over a felled branch and falls to her front knees, nearly jerking me over the tail of the gray before I get him stopped. The reins slide through my hands and trickle onto the ground with a soft slap.

"Whoa," I whisper. "Hooo, now."

I get down in a hurry, and it's all I can do to drag Old Ginger back to her feet, without her just laying over on her side and crushing Missy Lavinia, who I guess is still living, but I don't know for sure. Not a sound comes out of her.

"Hooo, now. Easy," I whisper and steady a hand on Ginger's neck. She's got no more in her. Not tonight.

The smell of wet charcoal sifts up in the damp. I move toward it and find what's left of a wagon camp against a upturned tree. Roots reach toward the moon like hands with skinny fingers and long, pointed claws. It's shelter, at least, and the tree's been dead awhile. I can break off dry timber to start a fire.

My bones complain while I go to work at it, rake the ground to scare off any critters, untie the poke and lay the oilcloth flat to sit on, hobble the horses so they can't run off if they get spooked. Last thing, I pull Missy Lavinia and Juneau Jane down, drag them over, and pile them against the tree. They smell so bad, at least the mosquitos don't want them. Their skin's cold from the night and the wet, but both still draw breath. Juneau Jane groans like I hurt her. Missy Lavinia don't move or twitch or make a sound.

Dog stays by my side every step, and though I never been easy round a dog, I'm grateful for his company. **Ain't fair to judge all of something by just a few, Hannie,** I tell myself, and if I survive this day, I've learned something from it. This half-growed pup is a good dog. Got a sweet, kind heart and only needed somebody to be kind back.

**A good heart can't ever let the bad get in,** Mama's voice whispers in my head. **You got a good heart, Hannie. Don't let the bad get in you. Don't open the door to it, no matter how much it comes knockin' or how sweet it sounds askin'.**

I try to coax some water down Missy Lavinia and Juneau Jane, but their eyes roll back and their mouths hang slack and the water just dribbles out over their swelled-up tongues. Finally, I give up and just lay them against the roots again. I drink and eat and hang the dry meat in a tree a little ways off and hunker down. Whatever else happens to us tonight, it'll have to be in the hands of the saints. My hands are too weary to fight, now.

I say the Our Father and wait for sleep to come to me. I don't even make it all the way through.

In the morning, I hear voices. I open my eyes, thinking it's Tati, and John and Jason, already at the fire, stirring up a meal. Summertime, we cook outside to keep the hot out of the cabin.

But sunlight comes bright through the lids of my eyes, little needle points of shadow and color in pretty patterns like Old Missus's Turkish carpets. How's the sun so far up this early in the morning? Every day but Sundays, we rise at four, just like the work gangs did back in the old times. Only there's no overseer's bugle to chase us from our beds. No more field hands with the little homemade box ovens balanced on their heads, carrying coals from the fire, with meat and a sweet potato inside, to be left at the edge of the field and finish cooking for the first few hours of the day.

Now that we're croppers, nobody can make us squat in the dirt and eat like animals do. We sit in a chair, take our meals at a table. Proper. Then we go to work.

I open my eyes, and the sharecrop farm is gone. I trade it for mud-spattered horses. A dog. Two gals slumped together in a bed of oilcloth, half dead or dead, I don't know yet.

And voices.

I'm all the way awake then. I get up in a squat and listen. Ain't close, but I hear somebody. Can't make out the words.

Old Ginger's got her ear cocked toward the road. Dog is up on his feet, looking that way. The gray has his nostrils wide, sniffing. He nickers down in the throat, soft like a whisper.

I scramble to my feet, slip a hand over his muzzle. **"Shhhhh,"** I whisper to him and the dog.

That them sawmill men coming for us?

I put the other hand on Ginger to keep her still. Dog creeps to my feet, and I hook a leg over him, squeeze him twixt my knees.

Out on the road, wagon springs creak and rock. Hooves make a **squish-pop, squish-pop, squish-pop** in the wet dirt. A wheel bounces in a rut. A man grunts. Could be them woodcutters got their mule back.

I lay my head against the gray's muzzle, close my eyes and think, **Don't move. Don't move. Don't move,** while the wagon goes right on by. It's disappearing past the bend by the time I dare let loose of the horses and go look. I don't follow after it. More than likely all I'd get is trouble. I'm still toting two girls who can't explain theirselves and traveling with horses too fine for me to own.

Missy Lavinia and Juneau Jane hadn't changed. I tip them up against the felled tree, try again to put water down them from the canteen. Juneau Jane flutters her eyes open just a touch, swallows a little, but she retches it up, soon as I set her against the roots. No choice but to turn her over on her side and let it come back out.

Missy Lavinia won't take any at all. Won't even try. Her skin's the color of deadwood, gray and puffy, her eyes matted and her lips swole-up, cracked and sealed over with blood, like they been burned. Both of the girls been fed a poison. That's all it could be. Poisoned with something to kill them or just to keep them quiet in them boxes.

Missy's got a hard, swole-up knot poking out of her head, too. I wonder if that's why she's worse than Juneau Jane.

I know about poisons like the ones old Seddie conjures from the roots and the leaves, the bark of a certain tree, the berries of this plant or that one. She'd give somebody the right one, depending if she wanted to make them too sick to work, or too addled, or too dead.

**Keep clear a' that ol' witch woman,** Mama told Epheme and me when we first went up to the house to nursemaid Missy Lavinia. **Don't look Seddie's way. And don't let her get thinking Ol' Missus favors you better than her. She'll slip a poison on you. You keep clear of Ol' Missus, and Young Marse Lyle, too. Jus' do your work and be good to Old Marse, so's he'll let you come visit me on Sunday afternoons.**

Every Sunday evenin', she'd tell us the same thing before she had to send us back.

No way of knowing if somebody's to live or die after a poison. Just wait while the body decides how strong it is, and the spirit chooses how much desire it has for its earthly home.

I need to find us a hiding place, but I don't know where. Another day lopped over the back of a horse might be more than Missy and Juneau Jane can bear up to. And the breeze smells of rain.

It's a chore, getting all us back moving again, but I manage it. I'm weary before even starting on the day, but to save the horses and to keep us clear of the road, I start off afoot, leading the sorrel and the gray behind like pack mules.

"Let's go, dog," I say, and we do.

I put one foot down and then the next, pick my way through the woods, poking the ground with a stick to check for bogs and suck holes, and push off the sharp palmetto leaves. Keep on like that far as I can till a long, wide blackwater slough blocks the way and I got no choice but to start back toward the road again.

The dog sniffs his way to a path I didn't see at first. There's tracks along the banks of the bog. Big ones . . . man tracks. Smaller ones, also. A child or a woman. Just the two of them, so they're not the men from the sawmill. Maybe folks fishing or hunting gators or seining crawfish.

There's been people here at least, and pretty recent.

I stop on the trail when the road comes in sight up the hill, and I listen hard. No sounds but the bayou. The **pop-pop** of bubbles in the mud, the heavy-throated bullfrog, the skeeters and the blackflies buzzing. Dragonflies hum back and forth over stands of saw grass and muscadine vines. A mockingbird sings his borrowed songs all hooked together like different-colored ribbons tied end after end.

Dog pushes through the brush into the clear of the road, stirs up a big ol' swamp rabbit and gives a howl and bounds off after it. I wait and listen some more to see if another dog might answer, if there's a farm or a house near, but no sound comes.

Finally, I follow the footprints up the slope.

The tracks turn and go down the road. Two people, still heading someplace afoot. Both got shoes on. The big tracks travel along straight, but the little ones wander to and fro, on the road and off it, showing there was no hurry at all. Don't know why it's a comfort, but it is. The footprints don't go far before they turn off the road and start up some high ground to the other side. I stand and look, try to set my mind on whether I should follow or keep on straight. A swish of breeze blows from the dark sky ahead, and answers my question. A storm's rising. We need shelter, a place we can lay up. That's all there is to it.

Dog comes back. Didn't catch the rabbit, but he's got a squirrel he wants me to have.

"Good dog," I tell him and gut the squirrel quick with the old hatchet, then tie it to one of the saddles. "We'll have that later. You catch another one if you see it."

He smiles in a dog way, and swings that ugly bare-skin tail of his, and starts off down the road along the foot tracks, and I follow.

The trail takes us up a little hill, then down again, 'cross a shallow creek where the horses stop to drink. After a while, more tracks come in from other directions. Horse tracks. Mule tracks. People tracks. The more that come together, the more they make a clear path, trod through the woods, down into the soil. People been walking in this way a long time. But always walking, or riding a horse or mule. Never a wagon.

Me and the gray and Ginger and the dog add our tracks to all that's passed through before.

Rain catches us just after the trail gets better. Rain in kettlefuls and pails. It soaks through my clothes and runs rivers off my hat. Dog and the horses clamp their tails and arch their backs against it. I tip my head down, fighting the misery, and the only good thing is it washes the stink off of me and the saddles and the horses and Missy and Juneau Jane.

Now and again, I squint against the curtains of water, try to see, **Is there anything around?** But I can't make out five foot ahead. The path turns to mush. My feet slide. The horses slip round. Old Ginger stumbles and flounders on her knees in front again. She's so fretful about the rain, she gets right back on her feet.

We start up another rise, little rivers washing all around us. Water flows through my shoes, burns on the blisters there at first, then just turns my feet cold, so I can't feel them at all. My body quakes till it feels like my bones might break in two.

Juneau Jane moans long and loud enough I hear it, even over the storm. Dog hears it, too, circles in behind her. Next thing, he's back to lead the way, but I'm blinded enough that I trip over him and fall hands first in the mud.

He yelps, squirts out from under me, and skitters off running. It's only when I'm climbing to my feet and pulling my hat out of the mud that I figure out why. There's a place here. Little old place tucked in the trees, low roofed and built of cypress logs chinked with straw and tabby. The trail meets a half dozen other trails from other directions and leads us right to the front door of that little house.

Nobody answers when I step on the porch beside the dog, and call out, and pull the horses up close where they can shelter their heads at least.

Once I open the door, I know why, and what this house is. This the kind of place the slaves built with their own hands, way deep in the swamps and the woods, where their masters wouldn't find it. Sundays, when the work gangs didn't go to the fields, off they'd sneak to these hideaways, one by one, two by two. Meet up for preaching, and singing, and shouting, and praying, where they couldn't be heard, where the owners and the overseers couldn't stop them from crying out for freedom and how their deliverance was coming one day soon.

Here in the woods, a colored man was free to **read** from the Bible, if he could read, or listen to it if he couldn't, not just be told that God gave you to your masters so that you could obey.

I thank the saints and get us out of the weather, quick as I can. Dog follows me back and forth 'cross the dirt floor, the two of us leaving trails of water and mud on the straw that's been laid down. Can't be helped, and I don't suppose God or anybody would blame us.

Slabwood benches stand in quiet rows. Up front for the altar, the floor's built up using four old doors that must've been on a Grand House back before the war. Three red velvet chairs sit behind the preacher's stand. On the communion table, there's a pretty crystal glass and four china plates, probably brung from a big house when the white folks went refugee because of the Yankees, leaving the place empty.

Behind the altar, a tall cut-glass window catches what there is of the daylight. It's out of one of the doors on the floor. Oilcloth stretched on frames covers the rest of the windows. Newspapers been nailed to the walls at the back of the room. The chink must be gappy in that part.

It's up there at the altar that I lay down Missy Lavinia and Juneau Jane, pull the velvet cushions off the chairs and put them under their heads. Juneau Jane shivers like a wretch, that wet shimmy stuck to her body with dirt and water and blood. Missy Lavinia is worse yet, and she still don't moan or move. I lean close to her nose to see, **Is she still breathin'?**

Just the least stroke of air stirs on my cheek. It's cold and feathery, and I got no good way to warm her up. Everything we have is soggy wet, so I strip us all down, hang the clothes to drip, and get a fire laid in the iron stove at the back of the room. It's a fancy little one from a ladies' parlor, with roses and vines and ivy leaves cast in the iron and a pretty skirt and bowed legs.

There's a cook plate up top. After the stove heats, I'll fix up that squirrel, feed Dog and me.

"Least we got kindle in here and plenty of split wood out front. Lucifers, too," I tell him. I'm thankful the floor is dry, and the roof don't leak. And when I get a good flame, I'm thankful for that, too. I crouch naked, bare and slick from the rain, and feel the fire's heat even before it comes. Just knowing there's an end to the cold makes it better.

After the stove's drafted good, I drag one of them velvet chairs to the back of the room. It's the big, wide kind for a lady to sit with her hoops, back when they wore such. A courtin' bench, so's she could arrange her skirts closer a bit if she wanted a beau to sit with her, leave it laid out, if she wanted to keep him off.

I pull my knees up in the chair, let my head rest, stroke my fingers back and forth against the red velvet. It's soft like a horse's muzzle. Soft and warm everyplace it touches my body. I sit and stare at the flame, thinking how good that chair feels.

Never sat in a velvet chair in my life. Not once.

I rub my cheek against it and soak the heat from the fire. My eyes get heavy and close, and I let go.

Two days of sleeping and waking and tending follow. Two days, I think. Might be three. I turn feverish myself late in the first day. Feverish, and tired, and even though I cook up the squirrel, I can't keep much of it down. It's all I can do to hobble the horses so they can forage, and get back in my dry clothes and wrap the other girls with the drawers and shimmies, and try from time to time to let the dog come and go or force a little water down Juneau Jane. Missy still won't take any, but her little half sister's getting stronger.

The first day I get my wits again, Juneau Jane opens her strange gray-green eyes and looks up at me from the red chair cushion, dark hair splayed out all over it like a nest of snakes. I can tell she's seeing me for the first time and can't make sense of where she is.

She tries talking, but I shush her. After all the days of quiet, even that much noise makes my head pound. "Hush, now," I whisper. "You're safe. That's all you got to know. You been sick. And you're still sick. You rest now. It's safe here."

I figure that much is true. Rain's been falling, day after day. Water must be up high everywhere, and whatever tracks we left behind, they're surely gone. Only worry is how long it might be till Sunday, when somebody comes. I got no idea by now.

Question answers itself when Dog sits up and barks me awake early in the morning. Scares my eyes wide open.

Outside, a voice sings,

**Children wade, in the water**
**And God's a-gonna trouble the water**
**Who's that young girl dressed in red?**
**Wade in the water**
**Must be the children that Moses led**
**God's gonna trouble the water. . . .**

The voice is deep and strong. Can't tell, **Is it a man or a woman?** But the song brings Mama to mind. She'd sing it to us when I was little.

I know I need to move, stop whoever that is from coming in here, but I can't help it. I listen at a few words more.

They come in a child's voice this time.

That's good. Good for what I got in mind to do next.

**Wade in the water, children,** the little voice sings loud, not afraid.

**Wade in the water,**
**And God's a-gonna trouble the water.**

Then the woman again,

**Who's that young girl dressed in white?**
**Wade in the water**

**Must be the children of the Israelite,**
**God's gonna trouble the water.**

I whisper the lines along with them, feel my mama's heartbeat against my ear, hear her say real soft, **This song 'bout the way to freedom, Hannie. Keep to the water. The dog, he can't find the smell of you there.**

The child sings the chorus again. It ain't far away now. They must be almost to the clearing.

I get up and hurry to the door, press my hand hard against it, get myself ready.

**Who's that young girl dressed in blue**
**Wade in the water . . .**

I swallow hard, think, **Please, let them be good people coming up the path. Kind people.**

They sing together, the big voice and the small one.

**Must be the ones that made it through**
**Wade in the water.**

Behind me, a scratchy whisper says, "Wade . . . wahhh-ter. Wade in . . . wahh-ter."

I look quick over my shoulder, see Juneau Jane pushing herself up off that red velvet cushion on one wobbly arm so weak it wiggles back and forth like a hank of rope, her eyes open halfway.

**And God's a-gonna trouble the water,** the child outside hollers into the air.

"Y-you d . . . don't, b-believe . . . be . . . been redeemed . . ." Juneau Jane sways, fighting to push out the words and stay upright.

A cold feeling travels all over me, then hot sweat breaks after it.

"Hush up! Quiet, now!" I hiss. I pull open the door, stagger to the edge of the porch, and hang against a post. Two people come out of the woods—a stout, round woman with hands like supper plates and big feet in black leather brogans, white kerchief on her head. With her comes a little boy child. Her grandson, maybe? He's skipping along with picked flowers in one hand.

The woman twirls a piece of feather grass at him, tickles his ear when he's dancing by. He laughs hard.

"D-don't come no closer!" I holler out. My voice is weak and won't carry far, but they stop sudden, look my way. The boy drops his flowers. The woman snakes an arm out and, quick, tucks him behind her.

"Who you be?" She stretches to get a better look at me.

"We got fever!" I yell across. "Keep away. We got sickness."

Woman backs up a little, pushes the boy with her. He hangs on to her skirt, peeks from it. "Who you be?" she asks again. "How you come in dat place? I don' know who you is."

"We travelin'," I answer. "Been struck with fever,

all us. Don't come no closer. Don't nobody come here, catch the sickness."

"How many you is?" She lifts her apron, wads it over her mouth.

"Three. Other two's worse off." It ain't a lie, but I sink against the post to look weaker. "Need help. Need food. Got money to give. You carryin' mercy in your soul today, sister? We travelers, come in need a' mercy."

## Lost Friends

Dear Editor—I am inquiring for my people. My mother was Priscilla; she belonged to Watson and he sold her to Bill Calburt, near Hopewell, Georgia. We lived near Knoxville. My name was Betty Watson. I left her when I was three years old. I am now 55 years of age. I learned how to read when I was 50. I take and read the SOUTHWESTERN, it is food for my soul. I am anxious and would be glad to hear something of my mother or my brother Henry. Some one help me. Write to me in care of Rev. H. J. Wright, Asbury M. E. Church, Natchitoches, where I am a member and a Sabbath school scholar.

BETTY DAVIS

—"Lost Friends" column of the Southwestern

## CHAPTER 14

BENNY SILVA—AUGUSTINE, LOUISIANA, 1987

See," LaJuna says as she pushes aside stacks of **National Geographic** magazines. She lays an **Encyclopaedia Britannica** on the billiard table, then flips up the cover, which has no pages or binding attached. It's been used to house—or hide—a package wrapped in a worn scrap of wallpaper, gold-and-white flocked at some time in the past, but the remaining stripes are more of a glue stain than anything else. Jute string holds the whole thing together.

"Miss Robin didn't even know about these, I don't think." LaJuna taps a finger to the bundle. "One time when I came in here—that was toward the end part, when the judge had good days and bad days with his mind—he says to me, 'LaJuna, climb on up there to that top shelf for me. I need something, but somebody took the ladder.' Now, that ladder'd been gone since the track broke, so I knew the judge wasn't having a good day with his mind. Anyhow, I did like he wanted, and he showed me what's in here. Then he looked at me and said, 'I shouldn't have let you see that. There's nothing good to come of it and no way I can set it right. I want you to put this back where it was. We won't touch it again unless I decide to burn it, which I quite likely should. Don't ever tell anybody it's here. If you do that for me, LaJuna, you can come take any **other** book anytime and keep it to read, as long as you like.' Then he had me get him one of the encyclopedias, and he cut the encyclopedia cover right **off** the pages and wrapped it around this whole thing, and then we put it away."

LaJuna picks at the knotted jute with chipped-up candy apple red fingernails, but the twine is stiff and tightly tied. "See if there's some scissors in that top drawer. Judge always kept a pair in there."

A pang of conscience forces me to hesitate. Whatever is inside that bundle must have been very private. It's none of my business. None. Period.

"Never mind." LaJuna's fingernails do the trick. "I got it."

"I don't think you should. If the judge didn't . . ."

But she's already laying open the wallpaper wrapping. Inside, there are two books, which she places side by side. Both leather bound, one black, one red. One thin, one thick. The black one is easy enough to recognize. It's a family Bible, the old-fashioned kind, large and heavy. The red leather book is much thinner and bound along the top like a notepad. Faded gold letters on the cover read

**Goswood Grove Plantation**
**William P. Gossett**
**Items of Significant Record**

"Now that little skinny book . . ." LaJuna's still talking. "That's stuff they bought and sold. Sugar, molasses, cotton seed, plows, a piano, land, lumber, horses and mules, dresses and dishes . . . all kinds of stuff. And, sometimes, people."

My mind goes numb. It can't quite register what I'm looking at, what this is. "LaJuna, it's not . . . we shouldn't . . . The judge was right. You need to put this back where it was."

"It's history, isn't it?" She's as casual as if we were talking about what year the Liberty Bell was cast or when the Magna Carta was written. "You're always telling us that books and stories matter."

"Of course, but . . ." Something so old should be handled with only freshly washed hands or white cotton gloves, for one thing. But if I'm honest with myself, I know it's not the archival concerns that bother me; it's the contents.

"Well, these are stories." She skims a fingernail along the edge of the Bible and opens it before I can stop her.

The **Family Record** pages at the front of the Bible, perhaps a dozen or more, are filled with the artful script of old dip pens like the ones I've collected for years. Names occupy the left column: Letty, Tati, Azek, Boney, Jason, Mars, John, Percy, Jenny, Clem, Azelle, Louisa, Mary, Caroline, Ollie, Mittie, Hardy . . . Epheme, Hannie . . . Ike . . . Rose . . .

The remaining columns list birthdates, death dates for some, and odd notations, **D, L, F, S,** plus numbers. Names are sometimes listed with dollar amounts beside them.

LaJuna's half-red fingernail hovers over one, not quite touching it. "See, this is all about the slaves. When they were born, and when they died and what number grave they were buried in. If they ran away or got lost in the war, they got an **L** beside their name and the date. If they got freed after the war, they got an **F,** and **1865,** and if they stayed on the place to be sharecroppers, they got an **S / 1865**." Her hands flip palms up, as matter-of-factly as if we're discussing the school lunch menu. "After that, I guess people kept their own notes."

A moment passes before I can process the information and stammer out, "You learned all that from the judge?"

"Yeah." Her features arrange in a way that conveys the slightest bit of uncertainty about the mysteries the judge left behind. "Maybe he wanted somebody to know how to read it, since he decided not to show Miss Robin. Can't say how come. I mean, she knew this place was built by people who had to be slaves. Miss Robin was way into doing research about Goswood. The judge just didn't want her to feel guilty about stuff that happened a long time ago, I guess."

"I guess . . . maybe," I echo. The lump in my throat is itchy and uncomfortable. Part of me wishes the judge would have taken responsibility for nailing shut the coffin on this piece of history and burning the book. Part of me knows how wrong that would've been.

LaJuna pushes on, dragging me along on a trip I don't want to take. "Now, see where there's no daddy listed? Just a mama and then somebody's born? That's where the daddy was probably a white man."

"The judge **told** you that?"

Her mouth thins and an eye roll comes my way. "Figured it out on my own. That's what the little **m** means—**mulatto.** Like this woman, Mittie. She hasn't got a daddy, but, **of course,** she had a daddy. He was the—"

That's it. That's all I can stand. "I think we should put this away."

LaJuna frowns, her gaze probing mine, surprised and . . . disappointed? "Now you sound like the judge did. Miss Silva, you're the one **always** talking about stories. This book, here . . . this is the only story most of these people ever got. Only place their names still are, in the whole wide world. They didn't even get gravestones with it written on there or anything. Look."

She flips back a page so that the heavy endpaper attached to the cover lies flat beside the flyleaf, open like butterfly wings. A grid of sorts has been drawn across them, sectioned off in somewhat orderly rectangles with numbers. "This"—she tells me, circling the grid with her fingertip—"is where they are. Where they buried all the slaves whenever they died. The old people and the kids and the little bitty babies. Right here." She grabs a pen and sets it on the desk below the book. "That's **your** house. You been living right there by these people, and you didn't even know it."

I think of the lovely orchard only a short walk from my back porch. "There's no graveyard out there. The city cemetery is over on this side." I place a deco-era stapler and a plastic clip to the left of the pen. "If the pen is my house, the cemetery's **here.**"

"Miss Silva." LaJuna cranes away. "I thought you knew **so** much about history. That graveyard over there beside your house, the one with the nice fence and all the little stone houses with people's names, that was the graveyard for white folks. Tomorrow, when I come to help you with the books, I can walk over and **show** you what's out behind your place. I went and looked for myself after the judge—"

A grandfather clock in the hall chimes, and both of us jump.

LaJuna jerks away from the table, pulls a broken wristwatch from her pocket, and gasps, "I gotta go. I just came over here real quick to get a book for tonight!" Snatching up a paperback, she dashes out the door. Her footsteps echo through the house along with "I gotta babysit for Mama on her shift!"

The door slams, and she vanishes.

I don't see her for days. Not at Goswood Grove House, nor at school. She's just . . . gone.

I walk the orchard behind my place alone, study the rise and fall of the ground, squat down and pull back the grass where it grows in little mounds, dig away a few inches of soil and find plain brown stones. A few of them still bear the faint shadow of carved markings, but nothing I can make out.

I sketch them in a notebook and compare them to the narrow, numbered squares on the hand-drawn graveyard map in the Goswood library. It matches up as well as could be expected after the passage of time has been allowed to absorb the truth. I find adult-sized plots and smaller ones—babies or children, buried two or three to a space. I stop counting rectangles at **ninety-six,** because I can't stand it any longer. A whole community of people, generations in some families, lie buried behind my house, forgotten. LaJuna is right. Other than whatever has been handed down orally among relatives, that sad, strange batch of notations in the Gossett Bible is the only story they have.

The judge was wrong to have hidden this book. That much I know. What I'm unsure of is how to proceed from here, or if it's even my place to. I'd like to talk more with LaJuna, to find out what other information she has, but day after day goes by and there's no opportunity.

Finally, on Wednesday, I go searching for her.

The quest eventually leaves me standing in front of Aunt Sarge's house, shod in the worn, lime-green Birkenstocks that go with absolutely nothing I own, but are kind to a big toe that was in the way when a stack of books tipped over at Goswood Grove House, seemingly with a mind of its own. A few other strange things have happened there during my many hours alone in the library, but I refuse to think much about them. I don't have time. All weekend, and for three days after school now, I've been sorting books at warp speed, trying to do what I can before anyone else discovers I've been given access and before I track down Nathan Gossett again to make him aware of what he actually has in that library.

I've fallen behind on laundry, grading papers, planning lessons, and just about everything else. I'm also dangerously low on pooperoos.

On the upside, with the change in classroom snacks, I have shed my old nickname and the kids are testing a new one—**Loompa,** owing to the Oompa-Loompas in the ever-popular book **Charlie and the**

**Chocolate Factory,** a copy of which has been added to our classroom shelves, courtesy of the judge's penchant for Book of the Month subscriptions. We've devised, after much class debate, a system of allowing weeklong checkouts from our new lending library. One of my extremely quiet backwoods kids, Shad, has the book right now. He's a freshman and a member of the notorious Fish family. He saw the movie after a family trip to visit his father, who's doing three years in federal prison on some sort of drug charge.

I'd like to learn more about Shad's situation—he consumes a lot of pooperoos, for one thing, and also covertly stuffs them in his pockets—but there aren't enough hours in the day. I feel as though I'm constantly doing triage on who needs my attention the most.

Which is why it's taken me days to venture into the LaJuna situation. I've just finished paying a call at the home address in her file. The man who answered the door of the ramshackle apartment informed me, quite curtly, that he'd kicked the **so-and-so** and her brats out, and I should get off his porch and not bother him again.

My next option is Aunt Sarge or Granny T. Sarge lives closest to town, so here I am. The one-story Creole cottage reminds me of my rental, but with renovations. The siding and trim have been painted in contrasting colors, creating a dollhouse effect in sunny yellow, white, and forest green. Seeing it strengthens my resolve to plead the case with Nathan for my rental house being spared. It could be as cute as this.

Tomorrow is farmers market day. I'm hoping to catch him.

First things first, though. Right now, I'm after LaJuna.

No one answers the door, but I hear voices coming from around back, so I make my way past an immaculate flower bed to a chain-link fence and leaning gate. Morning glory vines twine their way up the posts and back and forth through the wire, woven like living cloth.

Two women in tattered straw hats work along a row of tall plants in a vegetable garden that takes up most of the yard. One woman is heavyset and labors along, her movements slow and stiff. The other is Sarge, I think, though the floppy hat and flowered gloves seem out of character. I watch the scene a moment, and a memory teases my mind, then breaks through. I recall being a small child in a garden, having someone guide my stubby fingers over a strawberry as I pulled it from the plant. I remember touching each berry still clinging to the plant and asking, **Pick this one? Pick this one?**

I have no idea where that was. Someplace we lived, some neighbor warmhearted enough to play surrogate grandparent. People who were always home and spent a great deal of time out in their yards were my favorite targets whenever we'd land in a new town.

A yearning skates in unexpected, slams hard against

my heart before I can turn it around and send it packing. Every once in a while, even though Christopher and I had talked about it at length and agreed that kids weren't right for either one of us, there's that urge, the painful **What if. . . .**

"Hello!" I lean over the gate. "Sorry to bother you."

Only one garden hat tips upward. The older woman continues along the row. She plucks, and drops, plucks, and drops, filling a basket with long green pods of some sort.

That **is** Aunt Sarge in the other hat. I recognize the way she swipes her forehead with her arm before readjusting her hat and crossing the yard to me. "Got another problem with the house?" Her tone is surprisingly solicitous, considering that our last meeting ended unpleasantly.

"No, the house is fine. Sadly, I think you're right about its future rental status, though. If you hear of something coming open, a garage apartment or whatever, I don't need much, since it's just me."

"Well, if it's going to end up **just you,** it's better to know when he's only the fiancé, right?" She recalls our conversation during the roof recon, and I feel the tug of kinship again.

"Truth."

"Look," she offers, "I'm sorry I was hard on you the other day. It's just that it's not a far trip from believing you can change things in Augustine, to going nuts. That's all I was trying to say. I'm not much of a diplomat, which is mostly what cut short my military career. Sometimes, if you're not willing to blow smoke at people, you find yourself ditched on the side of the road."

"Sounds a little like the faculty in a college English department," I admit. "Minus the Humvees and camouflage, I mean."

Aunt Sarge and I actually chuckle. Together.

"Is this your house?" I say, by way of keeping the conversation going. "It's great. I'm a sucker for anything antique or vintage."

She thumbs over her shoulder. "Aunt Dicey's place. My grandmother's baby sister. I came by last spring to visit after . . ." A labored sigh, and whatever she was about to divulge is quickly rerouted to "Didn't plan on staying, but Aunt Dicey was in a mess. No propane in the tank, the plumbing cut off to most of the house. Ninety-year-old woman heating bathwater on the stove. Too many no-account kids and grandkids and great-grandkids, and nieces and nephews. Whatever Aunt Dicey has, if somebody asks for it, she'll give it. So, I just moved in."

She rubs the back of her neck, stretches it one way and then the other. A rueful laugh hisses between her teeth. "And here I am, picking okra in Augustine, Louisiana. My dad would turn over in his grave. Best thing that ever happened to him was getting drafted into the army and discovering a whole new world out there."

Obviously, there's a much bigger story under Sarge's

crusty exterior. "Looks like you've made a tremendous difference on the house."

"Houses are easy. People, not so much. You can't just strip out the lead pipe, re-run the wires, slap on a coat of paint . . . and fix things in a lot of these families."

"Speaking of family"—I avoid the sinkhole of what **can't** be done in Augustine—"the reason I stopped by is LaJuna. She and I had an accord of sorts last week. She promised not to miss any more school, and I told her that if she didn't miss, she could help me with a project I'm working on. That was Thursday afternoon. She didn't come to school on Friday, and I haven't seen her since. I went to the home address on file for her, and the guy there told me to get lost."

"That'd be her mama's old boyfriend. Tiffany hits him up when she needs a place to land. Tiffany's always hitting somebody up—been doing that since she snagged my cousin senior year of high school and had LaJuna. That's how Tiff gets by." She pulls a bandana from her pocket, takes off the hat and mops her neck, then fans some air under her T-shirt. "Tiff's hard on people. Left LaJuna here for years while she was in prison and never has done a thing to pay Aunt Dicey back."

"Can you tell me where they are? Living, I mean. LaJuna said her mom had a new job and they were doing fine." I know a little about intentionally misleading the adults in your life to keep secrets under wraps. Things that, if they knew, would send your whole world tumbling end over end. "I don't think LaJuna would break her promise. She was so excited about sorting"—I catch myself—"our project."

"Honey, you coming back?" Aunt Dicey calls out. "Bring your friend. She wants to help us pick, then she can stay over for some okra and fried green 'maters. That'll be good! Don't have much meat to put with it. Couple slices of roast left from my Mealsie Wheelsies. We can have that, too. Tell her to come on in here. No need in being bashful." Aunt Dicey cups a hand around her ear, listening for a response.

"She has things to do, Aunt Dicey," Sarge calls, loudly enough to be heard in the next town down the road. "And we have meat. I bought a ham."

"Oh, hi there, Pam!" Aunt Dicey says.

Sarge shakes her head. "She doesn't have her hearing aid in." She hustles me toward the car. "You'd better get out of here while you can. She'll tie you up until midnight, and I know that's not what you came here for. Listen, I'll do what I can about LaJuna, but her mama and I aren't each other's favorite people. She ruined my cousin's life. I've caught Tiffany over here more than once, looking to mooch food or money from Aunt Dicey. Told her if she shows up again, things'll get ugly. Tiff needs to pay her own bills, stop skipping out on work to hang with that loser ex-boyfriend of hers down in New Orleans, which, if I had to guess, is where she's at right now. Taking the baby for a visit with his daddy. LaJuna's probably stuck there, looking after the rest of the kids and trying to get her mama to go back to work before she gets fired."

I have a sudden and crushing picture of LaJuna's life. No wonder she's bossy with adults. She's parenting one.

Sarge angles an appraising look my way when we get to the car. "You need to know that it's not LaJuna's fault. Kid's stuck at the bottom of a well and has to drag four people up the rope with her. Multiply that by a half dozen different batches of kinfolk, and you'll see why some days, I just want to get in the car and drive. But man, I loved my granny and she loved her baby sister, Dicey . . . well . . . I don't know. We'll see."

"I get it." The problems here are deeply rooted. If the way of things was easy to change, people would've done it already. "Like throwing starfish back into the ocean."

"Huh?"

"It's just a story I had on the bulletin board of my old office. Perspective, sort of. I'll xerox a copy for you if I ever find it again."

Sarge leans over to peer through the Bug's window. "What's all that?" She's studying the library questionables I've stacked in the backseat in hopes of showing them to Nathan at the farmers market tomorrow morning—a few valuable old books I'm worried about, along with the plantation ledger and the family Bible with the burial records in it.

I consider trying to obfuscate, but what good

would it do? Sarge is looking right at the ledger that bears the Gossett name. "I wanted to make sure I got a chance to study these more closely . . . while I could. Coach Davis roped me into handling gate duty tonight at the football stadium. There's some kind of a fundraiser concert for the athletics department and I guess they were desperate for workers. Anyway, I thought I could do some reading in between, or after."

"You've been in the judge's house? **That's** where you got all this?" She slaps the car's hood. "Oh Lord." Her head falls back and the straw hat slips off, drifting soundlessly to the driveway. "Oh **Lord,**" she says again. "Did LaJuna let you in there?"

"Nathan gave me a key," I blurt, but I can feel the steam building next to me. Sarge is like a pressure cooker, about to blow.

"Put that stuff back where you got it."

"I'm looking for books for my classroom. Nathan said to take whatever I could use, but I don't think he has **any** idea what's in that house. The library closets are full. Half of the bookshelves are double stacked. Behind the first row of new books, there are old books, rare books. Things like those." I nod toward the seat.

"**This** is the project with LaJuna?" Sarge demands. "I don't care if she messes around in the gardens over there, but I told her to stay out of that house."

"She showed up the first day." I can feel my relationship with LaJuna potentially being shredded.

First I invade her secret place, now I'm getting her in trouble with her aunt. "She knows a lot about the place. Its history. The stories. She spent quite a bit of time with the judge while she was with her aunt . . . or great-aunt . . . your Aunt Dicey. There's an old hatch in the floor under the—"

"Stop. Don't. Not interested." If I didn't before, now I fully understand that I am into something much bigger than I can grasp. "Put that stuff back. Don't let LaJuna in that house again, either. If Will and Manford Gossett or their wives find out she's involved in this, Tiff won't be clinging to that new job at Gossett Industries, she'll be out. You get on their wrong side, you better start packing your boxes and rent yourself a moving van. Trust me."

"I can't just **quit.** I need the books, and they're sitting there going to rot."

"Don't think you're safe because **you** don't work for Gossett Industries, either. Manford's little blond trophy wife is **on** the school board."

"My understanding is that the house and land are Nathan's, though."

"Look, before Nathan's sister died, things might've been different." Shaking her head, she focuses on the pavement as if she's sorting her thoughts. "When Robin inherited that house from the judge, she stood guard over it. She cared about it. It was hers and she wasn't about to let her uncles steal it out from under her. But she's gone, and, yes, technically the house passed on to her brother, but the only reason

Nathan hasn't sold it is out of respect for his sister—because Robin fought Will and Manford for it until her dying day."

"Oh . . ." I murmur.

"It's a mess," Aunt Sarge says. "Stay away from the Gossetts. Stay away from the house. Don't take those books around town with you, and, whatever you do, don't show them to anyone at the football stadium. Put that stuff back where you found it. I'll try to get LaJuna straightened around about school, but you keep her away from Goswood."

I meet Sarge's gaze. A lot goes unsaid between us in that quick look before I climb into the car. "Thanks for the help with LaJuna."

"It'll depend on what's up with her mom." She rests a hand on the open window. "I know that story about the starfish. I get what you think you're trying to do. But around here, the tide's pretty strong."

"Point taken." Driving away, I lift my chin and set my jaw. I can't stay out of Goswood Grove House. I won't. I need a tide wall, that's all, and I'm going to build it with books.

I do heed Sarge's advice and cover the books in my car while I sell tickets at the fundraiser. I park where I can keep an eye on the Bug, because the door lock on the passenger side doesn't work.

Unfortunately, gate duty turns out to be more involved than I'd expected. I'm not just in charge of taking ticket money, I have to run around under the bleachers, flushing out teenagers who are wrapped around each other like twist ties. I'm pretty sure I cause permanent damage to a few potential romances.

Kids have changed a lot since I was one. It's a scary world in the hidden realms of the football stadium.

I am more than relieved when I get back to the Bug, and the books are safely where I left them. I plan to stay up late, ignore my prep work for school tomorrow, study these materials and take notes. I want every minute I can get with them, just in case tomorrow's planned conversation with Nathan Gossett doesn't go well.

I'm not the least bit prepared to find Sarge pacing back and forth on my porch when I pull into my driveway.

# CHAPTER 15

## HANNIE GOSSETT—LOUISIANA, 1875

"We got to **leave,** Juneau Jane." Ain't ever spoken to a white person that way in my life, but Juneau Jane ain't white, ain't colored. I don't know what to call her. No matter right now, because she could be the Queen of Sheba in a new pink dress and we'd still have to get from this place before things go bad. "Need you to help me push Missy Lavinia up on that horse, and we'll make our way back to the road. Won't be much longer before that old woman figures either we're dead or we told a lie about having the fever."

Four more days now, we been holed up here in this church in the wood. Four days of nursing, and feeding, cleaning the waste from feverish bodies and praying. Four days of leaving coins in the tree at the edge of the clearing, and hollering to the woman what I need for her to bring me. She's kindly, merciful and good. Even took the dog home with her so's to care for it proper. She'll be good to that dog, I know, and I'm happy for that, but the woman gets more nervous every time she sees us still here. Word must've spread about the fever, and folks'll be wondering, **Should they burn this place to the ground to save their family from the sickness?**

Them sawmill men could come sniffing after us, too. Can't take that chance.

Juneau Jane don't answer me. She just keeps on with whatever it is she's doing over there by that wall of nailed-up newspapers. Got herself facing into the corner, so's I can't see. She's mostly been a quiet thing since she come to. Confused and scared and twitchy, like the soldiers that wandered the roads after the war, their minds tangled, their nerves skittery and strange. When the mind's been lost from the body, it can't always find the way home. Might be that's the soul's way of preserving itself. Far as she'll say when I ask her, she don't remember a thing about how she came here, or what was done to them by that man with the patch eye or his helpers.

Missy Lavinia ain't said a word so far. She was a big, heavy rag doll when I washed her clean with a bucket from the rain barrel and got her dressed in the clothes I paid the old woman for. Boys' clothes and a hat. If we do see anybody on the road, it'll be a whole lot easier to explain ourselves that way.

"Time we move on." I keep talking while I gather up the food and quilt and wool blanket I bought from that woman. We can use them to sleep under or stretch over ourselves like a tent. "I got the horses caught. Saddled. You help me push Missy Lavinia up on that mare, now."

Still not a word comes, so I cross the room and touch Juneau Jane's shoulder. "You listening at me? What's over here in this corner, so important you ain't got time to answer? I saved your life, you know? Saved both your lives. Coulda left you two locked up in that poacher's room, that's what I coulda done . . . and should've, too. I don't owe you nothin'. I **said,** for you to come help." I'm about to the end of myself and the sun's just barely up past the trees. Might be time I just leave, let them shift for theirselves.

"Soon," she answers, low and flat, sounding older than the child she is. "But I must first complete my task."

She's got one of them newspapers pulled off the wall, and her bare foot set on top of it, and she's cutting the shape of her foot out of the paper, using the tip of the skinning knife the woman brung me.

"Well, I'm sorry if them shoes I got for you ain't to your pleasure. We hadn't got time for you to fix paper to pad them. You can stuff them with grass or leaves on the trail. I'd be grateful just to **have** shoes, if I was you. That woman couldn't even get me any to fit Missy Lavinia. Have to leave her barefoot for now, worry about that later. We need to leave from this place."

The girl turns them strange eyes my way. I don't like it when she does that. Gives me the shakes. She slips a hand under her leg, pulls out a pair of them newspaper feet that's already been cut and holds them out toward me. "For your shoes," she says. "To keep the conjures away."

A witch's fingernail slides up my back bone and down my rib bones, and along every other bone in my body, making a chill under my skin. I stay away from any and all conjures and even the talk of them.

**I don't believe in conjures, Lord,** I say in my mind. **Just so you know.** This being a church and all, it's best to make that plain.

I say to Juneau Jane, "How can a little paper keep a conjure off?" **I don't believe it, Lord, but it might be the quickest thing if I just do what she says.** I sit down in that chair, start kicking off my brogans. "If it'll get you to movin', I'll do it. But it ain't conjures that brung us all this trouble we're in. It was bad men, and you and Missy Lavinia and the addled brain plan you two hatched, and me being fool enough to dress myself up for a boy and go along with it."

"You need not have them if you prefer none." All of a sudden she's right talkable in that high-tone way of hers. Maybe even got a little sass. That's a good sign for her health, at least.

She tries to take my shoe newspapers.

I grab them up before she can. "I'll **do** it."

She pulls some more papers off the wall, folds them and tucks them down the boy shirt that bags where her new britches are tied up. The shirt rides so loose on her, the shoulder seams hang to her elbows.

"Hadn't oughta be stealing from a church house," I say.

"For later." She waves a hand toward the wall. "They have many."

I look up at the slab logs, at them pages stretched floor to ceiling. All that writing sectioned up in little boxes. I hadn't noticed them much while we been trapped in this room. Too busy. But somebody took the time to put them up there real careful, so that not a one covered over any part of the other. Don't seem like the way you'd do it to keep the weather from coming in.

"What's all that say?" I'm wondering it to myself, but I speak the question out loud.

"Have you not read them?" She goes on with fitting newspapers in her shoes. "Not in all this time?"

"Can't read." No shame in admitting that, I figure. "Some of us don't get a house to live in and money for clothes and food just handed out. Some pay our way in toil and sweat, since before the freedom, since **after** the freedom. Before the freedom, if Old Missus was to catch us trying to learn reading, she'd have us whipped good. **After** the freedom, we work from see to can't see every day of the planting time and the hoeing time and harvesting time. In between **them** times, light up the tallow candle or the pine knot, go to making socks, darning socks, or sew up clothes to wear, or clothes to sell. Whatever money we get goes to buy our goods at the plantation store and the seed for next year, and to pay the contract to Old Mister so the land will be ours one day. Glory! That day is comin', if I ain't wrecked it all for you and Missy Lavinia. No, I can't read. But I can work, and I can cipher good. Can do numbers in my head faster than most folks will on paper. What do I need to know past that?"

She lifts her skinny shoulders, keeps lacing up her shoes. "If you were to purchase your land, for instance, and there would, of course, be a paper requiring signature, how would one, unable to read the paper, avoid being hoodwinked?"

She's a smart-mouth little thing. Full up with herself. I think I liked her better when she was sickly. Quiet.

"Well, now that is the dumbest question. I'd just ask somebody to read it **for** me. Somebody I know's truthful. Save taking the time to learn reading, just for one little paper."

"But in what way would you be assured of the faithfulness of this person?"

"Well, ain't you a suspicious little thing? There's people that can be trustable for reading. Colored folks, even. More all the time, with them teachers from up north coming down and setting up the colored schools. Why, you can't turn over a rock these days, but you find **somebody** who can read." Truth is, though, Old Missus don't tolerate her people having to do with carpetbaggers or northerner teachers.

"And one might read for pleasure, as well. Enjoy stories."

"**Ffff!** I'd as soon somebody **tell** me a good tale. I know plenty of them kind. Tales from my mama, tales from Tati and the old folk. Some of them tales been told to me over **clothes** that was being sewed for **you.** I could sit right here and speak a dozen, just out of my head."

For the first time, she looks at me interested, but we ain't going to be together long enough for stories. I want no more to do with this business or her and Missy Lavinia, once we get back to Goswood Grove.

I finish up with my shoes. "Now, what's the words in our shoes say that's gonna keep a conjure off us? Explain me that."

"Not the words." She tries her shoes out. Seems happy enough with them now. "The **letters.** Before a conjurer can throw a conjure beneath your feet, all the letters in your shoe must be counted by him. In that amount of time, you are long gone away from the place, yes?"

I stand up and hear the crinkle under my feet. Feels funny. "Guess I should've counted the letters before I put them in there. That way, I'd know how long I got to run away **if** a conjurer wanders along by and says, 'Hold up, there, and let me count them letters a minute.' "

She gives me a smart face, braces up her skinny arms, elbows out. "And yet, you have added them in your shoes."

"To get you to hush up and start moving, only." I look at the rest of the papers on the wall. I hope they wasn't important. "You at least plan to tell me what them papers say, before we go? I'd like to know we didn't take something matterful."

She wiggles round, grabs the butt of her knee britches and tries pulling it down, then yanks the whole thing up higher. This girl ain't ever had a pair of britches on in her life, I bet. "They are seeking lost friends."

"The papers?"

"Those by whom the advertisements were placed in the newspaper." She moves to the wall, points to the top corner of one of the pages. It's all in little squares, like the Bible Old Marse would bring when somebody was to be put under the sod in the burial ground. There in the front pages, he'd make a square and write the grave number in it.

Juneau Jane's hand ain't much darker than the water-stained newspaper, as she runs a finger along the top block. "Lost Friends," she reads. "We receive many letters asking for information about lost friends. All such letters will be published in this column. We make no charge for publishing these letters to subscribers of the **Southwestern.** All others will please enclose fifty cents. . . ."

"Fifty cents!" I puff out. "For marks in a newspaper?" I think of all the things fifty cents will do.

She turns over her shoulder, frowns at me. "Perhaps we should be on our way."

"Tell me the rest." There's an itch in my mind, but I can't guess why that is.

Standing at the wall in her droopy britches, she looks up again. "Pastors will please read the requests published below from the pulpits and report any cases where friends are brought together by means of letters in the **Southwestern.**" She moves down the wall a bit. "It's a newspaper for churches. Colored churches."

"Colored churches got a **newspaper**? Down here in the state of **Louisiana**?"

"Many states," she answers. "This newspaper is delivered to many states. The **Southwestern Christian Advocate.** It's a paper for the pastors."

"And they read it to the people? All over everywhere?"

"I would assume so . . . if it has found its way to this place."

"Well, I never. What's it say? In all them squares?"

Juneau Jane points to one. It's a small block compared to some others. "Dear Editor," she reads out loud. "I wish to inquire about my people. They left me at a trader's yard in Alexandria, with a Mr. Franklin. They were to be sent to New Orleans. Their names were Jarvis, George, and Maria Gains. Any information of them will be thankfully received. Address me at Aberdeen, Mississippi. Cecelia Rhodes."

"My Lord," I whisper. "Read me another."

She tells the story of a little boy named Si, five years old when a Mister Swan Thompson passed and all his worldly goods, including the folks he owned, were divided up by his son and daughter. "It was in eighteen . . ." Juneau Jane stands on tiptoes to read the paper. "Eighteen thirty-four. Miss Lureasy Cuff was standing in the house and talking to my mother and saying, 'I think Pa should give Si to me because I raised him to what he is.' Uncle Thomas drove the wagon when Mother left. She had two children then, Si and Orange. Address me at Midway, Texas. Si Johnson."

"My Lord," I say again, louder this time. "He'd be a old man by now. A old man, off down in Texas, and him still looking. And word's come all the way to here, in that paper."

My mind swells like the river after a hard rain. Grows and turns and runs and picks up everything that's been heavy in my soul, that's been laid up on the banks for months and years. I float myself along to where I ain't been able to let myself go before. Are my people up there on that wall? Mama, Hardy, Het, Pratt . . . Epheme, Addie? Easter, Ike, and Baby Rose? Aunt Jenny, or li'l Mary Angel, who I saw the last time in that slave pen when she was just three years old and the trader's man carried her off?

She'd be growed big by now, Mary Angel. Just three years younger than me. Fifteen, I guess. Maybe she's gone to one of them schools for colored folks. Maybe she'd write in one of them little squares on the newspaper. Maybe she's there on that wall, and I don't even know it. Maybe they all are.

Need to find out. Learn what each of them little squares say. "Tell it to me. All that's up there," I ask Juneau Jane. "I can't go from this place without knowing. I lost my people, too. When the Yankees kept coming up the river in their gunboats, Old Mister made a plan for all us to go refugee in Texas till the Confederates could win the war. Missus's nephew Jep Loach stole some of us away, instead. Sold us all along the road, in ones and twos. I was the only one the Gossetts got back. The only one in my family that ended up refugee in Texas with him."

We can't leave this place. Not today. When the woman and the child come, I'll think what to tell them, but hearing all them papers matters most.

"What's that next one say?" First time in my life I ever been hungry for words, but I'm hungry for these like I been starved since a six-year-old child. I want to know how to look at the scratch marks up there and turn them into people and places.

Juneau Jane reads me another. Then another, but I don't hear her Frenchy voice. I hear the rasp of a old woman, looking for the mama she ain't seen since she was a little child like Mary Angel. Still carries that pain in her heart, like the wounds on the body, blood all dried up, but only way they'll heal is to find what's been lost.

I stand next to Juneau Jane, pick one square, then a different one, then another far across the wall.

> A sister sold from her brothers in South Carolina.
>
> A mother who carried and bore from her body nineteen babies, never let to keep any past four years old.
>
> A wife, looking for her husband and her boys.
>
> A mama whose son went off with his young master to the war and never come back.
>
> A family whose boy went to fight in the colored troops with the Federals, them left with no way to know, did he die and was put under the ground on some blood-covered field, or is he living yet, in a place far off, up north even, or just wandering the roads, still lost in his own mind?

I stand there looking at the wall, counting the squares in my head, ciphering. There's so many people there, so many names.

Juneau Jane drops off her tiptoes after a while, rests her hands on her britches. "We must depart this place, you said this yourself. We must travel from here while enough time remains to us. The horses are saddled."

I look over at Missy Lavinia, who's huddled herself in the far corner of the building, the quilt clutched up to her neck. She's staring at the little rainbows tossed over the room by that one pretty cut-glass window. "Might be if we wait a day, Missy would come to her mind by then, be less trouble to us."

"You made mention of your concern that the old woman who brings our goods has become suspicious."

"I **know** what I said," I snap. "I've done some more considering on it. Tomorrow would be best."

She argues with me again. She knows we can't be safe here much longer.

"You just a little fancy girl," I spit out finally, sharp, bitter words that pucker my mouth. "Prissy and been spoiled all your years so far, be some man's pet the **rest** of your years. What do you know about the things in them papers? About how it is for my kind? How it is to yearn after your people and never know, are they alive, are they dead? You ever going to find them again in this world?"

She can't see that the squares on the paper are like the holding pens in a trader's yard. Every one, a story. Every one, a person, sold from here to there. "Long time after the war, **long** time, on **all** the plantations, the mamas and the pappies, they still come—just walk up the road one day, say, 'I am here to get my children. My children belong to me now.' Some been tromping over the whole country, gathering up their kin. The old marses or missuses can't stop them after the freedom. But **nobody** ever comes up the road for me. I wait, but they don't come and I can't guess why. Maybe this is the way I find out." I stab a finger toward the papers, say again. "I **got** to know, or I ain't leaving here. I won't."

Before I can do a thing about it, Juneau Jane starts ripping down papers. "We'll bring them with us, for reading as we go." She even picks up the cut scraps from the floor.

"It's thievin'," I say. "Be wrong to take them from here."

"Then I will burn them." She hurries to the stove, cat quick, and opens the door. "I will burn them, and we will have nothing left for disagreement."

"I'll pull your little skinny arms off your body first."

"These have been read previously by the people coming here." She stands holding them by the stove. "And when we finish reading them, we will leave them with people who, perhaps, have not yet seen them. Would they not be of greater use there?"

I can't argue against that, and part of me don't want to, so I let it be.

We're gone long before middle morning comes, and they'll see we've left one of Missy's dollar coins for the use of their church house . . . and for the papers.

We make a sight, traveling down the road, all three of us dressed in too-big britches. Juneau Jane's got her long hair stuffed down the back of her shirt to hide it. Missy Lavinia's feet dangle bare and pink while I ride behind her on Ginger. Old Missus would be up on her shoutin' bench about those feet and ankles showing, if she could see. But Young Missy don't say a thing, just hangs on and stares off into the woods, her face as pale and blank as the little patch of gray-blue sky up above the road.

I'm beginning to wonder, why hadn't she come back to her mind, started talking again, like Juneau Jane? Is Missy gone for good? Is that bump on Missy's head the difference, or does Juneau Jane just carry a stronger will?

Up ahead, Juneau Jane talks in French to her horse, laying over his mane with her arms strung along his neck.

When we stop in the afternoon for water and food, and to rest the horses, I come back out of the woods after my necessary, and there's Juneau Jane with the skinning knife in one hand and a hank of something black in the other. All round her, like the wool sheared off a sheep, lays that long dark hair. She's sitting in a nest of it, one side of her head looking like a shaggy baby bird's. Maybe her mind's not so much healed as I thought.

Missy Lavinia is sprawled out nearby, her eyes shifting up and down a little, lazy-like, watching that knife do its deed.

First thing that goes through my thoughts is, **Old Missus would have a fit about this, Hannie. You turned your back, left the child alone with**

**a knife. It's never the child's fault for doing bad. It'll be your fault for not watching closer. You're the nursemaid.**

I remind myself that I ain't, and Juneau Jane ain't my trouble, but still, I say, "What'd you do that for? Old Missus . . ." It's halfway out of my mouth before I remember that Old Missus would flick this child off her porch like a tick. Squash her twixt two fingernails. "Could've just kept it tucked up under your hat till you get home. Your mama won't like what you done. Your papa, either, when he comes back. Reason he always loved you best, is you always was a pretty little thing."

She goes right on with her business.

"And he'll come back, you just watch. If them bad men told you he was gone for good, they just lied because Missy paid them to. Bad men lie easy as breathin'. And your papa **won't** like that . . . what you're doing."

Even I know that the only thing this girl's got of value is the way she looks. Her mama will be watching for a man with money who's interested in the girl. Ain't as many of them as there used to be, but there's still some. In the old days, they'd be trotting this child out at the quadroon balls by now, letting her get **seen** by all the rich planters and their sons. They'd be having conversations, working out a bargain with a man who'd keep her for hisself, but couldn't ever marry her, even if he wanted.

"Take a long time for hair like that to grow back."

She stares right through me, whacks off the hank in her fist, tosses it down like it's the head of a snake, keeps right on. Grab, pull, cut. Must hurt, but she's stony as them carved lions that sat on the gateposts at Goswood Grove before the war. "I'll not be returning. Not until I've found Father, or the proof of my inheritance."

"How you gonna do that?"

"I have decided to go to Texas."

"Texas?" That settles my question of this girl's mind. "How're you getting to Texas? And once you're there, where you plan to find your papa? Texas is a big place. You ever **seen** any of it? Because, I been there when Old Mister took us refugee. Texas is a wild land, full with rough men, and Indians that'll cut that hair off your head **for** you, and the skin with it."

A shudder runs through me, end to end. I remember Texas, and not in any good way I can think of. Not going back there. Ever.

But something else whispers in me, too: **Texas is where some of your people was carried off to. Where you left Mama.**

"My mother received word from Papa upon his arrival at the river port of Jefferson, Texas. He had engaged his solicitor there to defend the Gossett properties nearby, which **her** brother"—she gives a shrug toward Missy Lavinia, to let me know we're talking about young Mister Lyle now; just the mention of that boy darkens my mind—"had unlawfully sold. Those lands are my inheritance, and Papa's intent was that, once a settlement was reached in the lawsuit, the proceeds would be transferred to me, so as to assure my provision. The solicitor was to dispense with the legal matter immediately and if possible cause Lyle to return to Jefferson, that our papa might take him in hand. In his letter, Papa spoke with great concern of Lyle's rash behavior and the company he had been keeping of late."

I get a shiver, a bad feel. "Did your money come? Or word from Old Gossett that he'd **got** a hand on his son?"

"No further word arrived from Papa's solicitor, a Mr. Washburn, or from Papa. Papa's agent in New Orleans now puts forth that the letter in my mother's possession is invalid and perhaps fraudulent, and until corroborating documents **or** Papa might be found, nothing more will be proceeded with."

"It was that Mr. Washburn Missy was taking you to see in the building at the river landing, ain't that so?" I try to line it all up in my mind, but with Lyle's name in it, there's no good way. "You remembering any more about that, yet?" Every time I ask her that, she just shakes her head.

She does that same thing again, but a little quake goes 'cross her shoulders, and her eyes skitter away. She's remembering more than she wants to say. "I believe Lavinia knows no more of Mr. Washburn than I, and that the man has remained the entire time in Texas, even as **she** claimed he would be present to speak with us at the river landing." Her eyes go cold and turn Missy's way. "She bandied his name so as to lure me to the place and to have me waylaid there, but her arrangements went awry, and she was betrayed, as well."

My stomach turns over. Would Missy do such a thing to her own half sister? Her blood kin?

Juneau Jane goes back to chopping hair. Scraps of afternoon sunshine flick off the knife blade and skim the tree roots and the moss and the palmetto leaves. "I will ask in Jefferson Port of Papa and pay a call to the office of Mr. Washburn and then discern what I must do next. I pray that Mr. Washburn be found an honest man, unaware that Lavinia had bandied his name. I pray also that I find Papa, and he is well."

**That girl hadn't got the first idea what she's saying,** I tell myself and stand up. **Best to quit talking, now. Need to move along. Still a few hours left before dark.**

Don't know why I stop or why I turn round. "So, how you plan on getting to Texas?" Don't know why I say that, either. "You got money? Because I learned my lesson about stealing away on them boats. They'll drown you for that."

"I have the gray horse."

"You'd **sell** your horse?" She loves that horse and it loves her.

"If I must. For Papa." She chokes on the last words, then swallows hard and stiffens up her mouth.

Comes to me then that, of the three children, this

is the only one that maybe loves Old Gossett, instead of just looking to gain from the man.

We go quiet awhile. I feel my blood rushing through the muscles and flesh, hear it beat in my ears, wanting to be heard. Calling out.

"I think I might just take myself to Texas." The words come in my own voice, but I don't know who spoke them. **One more sharecrop season, Hannie. One. And that patch of ground at Goswood is yours. Yours and Tati's and Jason's and John's. You can't leave them like this, shorthanded with a crop to make. Nobody to help with the sewing and the knitting for extra money. How they gonna pay the note?**

But I think of the squares on the paper. Mama. My people.

Juneau Jane stops cutting and runs the blade along her palm, not hard enough to draw blood, but it marks her. "Perhaps . . . we might make the journey together."

I nod and she nods. We sit that way, tangled in the idea.

Missy Lavinia lets out a big ol' snort. I glance her way, and she's slumped over in the soft, wet moss, sound asleep. Juneau Jane and me look at each other, both thinking the same thing.

**What're we gonna do about her?**

## Lost Friends

Dear Editor—I desire to inquire for my mother, if possible to find out her whereabouts. Her name is Malinda Gill. We were separated in 1843, in Wake county, North Carolina, when I was about 2 or 3 years old. We belonged to Col. Oaddis (who is my father), he sold us to Israel Gill; my mother being high-tempered, Gill sold her and kept me. Rev. Purefile, who carried her to Roseville, where he kept a hotel. When Israel Gill bought mother from Col. Oddia we lived in Raleigh, N.C., then Gill moved with me to Texas. Any information of her whereabouts will be thankfully received. Address me at San Felipe, Texas, care of Mr. C. H. Graves.

HENRY CLAY

—"Lost Friends" column of the Southwestern August 2, 1883

## CHAPTER 16

### BENNY SILVA—AUGUSTINE, LOUISIANA, 1987

I have a sense of déjà vu as I stand in the farmers market parking lot, watching Nathan Gossett's truck pull in. Except I am exponentially more nervous this time. After a long confab with Sarge last night at my house and a few phone calls, incredible plans are falling into place, but most of them depend on Nathan's cooperation.

Was it only a week ago that I ambushed him, seeking permission to enter Goswood Grove House? He couldn't possibly know what that key has led to. I hope I can do a coherent job of sharing the vision with him.

In hindsight, a good night's sleep might have been

a wise idea, but nerves and caffeine will have to do. Sarge and I were up late, scheming and arranging for a few volunteers.

I clench and unclench my fingers, then shake out my hands like a sprinter about to run the hundred-yard dash. This is for all the marbles. I'm ready to put forth a sound argument, and, if necessary, grovel. Although I must be quick about it. I need to have my act together at school this morning. A very special guest speaker has been arranged for my freshmen, sophomore, and combination junior/senior classes today, courtesy of my new friend Sarge.

If all **that** goes well, we'll have the speaker come back another day to talk with my first and second period seventh and eighth graders. With some luck, my students are about to embark on a journey that none of us could've imagined two weeks ago. One that the dreamer in me truly believes has the potential to plant seeds. Sarge is not nearly so optimistic about it, but she is at least willing to come along for the ride.

Nathan stiffens defensively when he spots me crossing the parking lot on an intercept course. His lips circle around an exhale of air and sound. The muscles in his cheek tighten, momentarily obliterating the little cleft in his chin. He's sporting a five o'clock shadow, which, I am suddenly aware, does not look bad on him.

The observation hits me by surprise, and I find myself blushing when first we speak.

"If you're here to give me a report, I don't need

one. I don't want one." He lifts both hands, palms facing outward, a gesture that says, **I have no further involvement in this.** "I told you, I don't **care** what comes out of the library. Take what you can use."

"It's more complicated than I thought. With the library, I mean."

He winces in a way that says he regrets having given me that key.

At this point, full steam ahead is my only option. "I've already stocked some shelves in my classroom. Your grandfather was **quite** a book lover." I stop short of saying that the judge was a book **hoarder**—I've met a few in my bookstore years. I'd be surprised if there weren't more books in other rooms of the house, but I haven't snooped. "I have multiples of things like encyclopedia sets and Reader's Digest Classics. Is it okay if I donate some of those to the city library just down from the school? I hear their collection is pretty outdated. They don't even have a full-time librarian. Just volunteers."

He nods, loosening up a little. "Yeah, my sister was . . ." He shakes off whatever he was about to say. "She liked that old building."

"She had good taste. Those Carnegie grant libraries are amazing. There aren't very many in Louisiana." I could talk at length about why that is, and about the reasons **this** particular Carnegie library is special—I learned a ton last night with Sarge—but I'm conscious of time ticking by. "It's sad to see one in danger of shutting its doors for good."

"If some of my grandfather's collection can help, then great. The man was compulsive about some things. He was famous for letting kids come give sales pitches in his court chambers between cases. He ended up with a lot of encyclopedia sets and Book of the Month subscriptions that way. Sorry, I might've told you that already." A rueful shake of his head sends nutmeg-brown bangs drifting over the delineation mark between a tan and the part of his face that is regularly shielded by a hat or cap. "You really don't need to come ask me. There's no sentimental attachment on my end. My dad died when I was three. Mom was from a family that wasn't considered **of his class,** so Augustine was the last place she wanted to spend time after he passed. My sister had more ties here because she was ten years old when Mom relocated us to Asheville, but I didn't and don't."

"I understand." **And yet, you've moved back to Louisiana to live.**

I would never ask, of course, but why has Nathan, raised far from the bayous and the deltas, settled himself within a short drive of the ancestral homeplace he says he cares nothing about and can't wait to dispose of? No matter how much he wants to see himself as disconnected from this town, it has some sort of hold on him.

Perhaps even he doesn't understand what that is.

I feel a weird pang of jealousy toward his ancestral connection to a place. Maybe that's one reason I'm keen to dig into the mysteries of Goswood Grove. I crave the sense of heritage that rises like mist from wet ground there, old secrets kept closely guarded.

Like Nathan's, I suspect.

The alarm on my wristwatch goes off. I've set it to give me a five-minute warning before my drop-dead time for making it to school.

"Sorry," I say, and fumble to silence the noise. "Teacher thing. We segment the day between bells and beeps."

When I return my attention to him, he's focused on me, as if there's a question he's pondering, but then he changes his mind. "I really can't tell you anything about whatever's in that library. Sorry."

I plunge into a description of old books, undoubtedly valuable, and historical documents, as well as plantation records that detail events, offering facts that may not be recorded anywhere else. Things that, quite possibly, no one outside the family has looked at in a century or more. "We need some guidance on how you'd like to handle those items."

"We?" He retracts suspiciously. Suddenly, the air is so taut it could tear at any moment. "The one thing I did ask was that you keep this between us. The house is—" He clips the sentence forcefully, with effort. Whatever he was about to say is mitigated to "I just don't need the hassle."

"I know that. It wasn't my intention, but things have snowballed some." I forge ahead, daunted but desperate. These are decisions that **must** be made by someone in the family. "Is there any possibility you and I could get together and you could look at some of it? I could meet you at Goswood Grove." That's a no-go, I can tell, so I quickly improvise, "Or at my house? I'd be happy to bring some things over there. They're important. You really need to look them over."

"Not at Goswood Grove House," he says sharply. His eyes blink closed, remain that way a moment. His voice drops when he adds, "Robin was there when she died."

"I'm sorry. I didn't mean to—"

"I could come tomorrow evening—Friday. To your house. I have plans back in Morgan City tonight."

Relief softens the muscles along my spine, pulls the knots loose. "Friday is perfect. Six o'clock or . . . well, anytime after four-thirty. You choose."

"Six is fine."

"I could pick something up for us from the Cluck and Oink, if that sounds good? I'd offer to cook, but I really haven't settled into the place yet."

"Sounds good." But if I had to gauge his countenance right then, I'd say **good** isn't an apt description. Goswood Grove hangs around his neck like an albatross; the questions of its future care and feeding and the difficult memories it embodies are things he wants to avoid.

I understand that better than he probably thinks I do. I can't possibly explain the reasons to him, so I thank him profusely and then reconfirm our time.

As we part, I leave with the sense that he's sorry he ever met me.

Traveling back to school, I try to imagine his life, shrimp boating and whatever else he devotes his time to down there in Morgan City. Girlfriend? Buddies? What does his normal day look like? How does he spend his evenings and nights? His sister has been dead only two years, his grandfather, three. Both passed away while living in that house. What am I treading on by dragging him back to Goswood Grove and a grief that is clearly still fresh?

It's an uncomfortable question, and I do my best to push it out the Bug's window, let it sail away on the breeze as I speed across town, a woman on a mission.

I'm so filled with anticipation about what I have planned for my high school classes that I catch myself watching the clock during the first two periods of the morning, wrangling seventh and eighth graders.

My guest speaker arrives right on schedule, at the end of my conference period. I do a quick double take as she enters my classroom, fussing with a small drawstring purse. She's decked out in a white blouse with a high lace collar and a bow at the neck, an ankle-length black skirt, and short black lace-up boots. A jaunty, flat-brimmed straw hat crowns her thick gray hair, which is pinned into the same loose bun she wears behind the counter of the Cluck and Oink.

She smooths her skirt nervously. "How's this look?" she queries. "It was my costume from the Founder's Day float, back a few years. Put on a little weight since then. Too much barbecue and pie."

"I didn't mean for you to go to so much trouble,"

I say, though I can hardly stand still long enough to talk. "I just want you to tell them the story of the library. How your grandmother and the ladies of the New Century Club were responsible for putting it there."

She smiles and sends a quick wink my way, then adjusts the hairpins on her hat. "Don't you worry, sugar. I brought pictures to show and a copy of the letter my grandmama helped write to Mr. Carnegie. But these kids oughta hear the story from my grandmama herself."

Suddenly, the costume makes sense. I'm stunned and jubilant all at once. "That's brilliant."

"I know." She agrees with a definitive nod. "You said you wanted these young folks to see history. Well, I'm about to give them a piece of it."

And she does. She even hides in my supply closet until the class is settled in and I've taken roll. They're suspicious when I tell them we're having a guest speaker. They're not enthusiastic. Until they see who's here.

"Granny Teeeee!" They squeal like first graders.

She shushes them with one finger and a stern shake of her head. I wish I could do that. "Oh, no, not Granny T," she says. "This is the year 1899. Granny T is a little baby named Margaret Turner, only one year old. And Baby Margaret's mama, Victory, is a young married woman, and I am **her** mama, little Margaret's grandmama. I was born in the year 1857, so that makes me almost forty-three years old right now. I was born into slavery, right out on the Gossett place, and it was a hard life when I came up as a child. Had to work picking cotton, cutting cane, and hauling water to the field by hand, but that's a long time ago now. It's 1899, and I just took my savings and bought a little building to start myself up a restaurant, because I'm a widow woman now, and I have to earn my way on my own. I have nine children, and some are still at home to take care of.

"Now, I don't mind that it's hard work, except there is one thing that does trouble me much. I promised my departed husband that all our children would be educated, but the colored school only goes six months out of the year here, and the town library is small, and it is just for the white folks. The only other library is a little closet-sized shed room out back of the black Methodist church, started about ten years ago. We're proud to have it, but it ain't much. Now, at the time, all the highfalutin' ladies in town, the wives of the bankers and the doctors and such, have what they call the Ladies New Century Club and their project is to build a bigger library . . . for the white folks. But guess what?"

She bends forward in a dramatic pause, and the kids lean over their desks, their mouths hanging slack in concentration.

"That is not the library you children passed by on the school bus today, in **nineteen** and eighty-seven. No, sir. I'm going to tell you about the time a handful of ordinary women, who worked hard for their living, baked pies and took in extra wash and canned peaches and sold everything else they could get their hands on and fooled everybody and built the fanciest library in town."

Reaching into her cart, she extracts a framed photo and holds it up for the kids. "And this is them on the steps of that beautiful library the day it was opened. These ladies here, they are the reason it happened."

She gives the students several framed photographs to circulate as she goes on to tell them about the town's New Century Club unanimously rejecting the notion of using one of the highly touted Carnegie grants to construct a new library, fearing that money came with a **free use for all citizens** stipulation, which could mean **regardless of color.** The ladies of their church applied for the grant instead, the black Methodist church donated land, and the Colored Carnegie Library eventually opened in a newly created building much grander than that of the other library in town. Thereafter, the Carnegie library's founders took the liberty of naming themselves the Carnegie Colored Ladies New Century Club.

"Oh, mercy!" Granny T finishes, "All those women of the original Ladies New Century Club, they were pea-green jealous, I'll tell you. That was back during segregation, you know, and the black folks never got the better part of anything, so for us to have a place so fine and finer than the town library, that was a blot on Augustine, they said. Wasn't much they could do about it, except they did get the city to rule against the permit for the library to have a sign. That way, nobody coming through would know what it was. And so we put a statue of a saint on top of the marble base that was made to hold the sign, and for years, the building stood there that way, but it couldn't stop the magic. In those hard times, it was a symbol of hope."

She has barely stopped talking when the kids begin asking questions. "How come it's just called 'Augustine Carnegie Library' now?" one of the country kids wants to know.

Granny T points the lecture finger at him and nods. "Well, now, that is a good question. Y'all been passing around the pictures. Why do you think the old saint had to move on, so a new sign saying only 'Augustine Library' could go up on that marble base?"

The kids try out a few wrong answers. I'm momentarily distracted, thinking about Councilman Walker's visit to my front porch with his dog, Sunshine. The library saint lives in my oleander bush, thanks to Miss Retta. Now I appreciate him more than ever. He's a book lover, like me. Library history runs in his veins.

"Who's got the picture from 1961?" Granny T asks. "I bet you can say why it's just the Augustine Carnegie Library now."

"Segregation got over, Granny T," Laura Gill, one of my townie girls, answers shyly. Laura has never, absolutely never, spoken to me in class or in the hall.

She's clearly quite comfortable with Granny T—a relative or former Sunday school teacher, maybe?

"That's right, honey. And hooo-ee! Augustine might've fought other things as long as it could, but the city was sure happy to take over control of that library!" Memories dance behind Granny T's thick glasses. "It was the end of something and the beginning of another something. Now, black kids and white kids could sit together in the same room and read the same books. It was another chapter in the library's history. Another part of its tale. And a lot of people have all but forgot about that. They don't know the story of that building and so they don't appreciate it like they ought. But now, you kids . . . now you understand what it meant, and that it was hard won. And from here on, maybe you'll care about it in a different way."

"That's the reason I asked Granny T to come share with us today," I tell the kids, joining Granny T in the front of the classroom as the students pass around old photos. "There's so much history in this town that most people don't know. And, for the next few weeks, we're going to do some detective work, see what we can find out. I want each of you to discover the story of a place or an event in this town—something people probably aren't familiar with—and take notes, copy photographs, whatever you can gather, and write the story."

A few groans follow, but they're muffled. Mostly, there are murmurs of interest, mixed with questions.

"Who do we ask?"

"How do we find stuff?"

"Where do we go?"

"What if you don't know anything about anything here?"

"What if you ain't from here?"

A desk screeches and for a bare instant, I'm afraid some form of trouble is about to erupt right in front of our guest speaker. **Surely they wouldn't . . .**

I follow the sound to find Lil' Ray halfway out of his seat with one hand stuck in the air. "Miss . . . ummm . . . Miss . . ." He can't remember my real name, and he's afraid to call me by one of my dubious nicknames in front of Granny T.

"Lil' Ray?"

"So we gotta write about a place?"

"That's right. Or an event." **Please, please don't start a revolt.** If Lil' Ray rebels, so will his crowd of admirers. It'll be tough to get the class back after that. "This is going to be a big part of our semester grade, so it's important to work hard at it. But I want it to be fun, too. As soon as you've found your subject, let me know, so we won't have any duplicates, and we'll learn something different from each report."

I pan the room with my teacher eye, as in, **I mean it. Okay?**

Another squeal of desk legs. Lil' Ray again. "Miss . . . uhhh . . ."

"Silva."

"Miss Silva, what I meant was, instead of telling

about a place or a event, can we write about a **person,** because—"

"Oh, oh." Laura Gill interrupts—actually cuts him off—but she's got her hand in the air, as if that makes the interruption okay. "At this school in New Orleans, at Halloween time, they do this thing called **Tales from the Crypt.** I saw it in the newspaper last year at my cousin's house. They dress up like the person and stand there in the graveyard and, like, tell the story to everybody. How come we can't do that?"

The idea ignites something I'd only dreamed might be possible. Suddenly, fresh tinder is everywhere. My classroom is afire.

# CHAPTER 17

## HANNIE GOSSETT—RED RIVER, 1875

We gather what things we own, fold our quilt, and take down the scrim cloth we hung for shade from the sun that shines off the river in waves and ripples, mile after mile. For days now, our camp's been steaming upwater on the Red, fighting snags and grasshoppering over sandbars to get crosswise through the rest of Louisiana and out of it. We're in Texas now, for good or for worst.

Home's gone. Too far for looking back or going back. The horses been sold off, and I hope the man treats them good. Was hard to see them go, hardest on Juneau Jane, but that money's the only way we could buy goods and deck passage on this side-wheeler.

Still ain't sure if I chose right in getting on this boat with her, but before we did, I had Juneau Jane write a letter and post it back to Tati and Jason and John. Wanted them to know not to worry over me. I've gone off to see after word about Old Mister. I'll be back before time comes to harvest the crop.

I don't tell about hoping to find news of my people. Ain't certain how Tati would take that. Nor Jason and John, so it's best not to say. They been my only people for most of my life. But there's another life deep inside of me, one long back in a little slabwood cabin with the bed full of knees and elbows and so many voices you can't listen at them all at once.

Juneau Jane's read the newspaper pages, all the little squares, out loud more times than I can keep count of. The roustabouts and the crew—colored men mostly, except for the officers—come down to our little deck camp. Time after time, they ask what the squares say. A few look for theirselves, read the rows of little boxes with a killing hunger and a wish to finally have what's needed to satisfy it.

So far, only one man's found hope, a gal who might be a sister. He said to Juneau Jane, "Now, if I git you some paper and somethin' to write wit', maybe you'd write me a letter I could send off when we make Jeffe'son Port? I'd pay for the trouble." She promised she would, and off that roustabout went, whistling and singing, "Lord, Lord, ain't you good! Ain't you been good to me!"

The white folk on the **Katie P.** are mostly poor,

hoping to find something better in Texas than what they left behind. They looked at that singing roustabout like he was touched in the head. But they didn't look long. The notion's gone round that we been selling voodoo spells and potions under our scrim tent, and that's why the men come and go so much. Folks whisper about the strange silent ways of the big, barefooted white boy with us, and they don't want no part of it.

We still got Missy in tow. Wasn't any choice about it. The river landing where we boarded this boat was nothing more than the leftovers of a trader town shelled flat in the war. Couldn't leave Missy there in this kind of shape. If we don't find Old Mister in Jefferson, we figure to put Missy in the hands of the lawyer man, let her be his burden then.

As we're moving off the Red and into Caddo Lake, then winding up through Big Cypress Bayou toward Port of Jefferson, the **chug-puff-slap, chug-puff-slap** of steamboats echo from all directions. The **Katie P.**'s shallow hull rocks on the wakes when we pass another boat, them going out loaded down with cotton, corn, and bags of seed, and us coming in with all manner of goods from sugar and molasses in pony kegs, to cloth, kegs of nails, and glass windows. Their folks wave, and our folks wave.

Even from a long way off, we hear and see the port coming up. Boat whistles blow a commotion. Bright-colored buildings with heavy iron balcony rails peek through the standing cypress and grapevine on the riverbank. The town noise fights over the rattle of the **Katie P.** and the steam off the boiler. Never heard such racket in my life, nor seen so many people. Music and yelling, horses squealing, oxen bellowing, dogs barking, carts and wagons bouncing along redbrick streets. This's a flaunty place. Busy and big. The farthest river port you can get to in Texas.

A dark feel slides over me. First I don't know the reason, but then I do. I remember this town. Didn't come in by river last time, but this's where the sheriff's men brung me as a child after the Jep Loach trouble. They put me in the jailhouse for safekeeping, waiting on my lawful owners to come fetch me back.

The memory strikes me now, as I fold up the Lost Friends papers and put them in our pack. There's names written in all the edges of the papers, with a lead pencil a boatman stole off a gaming table in the cabin upstairs. Juneau Jane has put down the names of the men on the **Katie P.** who're looking for their people, and all the names of the folks they're missing. We made the promise to ask after them wherever we go. If we find news, it can be sent back to Jefferson in the mail, care of the riverboat **Katie P.**

The men brung us a few pennies here, a dime there, a box of Lucifers for starting fires, tallow candles, biscuits and corn pone from the boat's galley. "To help your travels," they'd say. We didn't ask for it, but they gave it over. Been eating better on this trip than in my whole life. Can't recall a time when my belly was full days in a row like this.

I'll miss the **Katie P.** and her men, but it's time to go.

"Need to get **her** on her feet," I say of Missy Lavinia, who just sits till you pick her up and move her like a rag doll, from one place to the other. She don't fight, but she don't help, either. The worst is taking her to the stalls at the back of the boat to do her necessary, couple times a day like a little child, which Juneau Jane won't do. Folks clear a path when they see us come, don't want to get close to Missy. She hisses at them if she feels like it, sounds like the boiler of the **Katie P.**

Makes things easier, getting off the boat at the landing, though. Other passengers back off and Juneau Jane and me get the whole gangplank to ourselves. Even the deckhands and the cabin crew stand away. Mostly they're kind enough, though, and slip us little tokens and another penny and dime as we pass.

They lean close to whisper the reminders.

" 'Member to keep a ear for my people, if you're able. Surely do appreciate it much."

"My mammy's name, July Schiller . . ."

"My sister is Flora, brothers Henry, Isom, and Paul . . ."

"My brothers were Hap, Hanson, Jim, and Zekiel. All born as Rollinses, owned by Perry Rollins in Virginee. Pappy was Solomon Rollins. A blacksmith man. All been sold south twenty-year ago, now, marched off in a trader's coffle to settle a debt. Never thought to see them again in this world. You boys tell their names for me everyplace you go, I'd be grateful. And I'll keep puttin' you in the Lord's way, so He don't forget about you, neither."

"My wife name Rutha. Twin gals Lolly and Persha. Bought off Master French's place by a man name Compton."

Juneau Jane steers over to a stack of cordwood and asks me for the Lost Friends papers, so she can make sure we ain't forgot anybody.

"I got them safe." I pat our pack. "We already wrote down all the names they just reminded us of. Besides, I got the list in my mind, too." I know about remembering names. Been doing that since six years old and Jep Loach's wagon, not so far from this place.

Juneau Jane perches herself on a log and waits for me to hand over the bundle. "What is preserved in writing is safe from failures of the mind."

"People **lose** papers." We ain't been friends on this journey, her and me. Just two people in need of each other right now. That's all it is. All it's ever gonna be. "My mind is sure to go along wherever I do."

"People lose their minds, too." She gives a hard look toward Missy, who's plunked herself down alongside the woodpile. There's a little green snake winding through the grass toward her britches leg. Her hat's tipped like she's watching it, but she don't even move to chase it off.

I take a stick and shoo the thing away, and think Juneau Jane would've just let it crawl right on to where it was headed. She's a mysterious thing, this fawn-skinned girl that's a pitiful skinny, big-eyed boy now. Sometimes she's like a quiet, sad little child. It's then that I think, **Maybe it ain't so easy for a yellow girl to make a life, either.** Sometimes, she just seems cold. A wicked, devil-fired creature like her mama and the rest of their kind.

Bothers me that I can't cipher her out, but she could've left me and Missy behind at the river landing, and she didn't. She paid the fare for us with her horse money. I wonder at what that means.

Sitting down beside her on the woodpile, I hand over the Lost Friends pages and the pencil and say, "Reckon it don't hurt to check. Ain't like we know where we're going, anyway. Somebody comes by—fine white folk, I mean—you try asking real nice, where can we find that Mr. Washburn?"

A thought comes into my head while she checks over her work. "How're we gonna talk to this lawyer man about your papa's papers if we do find him?" I look her over, then look down at myself. "Right now, I'm a colored boy, and you're a ragged little rat off the river." Been so caught up with the Lost Friends on the boat, I hadn't thought past us getting onshore. "No lawyer man will talk to us."

She hadn't thought that far, either, I can tell.

She chews the pencil end, looks up at all them fancy brick buildings, double-deckers, most of them. Some even triple. A gunshot fires off, cracking through all the noise of the town and the river port. We both jump. Men stop and look around, then go back to work.

Juneau Jane tips up that pointy little chin of hers. "I will speak with him." Her lips rise at the corners, her nose, which is her papa's turned-up nose, crinkling. "Were I to inform him I am William Gossett's daughter and heir, he would undoubtedly assume me to be Lavinia. I believe she was not truthful in saying they had made his acquaintance in New Orleans recently, given that the man resides here in Jefferson, and this is where Papa engaged his services not long ago."

A laugh puffs out of me, but there's fear in my belly. Back home, what she's aiming to do can get you dead in a hurry. If you're colored, you don't go pretending to be white. "You're a colored girl, case you hadn't noticed."

"Are we really so different?" She stretches one arm beside Missy's. Their skin ain't the same, but not too far off that you'd guess the truth, either.

"Well **she's** older than you." I wave a hand at Missy. "You're a child in short skirts, still. You ain't even got you no . . . well, you don't look much as **fourteen,** yet. Even if Missy **was** lying when she told you she'd met the man before, you ain't gonna pass for Missy."

Her eyes hold at half-mast, like I am thickheaded. I want to swat that look from her face. That is the exact way Missy Lavinia used to do when she was a little child. These two girls are more sisters than they know. Some things run in the bloodline just as sure as that little turned-up nose. "They skin you alive, if you get caught at this. Skin me alive, too."

"What choice have I otherwise? I must obtain word of Father or proof of his intentions for my provision. Lavinia would leave me penniless, with no choice but that my mother bargain me off to a man." The frost that always covers her over cracks a little now. There's pain underneath, and fear. "If Papa **is** gone, an inheritance becomes my only hope."

She's right, I know. Her papa is the only hope for all us. "Well, we have to get you a dress, then. Dress, and a corset, and some padding to stuff it, and a bonnet to cover that hair." I hope this plan don't get us killed or put in jail or worse. Then who'll carry the Lost Friends around? "But you promise me, I do this thing with you, no matter what we find out, you won't pull foot out of here and leave me stuck with her." I nod over to Missy Lavinia. "She ain't my burden to bear. And it's you and her that got me into this whole mess. You owe me something. You and me, we stay together, till we figure out about your papa. And till we get Missy sent back home. If this lawyer man does have money waiting for you, you'll pay Missy's passage and find somebody to get her back to Goswood. We have us a bargain?"

Her bottom lip pokes out a little at the idea of having to do for Missy Lavinia, but she nods.

"And one other thing."

"No other things."

"And one other thing. When we do part company, whenever that is, the Lost Friends go with me. And meantime, you learn me how to read it and write down new ones for new folks."

We shake hands on it, and the bargain is struck. We're in this mess, together.

Least for now.

"Making you a woman sure will be a whole lot tougher than making you a boy." The words are hardly out my mouth when a shadow falls over me, and I look up and see a colored man, stout as a woodcutter, standing over us. He folds and unfolds a hat in his hands.

I hope he didn't hear what I just said.

3toward the **Katie P.** "I hear . . . heared it from a fella. You put me in the Loss F-friends, too?"

We look toward the landing nearby and see the singing man Juneau Jane wrote the letter for on the boat, and he's pointing somebody else our way. Word of us has spread.

Juneau Jane gets her pencil and asks the man who he's looking for. It's nobody we've got on our pages already.

She takes down names of the man's people, and he gives us a nickel before he goes back to work, loading seed bags onto a swamp boat. Then comes another man. He tells us where to go to buy some used clothes and goods cheap, and I decide I better strike off before the day's gone. Can't take Juneau Jane and

Missy Lavinia with me, since it's the colored town he's talking about.

"You stay here, and I'll go where he said to," I tell her and get a biscuit from our poke, and tuck Missy's reticule in my britches, then leave them with the rest of our goods. "Watch after Missy."

I know she won't.

It worries me some as I follow the man's directions and wind up in a little settlement down in a gully. First, I find a stitcher woman who sells mended clothes out the back of her house. I buy what's needed for Juneau Jane, but I wish I could buy a miracle, because that's needed most. The stitcher woman points me to a harness maker who mends shoes for people and fixes up old ones to sell, too. I have to guess at the size, but I get some for Missy, since her feet are gone raw and she don't watch where she's walking. I trade off that gold locket that was hers. Figure it can't be helped, and the chain's broke anyhow.

I decide against buying button boots for Juneau Jane. Too much money, and they're lady shoes she can't wear for a boy. We'll just have to hide her brogans under her dress hem while she talks to the lawyer. I go to a peddler store in a tent, looking for a needle and thread, in case we need to put a stitch or two in that dress to keep on Juneau Jane's skinny body.

I buy socks and another blanket and a cook pot. Buy some pretty peaches from a man with a basketful. He adds a nice plum to the top and don't even want me to pay for it, since I'm new here. Folks are kind in the colored town. They're all just like me, come off plantations after the freedom, took to working for the railroads, or the timber companies, or the riverboats, or the shops, or in the white ladies' big houses that're almost close enough to see from here. Some freedmen started up stores of their own, to sell to colored folk in this little gully town.

They're used to folks coming through, traveling. I ask after the names of my people while I make my bargains, and I tell about my grandmama's blue beads. "Ever know anybody here name of Gossett? Be free now, but slaves before the war. Ever seen somebody wear just three beads on a string?" I ask over and over. "Three blue glass beads, just big around as the tip of your little finger and real pretty?"

**Can't recollect so.**

**Don't believe I do, child.**

**Sounds right purdy, but no I ain't.**

**You seeking after your people, child?**

"Feel somewhat familiar about those, I do," a old man tells me when we stand aside to let a dray rumble by, filled with coal. White clouds lay over the man's eyes like sifted flour, so he has to lean close to me to see. He smells of pine sap and smoke, and he walks stiff and slow. "Think I have seen such before, but a long time ago. Can't say where, though. Mind's not good these days. My apologies, young sprout. God speed you along in your journey, all the same. Don't go by the names, though. There's many that've changed their names. Picked new ones after the freedom. You keep looking."

I thank him and promise I don't take it for discouragement. "Texas's a big place," I say. "I mean to keep asking." I watch him walk back toward the colored settlement, bent over and hobbling.

**I could stay here in the gully town,** I think to myself. **Stay here in the shadow of all them big buildings and fine houses and the music and the noise and all the different kind of folks, and wouldn't that be something? I could ask after my people, day after day to travelers who come through from the East and the West.**

The idea sparks in my head, a fire on wood that's been laid and waiting a long time. Be a whole new kind of life to leave behind mules and farm fields and table gardens and chicken houses, and stay in a place like this. I could get work. I'm strong, and I'm smart.

But there's Tati and Jason and John and Old Mister and Missy Lavinia and Juneau Jane to think about. Promises and sharecrop papers. Life never is just about what you want. Seldom ever.

I push my mind back to the task I'm at now and commence worrying how long I been gone from Juneau Jane and Missy and what'd happen if Missy walked off or stirred up trouble. Juneau Jane might not try to stop her, and probably can't anyhow. Missy's bigger and stronger by twice.

I head back, walking fast and taking care to keep

out of the way of farm wagons and shays and white ladies with market baskets and baby carriages. I work up a sweat under my clothes even though the day ain't warm. I'm just worried.

In my mind, young Gus McKlatchy says, **Well, that's the problem with postulatin', Hannibal. Brings up trouble that ain't happened yet and likely won't ever. Why bother with it?** I smile to myself and hope Moses didn't catch Gus and throw him off that riverboat, too.

I try to quit postulating while I make my way back to the port landing.

Missy and Juneau Jane still sit right by the cordwood. There's colored folks gathered round—a couple men standing, couple squatted down or sitting on the grass, a old man leaning on a young girl's shoulder, and three women. All peaceable enough. Juneau Jane's reading to them from the Lost Friends. She's got our quilt set out, folded in front of her. I watch a man drop a coin in it. There's three little carrots, too, plus Missy Lavinia's eating on one.

It takes some doing to get us away from there, but I know we need to move on in our task. I tell the folks we'll come back later with the Lost Friends. Then I push Missy's feet into the shoes I bought her, and thank heaven they mostly fit.

Juneau Jane ain't happy with me when I chase off the last of the people so we can go. "You hadn't ought to make a spectacle," I say while we start down the riverbank.

"News of us and the Lost Friends traveled as the men from our boat visited the town with their pay," Juneau Jane answers. "Others came. What would you have me do?"

"I don't know." That much is true. "Just that we don't want everybody in the Port of Jefferson talking about us."

We go on about our business, make our way down the river on a trail folks must use for fishing or hunting. At a brushy spot near the water, I get all us washed some, but work on Juneau Jane most.

The dress and petticoats are a sorry sight. The raggedy corset hangs on her like a sack, and the dress hem is too long. "You'll have to walk high on your toes, like you got heel boots on," I tell her. "Keep your feet up under the dress, don't let them old brogans show; that'll give us away. No Gossett lady would be in such poor shoes."

I finally undo everything and take the britches she's been wearing and wrap them round her middle inside the corset, and stuff the bosom part with the shirt she had on, then do up the laces again. It's better, some. Who knows if it'll fool anybody, but what choice have we got? I do up her spoon bonnet last, pull it up tight against her face to hide the hair, then I stand back and look.

The picture of her pushes a laugh out my mouth. "You . . . y-you . . . look like somebody been whittlin' on Missy Lavinia." I cough. "Look like some . . . somebody took her down to the nubbins." I get to laughin', and I can't stop. Can't even catch my breath. Juneau Jane stomps her little foot and scolds me to hush up before somebody comes wandering down here to see, what's the ruckus about? But the madder she gets, the harder I laugh.

All that laughing makes me miss Tati and Jason and John, and even farther back, my brothers and sisters and Mama and Aunt Jenny and my four little cousins and Grandmama and Grandpapa. With all the ways we labored hard, planting and chopping and hoeing and harvesting, we laughed, too. **Laughing carry you over a tough time,** that's something my grandmama used to say.

I go right from laughing to being heavy in my heart. Feel a lonesome burden all of a sudden. Lonesome for people I love. Lonesome for home.

"We best get on with this," I say, and we pull Missy Lavinia up, work our way back to town, follow the directions the folks gave Juneau Jane to the lawyer man's office. It ain't hard to find. Man's got him a big brick building, two floors high, with letters carved in a square stone up top. Juneau Jane looks at it and reads his name there. L. H. WASHBURN.

"Walk up on your toes," I remind her. "Keep them shoes under your hem. And talk in a lady voice. And act in lady ways."

"I am aware of how to conduct myself with propriety," she brags, but she looks scared to death under that bonnet. "I have been given deportment lessons. Papa insisted upon it."

I pass over that last part. Just reminds me how good she's had it all these years. "And whatever you do, don't take off that bonnet."

We go up to the front steps, and I check her over one more time, and in she walks. I find a place to sit in the shade with Missy. She's rubbing her stomach and moaning a little. I try to give her hardtack to quieten her, but she won't take it.

"Hush, then," I say. "Ought to be too scared to think about your belly, anyhow. Last time I stood outside a building while somebody went in, you and Juneau Jane wound up in a box, and I almost got shot dead."

I won't be falling asleep in some hogshead barrel this time, that's for definite.

I keep a narrow eye on that building while we wait.

Juneau Jane ain't gone very long, and I'm afraid that can't be good news, and it's not. The lawyer ain't even there; only a woman that keeps his office, and she's packing the place up, floor to rafters. Old Mister was by here sometime back, but he left the property settlement for the lawyer to argue out, then he went on to Fort Worth town, hunting for Lyle. Then, two weeks after Old Mister was through here, Federal men come to the office looking to get some files. The woman didn't know what, but Mr. Washburn went out the back door when he saw them Federals. Next day, he gathered up some things and left for Fort Worth hisself. Said he meant to see about opening up a office there, didn't know when he'd be back.

"She had nothing in the remaining files bearing Papa's name," Juneau Jane tells me. "She opened the box, that I might see for myself. There was only this. And it is just a book in which Mr. Washburn recorded the accountings of Papa's land here—the land that was fraudulently sold by Lyle. After the turn of the year, the notations ended, and so we must—"

"Ssshhh." I grab her with one hand and Missy with the other.

I'm looking right across the street at three men walking toward that building—two white, one tall, lean, and pecan-shell brown, his hand resting on the butt of a hip pistol. I'd know the long, steady stride of that man anyplace.

Moses looks my way while I'm pulling Missy and Juneau Jane back into the shadows. Can't see his eyes under the hat brim, but I feel them on me. His chin draws in a little, then his head cocks to study us.

He falls a step farther back from the other men, and I figure a bullet comes next.

A question bolts through my mind.

**Which one of us does he shoot first?**

## Lost Friends

Dear Editor—I belonged to John Rowden of St. Charles county, Missouri. I was called Clarissa. I was sold to Mr. Kerle, a planter. My mother was named Perline. I was the youngest of mother's first children. I had a sister named Sephrony, and a brother called Anderson. I don't know much about mother's second children. My step father's name was Sam. He was a house carpenter and also belonged to Mr. Rowden. I was eight or nine years of age when sold. When Polk & Dallas passed through the country. I remember hearing them say I was ten years old. I wish to inquire if I have any living kinfolks and exactly where they are now living, and their full names, so that I can write to them. I have written before but have received no reply. I am all alone in the world, and it would be a great happiness to me to know that I had some living kinfolks. If mother, sisters and brothers are dead, I think I must have some nieces and nephews living. Hoping with the help of God to hear from some of my family and that before long. I remain respectfully Clarissa (now Ann). Mrs. Ann Read, No. 246 Customhouse, St., bet Marais and Treme sts., New Orleans

—"Lost Friends" column of the Southwestern January 19, 1882

# CHAPTER 18

## BENNY SILVA—AUGUSTINE, LOUISIANA, 1987

I wake and look across the room, surprised to find myself curled in the worn recliner affectionately nicknamed **Old Snoozy.** My favorite fuzzy blanket, Christopher's gift to me last year on my birthday, lies askew over me. I snuggle it under my chin as I'm opening my eyes to the gentle sunlight on the old cypress-plank floors.

Loosening one arm, I wrist-rub my forehead, blink the farmhouse into view, look across the room at the stocking-clad man feet propped crisscross on the antique wooden box I rescued from a dumpster near campus a few years back. I don't recognize the socks on those feet, or the well-worn hunting boots kicked off on the floor nearby.

And then, suddenly, I **do.** And I realize the night has passed, and morning is here, and I'm not alone. In an instant of befuddled panic, I touch my arm, my shoulder, my folded-up legs. I **am** fully dressed, and nothing is amiss in the room. That's a relief.

The previous evening comes back slowly at first, and then faster, faster, faster. I remember gathering things from Goswood Grove House and even a few treasures from the city library collection, to be fully prepared for my meeting with Nathan. I remember that he was late getting to my place. I was afraid he'd decided not to show.

He stepped onto my porch with an apology and a boxed cake he'd picked up as a gift. "Doberge cake. It's sort of a Louisiana thing," he explained. "I feel like I should apologize for the intrusion. I'm sure you could've made more interesting plans on a Friday night."

"This looks like a pretty incredible apology." I took ownership of what felt like three pounds of dessert, while shifting back a step to allow him in the door. "But I'll admit, it's tough to compete with gate duty at the football stadium and preventing teenagers from making out under the bleachers."

We laughed the nervous laugh of two people uncertain where the conversation should go from there.

"Let me show you a little of why I asked you to

come," I said. "We'll grab some barbecue and iced tea in a minute." I purposely didn't offer wine or beer, for fear of making our meeting seem too much like a date.

It was hours before we even remembered the takeout food and the cake. As I'd been hoping, Nathan wasn't as disinterested in family history as he thought. The tangled past of Goswood Grove swept us up as we sifted through old first-edition books, ledgers listing years of the plantation's business transactions and harvest tallies, journals detailing day-to-day activities, and several letters that were tucked between the books on one of the shelves. They were just the chatter of a ten-year-old girl writing to her father about her daily activities at a school run by nuns, mundane in their day but fascinating now.

I saved the family Bible and brought out the more innocuous and pleasant things first. I wondered how he'd feel about the bits of heritage that were raw and difficult. Of course, in the clinical sense, he most certainly **knew** his family's history, understood what a place like Goswood Grove would have been in the era of slavery. But how would he feel about coming face-to-face with the human realities, even through the faraway lens of yellowed paper and faded ink?

The question haunted me, dredged up a few specters of my own, realities I'd never been willing to revisit, even to share them with Christopher, who'd had such an idyllic childhood, I guess I was afraid he'd look at me differently if he knew the whole truth about mine. When it finally did come out, he felt betrayed by my lack of candor in our relationship. The truth blew us apart.

It was late at night before I gave Nathan the old leather-bound Bible, with its records of births and deaths, the purchase and sale of human souls, the babies whose paternity was not listed because such things were not to be discussed. And the grid map of the enormous graveyard that now lay hidden beneath an orchard. Resting places unmarked other than possibly by fieldstone or a bit of wood slowly eaten away by wind and water and storms and seasons.

I left him alone with the words, went to clean up the dishes and put away the leftovers. I diddled around with drying the plates and refreshing our tea glasses while he murmured, to himself or to me, that it was so strange to see it all on paper.

"It's a horrific thing to realize that your family bought and sold people," he said, his head resting back against the wall, his fingers spread lightly alongside the writing of his ancestors, his face sober. "I never understood why Robin wanted to come here and live. Why she felt compelled to dig into it so much."

"It's history," I pointed out. "I'm trying to impress upon my students that everyone has history. Just because we're not always happy with what's true doesn't mean we shouldn't know it. It's how we learn. It's how we do better in the future. Hopefully, anyway."

In my own family, there were rumors that my

father's parents had held positions of note in Mussolini's regime, had aided in the axis of evil that supported a quest for world domination at the expense of millions of lives. After the war, his family quietly faded back into the population, but they'd managed to keep much of their ill-gotten money. I never even considered investigating whether those rumors were true. I didn't want to know.

I confessed all that to Nathan for some reason, as I returned to the living room and sat down beside him on the sofa. "I guess that makes me a hypocrite, since I'm forcing you into your family history," I'd admitted. "My father and I were never close."

We talked about parental relationships then—maybe both of us needed something else to focus on for a while. Maybe fathers lost early to death or divorce seemed like a more approachable topic than trafficking in human bondage and how such a thing could be continued generation after generation.

We pondered it as we thumbed through pages of the plantation's daily logs, a journal of sorts detailing activities of business and life—gains and losses in financial terms, but also in much more human ways.

I leaned close, struggling to decipher the elaborate script noting the loss of a seven-year-old boy, along with his four-year-old brother and eleven-month-old sister. They'd been left locked in a slave cabin by their mother, Carlessa, a field hand purchased from a slave trader. It undoubtedly wasn't her choice to report to the harvest at four in the morning to begin a day of cutting sugar cane. Presumably, she locked the cabin to keep the children from harm, to prevent wandering. Perhaps she checked on them when the gang broke at midday. Perhaps she gave her seven-year-old strict instruction on how to look after his younger siblings. Perhaps she nursed almost one-year-old Athene before hastily settling the baby down for a nap. Perhaps she stood on the doorstep, worried, weary, afraid, agonizing as any mother would. Maybe she noticed the chill in the room, and said to her seven-year-old son, "You just get you a blanket, and you and Brother wrap up. If Athene wakes, you walk her round, play with her some. I'll be back when dark comes."

Perhaps the last instruction she gave him was, "Don't you try to light that fire, now. You hear me?"

But he did.

Carlessa's children, all three of them, were taken from her that day.

Their horrific fate is recorded in the journal. It ends with a notation, written by a master or a mistress or a hired overseer—the handwriting varies, making it evident that the responsibility for keeping records was shared.

**November 7, 1858. To be remembered as a cruel day. Fire at the quarters. And these three taken from us.**

Those words, **a cruel day,** were left to interpretation. Were they an indication of the writer's remorse, sitting at the desk, pen in hand, the faint scents of ash and soot clinging to skin and hair and the fibers of clothing?

Or were they an abdication of responsibility for the circumstances that ended three young lives? The **day** was cruel, not the practice of holding human beings as prisoners, of forcing women to leave their children inadequately tended while they labored, unpaid, to fatten the coffers of wealthy men.

The children's burials were mentioned that same week, but merely in matter-of-fact terms to document the event.

The hour grew later and later as Nathan and I read through the daily logs, sitting side by side on the sofa, our shins touching, our fingers crossing each other's as we struggled to make out notations that time was slowly bleaching away.

I try to recall the rest, now as I wake, uncertain how I ended up across the room in the recliner asleep.

"What . . . what time is it?" I croak in a drowsy voice, and sit up and glance toward the window.

Nathan lifts his chin—perhaps he was dozing, too—and looks my way. His eyes are red and tired. His hair disheveled. I wonder if he has slept even a little. At some point, he did slip off his shoes at least, make himself comfortable. He's taken the liberty of borrowing a stack of blank paper from my school supplies. Several sheets of notes lie on my coffee table.

"I didn't mean to stay this long," he says. "I fell asleep, and then I wanted to copy the grid map of the graveyard. The thing is, there's the annexation deal with the cemetery association, but there are already people buried under that ground. I need to see if I can make some kind of estimate of where these begin and end." He indicates the plots marked in the book.

"You should've thrown something at me. I could have gotten up and helped you."

"You looked pretty comfortable over there." He smiles, and the morning light catches his eyes and a strange tingle slips through me.

Horror follows in its wake.

**No,** I tell myself. **Firmly and unequivocally, no.** I am at a strange, unmoored, lost, lonely, uncertain point in life. I now know enough about Nathan to realize that he is, too. We pose a risk to one another. I'm on the rebound, and he's . . . well, I'm not sure, but now isn't the time to find out.

"I just stayed and kept reading after you dozed off," he explains. "I probably should've gone into town and grabbed a room at the motel."

"That would've been silly, and you know there's only the one motel in Augustine, and it's awful. I bunked there my first night." It's sad, actually, that this is his family's hometown, where his two uncles seem to possess the lion's share of everything, and he, himself, owns not only my house but an enormous one down the way, and he's talking about staying in a motel.

"The neighbors won't start rumors, I promise." I deploy the old cemetery joke to let him know I'm in no way worried about damage to my reputation. "If they do, and we can **hear** them, **then** I'll worry."

A dimple forms in one suntanned cheek. It's endearing in a way I know I shouldn't further contemplate, so I don't. Although I catch myself idly wondering how much younger than me he might be. A couple years, I think.

And then I tell myself to stop.

His comment provides a perfect segue into shoptalk, which is a relief. We've been so busy on our journey of discovery with the Goswood Grove documents, I haven't even brought up my other reason for wanting some of his time—beyond the matter of the value of antique books, and what he feels okay about donating, and making some arrangements for the proper historical preservation of the plantation records.

"There's one more issue I need to talk with you about, before I let you get away," I say. "The thing is, I want to use all these materials with the kids in my classroom. So many of the families in this town go back for generations, and a lot of them are connected, in one way or another, to Goswood." I watch for his reaction, but he keeps that to himself. He seems to be almost dispassionately listening as I go on. "The names in so many of those ledgers, and records of purchases and sales, and births and deaths and burials—even enslaved people whose labors were rented from or to other plantations up and down the River Road, and tradesmen who worked here or sold goods to the Gossetts, a lot of those names—in some form or other have been handed down through families. They occupy space in my grade book. I hear them being announced on the loudspeaker during football games and talked about in the teachers' lounge." Faces scroll through my mind. Faces in all shades. Gray eyes, green eyes, blue eyes, brown eyes.

Nathan draws his chin upward and away slightly, as if he senses a blow coming and his reflex is to avoid it. He hasn't considered, perhaps, that these long-ago events have woven their threads into the here and now.

I know, if I didn't fully internalize it before, why there are black Gossetts and white Gossetts in this town. They are all tied together by the tangled history in this Bible, by the fact that the enslaved people of a plantation shared their master's last name. Some changed the name after emancipation. Some kept what they had.

Willie Tobias Gossett is the seven-year-old boy who was buried well over a century ago along with his four-year-old brother and baby sister, Athene—Carlessa's children, who perished in a burning cabin with no way out. All that lives on of Willie Tobias is a notation in the carefully kept plot map that now sits on the end table next to Nathan Gossett's hand.

But Tobias Gossett is also a six-year-old boy who wanders, seemingly unrestricted, the roadsides and farm paths of this town in Spider-Man pajamas, his name possibly handed down through generations like an heirloom—a coin or a favorite piece of jewelry—from long-dead ancestors who possessed no tokens to pass along, save for their names and their stories.

"There's a project the kids want to do for school. Something they sort of cooked up on their own. I think it's a good idea . . . a great idea, in fact."

Since he's still listening, I proceed with the description of my Friday morning guest speaker, and the tale of the Carnegie library, the kids' reaction, and how their ideas morphed from there. "And the thing is, it really just started out as a means of getting them interested in reading and writing. A way to take them from books on a class requirement list they don't see as relevant, and into personal stories—local history they may have brushed past all their lives. People wonder these days why kids don't have respect for themselves or their town or why they don't honor their names. They don't know what their names **mean.** They don't know their town's history."

I can see the wheels turning as he slowly rubs his stubbled chin. He's catching my excitement, I think. I hope.

I soldier on. "What they have in mind for the culmination of this . . . is this thing they call **Tales from the Crypt.** It's done in cemetery tours in New Orleans apparently. They'll research and write about someone who lived and died in this town, or even here on the plantation, an ancestor or someone they feel connected to across the centuries. For the big finale—maybe as a fundraiser even—they'll dress up in costume and stand by the tombstone as a living witness, and tell their story during a cemetery tour. It'd let everyone see **how** all the histories are intertwined. Why the lives of ordinary people mattered then, and why they **still** matter. Why it's relevant today."

He looks down at the book of plantation records in his lap, runs a thumb carefully along the edge of the page. "Robin would have loved this. My sister had all kinds of ideas about Goswood, about restoring the house, documenting its past, cleaning out the gardens. She wanted to open a museum that would focus on **all** the people of Goswood, not just the ones who slept in those four-poster beds in the big house. Robin was one for lofty ideas. A dreamer. That's why the judge left the place to her."

"She sounds like an incredible person." I try to imagine the sister he's lost. I summon her up in my mind. Same deep blue-green eyes. Same smile. Medium-brown hair like Nathan's, but seven years older, more fine-featured and slight-boned.

And so obviously loved. He looks heartbroken, just mentioning her. "You need her, not me," he admits.

"But we **have** you." I try to go at it gently. "I know you're busy and you live out of town and all of this"—I indicate the papers he's been up all night reading—"isn't something you were interested in. I'll be incredibly grateful if my students can have access to these papers for their research projects, but many of the kids are going to find their ancestors in the graveyard that's not marked. We need permission to use the land behind my house, and that land belongs to you."

An inordinate amount of time passes while he wrestles with the question. Twice, then three times, he starts to reply, then stops. He surveys the materials on the coffee table, on the end table, on the sofa. He pinches his forehead, closes his eyes. His lips thin to a grim line drawn by emotions he obviously feels the need to keep from showing.

He's not ready for all of this. There's a well of pain here for him, and I have no way of fully understanding all the wellsprings that feed it. His sister's death, his father's, his grandfather's, the human reality of Goswood Grove's history?

I want to let him off the hook, but I can't quite make myself say anything that would. I owe it to my students to pursue this before heaven-knows-what happens to these documents and Goswood Grove itself.

Nathan shifts forward on the sofa so that, for a moment, I'm afraid he's decided to walk out. My pulse ratchets up.

Finally, he props his elbows on his knees, sags between his shoulder blades, stares through the window. "I hate that house." He fists his hands together. Tight. "That house is a curse. My father died there, my grandfather died there. If Robin hadn't been so obsessed with fighting my uncles over the place, she wouldn't have ignored the symptoms with her heart.

I knew she didn't look good the last time I was there. She should've gone for tests, but she didn't want to hear it. She didn't want to face the fact that the house was too much for her to take on. She spent fourteen months fighting battles over her plans for it—battles with my father's brothers, with the parish, with lawyers. You name it, if it's around here, Will and Manford have their hands in it. That's what consumed my sister's final years, and that was what we argued about the last time I saw her." His eyes glitter as he recalls these events. "But Robin had promised my grandfather she'd take care of the place, and she wasn't one to go back on a promise. The only one she ever broke was when she died. She promised me she wouldn't."

The pain of his loss is raw, overwhelming, unmistakable, even though he tries to conceal it.

"Nathan, I'm sorry," I whisper. "I didn't mean to . . . I wasn't trying—"

"It's okay." He rubs his eyes with a thumb and forefinger, drinks in air, straightens, tries to toss off the emotions. "You're not from here." His eyes meet mine; our gazes grab and hold on. "I understand what you're trying to do, Benny. I admire it, and I see the value of it. But you have no idea what you're stepping into."

## CHAPTER 19

### HANNIE GOSSETT—TEXAS, 1875

I'm on my knees when I wake. The ground shakes and sways like I jumped a thundercloud to ride it over the land. Splinters needle through my britches and dig at my skin.

Off in the far fields, I see my people. Mama and all my brothers and sisters and cousins, they stand in the sunshine, their burden baskets set down while they raise their hands and look to see who it is calling out to them.

"Mama, Hardy, Het, Prat, Epheme," I yell. "Easter, Ike, Aunt Jenny, Mary Angel, I'm here! Mama, come get your child! I'm here! Can't you see?"

I reach out toward Mama, and then she's gone, and

I open my eyes to a starry dark sky. The wind batters my face, dusts it with hot bits of ash from the engine of the train that's carrying us west. Mama ain't out there and never was. She's just a dream again. The farther we go into Texas, the more I see her when I close my eyes.

Is that a sign?

Juneau Jane pulls me down hard. She's got a rope tied at my waist to be sure I don't wander off the edge of this flatcar in my sleep. It loops Missy Lavinia next, and then Juneau Jane. Wasn't any way to get shed of Missy in Jefferson, with Moses breathing down our backs. Don't know why he didn't fire on us in that street and kill us dead, all three. Don't want to know.

He just turned and walked on with them other men, and we found our way to the train, and got on it and put miles betwixt us.

This open car is a rough way to travel, the wind streaming hot cinders through the night sky over our heads. I've seen trains, but ain't ever been on one. Didn't think I'd like it, and I don't. But it was the way to get from Jefferson in a hurry. The trains go west, so full of stock and goods and folks, hardly a space can be had. Folks ride up top of the coach cars and in the stock cars with their horses, and in flatcars twixt the loads, like we're doing. They hop off here and there, sometimes when the train just slows down enough to drop a mail bag on a hook or pick one up, and blow the whistle.

We'll stay on this train to the end, past the little

town of Dallas, to Eagle Ford at the Trinity River, where the Texas and Pacific Railway ends till they get it open farther west. From Eagle Ford, we'll cross the river and walk or ride a wagon more than a day's travel, to Fort Worth town, to find Old Mister or the lawyer man . . . or what is to be learned of them.

I never laid my eyes on so much country. The farther west we ride on this rumblin', shakin' beast, the more the land changes. Gone is the shelter of the piney woods, the last part of Texas I knew from the refugee years. Here, the grass stretches out, mile by mile in low hills, the elms and the live oaks and the pin oaks cluster together along the creeks and in the folds of dry watersheds.

Strange land here. Empty.

I settle back in beside Missy, feel her grab at my clothes. She's scared of this place, too.

"You hush up now," I say. "Hush up and be still. You're all right." I watch patchy trees whirl by in the dark, their moon shadows laying over hills and flats without a farm light or a campfire, far as I can see.

Deep slumber takes me off, and Mama don't come, and I don't go to the trader's yard or watch little Mary Angel stand on the auction block. All inside me, there's nothing but peaceable quiet. The kind of quiet with no time passing in it.

Seems like just a blink's gone by before I wake up to noise, and Juneau Jane shaking my one arm, and Missy whimpering and digging her fingers into the other. There's music playing someplace and a gristmill chugging and grinding grain. My neck's crooked from my head laying on my shoulder, and my eyelashes stick from the wind and the dirt. I pull them apart and see it's dark yet. The moon's gone, but the stars still spatter the black sky.

The train scoots along in a slow, lazy sway, like a mama rocking her baby, too lost in the look of her child to think of the day's work done or the hard row ahead.

When the train stops, there comes a ruckus of men and women, horses, dogs, wagons, hand trucks. A barker calls out, "Pots, pans, kettles! Salt pork, bacon!"

Another yells, "Good buckets, sharp axes, oilcloth, shovels. . . ."

A man sings "Oh Shenandoah," and a woman laughs high and long.

No matter that good folk oughta be sleeping at this hour, the noise of people and animals seems to come from everyplace. Noise and noise.

We get off the train and move away from rolling wagons and scrambling horses and find a place on a boardwalk under a coal lamp. Wagons come too close to other wagons and folks holler out. "Watch yerself, thar," and "Haw, Bess. Haw, Pat. Git up! Git up, now!"

A man yells something in a language I don't know. A team of loose horses bolts out of the dark and down the street, harnesses flapping. A child screams for its mama.

Missy squeezes my arm so hard I feel the blood

swell up in my hand. "Stop that, now. You're troublin' me. Ain't walking all the way to Fort Worth with you hanging on me." I try to shake her off, but she won't have it.

A spotted bull trots into the torchlight and moves on by, easy as could be, nobody leading it, nor chasing it, nor minding it, far as I can see. The torch lamp glows off its white spots and the frightful, gray horns long enough a man could lay in them like a hammock. The lamp glow goes down into the middle of the bull's eye and bounces off and comes at us blue-red, and he snorts out dust and steam.

"This's a awful place," I tell Juneau Jane, and I worry Fort Worth might be worse, not better. Texas is bad wild, once you get past the river port. "I'd as soon start out walkin', and us be gone from here."

"But, the river is first," Juneau Jane argues. "We must wait until day, in order that we will know the means by which others cross the water."

"I guess." I hate to let her be right, but she is. "Might be, in the morning, we can pay a little to get on a wagon, anyhow."

We wander here and there, looking for a spot to huddle up. Folks chase us out, if they see us. What looks like three ragged boys, colored and white together, and one addle-headed being led by the hand, ain't something anybody feels kindly toward. Finally, we go down to the riverbank, where there's wagon camps, and we push up in some brush, and cower together like three lost pups, and hope nobody bothers us.

Soon's light comes, we eat a breakfast of hard pilot biscuits out of our pack and the last few bites of salted ham from the crew on the **Katie P.,** and then we hold the poke up overhead and cross the river at the shallows. It ain't hard to know the way, just walk along with the steady row of wagons fording the river and going west. A line of other folks passes us, traveling the other way, too, aiming for the railhead with their buckboards and farm wagons. Herds of spotted big-horned cattle tramp through, trailed by rough-looking men and boys in wide hats and knee boots. Sometimes, the herds pass for what seems like a hour at a time.

It ain't midway in the morning before Missy goes to limping in them new shoes from Jefferson. Sweat and road dust makes a plaster on her skin, clinging her shirt to her body. She takes up fussing and tugging at it and working loose the cloth that's binding her bosom flat. "You leave that be," I keep saying and swatting her hand away.

Finally, we move off into the grass while two wagons pass each other going opposite ways. Minute my back is turned, Missy plops herself down in the shade of a little pin oak. She won't get up no matter how we try to coax her.

I stand by the road and start looking for a wagon we can get on for a little pay.

A colored driver with a load of freight and a kindly face takes us up, and he's a talkish sort. Rain is his name. Pete Rain. His papa was a Creek Indian and his mama a escaped slave from a plantation that belonged to some Cherokees. The farm wagon and the team he owns all to hisself, and that is the business he does, hauling goods from the railroads to the settlements and then back from the settlements to the railhead, to ship east. "Not bad work," he tells us. "All you got to worry about is losing your scalp." He shows us bullet holes in the wagon and shares tales of bushwhacking and raiding parties with fearsome painted warriors.

He tells tales most of the day. Stories of the Indians up north of here, the Kiowas and Comanches, who roam down off their reservations when they choose and steal horses and burn farms and take captives, or leave cut-up bodies behind. "Doesn't seem to be any particular figuring to their ways," he says. "Just whatever they favor doing at the time. The war is over in the South, but there's still war here. You boys be watchful. Look out for road agents and bad sorts, too. You come across anybody that calls himself a Marston Man, you go the other way double fast. Their gang is worst of all, and growing in numbers each day."

By the time dark is settling in, Juneau Jane and me, we're looking twice at every bush and tree and sniffing the air for signs of smoke. Our ears stay sharp for sounds of Indians, and bushwhackers, and gangs of

Marston Men, whatever they might be. We're glad to share Pete Rain's camp. Juneau Jane helps with the horses and harness, and I take to boiling up a stew from rice, salted ham, and beans. Pete Rain shoots a rabbit, and we add that, too. Missy sits and stares at the fire.

"What's wrong with the boy?" Pete asks while we eat our meal, and I feed Missy spoonfuls, because she can't pick up stew with her hands.

"Don't know." That's mostly true. "He run onto a difficulty with some bad men and been this way ever since."

"Sad thing," Pete mutters, and rubs his plate out with sand and drops it in the rinse bucket before laying back to look at the stars. They're bigger and brighter here than ever I saw back home. Wider, too. The sky goes all the way from one end of the world to the other.

While Pete's quiet, I tell him about my three blue beads and ask after my people in case he knows of them. He don't, that he can say.

Juneau Jane tells him of the Lost Friends and he wants to know more, so she gets out the papers and leans to the fire. I sit over her shoulder and she moves her finger along the words for me while she reads. Pete don't know any of them names, either, but he says, "I got a sister out there someplace. Slave catchers stole her and killed my mama while I was off to hunt with my pap. That was the year eighteen and fifty-two. Don't reckon I'll ever find my little sister or that she'd even remember me, but you could put her name in the Lost Friends. I'll give you the fifty cents to get me a letter printed in that **Southwestern** newspaper, plus the mailing money if you'd post it for me while you're in Fort Worth. I don't linger in that place. Folks don't call it Hell's Half Acre for nothing."

Juneau Jane tells him she'll do what he asks, but instead of the papers, she gets out that ledger book from the lawyer's office and opens it. "The space on the papers is filled," she says. "Here, we have room."

"I'm appreciative of it." Pete rests his head in his crossed arms like a pillow and watches the trail of angel glow that runs across the night sky. "Amalee, that was her name. Amalee August Rain. She was too bitty to say it at the time, though, so I don't suppose she got to keep it."

Juneau Jane starts the book, saying the words she writes, **"Amalee August Rain, sister of Pete Rain of Weatherford, Texas. Lost in the Indian Nations, September, 1852, when three years old."** She tells the letters out loud, and I try to think how each one looks before the pencil makes it. A few I get right.

When I lay down that night, I think about alphabet letters and I point one finger against that wide black silk sky and draw them from star to star. **A for Amalee . . . R for Rain . . . T for Texas. H for Hannie.** I keep on till my hand falls and my eyes close.

In the morning when I wake and sit up on my blanket, the lantern sputters low on its shepherd's hook, and Juneau Jane sits under it in the dawn dark, her legs crossed and the book in her lap. The skinning knife is stuck beside her in the dirt, and the pencil's down to just a stub. Her eyes are weary and red.

"You been at that all night?" She never even moved her blanket over to the wagon.

"Indeed, yes," she whispers real soft, since Pete and Missy hadn't woke yet.

"Just writing that one letter so's to mail it for Pete in Fort Worth town?" I climb from my place and scrabble over to her.

"Something more." She holds the book up in the first of the light and the last of it, so's I can see. Page after page of it has words now. "I have written all of them." She shows me her work, while I look down in wonder. "These pages, by the beginning letter of the surname." She turns to a page with R, which is a letter I know, and there at the top she reads off, "Amalee August Rain."

I sit down beside her and she gives it over to me, and I turn through all the pages. "I'll be," I whisper. "A **book of lost friends**."

"Yes," she agrees and gives me a piece of tore-out paper with writing on it, which she says is the letter for Pete.

A yearning comes in me then, and though we oughta get a small cook fire laid and start on breakfast, I settle in the grass aside of her, instead. "Could you take out another paper from the book and write me one, while there's still some of the pencil left? I want a letter about my people . . . for the Lost Friends."

She lifts a eyebrow my way. "There will be time for this as we go on." She looks toward Missy and Pete Rain sleeping. In the post oaks overhead, the morning birds call up the dawn.

"I know. And I ain't got the fifty cents to get it in the paper, yet . . . or the money I can give for a stamp." Lord knows when I'll be able to spend all that on words in a newspaper. "But I just want to hold my letter, I guess. Till the time comes. Be like holdin' hope, in some way, wouldn't it?"

"I suppose it would." She goes to the back of the book, folds the cover flat and scratches her fingernail along the seam, then tears out a page careful and straight. "How would you have it read?"

"I want it fancy, sort of. So, if my people see it, they don't . . ." A tickle comes in my throat like a little bird just fluffed its feathers in there. I have to clear it out before I can talk again. "Well, I want that they'll think I'm smart. Proper, you know? You write it real proper, all right?"

Nodding, she puts the pencil stub to the page, bends low over it, blinks her eyes closed, then open again. I reckon they're parched tired after all night. "What would you have it say?"

I close my eyes, think long into my little-girl years. "And don't read them words back to me as you go," I tell her. "Not this time. Just write it for now. Start it with, 'Mr Editor: I wish to inquire for my people.' "

I like how it sounds friendly, but then I don't know what goes next. The words don't come in my mind.

**"Tres bien."** I hear the pencil scratch across the paper and then go quiet awhile. A dove sings its soft song and Pete Rain rolls over on his blanket. "Tell me about your people," Juneau Jane says. "Their names and what happened to them."

The lantern flame gutters and hisses. Shadows and light flicker 'cross my eyelids, tell my story back to me, and I tell it to Juneau Jane. "My mama was named Mittie. I am the middle of nine children and am Hannie Gossett." The chant starts in my mind. I hear Mama and me say it together under the wagon. "The others were named Hardy, Het, Pratt . . ."

I feel them with me, now, dancing in the pink-brown shadows behind my eyes, all us remembering our story together. When I'm through, my face is wet with tears and cool from the morning breeze. My voice is thick from the lonely that comes with how the story ends.

Pete Rain stirs on his pallet with a grunt and a sigh, and so I wipe my face and take the paper Juneau Jane gives me. I fold it to a square I can carry. Hope.

"We might send it in Fort Worth," Juneau Jane says. "I have yet a bit of money from the sale of my horse."

I swallow it down hard again, shake my head. "We best keep that for survivin' just now. I'll send this letter when I can pay its way. For now, it's enough just to know I got it with me." A coldness goes deep in my bones as I look off into the long stretch of sky to the west, where the last stars still labor against the dawn gray. My mama used to say they were the cook fires in heaven, the stars, that my grandmama and grandpapa and all the folk that went before us lit up the fires of heaven each night.

The letter feels heavier in my hand when I think of that. What if all my people are already up there, gathered at them fires? If nobody answers my letter, is that what it means?

Later on in the day, I wonder if Pete Rain thinks the same thing of his letter. We show it to him in the wagon, when we're riding the last few miles to Forth Worth. "You know, I believe I'll mail that with the fifty cents myself," he decides and tucks it in his pocket, his face pinched and sober. "So I can say a prayer over it first."

I decide I'll do the same for my letter, when it's time.

Before we part ways in town, Juneau Jane tears a scrap out of the newspapers and gives it to Pete Rain. "The address for sending your letter to the **Southwestern,**" she says.

"Thank you. And you boys, you tread lightly here," he warns us again, and tucks the scrap away, too. "Fort Worth's not the worst town for colored folk, not bad as Dallas, but not peaceable, either, and the Marston Men like this place more than most. Watch the squatter camps down along the river below the courthouse bluff, too. You can get by with pitchin' camp there, but don't leave your belongings behind.

Nothing's safe down in Battercake Flats. Too many folks in need, all in one place. Tough times in Fort Worth town, since the railroad's gone bust and can't build the line on through to here. Tough times make good people and bad people. You'll see both.

"You need help, go visit John Pratt at the blacksmith shop, just off the courthouse. Colored fella, good man. Or the Reverend Moody and the African Methodist Episcopals at the Allen Chapel. Mind the whorehouses and the saloons. Nothing but trouble there for a young man. You want my advice—don't stay long in Fort Worth. Move on to Weatherford or down Austin City way. There's more future in it."

"We have come to find my father," Juneau Jane tells him. "We have no plan to remain after." She thanks him for the ride and tries to pay him for the trouble, and he won't take it. "You gave me back a hope I surrendered long ago," he says. "That's enough, right there."

He clucks up the horses and travels on, and there we stand. It's the middle of the day, and so we huddle off twixt two board-and-batten-sided buildings and eat our lunch of more pilot biscuits and peaches that won't last much longer in our poke.

A racket takes our eyes to the street. I look up and expect that it'll be cattle or wagons, but it's a detachment of Federal soldiers, riding down the street in lines, two by two. Cavalry. They don't much resemble the ragged Federals of the war, who wore blue uniforms patched up and stitched over holes, stained with dirt and blood and held together with carved circles of wood where the brass buttons went missing. The soldiers back then rode bone-thin horses of whatever kind they could buy or steal, as horses got hard to come by with so many killed in battles.

These soldiers today travel on matched bays, the whole bunch of them. The yellow cavalry stripes on their pants show bright, and the black bill caps sit square and level. The brass plates on their rifles shine at the sun. Scabbards, buckles, and hooves raise a clatter.

I step back in the shadows. A tightening starts deep in my middle and works its way through me. Ain't seen soldiers anytime lately. Back home, if you spot one you don't dare look his way or stop to talk. No matter that the war is over and **been** over all these years, you get seen talking to the Federals, folks like Old Missus don't like it.

I pull Juneau Jane and Missy back, too. "We got to be careful," I whisper and hurry them away to the other end of the alley. "That woman in Jefferson said it was the Federals come looking for Mr. Washburn and his papers. What if they're looking for him here, too? Some of that trouble Lyle brought on, maybe." I'm surprised by my own mouth for a minute. I didn't call him Young Mister or Marse Lyle, or even Mister Lyle, just **Lyle,** like Juneau Jane does.

**Well, he ain't your marse,** I tell myself. **You are a free woman, Hannie. Free to call that snake by his given name if you want to.**

Something inside me gets bigger, just then. Not sure what it is, but it's there. Stronger now. Different.

Juneau Jane don't seem worried about the soldiers, but it's clear her mind's on other things. She looks down the hill, where shanties made from all manner of wagon parts, downed branches, slabwood, barrel staves, crates, and sawed trees squat low on the muddy banks of the Trinity River. The frames lean toward the water, covered in hides, oilcloth, tarred scrim, and pieces of bright-colored signs. A little brown boy pulls wood off one shack so he can feed the cook fire at another.

"I could manage a change of clothing down there, before seeking Mr. Washburn. Some of the huts appear vacant," Juneau Jane says.

What's she thinking? "That's got to be Battercake Flats. Where Pete told us not to go." But arguing don't do no good. She's already finding her way to the path. Can't let her walk down there by herself, so I go along, dragging Missy with me. Missy might scare somebody, at least. "Get me killed. Get me killed in Battercake Flats," I call ahead to Juneau Jane. "Ain't the sort of place I want to meet my maker, that's for definite sure."

"We will not leave our belongings," she says, marching right ahead on them skinny spider legs.

"We will if we're dead."

Two soot-smudged white women in threadbare clothes come up the path. They inspect us over real careful, studying our bundles to see, can they steal something? I grab hold of Missy's arm like I'm worried, say to her, "Now, you leave them two women be. They ain't hurting you."

"You'ns in need a' som'pin'?" one of the women asks. Her teeth are rotted off into sharp points. "Got us a camp jus' thar. Hungry fer some hot grub, err ya? We don' mind to share our'n. Carryin' any coin, err ya? You gimme jus' a little, Clary, here, she'd skee-daddle on over to the merkateel store, git us'ns some coffee. Drunk up the las' of our'n in camp. But it ain't far . . . to the merkateel."

I look yon, and there's a man standing and watching us. I back off the path and pull Missy with me.

"No reason for to be so skeert and skitterish." The woman smiles, her tongue working the holes where teeth are gone. "We's right friendsome folk."

"We have no need of friends," Juneau Jane says and moves away to let the woman pass.

The man down the hill stays watching. We wait till the women round the courthouse, then we turn and go that way, too. Back up the hill.

I remember what Pete said. There's good people, and there's bad people. Here in Fort Worth town, round every corner we turn, seems like somebody's looking us over, seeing if we're worth the trouble to steal from. This is a place of plenty and none, this Fort Worth. A town you've got to know the way of to be safe in it, and so we go to the blacksmith shop to find John Pratt. I leave Missy and Juneau Jane outside, and step in just myself. He's kindly, but can't say about Mr. Washburn.

"Been many folk leave the town since the railroad didn't come on," he says. "Lot of people had been speculatin' on that. Shucked out when the news come. Hard times, right now. But there's some who moved in to grab up what can be bought cheap. Could be your Mr. Washburn is that kind." He tells us how to get to the bathhouses and the hotels, where most folk new to town would go if they had money. "You ask around there, you'll likely find news of him, if there's any to be had."

We go along as he told us, asking anybody that's willing to talk to three wandering boys.

A yellow-haired woman in a red dress calls us to the side door of a building, says she runs the bathhouse, and she offers a bath cheap. They got hot water ready and nobody to use it.

"Slim times, right now, boys," she tells us.

The sign in the window says my kind ain't welcome there and Indians ain't, either. I know that because Juneau Jane points and whispers it in my ear.

Lady in the doorway looks us over good. "What's wrong with the big boy?" She folds her arms and leans closer. "What's wrong with you, big'un?"

"He simple, Missus. Simpleminded," I say. "Ain't dangerous, though."

"Didn't ask you, boy," she snaps, then looks in Juneau Jane's face. "What about you? You simple?

You got Indian blood in you? You a breed or you a white boy? Don't take no coloreds ner Indians in here. And no Irish."

"He a Frenchy," I say, and the lady hisses air to shut me up, then turns to Juneau Jane. "You don't talk for yourself? Kind of a pretty little boy, ain't ya? How old are you?"

"Sixteen years," Juneau Jane says.

The lady throws back her head and laughs. "More like twelve years, I'd say. You ain't even shavin' yet. But you sure sound like the Frenchies, all right. You got the money? I'll take it. I don't got nothin' against a Frenchman. Long's you're a payin' customer."

Juneau Jane and me move off from her. "I don't like the look of it," I whisper, but Juneau Jane's got her mind made up. She takes the coins she needs and the bundle with her woman clothes and lets me keep the rest.

"We'll be out here. Right here, waiting," I say, loud enough for the lady to hear. Then whisper behind Juneau Jane's head, "You get inside, you look for where there's another door. See that steam rising out behind the building? They got to be emptying buckets and washing clothes back there. You slip out that way when you're done, so she don't see you in your lady clothes."

I grab Missy Lavinia's arm, steer her away and figure I might as well look for some of my own kind to ask after Mr. Washburn. Down the boardwalk, a boy's hollering for boots to shine. He's a skinny brown thing maybe about Juneau Jane's age. I work my way over there and ask him my question.

"Might know," he says. "But I don't give answers free, 'less I'm shinin' shoes at the same time. Them shoes you got ain't worth shinin', but you gimme five cents, want it done, I'd do it, but back in the alley, though. Can't have the white folk think I do colored shoes. Won't let me to use my brushes on them after."

Nothing comes free in this town. "Reckon I can find out someplace else to ask . . . unless you want to trade for it."

The eyes go to slits in his tan-brown face. "What you wantin' to trade?"

"Got a book," I say. "Book to write the names of people you lost in the war, or who was sold from you before the freedom. You missing any of your people? We can put their names in the book. Ask after them all the places we go. You got three cents for a stamp, and fifty cents for the advertisement, we can write up a whole note about your people, and send it to the **Southwestern** newspaper. It goes by delivery all over Texas, Louisiana, Mississippi, Tennessee, and Arkansas, to the churches where they can call it out from the pulpit, case your people are there. You missing any people?"

"Ain't got none at all," the boy says. "My mam and pap's both killed by the fever. Never remembered neither one of 'em. Got no people to look for."

Something tugs my pants, and I look down, and

there's a old colored woman, sitting cross-legged against the wall. She's wrapped in a blanket, her back so humped she can scarce turn her face up to get a look at me. Her eyes are cloudy and dull. A basket of pralines sits in her lap, with a sign I can't read, except some of the letters. Her skin is dark and cracked as dry leather.

She wants me to come close. I go to squat down, but Missy Lavinia tries to pull my arm. "Stop troubling me," I tell her. "You just stand there."

"I can't buy your goods," I tell the woman. "I'd do it if I could." She's a poor, ragged thing.

Her voice is so quiet, I have to lean close to hear her over the racket of men and wagons and horses passing by. "I got people," she says. "You help me seek my people?" She reaches for the tin cup that sits with her, shakes it, and listens hard for the sound. Can't be more than a few cents in there.

"You keep them coins," I say. "We'll put you in our book with the Lost Friends. Ask after your people anyplace we go."

I move Missy Lavinia over to the wall. Set her down on a painted bench in front of a window. She's white, so she can sit there, I reckon.

I go back and rest on my knees beside the woman. "Tell me about your people. I'll remember it, and soon's there comes a chance, I'll get it in our **Book of Lost Friends.**"

She says her name is Florida. Florida Jones. And while the music plays someplace nearby and folks stroll on the boardwalk, and a smith's hammer sings out **whang-ping-ping, whang-ping-ping,** and horses snort and lick their muzzles, dozing lazy at the hitch racks, Florida Jones tells me her tale.

When she's done, I say it all back to her. All seven names of her children, and the names of her three sisters and two brothers, and the places where they been carried off from her and who by. I wish I could write it down. I'm carrying the book and what's left of the pencil, but I can't make enough letters and how they sound. Don't know how to work the pencil, either.

Florida's thin hands reach out, cold on my skin. Her shawl falls away, and I see the brand on her arm. **R** for runaway. Before I think what I'm doing, I touch a finger to it.

"I gone off seekin' my children," she tells me. "Ever'time they take one, I go seekin'. Stay seekin' long's I can, till they find me, or the pattyrollers cotch me, or the dogs git on me, bring me back home to that place I hate and that man I been made to be with against my wants. Once I get over the punishin', Marse say, 'Make another baby, you two, or else . . . ' and then that man get on me and pretty soon, I'm ripenin' up again with another one. Love that sweet, pretty thing when it comes. Ever'time, Marse tell me, 'Florida, you get to keep this one.' And ever'time, he find hisself in need of money, off they go. And he say, 'Well, that one was too fine to keep, Florida.' And I just sit and cry out and mourn till I can get away and go searchin'."

She asks if I could write a letter for her and mail it to the **Southwestern** newspaper. Then she hands over her cup for me to take the money.

"It ain't enough yet, to pay for the paper," I tell her. "But we can go on and get the letter ready. And the day's early, yet. Might be we could help you sell the rest of your—"

Commotion in the street stops me. I turn in time to hear a woman scream and a man holler as a wagon just misses somebody. A horse tied at hitch sits back against the reins and breaks the slobber leathers and somersaults over its tail, its hooves kicking and thrashing the air. Other horses spook and pull and tug their reins free and wheel off. One smacks into a man riding a ewe-necked chestnut colt that looks barely old enough to be under saddle.

"Har!" the man hollers and jerks up the rawboned colt, puts the spurs to it and whips it over and under with his long bridle reins. The colt downs its head and goes to bucking—just misses barreling right into Missy Lavinia, who's wandered from the bench. She's standing in the street, just staring off. The wagon team bolts and the driver fights to gather them up before there's a runaway. Folks on foot and dogs scatter in every direction. Men run to the hitch rails to grab their horses, and loose mounts hightail down the street, the reins flying free.

I jump up and go to running while the colt and its rider kick up dust clouds, them hooves sailing past Missy, but she just stands there looking.

Somebody calls from the boardwalk, "Yeehaw! Look at 'im buck!"

I get to Missy Lavinia just before the colt finally lands spraddle-legged, buckles in the knees, and goes down hard, rolling over the top of its rider, who hangs on and comes halfway back up when the colt does. "Git on yer feet, you broom-tail dink." The man whips the horse on the face and ears till it finds its legs again, then he spurs it toward Missy Lavinia. "Git out the street! Ya spooked my horse!" He grabs a rope from his saddle, meaning to hit her with it, I guess.

Missy throws her chin out and bares her teeth and hisses at him.

I try to move her up on the boardwalk where he can't run us down, but she won't budge, just stands there hissing.

The rope comes down hard. I feel it whip my shoulder, hear it sing side to side through the air, slapping saddle leather and horseflesh and whatever else it can reach. The rider reins the colt round, while the wild-eyed thing bawls and snorts and balks. It comes sidewards and spins and fights for its head, knocking into Missy Lavinia. She goes down into the mud, and I fall atop of her.

"Please! Please! He addle-headed! He addle-headed! He don't know!" I yell and throw my hands out front of us as the rope sings again. It hits my fingers hard, and I grab on, desperate to stop it. The rawhide honda whips back and hammers my cheekbone.

Lights explode in my eyes, and then I'm falling down a deep hole into the black. I take the rope with me, hang on to it for all I'm worth. I hear the cowboy yelp and the colt stagger and then the thump of its heavy fall. I smell the gush of its breath.

The rope jerks me up before I can let go, and I fly forward off Missy. Next thing I know, I'm belly-down in the street and looking in that horse's eye. It's big and black, shiny like a drop of wet ink, white and red at the edges. It blinks one time, slow, looking into me.

**Don't be dead,** I say in my mind and see the rider pushing hisself out from under the laid-over colt. Other men run over, pulling at the ropes that've got the poor thing tangled. One more blink, and they shoo the horse to its feet, and it stands there splayed and heaving, better off than the man, who's on one leg. He tries to stand but folds, and howls and goes halfway down before somebody catches him.

"Gimme my rifle!" he yells out, struggling for the scabbard on his saddle. The colt spooks and buggers away. "Gimme my rifle! I'm-a git rid of us a halfwit and its boy! You be needin' a shovel to pick up what's left when I git through."

I shake the fog out of my head. Need to get up, get away before he puts a hand on that gun. But the world spins, everything moving like a dust devil—old Florida, the sorrel colt, a red-and-white-striped pole by a store, the sun shining on a window glass, a woman in a rose-pink dress, a wagon wheel, a barking dog on a leash, the shoeshine boy.

"Hang on. Now just hold on," somebody else says. "Sheriff's comin'."

"That halfwit tried to kill me!" the man hollers. "Him and his boy tried to kill me and steal my horse. He's broke my leg! He's broke my leg!"

**Go, Hannie, run,** my mind shouts. **Get up! Run.**

But I don't know which way **is** up.

## Lost Friends

Dear Editor—Please allow me space in your valuable paper to inquire for my brothers and sisters. We belonged to Mr. John R. Goff, of Tucker county, West Virginia. I was sold to Wm. Elliott, of same State. My sister Louisia was sold to Bob Kid, and was sent here to Louisiana. My brothers' names are Jerome, Thomas, Jacob, Joseph and Uriah Culberson. The sisters were Jemima, Drusilla, Louisa, and Eunice Jane. Jerome, Joseph, and Eunice Jane I know are dead. Uriah is still living near the old home. Thomas went with the rebel army. Jacob and Drusilla are I know not where. I married Jas. H. Howard in Wheeling, W. Va., in 1868, and moved here in 1873. My sister, Louisa is here living with Gilbert Daigre, her former owner, as his wife. I am very anxious to know their whereabouts, and any information that will enable me to find them will be thankfully received. Atlanta, Ga., Richmond, Va., and Baltimore, papers please copy. Address me at Baton Rouge, La.

JEMIMA HOWARD

—"Lost Friends" column of the Southwestern
April 1, 1880

## CHAPTER 20

### BENNY SILVA—AUGUSTINE, LOUISIANA, 1987

Few things are more life affirming than watching an idea that was fledgling and frail in its infancy, seemingly destined for birth and death in almost the same breath, stretch its lungs and curl its fingers around the threads of life, and hang on with a determination that can't be understood, only felt. Our three-week-old history project, which the kids have dubbed **Tales from the Underground,** in a mixture of the original **Tales from the Crypt** idea and an homage to the Underground Railroad, the freedom chain that helped escaped slaves make their way north, has found its feet.

On Tuesdays and Thursdays in the classroom,

we're reading about heroes of the Underground Railroad like Harriet Tubman, William Still, and the Reverend John and Jean Rankin. The room that was once so deafeningly raucous I couldn't hear myself think, or so quiet I could hear—even over my own reading of **Animal Farm**—the clock ticking and the soft wheeze of students napping at their desks, is now noisy with tapping pens and pencils and snatches of lively, perceptive debate. Over the past two weeks, we've talked at length about the national and political conditions of the antebellum time period, but also about the local histories we're uncovering on Mondays, Wednesdays, and Fridays, when we line up and march two blocks down the street, not always in an orderly fashion, to the old Carnegie library.

The library itself has become a partner in our **Tales from the Underground** project, adding colorful local history to our discussions, not only because of the story of how the grand old building came to be but also what it meant and how it served for decades. Upstairs in an old theater-style community room, aptly dubbed the Worthy Room, framed photos on the walls testify to a different life, a different time, when Augustine was officially divided along the color line. The Worthy Room hosted everything from stage plays, political meetings, and performances by visiting jazz musicians, to soldiers mustering for war and Negro league baseball teams forbidden to bunk at the hotels and in need of a place to sleep over.

In the nearby Destiny Room, with a couple weeks of hard work by the kids, borrowed folding tables from the church next door, and the help of some legacy descendants of the library's Ladies New Century Club, we've created a temporary research center of a sort. It's the first time this much of the area's historical information has been gathered in one place, as far as we know. Over the years, Augustine's history has been tucked away in desk drawers, attics, file boxes at the courthouse, and dozens of other out-of-the-way spaces. It has survived mostly in bits and snatches—in faded photos, family Bibles, church baptismal records, deeds of sale for land parcels, and memories passed down from generation to generation as children sat at the knees of grandparents.

The problem is, in today's world of fractured families, readily available cable TV entertainment, and video games that can be plugged into home television sets for hours of Pong and Super Mario Bros. and Mike Tyson's Punch-Out!!, the stories are in danger of fading into the maelstrom of the modern age.

And yet, something in these young people **is** curious about the past, about what led to those who are here now and what . . . or who . . . came before.

Aside from that, the idea of dead people, and bones, and graveyards, and playing dress-up to bring ghosts to life is too much even for my most closed-off kids to fully resist. Perhaps it is the presence of Granny T and the other New Century ladies, but my students are all business in the Destiny Room and cooperative in sharing the ten pairs of white cotton gloves loaned to us by the church's bell choir. And thanks to a speaking appearance by a history professor from Southeastern Louisiana University, the kids understand the fragility of old documents and why using the gloves really does matter. They're careful with the materials we've borrowed from the library's archives and the record cabinets of local churches, as well as those we've transported from Goswood Grove and the attics of various families around town.

Other than during the library's short public hours, we are alone in the place, so noise doesn't matter. And we **are** noisy. Ideas circle the room like honeybees, buzzing from landing place to landing place, gathering the nectar of inspiration.

Over the past three weeks, each day has brought new discoveries. Breakthroughs. Little miracles. I never imagined that teaching could be this way.

I love this job. I love these kids.

I think they're starting to love me back.

A little, anyway. They've given me a new nickname.

"Miss Pooh," Lil' Ray says as my fourth-period freshman class makes the short trek over to the library for another Monday session.

"Yes?" I squint upward into the patches of sunlight and leaf shadow slipping over his chubby cheeks. He is a mountain of a kid, in the middle of the adolescent growth spurt that seems to hit boys about this age. I'd swear he was three inches shorter yesterday. He must be at least six two, yet his hands and feet are still huge for his body, as if he still has a lot to grow into. "You could put some chocolate chips in these." He holds up the pooperoo he's eating while we walk. He's struggling to choke it down with no drink. Food is not allowed in the library, but there is an art deco drinking fountain on the way in. "I think that'd be good."

"Then they wouldn't be so healthy for you, Lil' Ray."

He chews another bite like he's trying to process gristle.

"Miss Pooh?" He opens another topic. I'd like to believe that they've given me this delightful nickname because I am cuddly and charming in an **oh, bother** sort of way, à la Pooh Bear. But really, they've named me after the lumpy oatmeal cocoa cookies.

"Yes, Lil' Ray?"

His gaze rolls upward, scans the trees as his tongue swipes the leftovers from his bottom lip. "I been thinkin' about something."

"That's a miracle," LaJuna smarts off. She returned as unceremoniously as she left and has been back in class for two and a half weeks now. She's staying with Sarge and Aunt Dicey. Nobody, including LaJuna, knows how long that will last. She's strangely lackluster and negative about the **Tales from the Underground** project. I don't know if that's because of her current life situation, or because the project developed while she was AWOL from school, or because she doesn't like the fact that dozens of other students have horned in on her exploration of the secrets the judge left hidden in Goswood Grove House. That place was sacred territory for her, a refuge since her childhood.

Some days, I feel like I've betrayed a fragile trust with her or failed some important test, and we'll never get to where I'd like to be. But I have dozens of other students to think about, and they matter, too. Maybe I'm being naïve and idealistic, but I can't help hoping that **Tales from the Underground** has the potential to bridge the gaps that plague us here. Rich and poor. Black and white. Overprivileged and underprivileged. Backwoods kids and townies.

I wish we could bring the school at the lake in on it, draw together students who live within a few miles of one another yet inhabit separate worlds. The only reasons they comingle are to battle it out on the football field, or sit in close proximity over boudin balls and smoked meat at the Cluck and Oink. But during what have turned into regular Thursday evening update sessions at my house, Nathan has already warned me that Lakeland Prep Academy is one of the places I need to stay away from, and so I have, and will.

"So, Miss Pooh?"

"Yes, Lil' Ray?" There is no short discussion with this kid. Every conversation goes this way. In stages. Thoughts move carefully through that head of his. They percolate while he seems lost in space, looking at the trees, or out the window, or at his desktop as he painstakingly manufactures spit wads and paper footballs.

But when the thoughts finally do emerge, they're interesting. Well developed. Carefully considered.

"So, Miss Pooh, like I said, I been thinking." His oversized hands wheel in the air, pinkie fingers sticking out as if he's practicing to drink tea with the queen. The thought makes me smile. Every one of these kids is so unique. Filled with incredible stuff. "There's not just dead grown-ups and old people in that cemetery, **and** in the cemetery books." Consternation knits his brows. "There's a lot of kids and babies that hardly even got born before they died. That's sad, huh?" His voice trails off.

Coach Davis's star lineman is choked up. Over infants and children who perished more than a hundred years ago.

"Well, of course they did, numb nut," LaJuna snaps. "They didn't have medicine and stuff."

"Granny T said they'd mash up leaves 'n' roots 'n' mushrooms 'n' moss 'n' stuff," skinny Michael pipes up, anxious to do his job as Lil' Ray's wingman-slash-bodyguard. "Said some of that worked **better** than medicines do now. You didn't hear that, homegirl? Oh, that's right, you skipped that day. Show up, you might know the stuff, like the rest of us, and not be raggin' on Lil' Ray. He's trying to help the **Underground** project. And there's you over there, wanting to tear it down."

"Yeah." Lil' Ray straightens from his ever-present slump. "If losers would stop saying loser stuff, **I** was gonna say that we can play people **our** age, or people that're older, like we can color our hair gray and all. But we can't play **little** kids. Maybe we oughta get some little kids to come and help, and do some of the kid graves. Like Tobias Gossett. He lives down from us in the apartments. He ain't got nothing to do, mostly. He could be that Willie Tobias that's in the graveyard. The one that died in the fire with his brother and sister because his mama had to leave them home. People oughta know, maybe, you can't leave little kids by theirselves, like that."

The lump that was in Lil' Ray's throat transfers to mine. I swallow hard, trying to get it under control. A sudden uprising of opinions erupts for and against that plan. Copious slurs, a dis of poor little Tobias, and a dusting of mild curse words add to the debate, but not necessarily in a productive way.

"Time-out." I use the referee hand signal to make my point. "Lil' Ray, hold that thought a minute." Then I address the rest of them. "What are classroom rules?"

A half dozen kids roll their eyes and groan.

"Do we **gotta** say it?" somebody pipes up.

"Until we start remembering to follow it, yes," I insist. "Or we can go back to the classroom and diagram sentences. I'm good either way." I make the motion of a choir conductor's baton. "All together now. What's Article Number Three of our Classroom Constitution?"

An unenthusiastic chorus responds, "We encourage vigorous debate. Civil debate is a healthy and democratic process. If one cannot make one's point without yelling, name-calling, or insulting others, one should develop a stronger argument before speaking further."

"Good!" I take a mock bow. We've carefully drafted the Classroom Constitution as a group, which I've blown up on the copier, laminated, and permanently affixed to one side of the chalkboard. I've also given every kid a portable copy. They get extra points for knowing it.

"And Article Two? Because I have so far detected three—count them, **three**—violations of that one in this recent conversation." I turn and walk backward, directing the choir again. Thirty-nine annoyed faces silently say, **You are insufferable, Miss Silva.**

"If the word is derogatory or improper in polite company, we don't use it in Miss Silva's class," the troupe murmurs as we near the library steps.

"Yes!" I pretended to be wildly delighted with their ability to commit the constitution to memory. "And better yet, don't use it **outside** of class, either. Those words make us sound average and we don't settle for average because we are . . . **what**?" I point the pistol fingers—our school symbol—their way.

"Outstanding," they drone.

"Alrighty then!" An uneven joint in the sidewalk foils my mojo, and I slip sideways on my platform clogs and almost go off the curb. LaJuna, Lil' Ray, and a quiet nerdy girl named Savanna rush forward to catch me, while the rest of the class erupts in snickers and giggles.

"I'm good. I got it!" I say and pause to recover my shoe.

"We oughta add 'Don't walk backward in clogs' to the Classroom Constitution." It's the first lighthearted thing LaJuna has said since she came back to school.

"You're funny." I wink at her, but she's angled herself the other way. The rest of the group has paused to keep from running me down, but they are also focused on the library steps.

I turn around and my heart gives a **flit flit flutter,** like a butterfly rising. There stands Nathan. I let a brightly colored "Hey!" fly out before I can swat it down. Heat pushes into my cheeks as a random observation darts across my consciousness. The aqua T-shirt nicely complements his eyes. He looks good in it.

And the thought ends right there, like a sentence cut short, left dangling without punctuation.

"You said to . . . come by. If I had the chance." Nathan seems uncertain. Maybe he feels the weight of having an audience, or maybe he senses my self-consciousness.

Thirty-nine sets of curious eyes watch us acutely, reading the situation.

"I'm glad you did." Do I still sound too bubbly? Too pleased? Or just welcoming?

I'm acutely aware that until now, our association has always been over Cluck and Oink takeout at my house. In private. Since our first all-night research session, we've just drifted into a Thursday evening thing, as it's a convenient night for both of us. We look over the latest findings from Goswood Grove, or pieces of the kids' research, or various documents that Sarge and the New Century ladies have managed to dig up at the parish courthouse. Whatever's new in the **Underground** project.

Then we walk the old plot maps of the plantation graveyard and a potter's field that lies between the orchard and the main cemetery fence. Occasionally, we wander to the quiet, moss-covered stones, concrete crypts, and ornate brick and marble structures that hold the aboveground gravesites of Augustine's most prominent citizens. We've visited the resting place of Nathan's ancestors in a private section of stately mausoleums, the elaborate marble structures encircled by an ornate wrought iron fence. The statues and crosses cresting their interment places, including those of Nathan's father and the judge, reach skyward, far above our heads, denoting wealth, importance, power.

Nathan's sister is not buried there, I've noticed,

but I haven't asked why or where she is. Maybe in Asheville where they grew up? I suspect that the pomp of the Gossett family plot wouldn't have suited Robin, from what little I know of her. Everything about that place is meant to provide some sort of immortality here on earth. And yet the Gossetts of old have not altered the terminal nature of human life. Like the enslaved people, the sharecroppers, the bayou dwellers, and the ordinary workingmen and women in the potter's field, they've all come to the same end. They are dust beneath the soil. All that is left behind lies in the people who remain. And the stories.

I wonder, sometimes, as we wander that graveyard, what will remain of me someday. Am I creating a legacy that matters, that will last? Will someone stand at my grave one day, wondering who I was?

During our walks, Nathan and I have fallen off into deep conversations about the broader meanings of it all—in the hypothetical sense. As long as we don't stray too near the topic of his sister, or the possibility of his visiting Goswood Grove House, he's relaxed and easy to talk to. He tells me what he knows about the community, what he remembers about the judge, what little he recalls about his father. There isn't much. He speaks of the Gossett family in a distant way, as if he is not part of it.

Mostly, I keep my history to myself. It's so much easier to talk in the more abstract, less personal sphere. Even so, I look forward to our Thursday evening get-togethers more than I want to admit.

And now, here he is in the middle of a workday—a time when he would normally be out with his boat—to see for himself the topic I talk about most when we're together. These kids, my job, the history. I'm afraid he is partially motivated by a need to learn more, in case this whole thing becomes a battleground with the rest of the Gossett clan, as he has repeatedly warned me it might. At that point, he'll run interference or try to mitigate the damage or something. I'm not sure what.

"I don't want to get in your way. I had to be in town today to sign some paperwork." He pushes his hands into his pockets and glances toward the student horde, which is bunching up behind me like a marching band with a fallen majorette at the fore.

Lil' Ray swivels to get a better view. LaJuna does, too. They're like two plastic pink flamingos with necks curving in opposite directions, a question mark and a mirror image.

"I've been hoping you'd stop by sometime. To . . . see us in action." I restart the forward momentum. "The kids have sifted out even more amazing information this week, not only through the books and papers from Goswood but from the city library and the courthouse. We even have boxes of family photos and old letters and scrapbooks. Some of the students are doing interviews with older people in the community, using oral histories. Anyway, we can't wait to share a little bit of it with you."

"Sounds impressive." His praise warms me.

"I'll show him round if you want," Lil' Ray is quick to offer. "My stuff is good. My stuff is **boss,** like me."

"You ain't boss," LaJuna grumbles.

"You best just shut your big, nasty mouth," Lil' Ray protests. "You're gonna get the Nativity Rule evoked on you, huh, Miss Silva? I think we should do some evoking right now. It's been two times LaJuna's disrespected me. Article Six—Nativity Rule. Times **two.** Right, Miss Pooh?"

LaJuna answers before I can. "What**ever.** It's Negativity Rule, and **in**voked, idjut."

"Oh! Oh!" Lil' Ray bounds three feet in the air, lands in a knee-down half split, pops up, snaps his fingers, and points at her. "And that's Article Three, Civility Rule. You just call me **idjut.** Dished out an insult instead of gave a civil argument. That's against the Article Three. Right? Huh? Huh?"

"You dissed me, too. You said I had a big, nasty mouth. Which one of your lame rules is that breaking?"

"Time-out," I snap, mortified that this is happening in front of Nathan. The thing about so many of the kids here—country kids, town kids, a sad majority of these kids—is that their norm is constant drama, constant escalation. Conversations start, grow louder, get ugly, get personal. Insults fly and then lead to pushing, shoving, hair pulling, scratching, throwing punches, you name it. Principal Pevoto and the school security officer break up multiple altercations daily. Broken homes, broken neighborhoods, financial stress, substance abuse, hunger, dysfunctional relationship patterns. All too often, children in Augustine grow up in a pressure cooker.

I think again about the world my mother came from in her rural hometown, the world she thought she'd left behind. But watching the young people here, I'm reminded of how much she unwittingly brought with her. My mother's relationships with men were impulsive, careless, loud, and filled with volatility, manipulation, and verbal abuse that went both ways and sometimes turned physical. My interaction with her was the same way, a mixture of full-on love, habitual put-downs, crushing rejection, and threats that might or might not end up being carried out.

But now I realize that, even with the rocky, unpredictable home life I experienced, I was lucky. I had the benefit of growing up in places where people around me—teachers, surrogate grandparents, babysitters, friends' parents—decided I was worthy of their time, their interest. They provided examples, role models, family meals at dinner tables, reprimands that didn't come with a swat or a cutting remark or end in the questions **Why don't you ever listen, Benny? Why are you so stupid sometimes?** People around me invited me into homes that operated on a schedule and where parents spoke encouraging words. They showed me what a stable life could look like. If they hadn't bothered, how would I have even **known** there was another way to live? You can't aspire to something you've never seen.

"Sixty-second quiet cooldown," I say, because I need it as much as the class does at the moment. "Nobody say anything. Then we'll analyze **why** this wasn't a good conversation. We can also review the Articles of Negativity and Civility . . . if you want to."

An exquisite silence follows. I hear leaves rustling, birds singing, a telephone line squeaking softly as a squirrel runs along it. The flag pops in the breeze, its metal hook tapping out an uneven Morse code against the pole.

These are glorious moments of peace that live in the shadow of Article Six, the Negativity Rule, and the prescribed punishment for breaking it. The students detest having to pay back each negative comment by offering three positive ones. They would rather clam up than compliment one another. It's a sad reality, but I hope it's making the point that negativity has consequences and a huge cost. Making up for it takes three times the work.

"All right, then," I say, after thirty seconds or so. "Be warned. Negativity Rule is officially in effect. Next person to say something negative must atone with three positives. Shall we practice as a class?"

Replies come in droves.

"No!"

"Nope."

"Miss Silva! **Pah-lease.** We get it."

Nathan covertly catches my gaze, blinks with both surprise and . . . admiration? I feel slightly lighter than air, as if the murky Louisiana day has suddenly been infused with helium.

"I'll start," I tease. "You guys are so amazing. You are definitely, absolutely, positively among my six favorite classes."

They answer with groans and exhales. I have only six class periods, even counting my planning period, of course.

Lil' Ray hovers a big hand over my head as if he's going to bounce me like a basketball.

"We're number one, though," skinny Michael argues. " 'Cause we're the best. Freshmen rule."

I make the zipper sign across my lips.

"I could show your friend **my** project, too," Michael offers as we start up the library steps. "Dude, mine's **so** ace. I found my people all the way back to five generations. Daigre family's got some crazy history. Nine brothers and sisters, born enslaved in West Virginia and they end up all over the place. Thomas goes with the Confederate army. Why? I don't know. His sister Louisa, after the war is over, she gets married to the man who was her owner. Did they fall in love or did she have to do it? I don't know. Like I said, my **Tales from the Underground** is ace."

"Yeah, well mine's so ace, it's, like, **triple** ace," Lil' Ray claims, then senses the possible rub of the Negativity Rule. "I didn't say his was bad, though.

Just that mine's ace. Hard-core, y'know? I got my people traced way back. I got stuff from the Library of Congress in my project."

"My people were here before any of y'all's people," protests Sabina Gibson, who's actually on the rolls of the Choctaw tribe. "I win no matter what y'all find out. Unless you got, like, cavemen in your papers or something."

A battle of dueling ancestors ensues. It follows us past a lovely marble pedestal that holds the AUGUSTINE CARNEGIE LIBRARY sign, and up the concrete steps.

The group collects at the ornately molded doors, undoubtedly shiny brass at one time but now streaked with a sad patina of disuse. I shush the chatter before we head inside. I want the kids to practice reasonable library etiquette, even though the place will most likely be empty, save for our helpers from the New Century ladies.

Lil' Ray protests in a whisper that it was his idea to show **the guy** his project; therefore, he should get first dibs on our guest.

**The guy** doesn't answer, but looks at me in a way that says he's amicable to whatever we decide.

I realize I haven't made introductions, and while a few of these kids may realize who Nathan is, most of them don't know him. I introduce him, but as soon as I speak the name, the buoyancy of the group drops as if our collective shoes are slowly filling with cement. A silent undercurrent of apprehension stirs in our midst. A few suspicious glances slant his way, and a few curious ones. The Fish girl cups her hand and whispers in her friend's ear.

Nathan looks like a man who would prefer to walk back down the steps, leave this town behind, and never return. But something stops him—the same something that has brought him here today.

I suspect neither of us knows quite what that something is.

## CHAPTER 21

HANNIE GOSSETT—TEXAS, 1875

Missy Lavinia rocks on the bunk and cries and moans in the dark. She's wet herself because she won't use the slop jar in the corner, and carried on so much about it she retched up what was in her stomach, too. This whole low-slung jail building has gone to stinking. The night's so still, no air moves through the window bars to take out the smell.

**How'd I end up like this?** I ask myself. **Lord, how'd I end up here?**

The man in the next cell complains of the noise and the stink and beats on the wall twixt us and tells Missy to quieten down, she's near drove him crazy. Heard the deputies bring him in a couple hours past sundown—a liquored-up fool that's got hisself in trouble for stealing horses from the army. The sheriff of Fort Worth is waiting for the army to come fetch him. He's a Irishman, by the way he talks.

In the dark, I sit and finger the place on my neck where Grandmama's blue beads should be. I think of Mama and how everything's gone wrong since I lost the beads, and now maybe I'll never meet her or any of my people again in this world. Lonely perches like a buzzard on my head. It pecks at my eyes so all I can see is a blur outside the window as the half moon blows its breath over the stars, dimming them down.

I'm the alonest I've ever been. Last time I was locked up was when I was six years old, after I told my purchaser at the auction sale that I was stole away from Goswood Grove. Even though I was just a child, alone and scared in that jail after being turned over to the law for safekeeping, at least I had the hope that Old Gossett would fetch me and find Mama and the rest.

This time, ain't nobody coming. Wherever Juneau Jane is tonight, she don't know what's become of us. Even if she did, wouldn't be a thing she could do about it. By now, trouble might likely have found her, too.

"You s-s-shut that clabberhead u-u-up!" the Irishman horse thief hollers. "Y-you quieten 'im dow . . . down, or I'm-a . . . I'm-a . . ."

I sit myself beside Missy in the dark, and my belly heaves at the smell of her. "Hush, now. You ain't doing us no good. Hush up."

I lean my head back and tip my nose up to get at the night air, and I try to hum the song the woman and the child sung outside the church in the swamp. I don't sing the words, but in my mind, I hear them in Mama's voice.

**Who's that young girl dressed in white**
**Wade in the water**
**Must be the children of the Israelite**
**Oh, God's a-gonna trouble the water.**

Missy curls herself into a ball and sinks her head down on my knee, same way she did when I'd crawl into her crib to shush her baby cries at night. Only time she behaved sweet like that was if she was scared and wanted somebody.

I stroke my fingers over her thin, wispy hair and close my eyes, and keep on humming till the song and night finally leave me. . . .

When I wake up, I hear my name. "Hannie," the voice is quick, a sharp whisper. "Hannie."

I sit bolt up, listen. Missy stirs, but falls off my knee and back to her slumbering. The Irishman has gone quiet, too. Did I dream the voice?

The first, thin gray light sifts in the window. Dread comes with it. How long will they keep us here and what's to happen after? I'm afraid to know.

"Hannibal?" The voice comes again. I know it then. There's only one person who'd call me **Hannibal,** but that can't be, and so I know I'm inside one of my waking dreams. Even so, I stand up on the bunk, wrap my hands over the bars, and pull my chin to the windowsill to look out. To learn what the dream has to tell me.

I see his shape, standing in the morning dim, holding the rope on a donkey with a two-wheeled wood cart hooked to it.

"Gus McKlatchy? From the boat?"

"Sssshhh! Don't call any notice," he says, but there ain't another soul in my dream, except him.

"You come with a message for me? The Lord send you?"

"Well, I doubt it, since I ain't got religion."

I wonder, then, did they toss Gus off that boat sometime after me and the paddle wheel ground him under? Is that the ghost of Gus McKlatchy, standing there in his ragged shirt and floppy hat, knee high in the fog? "You a haint, then?"

"Not 'less somebody didn't tell me about it." He looks over his shoulders and sidles the donkey up close to the wall, then stands on the donkey's back to get near the window.

"What're you doing here, Hannie? Never thought to find you again, this side a' the sod blanket. Figured you's drowned in the river when that man, Moses, pitched you off't the deck."

My whole body shivers at the memory. I feel the water over my head, the big strainer tree pinwheeling along the river bottom, grabbing my britches and pulling me down. I feel Moses's breath on my cheek, his lips on brushing my ear. **You swim?** "I got free of the wake and made shore. I don't swim much, but I can swim."

"Well, I **knowed** that was you I seen get arrested yesterdey. You with some big, sapheaded white boy, but I couldn't comprehend the **how** of it, bein' as you got throwed from the boat back on the Red." Gus's voice gets louder as he's more excited. He checks round and quiets again. "You was one lucky chap, by the by. Next night on that boat, I seen a man get pistol-whipped, then they slit his throat and tossed him off the back. Heard them say he was a Federal man and sniffing round their business. That whole boat was folk with Confederate leanin's, if you know what I mean. Feller with the patch on his eye, they all called 'the Lieutenant,' like soldiers, like they don't know the war's been over ten years now. I kep' myself hid all the way to Texas, and I was pleasured to take my leave of them, I will say."

A knot ties itself in my throat. I'm not happy for where I am, but I'm grateful both Gus and me made it off that boat alive.

"I might could get you outta here, Hannibal," Gus says.

"I'm glad if you'd say how. We're in a mess. A pure mess."

He stops to think a minute, rubs the thick trail of freckles along his chin, then nods.

"I got me a job on a freight wagon headed down through Hamilton and San Saba, all the way to

Menardville. They's some danger in it, Indians and sech, but the pay's respectable good. I figure it'll git me farther south toward where all them cattle been runnin' wild since't the war, just breedin' and procreatin' so's all a fella's got to do is catch 'em up and make his fortune. You can come on along, the two of us partner up like we talked about. I might can git the boss man to advance you the pay for freight drivin' and bail you from jail, if you's to sign on for the trip. They're in sore need of drivers and guards. You handle a four-up heavy horse team all right?"

"Course I can." I let my mind drift to the notion. I could leave Missy Lavinia and Juneau Jane to their own troubles and go with Gus and ask after my people wherever we land. Gus would, sooner or later, figure out I ain't a boy, but maybe he don't even care. I'm strong, and I'm good. I can do the work of a man. "Drive mule teams, horse teams, ox teams, a plow. Know how to tack a shoe back on a hoof, and spot the colic coming on, mend a harness, too. You could tell your boss man that about me."

"I right will. As I made a mention of, there's some danger in it, just so's you know. Comanches, and Kiowas and all. Come down out of Indian Territory, and raid and kill some folks, then run back north, where the law can't get 'em. You any kind of good shot with a rifle?"

"I am." I been getting grub in the woods and the bayous at Goswood Grove for years now. Tati figured it was better to leave Jason and John to work the crop, since they'd be stronger. "Shot more squirrel and possum than you can count."

"You shoot a man if you had to?"

"I guess I would." But I got no idea. I think of the war. Dead men with faces gone, arms and legs and parts of bodies left like hunks of meat, floating on the river or being hauled home by friends or slaves for burial. Food for flies and worms and wild creatures.

"Best you be sure of it," Gus tells me.

"I reckon I'd do what I had to. I'd do about anything to get free of this place."

"I'll work toward it," Gus tells me, and I take that for a hope. A blessed assurance that, some way, my freedom is bound to come. "Meantime, I got something for ya." He digs in his pocket. "Don't know why I held on to it, 'cept you 'n' me was travelin' friends and maybe was to be partners in the cow business . . . before you's shucked off't the boat, that is. And I'd spoke that promise to you, that I'd ask after your people wherever the trail took me."

He stretches his hand out, and snaked across that dirty white palm sits a hank of leather cord and three little round dots.

My grandmama's beads, but how can that be so? "Gus, how'd—"

"That spot you's expulsed off the boat, I fetched these up from the deck. Seemed the least I could do was let your people know what become of you, if I's ever to happen on your people, that is. I been asking here and there, about folk name of Gossett, wears three blue glass beads on a string. Gus McKlatchy don't go back on a promise. Not even to somebody who's likely drowned and dead. But you ain't dead now, so far's the evidence would show at this present time, so these is yours."

I take the beads, feel that his skin is sweaty and warm where I brush across it. My fingers curl over the beads. **Hold on tight, Hannie. Hold on tight, in case these could be a dream.**

It's too fine to be real, having the beads back after all this time.

"I been asking round for you," Gus goes on. "About that Mr. William Gossett and that Mr. Washburn you made mention of, too. Didn't learn nothin'."

I hear him like he's talking from the other side of a long field, acres and acres away.

I hold the beads to my face, breathe them in, roll them against my skin. I feel the story of my people. My grandmama's story and mama's. **My** story. A pounding grows in my blood and gets faster. It fills me and carries me up till I could spread my arms and fly like a bird. Fly right out of here.

"The freight wagons is going in the right gen'ral direction, see?" Gus talks on, but I don't want him to. I want to hear the music in the beads. "Get there, find some work down thataway . . . Menardville, Mason, Fredericksburg, Austin City maybe. Finish saving up for us each a horse and tack. While we're down there, I could help in askin' after your people, if you desired it. Make some inquirin' in places where it might be risky for a colored boy to be poking his nose. I'm a right good asker. **Ask not, get not,** that's what we McKlatchys say."

I roll the beads against my skin, breathe and breathe. I close my eyes and wonder, **If I wish it hard enough, can I fly through them bars?**

A rooster crows far off, and someplace closer a bell sings to the morning sun. Gus grabs a breath. "I got to go." The donkey grunts as Gus jumps down. "Best git on about my business 'fore somebody catches sight of me here. You'll see me again, though. As I said, Gus McKlatchy don't break a oath."

I open my eyes and watch him leave, his head tipping back as he whistles a song into the morning dim. Bit by bit the fog off the river takes him over, till there's just the tune of "Oh! Susanna" and clap of the donkey's small, round hooves and the cart singing along with each turn of the hardwood wheels. **Sheee-clack-clack, sheee-clack-clack, sheee-clack-clack, sheee . . .**

When even that's gone, I fall back to the bunk and hold the beads in my fist and curl myself close to make sure the beads stay real.

Bright light pours through the window bars in squares by the time I wake again. It's already halfway across the floor. It'll go up the wall by sundown.

I open my hand and hold it high to where the light is warm and true. The beads catch sun and shine like a bird's wing.

They're still here. Still real.

Missy's awake and rocking back and forth and making her noise, but I just scramble up to my feet and stand on the bunk and look out the window. Rain's come sometime in the early hours, so I can't see the tracks of a boy nor a cart, but I hold the beads in my hand, and so I **know.**

"Gus McKlatchy," I say. "Gus McKlatchy."

Hard to see how a boy only twelve or thirteen years old can get us out from this place, but some days you take any hope you can find, even one as poor and skinny as that pie-eater white boy, Gus.

The day weighs a little less heavy on me while the squares of light trek over the floor. I think of Gus, someplace in this town. I think of Juneau Jane, who's not even got a dime to her name. All our goods, except Juneau Jane's lady clothes, stayed with me and now they're gone with the sheriff. Our money. Our food and goods and the derringer pistol. **The Book of Lost Friends.** Everything.

Missy moans and holds her stomach, and goes to fussing long before the jail man comes with our bucket of pot likker soup and two big wood spoons. One time a day. One bucket. That's all we get, sheriff said.

I hear the Irishman stirring from his bunk. He'll go to hollering now that he's woke up. Instead, as we eat our pot likker, he whispers, "Hey. Hey, you hearin' me, neighbor? Hearin' me now, are you?"

I unfold my legs and stand up stiff, then sidle forward a few steps by the wall, just far enough that I can see thick arms hanging out the bars, but he can't see me. His skin's red and baked from the sun. A fur of thick yellow hair covers over it, down to the knuckles. They're the hands of a strong man, so I stay to the wall.

"I hear."

"Who was it ye'd be conversin' with outside this morn'?"

No reason to trust him, so I answer, "Don't know."

"McKlatchy, I heard him sayin'." So, the man was listenin' at us. "Good Scottish name, there. Friend to Irish folk, like myself. My dear mam, she was Scots-Irish, she was."

"Can't say about none of that." What's this man want? He plan to tell the sheriff on me?

"The two of ye help me away from here, lad, I'd be beholdin'. Be of help to ye both, I could." The big hands turn a circle, hurried.

I stay to the wall, where I am.

"Some things I know," the Irishman says. "The man ye seek after, Will'am Gossett. I met the man, indeed. Southward of here a distance, in the Hill Country near Llano town. Offered the man a fine horse trade when his own went lame under him. I could be takin' ye to him, if ye'd help me gain my freedom. I fear your Mr. Gossett may run abreast of trouble, should soldiers down that way come upon him . . . as he was ridin' one their horses when we parted. Warned him, I did, to trade the beast for another when he reached the nearest town. He wasn't a man for listenin'. Neither was he a man for that Llano country. If ye'd help me get away from this place, I'd make it worth the while and aid in your searching. I could be of use to ye, friend."

"Don't reckon there's much way we could help you," I say, so's he'll know I don't believe it.

"Relay to the employer of your friend that I've a fine hand with a team and am troubled none by the risk of freighting. If only he may lift me from my current difficulty without my neck in a rope."

"They ain't gonna turn no army horse thief out of jail."

"There's many a deputy can be bought."

"I don't know nothing about all that, either." Can't believe a thing coming from a Irishman, anyhow. Irishmen tell tales, and they hate my kind, and the feeling runs both ways.

"The three blue beads," he tries next. "Heard you speaking of it, I did. Having tramped the Hill Country far and wide, I've seen such a thing. At a traveler's hotel and restaurant down Austin way, just along Waller Creek. Three blue beads on a string. Tied round the neck of a little white girl."

"A white gal?" I guess he ain't figured out I'm colored and anybody with my grandmama's blue beads would be, too.

"Red-haired, a bonnie little thing, but young. Eight, perhaps ten, I'd say. Serving water to tables outdoors in a courtyard under the oaks. I could take you to the place."

I turn and go back to the bunk. "That wouldn't be nobody I'd know."

The Irishman calls out, but I don't answer. He goes to swearing on his mama's soul that he ain't lying. I pay him no mind.

Before there's even time for the soup to cool in the pot, the army's come for him, anyhow. They drag him away, screaming so loud Missy covers her ears and crawls under the bunk in all the stink and mess.

The deputy shows up at our cell next, drags me out the cell door and there ain't a thing I can do about it. "You'll shut your yap, if you know what's good for you," he says.

The sheriff's in the front room and I start to begging and telling him I hadn't done anything. "You git," he says, and shoves our poke into my hands. Feels like everything's there, even the pistol and the book. "You've been hired for work that's to take you out of my town. See that I don't find your face here again, once J. B. French's freight wagons leave."

"But Mis—" I stop myself just short of saying **Missy.** "Him. I got him to see after, the big boy that come in with me. He don't have nobody else. He's harmless, he's just addle-headed and simple, but I—"

"You shut yer yap! Sheriff James don't need no word from you." The deputy kicks me hard in the back, sending me facedown onto the floor. I land on our pack and my knees and one elbow, then scrabble around to get up again.

"The boy is to be remanded to the State Lunatic

Asylum in Austin," the sheriff says, and the deputy opens the jailhouse door then kicks me into the street and throws our goods after me.

Gus is there waiting and helps gather up the poke. "We best git gone, before their minds go to reconsiderin' on your release," he says.

I tell him about leaving Missy, but he don't want no part of that.

"Look here, Hannibal. It was all I could do to get **you** out. You start trouble, they'll put you in again, and there won't be no help for that."

I stumble along, letting Gus pull me down the street. "Act right," he says. "What's got into you? You'll have us both in the stew. Mr. J. B. French and his foreman, Penberthy, they don't stand for no guff."

I follow along, try to reason out what to do next. The town streets, horses and wagons, colored folks and white folks, cowboys and dogs, stores and houses go past my eyes all in a mix, so I don't see any one thing. Then there's the alley by the courthouse and Battercake Flats. I stop and look down toward the bluff, remember sitting right there, Missy and Juneau Jane and me, eating lunch from our poke.

"This way." Gus nudges my shoulder. "Just down a bit in the wagon yard. They done packed up the one freighter, and the last of the crew is to ride up top of the load. We'll join with the wagons from Weatherford and then leave southward from there. We ain't got time to dally."

"I'll come on," I say, and push the pokes into Gus's

hands before he can say no. "I'll come on, but there's something I got to do first."

I turn and run, through the streets and the alleys, past yapping dogs and spooked horses at hitch rings. I know I shouldn't, but I go back to the place where all the trouble started. Where Old Florida and the shoeshine boy work their business, near the bathhouse. I ask them of Juneau Jane, and they say they ain't seen her, and so I hurry round the back. There, I stop and watch the workers come and go, hauling the water in and out in buckets.

A wide, round-faced colored woman comes out to take clothes off a alley line. She laughs and teases with some of the others. I move her way, thinking to ask her of Juneau Jane.

I don't even get near there before a man steps out on the gallery above. He tips his head back and blows smoke into the air from a cigar. It curls under the brim of his hat and slips away as he comes to the rail to tap ashes over. When he does, I see the melted scars along his face and the patch over his eye. Takes everything I have to turn around slow, not run, just walk. I squeeze my fists and hold my arms stiff and don't look back, nor left, nor right. I feel the Lieutenant watching me.

**No, he ain't. No he ain't,** I tell myself.

**Don't look.**

I round the corner and break into a blind run.

It's then I see that the side alley ain't empty. There's a man loading boxes on a pushcart. He's tall and lean and strong built, dusky like the shadows that cover us both. I know the sight of him even in the half light. You don't forget a man who's come close to killing you, twice over. Who would do it now, if he got the chance.

I try to stop and turn back, but the wash water runs down the alley in a little stream. I slip in the mud and go down.

Moses is on me before I can get to my feet.

## Lost Friends

Dear Editor—I was born in Henrico county, Va., some 70 years ago. My mother was Dolly, a slave belonging to Phillip Frazer, and I remained the slave of said Frazer until I was about 13 years of age. I had two younger sisters. Their names were Charity and Rebecca. They were 4 to 5 years old when I was sold to Wilson Williams, of Richmond. Mr. Williams some 6 or 7 months thereafter sold me to Goodwin & Glenn, negro traders; who sold me at New Orleans, La. I being at that time about 14 years of age, I subsequently became the property of many and divers masters in Louisiana and Texas, until freed by the emancipation proclamation of President Lincoln. I am now a resident of this city and a member of M. E. Church. I wish to hear from my sisters, Charity and Rebecca, whom I left back in Virginia and also from other relatives, if I have any; and avail myself of your columns as a means of inquiring concerning them. I can be addressed to the care of Rev. J. K. Loggins, St. Pauls church, Galveston, Texas.

MRS. CAROLINE WILLIAMS

—"Lost Friends" column of the Southwestern April 14, 1881

## CHAPTER 22

BENNY SILVA—AUGUSTINE, LOUISIANA, 1987

It's Thursday again, and I know, without even the first glimpse through the trees, that Nathan's truck will be parked in my driveway. My mind sprints ahead of the Bug, which is now sporting a new bumper, thanks to Cal Frazer, the local mechanic, and nephew of Miss Caroline, one of our New Century ladies. He loves old cars like the Bug, because they were made to be repaired and kept in use, not discarded in the trash heap after the digital clocks and automatic seatbelts die.

A city police car pulls out of its hiding place behind a billboard and trails me, and for once I don't break into a nervous sweat about whether I'll get stopped over the bumper issue. Even so, a mildly eerie feeling lingers as we traverse each curve together. It's like a movie scene in which the local law and small-town powerbrokers are indistinguishable from one another. They all have the same goal. To stop anyone new from upsetting the status quo.

As much as I'd like to keep the **Underground** project quiet until it's closer to fruition, it's hard when dozens of kids, a group of senior ladies, and a smattering of volunteers like Sarge are running around town scrounging for everything from courthouse records, old newspaper articles, family pictures and documents to poster board and costume materials. We've hit the first week of October, which puts the Halloween date for our pageant less than thirty days away.

I stop at the end of my driveway, just to see who's in the police cruiser, since it's way out here beyond the city limits. The driver is Redd Fontaine, of course. As the mayor's brother, and a cousin to Will and Manford Gossett, he claims everything as his jurisdiction. He drifts by in no particular hurry, looking past me toward my house.

I can't help wondering if he's scoping out Nathan's truck. The Bug and I hold our position, seeking to block the view until the police car passes by, then we roll on in. My pulse steadies at the sight of khaki shorts and a camo green chambray shirt peeking through the oleander where the garden saint hides. I know the outfit, even before I see Nathan on the porch swing. As far as I can tell, he has about five daily uniforms, all of them casual, comfortable, and in tune with south Louisiana's hot, humid weather. His style is a cross between mountain guy and beach bum. He does not do dress-up.

It's one of the things I like about him. I'm not all that fashion forward, either, although I am trying hard to make a good impression in my teaching career. **Dress for the job you want, not the job you have** was the oft-given advice of college career counselors. I think I want to be a principal someday. It's a new revelation and one I'm still growing into. Secondary education suits me in an unexpected way. These kids make me feel that I have a purpose, that getting up and going to work every day matters.

The Bug nestles quietly into its usual set of driveway ruts and sighs into silence as I turn off the ignition. On the swing, Nathan sits with one elbow comfortably propped, his fingers dangling. He's focused toward the cemetery, his eyes narrowed so that I momentarily wonder if he's catching a catnap. He looks . . . relaxed, unbothered and in the moment.

It's a lesson I'm trying to learn from him, this living squarely in the present. I am a planner and a worrier. I torment myself by mentally replaying my past mistakes, wishing I'd been smarter, wishing I'd been stronger, wishing I'd made different choices. I live too often in the realm of **what if.** I also expend time and mental energy continually trying to anticipate what sort of crouching tiger might be hiding around the next corner. Nathan's default seems to be to take life as it comes and contend with tigers if and when they appear. Perhaps it's the result of having been raised in the mountains by an artist mother he lovingly refers to as a **beatnik.**

I wish he would talk more about her. I've been seeking ways to understand him, but he doesn't give out much. Then again, neither do I. There's so little I can divulge about my family or my past that doesn't veer too close to the things I've spent most of my adult life avoiding.

The creaking porch steps snap him from his reverie. Cocking his head, he studies me momentarily. "Tough day?" he asks.

"Do I look **that** bad?" Self-consciously, I snatch up fuzzy black curls and tuck them into the French braid that looked nicely professional this morning.

He gestures to the empty half of the swing like it's a psychologist's couch. "You look . . . worried."

I shrug, but in truth I am nursing a worry and a little wound. "The approvals for the **Underground** project, I guess. I've described it to Mr. Pevoto a few times, but I'm not sure he's really hearing me, you know? He just kind of pats me on the head and tells me to get parent permission forms signed. I'm still missing quite a few. My plan was to take care of a bunch of them at parent-teacher night. Eleven people breezed through my classroom. Eleven. Total. From five sections of class daily, averaging thirty-six kids each, I got three moms, one dad, one couple, one aunt, one court-appointed guardian, and a foster mom. Two grandparents. Most of the night, I just sat there in an empty room."

"Awww, man, that's rough." His arm shifts from the back of the swing, and he pulls me into a shoulder hug, his fingers brushing the skin of my upper arm. "It must've stung a little, huh?"

"Yeah. It did." I sink into the comfort of the companionable gesture . . . or whatever it is. "I had bulletin boards all made with their writing and some photos. I wanted it to be nice for everybody, you know? But it was just me and a platter of cookies and Hi-C . . . and tasteful fall-themed plates and cups. I splurged at the Ben Franklin. Now I won't need to buy any paper goods for months."

I'm aware that I sound like I'm fishing for sympathy, and I hate it but I guess that's where I am at the moment. Parent-teacher night hurt and this . . . whatever we're doing right now, feels good.

"Awww," Nathan says again, with a friendly squeeze in the way of trying to buck me up. "I'll eat some of the cookies."

My head relaxes on his shoulder. It suddenly feels so natural. "Promise?"

"Promise."

"Pinkie swear?" I lift my free hand, then just as quickly let it fall. I used to do that with Christopher. Old habits. A specter rising up to remind me that tumbling into a new relationship to cure the melancholy of a broken one was my mother's life strategy, and it never worked. Nathan and I are friends. We're cohorts. It's better to keep it that way. He knows that, which is why, even when I've tried to fish for information about his past, he hasn't given it. I've even hinted that I'd love to see how things work on the shrimp boat. I've never been invited into that part of his life. Not even a peek. There's a reason for that.

I pull away, regaining a safe distance.

He sets his hand on the bench between us, then moves it farther from me, resting it uncertainly on his thigh, lightly drumming his fingers. We watch a wren hop along the porch rail then flit away.

Finally, Nathan clears his throat and says, "Oh, hey. Before I forget, I wanted to let you know that I've told my lawyer to nix the land sale to the cemetery association, at least in its present form. Obviously, it's wrong to start selling off cemetery plots where people were buried over a hundred years ago. The cemetery association will just have to find land for an annex someplace else. That means you don't need to worry about the house. It's yours, however long you want it."

Relief and gratitude spiral through me. "Thank you. You can't imagine what that means." The revelation nudges me squarely back to a safer frame of mind. I need this house, and my students need the **Underground** project. And any stumbling toward a romantic relationship between Nathan and me could complicate all of that.

I turn and prop a knee on the seat between us,

inserting yet more space, then move into conversation about the house. Sterile stuff. Nothing personal. We eventually trail off into the weather and what a beautiful day it is, and how it almost feels like fall. Almost.

"Of course, tomorrow it'll probably be ninety-five degrees again," Nathan jokes. "That's south Louisiana."

We commiserate over how strange it is to live in a place where the seasons are fluid, day-to-day. By now in Nathan's North Carolina mountains, the slopes would be spatters of flagrant yellow and amber, amid the myriad greens of tall pine. Back in Maine, which was a favorite of my many growing-up places, the orchard stands and hayrides would be running at full steam, ready for the bumper-to-bumper traffic of leaf peepers viewing the maples, sweet gums, and hickories. Crystalline frosts would sugar the mornings, and the first snows might tease the tips of dying grass. At the very least, the air would carry the unmistakable hint of coming winter.

"I didn't really think I'd miss having fall, but I do," I tell Nathan. "But then I have to say, if you're looking for some pretty impressive foliage, the gardens over at Goswood Grove are a good substitute." I'm about to go on about the antique climbing roses that cascade over fences, rambling up tall trees and what remains of an old gazebo, which I discovered just yesterday on my walk . . . when I quickly realize where I've driven the conversation.

Nathan's easy demeanor evaporates. He instantly

looks weighed down. I want to apologize, but I can't. Even that would point out that he's got deep issues over the house and what will become of it in the long run.

His gaze strays in that direction. I catch the clouded look, privately kick myself.

"So . . . I could whip up some grilled cheese and tomato bisque for us. How about hot chocolate, since we're celebrating fake fall and everything?" I'm like a football team, attempting a surprise onside kick to change the momentum of the game. "You hungry? Because I'm starved."

His attention hangs divided a moment longer. There's something he wants to say. Then the clouds part, and he smiles and offers, "Cluck and Oink would be easier."

"Well, that sounds mighty fine." My Louisiana accent is beyond pathetic. "You go grab us a side of pork, and I'll throw on some jeans while you're gone."

We're comfortably back to our usual Thursday night routine. Afterward, we'll walk off the food coma with a stroll through the graveyard, commenting on ancient tombs and wondering about the lives they represent. Or we'll walk the farm levee lane to get a view of the sunset across the rice fields, always carefully avoiding the portal to Goswood Grove, of course.

"Nah," he mutters as we stand up. I'm suddenly afraid that he's decided against dinner. "Let's just go down to the Cluck and eat. You've had a tough week. No sense in you having to clean up afterward." He must be reading the explosion of surprise on my face, because he quickly adds, "Unless you don't feel like it."

"No!" I blurt. But aside from his one library visit, which was just the kids and me and a few helpers, Nathan and I have kept to ourselves. "That sounds great. Let me do something with this hair real quickly."

"To go to the Cluck and Oink?" His forehead twists into a bemused serpentine shape.

"Point taken."

"You look great. Sort of Jennifer Grey in **Dirty Dancing** meets Jennifer Beals in **Flashdance.**"

"Oh, well, in that case . . ." I do a nerdy dance move my colleagues in the college English department once affectionately dubbed **Big Bird on Ice.** Nathan laughs, and we proceed to his truck. On the way to town, we chat about nothing important.

Entering the Cluck and Oink, I feel a pang of self-consciousness. Granny T is behind the cash register. LaJuna brings our menus, offers a shy hello, and tells us she'll be waiting our table.

Maybe takeout would've been a better idea. The library was one thing, but this looks too much like a date and sort of feels like one, too.

The girls' cross-country coach is in the corner. She checks me out in a way that's not friendly. She and the other coaches are annoyed with me. Some of the kids have been late for after-school practices because they're busy working on their **Underground** projects.

Lil' Ray emerges from the back room carrying a dish tub, spray bottles of pink cleaner looped over his belt like cowboy six-shooters. I didn't even know he worked here.

He and LaJuna cross paths in the narrow space between the waitress station and the kitchen door. They jostle and tease and then, where they think no one can see, melt into full-body contact and a kiss.

**When did that get started?**

I feel like my eyes have just been burned. **No. Please no.**

**No more.**

Heaven help me, I may not survive these kids. It's something, every time I turn around. Some new pitfall, pothole, roadblock, poor decision, or act of pure stupidity.

Lil' Ray and LaJuna are so young and they both have tremendous potential, but they're also dealing with huge challenges in their daily lives. When you're a kid in a tough family situation, you're painfully vulnerable to trying to fill the void with peers. As much as I'm in favor of young love in theory, I'm also aware of the potential fallout. I can't help feeling that Lil' Ray and LaJuna need a teenage relationship about as much as I need five-inch stilettos.

**Don't read too much into it,** I tell myself. **Most of these things come and go in a week.**

"So, I was thinking about the house." Nathan is talking. I rip my eyes away from the scene at the waitress station and try to ignore the glowering coach, as well.

"My house?"

The question hangs in the air while the bread boy stops at our table with an offering that would smell heavenly under any other circumstance. He sets down a well-used plastic basket, then loads it with corn muffins, breadsticks, and rolls, then adds butter, honey-butter, and a knife.

"Hey, Miss Pooh," he says. I'm so out of sorts, I haven't even looked up and noticed that the bread boy is **also** one of my students. A shaggy-haired kid from the Fish family. The others classify him squarely in the category with **the hoods.** Rumor is, he smokes weed, which his family grows in fields carved out of the backwoods somewhere. Generally, he smells like cigarettes, especially after lunch.

The Fish family receives no kindness in the teachers' lounge, either. White trash. **None of those Fish kids ever graduate from high school, so why waste your time?** was the exact quote. **Sooner they drop out, the better. Just a bad influence on the others.**

I offer up a smile. While Shad Fish, the next oldest boy in the family, is a bit more talkative, I wasn't even aware this senior Fish kid knew my name. Gar Fish has never spoken in class. Not once. Most of the time, he has his forehead propped in his hands, staring down at the desk. Even at the library. As a student, he's a complete slacker. He's not an athlete, either, so there's no coach defending his lack of academic effort.

"Hey, Gar." The poor kid has sisters named Star and Sunnie, and a little brother named Finn. People poke fun at the names constantly.

I had no idea Gar worked at the Cluck.

"I been . . . I been writin' . . . on my project," he says.

**Knock me over with a feather.**

A tentative glance flutters through the dark fringe of greasy, overgrown bangs beneath the Cluck ball cap. "Uncle Saul went over to the nursing home in Baton Rouge to say hey to Poppop. Me and Shad went on with him so we could talk to Pops, too. We don't got any family Bibles or anything like that at home."

He glances up self-consciously as the hostess seats new customers in the next booth. Gar shifts his back toward them before he goes on. "Pops told me some stuff about the family. They used to run a operation upwater from here. Biggest bootleggers in three parishes. Pops joined in at just eleven years old, after the revenuers took his daddy off. The family business got busted up after a while, though. Pops left home and went farther upriver to work for some uncles that had a sawmill. He remembers they had a room in the barn still with slaves' chains in it. Way back when, they'd catch runaways in the swamp, take them off to New Orleans and make money from it. You imagine that? Poachers. Like huntin' gators out of season. That's what my people did for their livin'."

"Huh." On occasion that's all I can say to the facts we've uncovered during our journey through the **Underground** project. The truth is frequently horrific. "The things we find in history are hard to understand sometimes, aren't they, Gar?"

"Yeah." His saggy shoulders slump. His eyes, a murky swampwater color, cast downward. There's a fairly pronounced bruise under the left one—no telling where he got that. "Might can I start over on my project? It's just that the Fishes do bad stuff and get in jail mostly. Maybe I can pick somebody out of the graveyard and talk about them? A rich guy or the mayor or something?"

I swallow the urge to get emotional. "Don't give up yet. Let's keep digging. Remind me tomorrow when we're at the library, and we'll work on it together. Have you looked into the other side of your family? Your mother's side?"

"Mama got put in foster care when she was little, so we didn't ever meet her people. They're from around Thibodaux, I think."

I shift uncomfortably in my seat, pinched by the thought of a child left unmoored in the world, at the mercy of strangers. "Well, all right, then we'll see what there is to learn. We'll start there tomorrow.

With your mother's last name. You can never tell where the—"

"Gold nugget might be unless you dig. Yeah, I know." He finishes the class mantra the kids and I have developed.

"Every family has more than one side to its history, right? What was her last name? Your mother's?"

"Mama was a McKlatchy before she married a Fish."

Nathan sets down the butter knife with a clank, straightens a bit. "My mother has some McKlatchys in her family. Distant kin, but they're all down around Morgan City, Thibodaux, Bayou Cane. We might be related way back."

Gar and I both gape at him. I had no idea that Nathan enjoyed family ties around here on his mother's side. Based on the descriptions of her as an outsider, I assumed she was from someplace far away. Nathan has an entire life south of here along the coast. A life with people in it. Kinfolk and family reunions.

"Maybe," Gar says, as if he's having a hard time processing a possible genetic connection to Nathan Gossett. "But I doubt it, though."

"Just in case you **might** be a relative," Nathan says, "do a little digging into Augustus 'Gus' McKlatchy. The old aunts and uncles used to talk about him at the family reunions when I was a kid. There's a good story there, if he's in your family tree."

Gar looks doubtful. "Hope your bread's good," he mutters, and shrugs, and then he's gone.

Nathan watches him walk away. "Poor kid," he says and looks at me in a way that silently adds, **I don't see how you can do this day in and day out.**

"Yeah, I kind of know how he feels." For some reason, maybe it's the new revelation about Nathan and the Fishes, but more of the Mussolini rumors from my father's family spill out. "It's strange how you can feel guilty for a family history you didn't have anything to do with, isn't it? My folks finally divorced when I was four and a half, then my father moved back to New York City. We don't keep in touch, but now I kind of wish I could ask him about it, find the truth." I can't believe I just said that, and to Nathan. With the **Underground** project invading so much of my mental space, family ties have been on my mind, I guess. The way Nathan's sitting there listening, nodding attentively, makes it seem all right.

He hasn't even touched the bread.

For an instant, I wonder if I could tell him the rest of it—everything. And if **that** wouldn't matter, either. Just as quickly, shame rushes in, and I squelch the notion. It'll change the way he thinks of me. Aside from that, we're in a public place. I'm suddenly aware of how quiet the women at the table behind us are. I hope they haven't been listening in.

Surely not. Why would they care?

I stretch upward a bit, and the blonde facing me lifts her menu, so that only her nicely highlighted hair is visible above the edge.

I push the bread toward Nathan. "Sorry. I don't know how I got off on that topic. Dig in."

"Ladies first." He scoots the basket back, pinches the knife handle between a thumb and forefinger and offers it to me. "As long as you're not a fiend on the jalapeño corn bread."

I chuckle. "You know I'm not." The corn bread is a takeout joke between us. I'll get out the plain sixty-cents-a-loaf grocery store bread before I'll eat corn bread. I know it's a southern staple, but I haven't acquired a taste for it. It's like eating sawdust.

We settle into the bread plate. Corn bread for Nathan, breadsticks for me. We'll split the rolls with our meal. It's become our routine.

My gaze has drifted again to the women at the next table, when LaJuna comes by to take our order. She lingers afterward, the pencil dangling. "Miss Silva." She's one of the few who has not succumbed to calling me Miss Pooh. It's her way of separating herself from the rest, I think. "Mama was supposed to come visit the other day and bring the little kids, so I could give my sister her birthday present and a cake Aunt Dicey and me made. But then we had to just talk on the phone, because Mama's car has trouble sometimes."

"Oh, I'm sorry." I clench my fingers around the napkin in my lap, twist opposite ways and wring out my frustration. This is at least the fourth promised **Mama visit** that has fallen through. Every time it happens, LaJuna is bubbly with excitement during the anticipation phase, then retreats into herself when the plans end in disappointment. "Well, I'm glad you got to talk on the phone."

"We couldn't very long, on account of collect calls cost too much on Aunt Dicey's phone bill. But I told Mama about my **Underground** project. She said when she was little, they used to say that way back, her great-great-great-grandmama had money and fancy clothes and she owned land and horses and stuff. Can I be her for my **Underground** project, so I can wear a pretty dress?"

"Well . . ." The rest of the sentence, **I don't see why not,** never makes it out of my mouth. The bell chimes on the front door and there's a sudden, palpable effect. The room feels as if the air has just been sucked out of it.

I see a woman nudge her husband and point surreptitiously toward the door. A man at another table stops chewing in the middle of a bite of brisket, sets down his fork, leans forward in his seat.

Across from me, Nathan's face goes slack, then rigid. I glance over my shoulder, see two men at the hostess stand, their designer golf clothes out of place against the restaurant's barn wood and tin interior. Will and Manford Gossett have aged since their portraits were hung at Goswood House, but even without the old photos and the family resemblance, I'd probably guess who they were, just by their demeanor. They move through the place like they own it, laughing, chatting, waving at people across the room, shaking hands.

They pointedly avoid looking our way as they breeze right past us and take their seats . . . with the women at the next booth.

## CHAPTER 23

### HANNIE GOSSETT—TEXAS, 1875

The rock bluffs, speckled with live oaks and cedar elms, and growed over in the valleys with pecans and cottonwoods, have turned to grass that rolls out, and out, and out. The hills stand yellow and barely green and hen-feather brown with soft pink tips. Stickery mesquites squat in lace-leaf patches. Flat padded cactus and limestone rock trouble the feet and legs of the horses, making us travel slow, even now that we're through the top of the Hill Country, with its farm fields and white rock barns and German church houses. We're gone on beyond all that. South past Llano town, out where there ain't a thing but scrap trees squatted in the low places like green stitches puckering a brown-and-gold quilt.

Seen antelope and wild range cattle with spotted hides all different colors, their horns thick as wagon axles. Seen a creature they call the buffalo. We stood the freight wagons up above a river and watched the wooly beasts wander across. Long time ago, before the hide hunters got them, there'd be hundreds and hundreds in a herd, is what Penberthy said. Don't anybody here call the freight boss **Mister.** Just Penberthy. That's all.

So I call him that, too.

I work the last two wagons in the train with Gus. We started as heelers on other rigs, but four men been lost from us already on this trip—one sick, one with a broke leg, one snake bit, and one that run off in Hamilton after news of renegade Indian raids to the south and settlers murdered in terrible ways. I try not to think on it much. Instead, I drive the wagon, and watch every rock and tree, and each stretch where land meets sky. I look for things moving, and I think mile by mile about Moses.

The man was true to his word. I can't say why, except that he ain't what I thought he was. He ain't the devil. He's the man who saved us—me and Missy Lavinia, and Juneau Jane.

"Go," he said, as the weight of his body pushed hard against mine in that alley by the bathhouse. His hand held tight over my mouth to keep me from calling out. Wouldn't've helped anyhow. Not likely anybody'd hear it in that bawdy, wild town, or think much of it if they did. Hell's Half Acre. Pete Rain was right. That name's well earned. The gravedigger must be the busiest man in Fort Worth.

Only reason we ain't laying under the soil there is Moses.

"Ssshhh," he said, and looked over his shoulder down the alley, then he leaned closer to whisper. "Go while you can. Get clear of this place, out of Fort Worth." His eyes were cool brass metal, his narrow face hardened by the lines of that long, thick mustache, his body heavy with sinew and bone and strong cords of muscle.

I shook my head, and he warned me again not to call out, and he took his hand off my mouth.

"I can't," I said and whispered to him of Missy and Juneau Jane and that they were the daughters of Mr. William Gossett, who had disappeared into Texas, and that us three had been split up in a bad way. "I got a job on a freight haul leaving out soon, headed for the Llano country, and then Menardville."

"I know of it," he answered, and sweat from under his hat drew trails down his skin.

I told him what the Irishman had said of Mr. William Gossett. "I got to get Missy and Juneau Jane somehow, and I'll take us away south, far from here."

A pulse beat under the sheen on his neck, and he looked around us again. There was noise nearby. Voices. "Go," he told me. "You can't help them from a pine box, and that's where you'll end up. I'll send them along, if I can." He turned me from the shadows toward the light and shoved me and said, "Don't turn back."

I ran through the streets and didn't stop and didn't catch a full breath till we'd rolled the freight wagons out of Fort Worth town.

We were still at our meet-up camp with the freighter line from Weatherford when a stout-built white man rode in, leading behind him Juneau Jane and Missy Lavinia on a big bay horse. He wore a cowboy's clothes, but the horses had the tack and brands of a Federal regiment.

"From Moses," the man said without looking at me.

"But how'd he . . ."

A quick shake of his head warned me I ought not ask questions, then he helped get Missy and Juneau Jane into my wagon before he went on forward to fix it with Penberthy. And that was all. Don't know what was said, and Penberthy never made a mention of it in all the days after.

Now we're young dogs in a pack, we three and Gus McKlatchy, who drives the wagon front of ours. We're low in the peck, but Penberthy's crew of drivers and wagon guards is mostly young, and more than half are colored or Indian or mixed blood. We three don't gather much notice. We get the trail dust, and the ruts at the water crossings, and the haze of churned-up grass and chaff that hangs over the prairie like a cloud after a half dozen wagons pass. If the Kiowa or the Comanches come upon this freight train, they'll take our wagon first, from the back. Likely we won't live to see what happens after. Our scouts, Tonkawas and colored men who lived with the Indians and married with them, travel out beside, and before and behind on their quick, sturdy ponies. They watch for signs. Nobody wants to lose the freight.

Nobody wants to be dead, either. Gus didn't lie about the risk of it.

At night, they tell stories in the camp. Dead by Indians is a particular bad dead. I've been showing Juneau Jane how to work the pistol and the carbine rifle that Penberthy give us to use. I even put the cartridges in Old Mister's derringer, case we get desperate enough to find out if it'll still fire. Evening after evening, Juneau Jane shows me and Gus letters and words, learns us about how they sound and how to write them, while she keeps on with **The Book of Lost Friends.** Gus ain't as quick to pick it up as me, but we both try. There's men on this train that're missing people, men who lived as slaves in Arkansas and Louisiana and Texas and Indian Territory before the war. There's folks in the towns we pass through, too, so we find plenty of chances to learn new words.

Time to time, some fresh names to add to the book even come to us from strangers on the road. We share talk or a camp and a meal, gather tales of Lost Friends or information about the way ahead of us, or get word of Indian troubles, or bad patches where road agents or them Marston Men look to rob and steal, or the nature of the rivers and watercourses. It's a mail wagoner on one of our last camp nights who warns us to take care in this area. He tells of horse thieving and cattle thieving and a range war twixt the German ranchers and the Americans that went in with the Confederates during the war.

"The Germans formed themselves a vigilante gang, call it the Hoodoos. Busted down the jail door in Mason a while back to get their hands on some fellas that'd been locked up for stealing loose cattle. Nearly killed the sheriff and a Texas Ranger. Shot one man in the leg, who had not a thing to do with the cattle, but was jailed for riding a stolen army horse. Poor sap was lucky they didn't hang him that night, too. The Hoodoos had strung up three of their prisoners before the sheriff and the Texas Ranger got it stopped. Now, the Hoodoos have shot another one, and his people have gathered a gang and gone warfaring over it. Troubles here lately with these Marston Men, too. Their leader calls himself 'the General.' Been stirring up another wave of Honduras Fever, telling diehard secessionist folk there's a new South to be built down in British Honduras, and maybe on the island of Cuba, too. Has won quite a few over to his cause. You can't tell who's who just by looking, either. You folks watch out. Ain't but a hare's hair between the law and the outlaws around here. This is dangerous country."

"I heared of them Marston Men," Gus says. "They was holding secret meetin's in a warehouse up to Fort

Worth town, recruitin' more folks. Fools on a fool's errand, you ask me. World don't turn backward. Turns forward. Future belongs to the man that faces hisself straight on."

Penberthy strokes his gray beard and nods. The wagon boss has put young Gus McKlatchy under wing, like a papa or a grandpapa would do. "That kind of thinking will take you far," he agrees, and to the mail wagoner, he says, "Thanks for the warning, friend. We'll be watchful over it."

"What was the name of the man who got his leg shot?" I pipe up, and everyone looks my way, surprised. I been purposeful to not call attention on this trip, but right now I'm thinking of the Irishman's story. "The one who's in jail for the stole army horse?"

"Don't rightly know. He survived the bullet to the leg, though. Strange sort for a horse thief, a gentlemanly type fellow. Reckon the army will hang him, if they haven't already. Yes, there's all sorts of bedevilment these days. World's not what it used to be, and . . ."

He goes on with his tales, but I tuck his news in my mind, think on it late into the night. Maybe the Irishman in Fort Worth wasn't fibbing about trading a stole army horse to a Mr. William Gossett, after all? If that was true, was the tale about the little white girl with the three blue beads real, too? I talk of it with Gus and Juneau Jane as we put in for the night, and we make a pact that once we get the freight to Menardville, we'll go over to Mason and see about the man who was shot in the leg, just in case there's a chance that man could be Old Mister or somebody who knows of him.

I close my eyes and drift and wake and drift again. In my dreams, I drive a freighter with a team of four black horses. It's Mr. William Gossett I'm looking for. But I don't find him. Moses comes instead. He steals into my dream like a panther you don't see, but you know it's stalking behind, or left, right, overhead, perched against the sky. You hear it stir and then it's on you, its body heavy against yours, breath coming fast.

You're stopped still, scared to look in its eye. Scared not to.

Overcome by the power of the thing.

That's how Moses sneaks into my mind, never letting me know for sure, is he my friend or my enemy? I feel every inch of him against every inch of me. See his eyes, smell his scent.

I want him gone . . . but I don't.

**Don't turn back,** he says.

I wake with my heart gone wild like the barrel drum. It crowds my ears, and then I realize it's thunder. The sound turns me itchy and fretful, unsettled as the weather. We break camp without breakfast and move out. We got two days yet to Menardville, long as there's no trouble.

Rain don't fall often in this dry country, but the next days, it comes like a kettle's getting tipped side to side over our heads. Thunder troubles the horses and lightning cuts the sky like a hawk's gold claws ready to scoop up the world and fly off with it.

The animals dance and worry the bits till the land gets soggy and the white caliche mud turns slick and soaks up over the horses' fetlocks. It sucks down the wagon wheels, and white-tinged water sprays out like milk as they turn, turn, turn.

I tip my head against the misery and think of Mr. William Gossett and try to work out if he could've come so far out into this bare land, and found hisself riding a stole horse, and then sitting trapped in a jail while men broke down the door and rushed in with hanging ropes and guns.

I can't even fancy him in such a place. What could bring him here into the wild?

But deep down, I know. I answer my own question. **Love.** That's the thing that would do it. The love of a father who can't give up on his only son. Who'd wander the entire wide world if need be to bring his boy home. Lyle didn't deserve that kind of love. He didn't return it, except with bad deeds and fast living and trouble. Likely, Lyle's already met his rightful end. Dead, shot, or hanged in some unplatted place like this one, his bones picked clean by wolves and left to fall to dust. Likely, Old Mister come down here chasing after a ghost. But he couldn't make hisself give up hope till he knew for sure.

The rain stops on the second day, quick as it hit. That's the way of it in this country.

The men shake out their hats and toss off their oilcloth slickers. Juneau Jane climbs out from under the wagon canvas, where she's hid during the storms, mostly. She's the only one here small enough to do that. Missy's wet clear through, because she won't keep a slicker on. She don't shiver or fuss or even seem to notice. Just sits on the tail of the wagon, staring off, like she is right now.

**"Quanto de temps . . . tiempo nos el voy . . . viaje?"** Juneau Jane asks one of the scouts, a half-Indian Tonkawa who don't speak English but Spanish. With knowing French, Juneau Jane's picked up their language some on this freight trip. I have, too, a little.

The scout holds up three fingers. I figure that means three hours more for us to travel. Then he raises a hand flat and passes it up and down over his mouth, the Indian sign that we got one more time to cross water.

The sun fights its way through the clouds and the day turns bright, but inside of me comes a darkening. The more we draw nigh on Menardville, the more it weighs heavy on me that we'll soon be after Old Mister again, and what if we find news of him but the news is hard for Juneau Jane? What if he's met a terrible end in this strange place?

What comes of us then?

Of a sudden, there's a patch of blue in the far-off sky, and I think of something. I think it right out loud. "I can't go back."

Juneau Jane tips her head my way, then climbs up from the wagon bed, settles in beside me, them cool silver coin eyes watching from under that floppy hat.

"I can't go back home, Juneau Jane. If we find news of your papa there in Mason, or if we find **him** even. I can't go back home with you and Missy. Not yet."

"But you must." She strips off her wet hat, lays it on her knee and scratches out her fuzzy hair. The men are far enough away right now, she can do that. Without the hat, a person might not take her for a boy, just lately. She's growed up some on this trip. "For the land. Your farm. It is the matter of greatest importance for you, no?"

"No. It ain't." A sureness settles itself in my soul. I don't know where it'll lead after this, but I know what's true. "Something was begun in me, way back when we stood in that little wildwood church and we looked at them newspaper pages. When we promised things to the roustabouts on the **Katie P.** and when we started **The Book of Lost Friends.** I've got to go on with it, to keep the promises we made."

I'm not sure how I'll do it without Juneau Jane. She's the writer. But I'm learning, and bound to get better. Good enough to scratch down the names and the places and to write letters off to the "Lost Friends" column for folks. "I'll be the keeper of the book after you go home. But I want you to promise me that when you make it back to Goswood Grove you'll help Tati and Jason and John and all the other croppers to get treated fair, just like the contracts say.

Ten years of cropping on the shares, and you gain the land, mule, and outfit for your own. Will you do that for me, Juneau Jane? I know we ain't friends, but would you swear to it?"

She sets her fingers over mine on the reins, her skin pale and smooth against the calluses worn into me by shovels and plows and the crisscross marks from the sharp, dry bracts of the cotton boles. My hands are ugly from work, but I ain't ashamed. I toiled for my scars. "I think we **are** friends, Hannie," she says.

I nod, and my throat thickens. "I wondered about that a time or two."

I chuck up the horses. I've let us fall too far behind.

We start through a draw and toward a long hill and the way is rough, and the horses take my attention. They're tired and wet, lathered under their collars from pulling in the mud. Their tails lash at flies that gather in the windless air. Up ahead, teams struggle with the rise and the slick earth, digging and sliding, digging and sliding. A wagon rolls back like it might come downhill. I turn my team off to the side to move out of the way, in case.

It's then I see that Missy's gotten herself off the wagon, and she's plopped down on her hindquarters, picking yellow flowers with not a worry in the world. I can't even push a shout from my mouth before a sorghum barrel busts its tie rope on the catawampus wagon and rolls downhill, kicking a spray of white rocks and mud and grass and chaff.

Missy looks up and watches it pass not ten foot

from her, but she don't move a inch, just smiles and swirls her hands in the air trying to catch the kicked-up fodder as it shines against the sun.

"Get out of there!" I holler, and Juneau Jane scrambles from the wagon seat. She runs in her too-big shoes, jumping grass moats and rocks, wiry as a baby deer. Swatting the flowers from Missy's hand, she tugs her off the ground and cusses her in French, and they start off afoot, away from the wagons and goods.

It's times like this I give up on thinking Missy is still inside that body, coming back bit by bit, and that she hears things we say, she just don't answer. Times like this, I think she's gone for good—that the poison, or the knock to the head, or whatever evil them men did to her, broke something and it can't be fixed.

Hearing her take that cussing from her daddy's mixed-blood girl, I tell myself, **If Missy Lavinia was anyplace in that big, stout body, she'd haul back and swat her half sister into next Sunday. Just like Old Missus would.**

I don't want to think what Old Missus will do with Missy Lavinia when they get home. Send her off to the asylum to live out her days, I guess. If there ever was any chance of finding her right mind again, it won't happen after that. She's a young woman still. A girl just sixteen. Those'd be long years, in such a place.

The question nips at me all the rest of the way to Menardville, which when we get there, ain't too much more than a few store buildings, a smith shop, a wheelwright, a jail, two saloons, houses, and churches. Juneau Jane and me make plans to leave out for Mason to see about Old Mister. It's just a day's hard horseback ride away, but longer afoot. Penberthy holds our pay and won't let us strike off. Says it's too dangerous walking, and he'll find us a better way to get there.

By morning, we know we won't go to Mason, after all. Folks tell Penberthy that the soldiers took the man who had the stole army horse to Fort McKavett, and there he still is, but he ain't even well enough to hang.

Penberthy fixes us a ride with a mail supply wagon bound on to the fort, just twenty miles south and west from Menardville. Our freight boss parts with us kindly and is good to his promises. He gives my wages and don't even hold out money for my bail in Fort Worth. He tells us to be mindful of what sort of men we get ourselves in with. "There's many a youngster succumbs to the promises of riches and fast living. Set the pay money deep in your pocket." He's hired Gus McKlatchy for another trip, so this is where we part ways.

We have our goodbyes with the crew. The one to Gus is hardest. He's been a friend to me. A real, true friend.

"I'd come on with you," he says before our wagon rolls out. "I'd like to see me a fort. Maybe even sign up and do some scoutin' for the army. But I'm bound to get me a horse and go to where all them wild cattle are just waitin' to be caught. One more trip back to Old Fort Worth, and I'll have enough to be well mounted and start making my fortune, gathering up a herd of my own."

"You watch out for yourself," I say, and he just grins and waves me off and says McKlatchys always land square footed. Our wagon rolls forward, and the load shifts under us. Juneau Jane grabs on to me, and I hang on to the ropes with one hand and to Missy with the other. "Gus McKlatchy, you watch out," I holler as the wagon rattles off, bound for Fort McKavett.

He pats the old sidearm in his belt and gives a grin that's all freckles and horse teeth. Then he cups his hands round his mouth and yells after me, "I hope you find your people, Hannibal Gossett!"

It's the last thing I hear before the town fades from sight and the San Saba River valley swallows us whole.

## Lost Friends

Information wanted of my mother, Martha Jackson, a mulattress who belonged to Judge Lomocks, in Fredericksburg, Virginia, and was sold in the year 1855. When last heard of was in Columbia, Mississippi, and keeping a millinery store. She had three sisters (octoroons, vis: Serena Jackson, born February 13th, 1849, Henrietta Jackson, born September 5th, 1853. Louisa Jackson, aged about 24 years; all were sold with their mother in Virginia. Any information from above named persons will be thankfully received by a bereaved and affectionate daughter. Address, Mrs. Alice Rebecca Lewis (Nee Jackson), 259 Peters Street, bet. Delord and Calliope, New Orleans, La.

—"Lost Friends" column of
the Southwestern
October 5, 1882

# CHAPTER 24

## BENNY SILVA—AUGUSTINE, LOUISIANA, 1987

It's Saturday night, and I'm worried, though I'm determined not to show it. We've been trying to have a dress rehearsal of our **Underground** project all week, but the weather has been working against us. Rain and more rain. Augustine, Louisiana, is like a bath sponge after the tub drains. The rain has finally stopped, but the cemetery is wet, the city park is puddled under, my yard is a swamp, the orchard behind my house is covered in ankle-deep mud. Yet, we have to do something. Our last couple weeks before Halloween weekend—and the **Underground** project—are rapidly ticking away. The school's agriculture department is hosting a Halloween party and haunted house fundraiser in the school's shop barn that same weekend, and they've already put their flyers out. If we want to compete, we have to start advertising.

Before we do that, I need proof that we're actually going to pull off the performance of this project. So far, the kids are all over the map with it. Some are ready. Some are struggling. Some keep changing their minds about whether they want to participate in the performance portion. It doesn't help that many of them get little encouragement or assistance at home and have no money for costumes or materials.

I'm losing hope, wondering if we should shift to doing written reports or presentations in class. Something more manageable. No living history pageant in the graveyard. No advertising. No community involvement. No risk of humiliation or crushing public disappointment for the ones who really have tried hard.

I've commandeered the old football field for our attempt at a dress rehearsal. It's on fairly high ground, and I see townie kids playing games of tag and sandlot ball here fairly often, so I figure it's up for grabs.

In the sunset glow, we've positioned the Bug and a few other rattletrap student cars so we can turn on headlights for illumination. I have no keys to the stadium lights that hang bent and broken above the old concrete bleachers, and they probably don't work anyway. A couple of lopsided streetlamps blink overhead, and that's it. I've spent the last of a small historical society grant to equip the kids with dollar store lanterns that look surprisingly like the real thing. They house cheap little tea candles, but even getting those to stay lit has turned out to be a challenge.

Someone thought a string of Black Cat firecrackers would be a great addition to tonight's fun. Ten levels of chaos broke out when they started popping. Kids ran everywhere, screamed, laughed, tackled one another. The cardboard mock tombstones we've worked on this week have been inadvertently trampled. Some of them were really nice. A few kids even went to the graveyard and made charcoal rubbings of the actual monuments they based their reports on.

Our new lanterns now twinkle cheerfully in the muck, half of them kicked upside down and sideways, victims of the fireworks scramble.

**This is all too far out of the norm for them,** the voice in my head says. **It's more than they can handle.**

**If they can't complete a rehearsal, then any kind of a public performance is a no go.** It's partly my fault. I never anticipated how much the group dynamic would change with all my classes, multiple age groups, and even little brothers and sisters and cousins gathered together to reenact their chosen characters.

"Come **on,** you guys. Let's not screw it up now." I try to sound forceful, but really I'm biting back the sting of discouragement. This is unfair to the ones who really wanted this to work. Including me. "These are **people** we're talking about. They were real living, breathing people. They deserve respect. Grab your tombstone and your lantern, and get with the program. If you have a costume with you and you don't have it on, put it on over your clothes. **Now.**"

My orders gather very little response.

I need help beyond just my few senior adult volunteers, who are largely confined to a sidewalk because the field is muddy and slick, and we don't want anyone to fall. I did ask one of the history teachers/assistant football coaches to dovetail with us for this project, but he waffled, reminded me that it's still football season, and said, "Sounds complicated. Did you get school board approval for this?"

There's been a knot in my stomach ever since. Do teachers go running to the school board every time they want to do a class activity? Principal Pevoto knows about our **Underground** project . . . sort of. I'm just afraid he's not fully processing the scale. He always has a ton on his mind and is moving so fast it's like talking to a buzz saw.

I wish Nathan were here. The kids keep asking about him. After our awkward brush with his uncles and the blondes last week, chatter and speculation is all over town. When Nathan took me home, he mentioned that he'd be tied up the latter part of this week and through the weekend. He didn't give me a reason; he wasn't really in the mood to talk. Eating barbecue while half of the town whispers about you will do that.

I haven't seen him since a week ago Thursday, though I finally broke down and dialed his number a couple times, then hung up before the answering machine could beep. Yesterday I left a message about tonight's rehearsal. I keep glancing around, hoping he'll show. I know it's silly and right now I've got bigger things to worry about.

Like Lil' Ray, sneaking across the practice field—if a 280-pound teenager can sneak—attempting to join the group late without being noticed. LaJuna trails along in his shadow, carrying what I assume to be their cardboard gravestones. She's wearing a ruffly pink prom dress with a hoop skirt petticoat underneath and a white lace shawl. He's wearing slacks and a fancy paisley silk vest that might be someone's long-outdated wedding attire. A gray jacket and top hat are carefully crooked in his arm.

Their costumes aren't bad—Sarge mentioned helping LaJuna with hers—but their tardiness nags at the back of my mind. The two of them jostle and bump up against each other as they blend into the group. I watch her hang on his arm, possessive, pleased with herself. Needy.

I understand where she's coming from. My own memories of those early teen years are real and fresh, even though they're over a decade old. So is my awareness of the potential risks. My mother started making me aware long before I was LaJuna's age. She wasn't shy on topics of sex, teenage pregnancy, the problem of bad choices in relationship partners, of which she'd made quite a few over the years. She was quick to point out that the thing girls in her family did best was get pregnant early, and with loser guys who weren't mature enough to be decent fathers. That was why she'd left her hometown. Even that didn't save her. She still got pregnant with the wrong man . . . and look where that landed her. Stuck working her tail off as a single mother.

The trouble was, it hurt to hear that. It reinforced all my insecurities and the fear that my very existence in this world was an inconvenience, a mistake.

**Maybe you should have a talk with LaJuna.** I shuffle this to my mental in-basket, along with a dozen other things. **And Lil' Ray. Both of them.**

**Are teachers allowed to do that? Maybe discuss it with Sarge, instead.**

But right now we have a rehearsal to accomplish or a graveyard pageant to cancel, one or the other.

**"Listen!"** I yell over the noise. "I **said,** listen! Stop **playing** with the lanterns. Stop talking to each other. Stop hitting each other over the head with tombstones. Put the little kids down and quit tossing them around. Pay **attention.** If you can't, then let's all just head home. There's no point going any further with the **Underground** pageant. We'll just settle for research papers and presentations in class and be done with the whole thing."

The rumble dies down a little, but only a little.

Granny T tells them to hush up, and she means it. She'll report to their mamas about how bad they've been. How they wouldn't listen. "I **know** where to find your people."

It helps a bit, but we're still a zoo. Some kind of wrestling match is breaking out on the left side of the group. I see boys jumping up and doing headlocks and laughing. They stumble and mow over a couple seventh graders.

**You should've known this would happen.** My inner cynic delivers an opportune gut punch. **Unicorns and rainbows, Benny. That's you. Big ideas.** The voice sounds a lot like my mother's—the mocking tone that frequently sharpened the edge during arguments.

"Cut it **out**!" I yell. I notice a car driving along the street at the field's edge. It drifts by, the driver leaning curiously out his window, scrutinizing us. The knot in my stomach works its way upward. I feel like I've swallowed a cantaloupe.

The car on the street turns around and cruises past again. Even more slowly.

Why is he looking at us like that?

A shrill whistle pierces the air behind me and bisects the chaos. I turn to see Sarge striding around the school building. I thought she was tied up babysitting tonight, but I'm insanely glad that reinforcements have finally arrived.

Her second whistle rises above the din and splits eardrums. It achieves an admirable degree of crowd noise reduction. "All right, you oxygen thieves, it's cold out here, and I've got better things to do than **stand around** and watch **you morons** jump on each other. If this is the best you've got, you are a **waste** of time. **My** time. These **ladies'** time. **Ms. Silva's** time. You want to act like losers, then go home. Otherwise, clamp your jawbones to the tops of your mouths, and **do not** release them unless you have raised your hand high and Miss Silva has called on you. And do not raise your hand unless you have something intelligent to say. Is that understood?"

There's complete silence. A pure, unadulterated hush of glorious intimidation.

The kids hover on a razor's edge. Leave? Go do whatever they'd normally be doing on a Saturday night in October? Or knuckle under to authority and cooperate?

"I can't **hear** you," Sarge demands.

This time, they answer in an uneasy, affirmative murmur.

Sarge rolls a look my way, grumbles, "That's why I'm not a teacher. I'd already be grabbing ears and knocking heads together."

I pull myself up like a rock climber after a fall to the bottom of a canyon. "Well, do we quit here, or do we go on? You guys decide."

**If they leave, they leave.**

The reality is that nobody expects much at this school, anyway. Pick any hall, half of the teachers are just coasting by. All that's really required is that the kids are kept from making too much noise, wandering loose, or smoking on campus. It's always been that way.

"We're sorry, Miss Pooh." I don't even know which

boy says it. I don't recognize the voice, but it's one of the younger ones, a seventh grader, maybe.

Others follow once the logjam is broken.

A new direction takes hold. Sarge's oxygen thieves turn away without further instruction, and take up their tea light lanterns, sort out their tombstones, and find their places on the field.

My heart soars. I do my best to hide it and look appropriately stern. Sarge stands at ease and sends a self-satisfied nod my way.

We progress along with the program, not like a well-oiled machine, but we sputter through as I walk around, simulating an audience.

Lil' Ray has crafted two tombstones for himself. He is his five times great-grandfather, born to an enslaved mother at Goswood, eventually becoming a free man, a traveling preacher. "And I learned to read when I was twenty-two and still a slave. I sneaked off in the woods, and I paid a free black girl to teach me. And it was very dangerous for us both, because that was against the law back then. You could get killed and buried, or whipped, or sold off to a slave trader and marched away from all your family. But I wanted to read, and so I did it," he says, and punctuates the sentence with a definitive nod.

He pauses then, and at first I think he's forgotten the rest of his story. But after the barest breaking of character and a slight twitch of a smile that says he knows he has the audience enrapt, he takes a breath and continues. "I became a preacher once black folks could have their own churches. I was the one who built up many of the congregations in this whole area. And I'd ride the circuit to different ones all the time, and that was very dangerous, too, because, even though the patrollers of slavery days were gone away, the Ku Klux Klan and the Knights of the White Camellia were on the roads instead. I had a good horse and a good dog, and they'd warn me if they heard somebody or smelled somebody. I knew all the places to hide and all the people who would hide me, too, if I needed it.

"And I married the girl who had taught me to read. Her name was Seraphina Jackson, and she used to worry to death when I was gone from our cabin in the swamp woods. She'd hear the wolves sniffing and digging around the walls, and she'd sit up all night with a big rifle we had found by a stone fence on a old battlefield. Sometimes, she'd hear gangs of troublemakers go by, too, but they did not menace her or my children. Why? Because the reason she was a free woman before emancipation is, her daddy was the banker."

Lil' Ray alters his posture, puffs his chest, puts on his top hat, and changes tombstones. His lashes droop to half-mast and he eyes us down his nose. "Mr. Tomas R. Jackson. I am a white man and a rich man. I had seven slaves in my big house in town, and years later when it burned down, that's the land where the Black Methodist Church and the library got built. But I also had three children with a free black woman, and so they were free, too, because the status of the child followed that of the mother. I bought a house for them and a sewing shop for her because the law wouldn't let us marry. But I didn't marry anybody else, either. Our sons went to college at Oberlin. Our daughter, Seraphina, got married to a freedman she taught to read and so she became a preacher's wife, and she took care of me when I got old, too. She was a good daughter and she taught lots of people to read until she got too old and couldn't see the letters anymore."

By the time he's finished, I can't help it, I'm in tears. Beside me, Sarge clears her throat. She's got Granny T on one arm and Aunt Dicey on the other, because they insisted on coming out here, and she doesn't want them to take a tumble.

We move to LaJuna next. "I am Seraphina," she says. "My daddy was the banker. . . ."

I eventually deduce that she has abandoned her own research project on family roots, to take on a role from Lil' Ray's family, now that they are a couple and all.

We'll have a talk about that later.

I let her finish, and we move along. A few of the life histories are more complete than others, but there's something magnificent in each one. Even the littlest participants manage to stumble through. Tobias tells, in only a few lines, the story of Willie Tobias, who died along with his siblings so tragically young.

I'm wrung out by the end of the rehearsal, and

stand with the volunteers, unable to process my thoughts into words. I'm amazed. I'm elated. I'm proud. I love these kids in a deeper way than ever before. They are incredible.

They've also attracted a bit of an audience. Cars have pulled in along the road's shoulder, where the armchair quarterback dads usually stop to watch middle school football practices. Some of tonight's observers are undoubtedly parents who've come to give kids a ride home. Others, I'm not so sure of. The sleek SUVs and luxury sedans are too upscale for this school, and the people stand in bemused groups, watching, talking, pointing occasionally. The body language looks ominous, and I think I spot the mayor's wife in her exercise clothes. A police department vehicle drifts around the corner and pulls in. Redd Fontaine swaggers forth, belly first. A few of the bystanders walk over to check in.

"Mmm-hmmm, that's trouble," Granny T says. "Meetin' of the BS—the Busybody Society—going on over there. And mmm-hmm, there goes Mr. **Fon**taine, struttin' down the way to see, can he find anybody with a bad taillight or a license tag out of date and write some citations? Just there to throw his considerable weight around. That's all he's up to."

A rust-mottled truck at the far end pulls out and rattles away before Officer Fontaine can get there. Some poor student's ride home just vacated the area.

"Uh-huh," one of the other New Century ladies murmurs in disgust.

Heat boils under my jacket and spills out my collar. I'm livid. This night is a triumphant one. I refuse to let it be spoiled. I am not putting up with this.

I start across the field, but I'm waylaid by kids asking how I thought things went, and if it was good, and what they should do with their lanterns, and how can they get costume materials if they don't yet have what they need? With our dress rehearsal having gone well, the ones who had been lackluster are psyched up.

"We do okay?" Lil' Ray wants to know. "Are we gonna get to have our **Underground** pageant? Because LaJuna and me got the advertising posters all figured out. Our manager at the Cluck says if we write up something for a flyer, he'll take it over to the Kinko's and get copies made for us when he goes to Baton Rouge to the restaurant supply. Color paper and everything. We're okay to do it, right, Miss Pooh? 'Cause I got these threads from my Uncle Hal, and I am lookin' **fine.**" He shakes LaJuna loose and does a slick 360-degree heel spin so I can get the full effect.

His smile fades when LaJuna is the only one who laughs. "Miss Pooh? You still mad at us?"

I'm not mad. I'm focused on the cars and the bystanders. What is going **on** over there?

"We okay?" LaJuna prods, reattaching herself to Lil' Ray's arm. She looks cute in the prom dress. It's narrow in the waist and low-cut. Too low-cut. And she looks **too** cute in it. Teenage pheromones thicken the air like smoke from a spontaneous combustion about to burst forth in full flame. I've seen the sort of mischief that goes on under the bleachers at the football stadium. I know where this could be headed.

**Don't assume the worst, Benny Silva.**

"Yes, we're okay." But I have a feeling the activity along the road means we might not be. "You guys were incredible. I'm really proud of you . . . most of you, anyway. And the rest, well, you guys help each other out, and let's get this thing in shape."

"Yeah, who's jammin' now?" Lil' Ray says and struts away in his top hat. LaJuna picks up her skirts and trails along behind.

Sarge, passing by with a box of tea light lanterns, leans close to me and whispers, "I don't like the looks of that." She motions toward the street, but before I can answer, her attention veers to LaJuna and Lil' Ray, fading into the night together. "Don't like the looks of that, either." Then she cups a hand to her mouth. "LaJuna Rae, where do you think you're off to with that boy?" She strikes out in hot pursuit.

I watch as the audience fades away, parents leaving with their kids and uninvited bystanders idling down the street in their vehicles one by one. Redd Fontaine hangs around long enough to write some poor parent a ticket. When I try to intervene, he advises me to mind my own business, then asks, "You get permission to have all them kids hanging around here after hours?" He licks the end of his felt-tip pen, then goes back to writing in his ticket book.

"They're not hanging around. They're working on a project."

"School property." All three of his chins wiggle toward the building. "This field's for school activities."

"It's a class project . . . for **school.** And, besides, I see kids playing sandlot ball here all the time after hours and on the weekends."

He stops writing, and both he and the unfortunate driver—one of the grandparents who showed for parent-teacher night—look my way. His eighth-grade granddaughter slinks in the passenger door and melts into the seat while the officer's attention is diverted.

"You tryin' to argue with me?" Officer Fontaine shifts his bulk in my direction.

"I wouldn't dream of it."

"You gettin' smart with me?"

"Absolutely not." **Who does this guy think he is?** "Just making sure all my kids get to where they're supposed to be."

"Why don't you make sure you clean up that field?" Fontaine grumbles, then goes back to his work. "And put out them candles before you set a grass fire and burn down the whole place."

"I think, with all the rain, we're pretty safe," I bite out and give the grandparent an apologetic look. I've probably just made things worse for him. "But thanks for the warning. We'll be **extra** careful."

Sarge is waiting for me when I return to the

sidewalk by the school building. LaJuna and Lil' Ray frown in tandem nearby. "Well?" Sarge asks.

"I'm not sure," I admit. "Really, I have no idea."

"Doubt we've heard the last of it. Let me know if you need me." Sarge nabs LaJuna to take her home. That's one less thing to worry about, at least. Lil' Ray wanders off into the night in his top hat, solo.

At home the house is too quiet. The windows seem dark and eerie for the first time ever. As I walk up to the porch, I reach through the oleander and touch the saint's head, give it an extra rub for luck. "You'd better go to work, pal," I tell him.

The phone is sounding off when I come in the door. It stops on the fourth ring, right as I grab the receiver from the cradle.

"Hello?" I say. No one's there.

I dial Nathan's number before I can rethink it. Maybe that was him. I hope that was him. But he doesn't answer. I blurt out an abbreviated version of the evening's story, the thrill of victory, the agony of Redd Fontaine, then I finish with, "Well . . . anyway . . . I was hoping to catch you. I just . . . really wanted to talk."

Wandering through the house, I turn on all the lights, then stand on the back porch, watching fireflies and listening as a pair of whip-poor-wills call to one another across the distance.

Headlight beams strafe the backyard. I lean over in time to see the city police car circle the cemetery, then pull back onto the highway. An uneasy, off-centered feeling simmers inside me, as if I'm coming down with something but it just hasn't hit yet. I'm wondering how bad it will get before it's over.

Resting my head against a dry, crackled porch post that's seen better days, I look at the orchard and the star-spattered sky blanketing the trees. I ponder how we can put a man on the moon, fly shuttles back and forth to outer space, send probes to Mars, and yet we can't traverse the boundaries in the human heart, fix what's wrong.

**How can things still be this way?**

**That's the reason for** Tales from the Underground, **I tell myself. Stories change people. History, real history, helps people understand each other, see each other from the inside out.**

I spend the remainder of the weekend watching an increasing number of cemetery visits, not just by the police. Apparently, ordinary citizens feel the need to stop by and make sure the local youth, or I, have not disturbed the place. Redd Fontaine wanders through in his cruiser from time to time as well. And more hang-up calls ring my phone, until finally I quit answering and start letting the machine get it. At bedtime I turn off the ringer, but I lie awake on the sofa, watching for light to skim through the blinds, and tracking the fact that the calls and Fontaine's graveyard drive-bys never happen at the same time. Surely a grown man, a police officer, couldn't be that juvenile.

By Sunday afternoon, my nerves are shot, and

I'm pretty sure that if my brain drums up one more gloomy scenario, I'm going to walk out into the rice field and throw myself to the alligator. Even though I've told myself I won't and shouldn't, I pick up the phone to call Nathan's number once more. Then I put it back down.

I think about going over to Sarge's house to talk to her and Aunt Dicey, and maybe Granny T as well, but I don't want to alarm anyone. Maybe I'm overreacting. Maybe the cop is just trying to make a point because I picked a fight with him. Maybe the uptick in graveyard visits this weekend is mere coincidence, or maybe the kids' interest has sparked others' curiosity.

In desperation, I wander the grounds at Goswood Grove, searching for unicorns and rainbows . . . and, perhaps, Nathan, whom I do not find, of course. I watch for LaJuna, as well. She doesn't show up. She is probably focused on her new romantic relationship. Hopefully she and Lil' Ray are off somewhere rehearsing their performance for the **Underground** pageant.

Hopefully, there will **be** an **Underground** pageant.

**There will be,** I tell myself. **There will. We're doing this. Positive thoughts.**

Unfortunately, despite all my efforts at staying upbeat, Monday is a unicorn killer. By ten A.M., I'm in the principal's office. The summons showed up in my second-hour class, and so now this is how I get to spend my conference period, receiving a grilling about my activities with the kids and a dressing-down from Principal Pevoto, with the aid and supervision of two school board members. They're positioned in the corner of the office like storm troopers on a raid. One of them is the blonde from the next booth at the Cluck and Oink. Nathan's aunt-in-law, the second or third trophy wife of Manford Gossett.

She doesn't even have a kid in this school. Hers are—no surprise—enrolled out at the lake.

The only thing more annoying than her condescending demeanor is her high-pitched voice. "What in the **world** such a thing has to do with the district-approved curriculum, which the district pays **good** money to have developed by an experienced curriculum specialist, I can't even begin to see." Her southern accent makes the words sound tactful and sugary sweet, but they're not. "Our prescribed curriculum is something for which an **inexperienced** first-year teacher, like yourself, should be grateful. You would do well to follow it to the letter."

I'm also realizing why she looked vaguely familiar to me in the Cluck and Oink. She was the one who passed right by me on the first day of school, when the pipe truck took the front bumper off my Bug. She looked straight at me, our gazes locked in shock and horror at what had almost happened. You don't forget a moment like that. And then she drove on like she hadn't seen a thing. The reason? That was a Gossett Industries truck. At the time, I didn't know what that meant, but I do now. It means people can come within inches of mowing you over, and nobody sees a thing, nobody says a thing. Nobody dares.

Sitting here now, I'm clutching the seat of a poorly padded office chair, so hard my fingernails are bending backward. I want to jump up and say, **Your truck almost ran me down in the street and nearly hit a six-year-old kid, and it didn't stop, and you didn't stop. Now, all of a sudden, you care about this school? These kids?**

**I can't even get the classroom materials I need. I have to schlep cookies to school, so my kids won't sit there hungry while they're trying to learn.**

**But you just keep wagging your pricey manicure and that horse-choking diamond bracelet at me. That helps make it all seem so much more right.** I grit my teeth against the words. They're right there behind the barricade. Right, right, right . . .

There.

Principal Pevoto knows it. He looks at me, shakes his head almost imperceptibly. It's not his fault. He's trying to save jobs here. Mine and his. "Miss Silva is inexperienced," he offers in the sort of soothing tone a nanny would use to placate a spoiled brat. "She didn't have any way of **really** understanding the sort of approvals that might be needed before taking on a project of this . . ." He glances apologetically at me. He's on my side . . . except that he can't be. He's not allowed. "Scale. In her defense, she did mention it to me. I should have asked further questions."

I cling to the chair, but it's about to become an ejection seat. I can't take anymore. I can't.

**What do you care, lady? Your kids are too good for this school.**

In my mind, I'm standing in the middle of the office, screaming those words with righteous indignation. **Most** of the board members don't have kids here. They're business owners, lawyers, doctors in town. They serve on the board for prestige and for control. They want to regulate things like the district's dividing lines and requests for property tax hikes and bond issues and student transfers to the district's flagship school on the lake—things that might cost them money, because they own property and most of the businesses here.

"We **do** provide every new teacher with a copy of the employee manual, which contains all the school policies and procedures." The lovely Mrs. Gossett, who has not deemed me worthy of permission to use a first name, pops a shiny silver alligator-skin pump off her heel, lets it dangle on her toe as she twitches her foot. "The new employees sign the paper saying they've read it, don't they? It goes in their file, doesn't it?"

Her little lickspittle, a trim brunette, nods along.

"Of course," Principal Pevoto answers.

"Well, it's very plain in the manual that **any** off-campus activity involving a student group or club requires board approval."

"To walk two blocks to the city library?" I spit out.

Principal Pevoto delivers an eye flash my way. I am not to speak unless spoken to. I've been warned already.

The blonde swivels her pointed chin with robotic precision, click, click, click. I am now directly in her crosshairs. "To promise these children that they will be holding some sort of . . . pageant . . . **off** campus, **after** school hours, most certainly **is** flouting the rules. And flagrantly, I must say. And in the city graveyard, of all places. Good gracious. **Really!** It's not only ridiculous, it's obscene and disrespectful to the dearly departed."

I'm losing it. Mayday. Mayday. "I've asked the cemetery's residents. They don't mind."

Principal Pevoto draws a sharp breath.

Mrs. Gossett purses her lips. Her nostrils flare. She looks like a skinny Miss Piggy. "I wasn't **teasing;** did you think I was? Though I am trying my very best to be nice about this. While that cemetery may not mean **anything** to **you,** being from . . . well, wherever you are from . . . it surely does matter to this community. For historic reasons, of course, but also because our family relations are laid there. Of **course** we don't want them disturbed, their graves desecrated to . . . to entertain young miscreants. It's hard enough to keep **these kinds** of kids from committing mischief out there, much less encouraging them to think of our cemetery as a playground. It's careless and insensitive."

"I was hardly—"

She doesn't even let me finish before she stabs a

pointy little finger toward the window. "Some years ago, several expensive grave markers were tipped over in that cemetery. Vandalized."

My eyes go so indignantly wide, they feel like they're about to pop out of my head. "Maybe if people understood the history, knew about the lives those stones represent, things like that wouldn't happen. Maybe they'd even be **preventing** things like that from happening. Some of my kids have ancestors buried there. Most of them do—"

"They are not **your** kids."

Principal Pevoto hooks a finger in his collar, tugs at his tie. He is as red as the volunteer fire truck he mans on weekends. "Miss Silva . . ."

I blaze forward. I can't stop myself now that I've started. I feel everything, all our plans slipping away. I can't let it happen. "Or they have ancestors buried next door. Under graves that were left unmarked. In a graveyard that my students are painstakingly working to enter into the computer, so the library can have records of those who lived their lives on that land. As **slaves.**"

That does it. I have tripped her trigger now. This is the real issue. Goswood Grove. The house. Its contents. The parts of its history that are hard. That are embarrassing. That carry a stigma no one quite knows how to talk about, and tell of an inconvenient heritage that still plays out in Augustine today.

"That is none of your business!" she snorts. "How dare you!"

The sidekick shoots from her chair and stands with her fists balled as if she's going to take me down.

Principal Pevoto rises, leans halfway across his desk with his fingers braced like spider legs. "All right. That is enough."

"Yes, it **is,**" Mrs. Gossett agrees. "I don't know **who** you think you are. You have lived here for . . . what . . . two months? Three? If the students at this school are ever to rise above their upbringing, become productive members of society, they must do it by leaving the past behind. By being practical. By gaining vocational training in some sort of work they are capable of. Most of them are lucky if they can achieve the functional literacy skills needed to fill out a job application. And how dare you insinuate that our family is uncaring in this regard! **We** pay more taxes to this school district than anyone. **We** are the ones who employ these people, who make life in this town possible. Who work with the prisons to give them jobs when they're released. You were hired to teach **English.** According to the **curriculum.** There will be no graveyard program. Mark my words. That graveyard is run by a board, and they will in no way allow this. I will make certain of that."

She pushes past me, the foot soldier following in her wake. At the door, she pauses to fire off one more volley. "Do your **job,** Miss Silva. And mind **who** you're talking to here, or you'll be lucky if you still have a job to worry over."

Principal Pevoto follows with a quick calm-down

lecture, telling me everyone stumbles in their first year of teaching. He appreciates my passion, and he can see that I'm building a rapport with the kids. "That'll pay off," he promises wearily. "If they like you, they'll work for you. Just, in the future, stick to the curriculum. Go home, Miss Silva. Take a few days off and come back with your head clear. I've called in a sub for your classes."

I mumble something, the bell rings in the hall, and I wander from the office. Halfway back to my classroom, I stop and stand, shell-shocked. I realize I'm not **supposed** to go back to my classroom. I'm being sent home in the middle of the school day.

Kids flow past, parting around me in a strange, raucous tide, but I feel as if they're far away, as if they don't even touch me, as if I've disappeared from the world.

The halls have cleared and the tardy bell sounds before I come to myself and continue toward my classroom. Outside the door, I gather my wits before slipping in to grab my things.

There's an aide watching my kids, I guess until the sub can arrive. Even so, they fire off questions. **Where am I going? What's wrong with me? Who will take them over to the library?**

**We'll see you tomorrow. Right? Right, Miss Pooh?**

The aide gives me a sympathetic look and finally starts yelling at them to shut up. I slip away and arrive home and don't even remember how I got there. The house looks forlorn and empty, and when I open the car door, I hear the phone ring four times, then stop.

I want to run inside, rip it from the cradle, choke it with both hands, and scream into it, "What is wrong with you? Leave me alone!"

The message light is blinking on the answering machine. I touch the button like it's the sharp end of a knife. Maybe this thing is escalating and now . . . whoever . . . is issuing anonymous threats on tape. Why would they bother when they can do their work right out in the open via the school board and Principal Pevoto?

But when the message starts, it's Nathan. His voice is somber. He apologizes for the delay in getting the messages I left on his machine—he's at his mother's in Asheville. The last few days have been both his sister's birthday and the anniversary of her death. Robin would've been thirty-three this year. It's a tough time for his mom; she ended up in the hospital with blood pressure problems, but everything's all right now. She's back home, and a friend has come to spend some time with her.

I dial the phone number and he answers. "Nathan, I'm sorry. I'm so sorry. I had no idea," I blurt out. I don't want to heap an additional worry on his shoulders. My job catastrophe and the school board hatchet job seem less consequential when I think of Nathan and his mother, mourning the loss of Robin. The last thing he needs right now is a Gossett fight.

I'll muster other forces. Sarge, the New Century ladies, the parents of my kids. I'll call the newspaper, start a picket line. What's happening is wrong.

"You okay?" he asks tentatively. "Tell me what's going on."

Tears grip my throat, tighten it like a vise. I'm frustrated. I'm sad. I swallow hard, pummel my forehead with the palm of my hand, thinking, **Stop.** "I'm fine."

"Benny . . ." An undercurrent says, **Come on. I know you.**

It breaks me open and I pour out the story, then end with the morning's heartbreaking conclusion, "They want to shut down the **Underground** project. If I don't cooperate, I'm out of a job."

"Listen," he says, and I hear thumping noises in the background, like he's in the middle of something. "I'm heading to the airport to try catching a standby flight. I've got to run, but Mom told me Robin was working on some kind of project before she passed away. She didn't want my uncles there to find out about it. Don't do anything until I get back."

# CHAPTER 25

## HANNIE GOSSETT—FORT MCKAVETT, TEXAS, 1875

It's hard to know the man sunk down in the mattress as being Mister William Gossett. Plain white sheets rumple round his body, sweated down and wrinkled in tight bunches where his hands been grabbing on and trying to wring out his pain like dirty wash water. His eyes, once blue as my grandmama's glass beads, are closed and sunk down in sallow pits of skin. The man I remember bears no resembling to this one in the bed. Even the big voice that'd call out our names, now it just moans and moans.

The memories come back on me when the soldiers leave us with him in the long hospital building at Fort McKavett. Back before the freedom, there was always a big Christmastime party where Marse had gifts wrapped for each one of us—new shoes made there on the place and two new sack dresses for work, two new shimmies, six yards of fabric per child, eight for women and men, and a white cotton dress with a ribbon sash so's the Gossett slaves would look finer than all the others, going off to the white people's church. That party, all us together, every one of my brothers and sisters, and mama and Aunt Jenny Angel and my cousins, and Grandmama and Grandpapa. Tables of ham and apples and Irish potatoes and real wheat bread, peppermint candy for the children, and corn liquor for the grown folk. Those were better times in a bad time.

That man in the bed loved the parties. It pleasured him to believe that we were happy, that all us stayed with him because we wanted to, not because we had to, that we didn't want to be free. I imagine that's what he told hisself to make it right.

I stand back from the bed now and remember all that, and I don't know what way to feel. I want to think, **This ain't none of your affairs, Hannie. Only thing you need from this man is to know, where's the cropper contract that'll make sure Tati and Jason and John get treated fair? He's took up enough of your life, him and old Missus.**

But that wall won't stay built up in me. It's set on sand, and it shifts with his every ragged breath, trembles along with his thin, blue-white body. I can't work up the tabby I need to mortar it solid. Dying is a hard thing to get done, sometimes. This man is having a tough time with it. The leg wound from back in Mason festered while he sat in the jail. The doctor here took off the leg, but the poison's gone into his blood.

What I feel, I guess, is mercy. Mercy like I'd want for myself if it was me in that bed.

Juneau Jane touches him first. "Papa, Papa." She falls to his side and takes his hand, and presses her face to it. Her skinny shoulders quake. After coming all this way and keeping brave, this is the thing that breaks her.

Missy Lavinia's got hold of my arm with both hands. Tight. She don't move one inch closer to him. I pat her the way I would've when she was tiny. "Now, you go on. He ain't gonna bite you. Got blood poison from the bullet, that's all. It ain't nothing you can catch from him. You sit here on this stool. Hold his hand and don't start that squeaking noise you did on the freight wagon, or fuss, or cry, or make any commotion. You be kind and give him comfort and peace. See if he'll wake up a little to talk."

She ain't willing, though. "Come on, now," I tell her. "That doctor said he won't wake up much anymore, if he does at all." I put her down on the stool and lean over crooked because she's weighing on my arm, digging her fingers into it.

"Sit up, now." I pull her hat off and set it on the little cabinet shelf over the bed. Every plank-wood bunk in the room, maybe a dozen on each wall, looks same as this one, but the rest have mattresses rolled up. A sparrow flits round the rafters like a soul trapped inside flesh and bone.

I smooth down Missy's thin, wispy hair, pull it behind her head. Wish her daddy didn't have to see her this way, if he does wake, that is. The doctor's wife was scandaled by the sight of us when we said these were the man's daughters who'd come to find him. She's a kindly woman and wanted Missy Lavinia and Juneau Jane to wash up and borrow proper clothes to wear, but Juneau Jane wouldn't go anyplace except to the bedside. I guess we'll be in boys' clothes awhile longer.

"Papa," Juneau Jane cries, shaking head to toe and praying in French. She signs the cross on her chest, over and over again. **"Aide-nous, Dieu. Aide-nous, Dieu . . ."**

He tosses and blinks and thrashes on the pillow, moans and moves his lips, then quiets and pulls long breaths, drifts farther away from us.

"Don't expect overmuch," the doctor warns again from his desk by the fireplace at one end of the room.

The wagon driver told us the tale on the ride upriver. He takes the route regular, to the fort and to Scabtown that's across water from the fort. Old Mister was brought here from the jail in Mason to plead his case and tell the post commander what he knew about the man who sold him the horse that was the army's, but he didn't make it that far. Somebody bushwhacked them on the way, shot one soldier before they could get to some cover to fight it out. The soldier died right off, and Old Mister was nicked in the head. He was in pretty poor shape by the time he got carried on into the fort. The post doctor worked on Old Mister in the hopes to revive him and learn if he knew who had set on them and why. They supposed it might be somebody Mister knew and maybe even the horse thief who'd sold the stole army horses. They wanted to catch him pretty bad. Even more if he'd killed a soldier.

I can tell them about the Irishman, but what will it help? He was already in the army's hands in Fort Worth town, so he ain't the one who done the bushwhacking. If Old Mister knows the man to blame for it, he won't tell. The only person Mr. William Gossett might know down here is the one he come all this way seeking. A son who don't want to be found.

I hold my peace about it, keep quiet all day and the next day and the next, though I'd like to tell them of Lyle, and how Old Mister sent him from Louisiana two years back, a boy only sixteen, running from a charge of murder. And how Lyle had care of the land in Texas, the land that was meant for Juneau Jane's inheritance someday, and Lyle sold it when it didn't belong to him. A boy who'd do that might shoot his own papa.

I don't tell a soul. I'm afraid it won't go good for us here if I do. I keep my secrets while our days pass at the fort, Old Mister trapped twixt living or dying.

The doctor's wife looks after us and gets us into proper clothes, collected up from the other wives at the fort. We look after Old Mister and each other.

Juneau Jane and me spend time with **The Book of Lost Friends.** Regiments of colored cavalrymen live here at the fort. Buffalo soldiers, they're called. They're men that hail from far and wide, and men who travel far and wide, too. Way out into the wild lands. We ask after the names in our book, and we listen to the soldiers' stories, and we write the names of their people in the book and where they were carried away from.

"Stay clear of Scabtown," they tell us. "It's too rough a place for ladies."

Feels strange to be womenfolk again, after all this time as boys. It's harder, in a way, but I wouldn't go out from the fort or to that town anyhow. A knowing's been brewing in me again. I feel something coming, but I can't say what.

It's a bad thing, though.

The knowing keeps me close to soldiers and never out farther than the hospital building, which sits away from the others so's not to spread sickness if there is some. I watch the officers' wives move round, and their children play. I watch the soldiers drill, form up their companies, play bugles, and leave to the West in long lines, side by side on their tall bay horses.

I wait for Old Mister to breathe his last.

And I watch the horizons.

We're two weeks at the fort on the day I look out from the room the doctor's wife has us three girls sleeping in, and I see one man alone, riding in off the prairie at the break of day, no more than a shadow in the bare light. The doctor has said Old Mister's body won't last through today, tomorrow at longest, so I think maybe that rider is the death angel, finally come to bring us peace from this trial. Old Mister's been troubling my dreams. A restless spirit that won't leave me be. He wants to tell something before he goes. He's holding a secret, but his time's run out.

I hope he can let go of it and won't haunt me after he's departed his earthly shell. That thought troubles my mind as I study the death angel on his horse gliding through the early fog. I'm up and dressed in a blue calico like the one we bought for Juneau Jane back in Jefferson. The hem hangs a little short on me, but it ain't unseemly. I don't need to pad out the bodice like we did with Juneau Jane.

I'm pulled from the window when Missy wakes and goes to gagging and holding her mouth. I'm almost too slow with the washbasin to stop her from messing the floor.

Juneau Jane staggers out of bed and dips a cloth in the pitcher and hands it to me after. Her eyes are red and hollowed out. The child's heart is weary from all this waiting. **"Nos devons en parler,"** she says, and nods at Missy. **We need to talk about it.**

"Not today," I tell her, because I understand enough

of her Frenchy talk, now. We use it round the fort when we don't want others to know what we say. This place is crowded with folks who wonder at the secrets we might hold. "We ain't talking about Missy today. Be time enough for it tomorrow. Her trouble ain't going nowhere."

**"Elle est enceinte."** No need for Juneau Jane to explain that last big word to me. We both know Missy is carrying. Her monthly hasn't come in all this time we been traveling. She's sick most mornings, and so tender in the breasts, no way she'd let me bind her up, even if we were still wearing boys' clothes. She fusses and squirms just over a corset tied loose, which she's got to have to be decent here.

Juneau Jane and me have left it unsaid till now, ignoring it separate and hoping that'd make it not true. I don't want to think about how it happened, or who the baby's father might be. One thing's certain, it won't be long before the doctor or his wife figures us out. We can't stay here much longer.

"Today is for your papa," I say to Juneau Jane. The words catch in my throat, hang there with little hooks like sandburs from a dry field. "You fix yourself up real pretty now. You want that I help you with your hair? It's growed out a little."

She nods and swallows hard, sits down on the edge of the little bed where she slept. There's two iron steads and ticking mattresses. I take a pallet on the floor. That's the only way folks let two white women and a colored girl stay in the same room—if the colored girl sleeps like the slaves did, at the foot of the bed.

Juneau Jane sits stiff, her shoulders poking from her cotton shift. Tight cords of muscle run under her skin. Her chin puckers, and she bites her lips together.

"It's all right to cry," I tell her.

"My mother did not approve of such things," she says.

"Well, I think I don't approve of **her** much." Over time, I've gathered a low opinion of this girl's mama. My mama might've been stole away from me young, but while she could, she spoke all good things into me. Things that lasted. It's the words a mama says that last the longest of all. "And anyhow, she ain't here, is she?"

**"Non."**

"You ever going back to see her?"

Juneau Jane shrugs. "I cannot say. She is all I have left."

My heart squeezes up. I don't want her to go back. Not to a woman who'd sell off a daughter into the hands of any man offering a money settlement to have her for a mistress. "You've got **me,** Juneau Jane. We're kin. Did you know that? My mama and your papa had the same daddy, so they were part brother and sister, though nobody talks of such. When my mama was just a tiny baby, my grandmama had to leave her and go to the Grand House to be wet nurse to the new white baby. That man laying there in the hospital now? He's half uncle to me. You ain't alone in this world after your daddy's gone. I want you to know that today." I go on and tell her more about Old Mister and my mama being born only months apart, half brother and sister. "You and me, we're cousins some way."

I hand her the mirror to hold, and when she looks at the two of us in it, she smiles, then rests her cheek against my arm. Tears fill soft gray eyes that turn upward at the edges like mine.

"We'll be all right," I say, but don't know how. We're two lost souls, her and me, wandering the world far from home. And where is home now, anyway?

I go to work on Juneau Jane's hair and turn back to look out the window again. The sun has crested the ridge, driving the fog off the hillside. The shadow man has turned to flesh and blood. Not the death angel, but somebody I know.

I lean over to see him better, watch as he pulls off his gloves, tucks them in his belt, and talks to two men down in the yard below. That's Moses. I've learned some things of him since we been at the fort awhile. Heard tales. Men will talk when it's a colored girl nearby, not a white woman. They think a colored girl can't hear. Can't understand. Knows nothin'. The doctor's wife is one to talk, too. She gathers with the women of the fort for coffee and tea in the hot afternoons, and they chatter of all their husbands said over suppers and breakfasts.

Moses ain't what I thought that first time I saw

him at the riverboat landing back in Louisiana. Not a bad man, nor a lawbreaker, nor a servant to the man with the patch on his eye, the Lieutenant.

His name ain't even Moses. It's Elam. Elam Salter.

He is a deputy U.S. marshal.

A colored man, a deputy U.S. marshal! I can hardly imagine, but it's true. The soldiers here tell tales of him. He speaks a half dozen Indian tongues, was a runaway from a plantation in Arkansas before the war and went to the Indian Territory. He lived with the Indians and learned all their ways. He knows the wild country, inch by inch.

He wasn't among them bad men to help in their wicked deeds, but to hunt the leaders of that group we've been hearing about, the Marston Men. Elam Salter has tracked them 'cross three states and all through Indian Territory. The wagon driver on the freight trip told it true. Their group's stirred evil talk and got folks rabid mad.

**Their leader, this Marston, will stop at nothing,** the doctor's wife told her ladies. **Surrounds himself with murderers and thieves. His followers would go with him straight off a cliff and never look twice, that's what I heard.**

**Elam Salter will chase them from heaven's gate to the devil's parlor,** a buffalo soldier said of him. **Up through the Indian Territory where the Kiowas and Comanches pitch their camps, down into Mexico where the federales would kill any U.S.**

**lawman they could, and out west of here where the Apaches roam.**

Elam Salter keeps his hair shaved off so he's not worth scalping. Takes that razor to his head every week unfailing, they say.

Men gather to him now, buffalo soldiers and white soldiers greeting the deputy marshal as a friend. Looking on from the window, I think of those moments in that alley, his body pressing me to the wall, my heart pounding against his. **Go,** he said and turned me loose.

That might've been my dying day, otherwise. Or might be I would've found myself chained in the hold of a ship bound for British Honduras with the arston Men, a slave again, my freedom gone. The fort women say they steal people—colored folk, white women, and girls.

I want to thank Elam Salter for saving us. But everything about him pulls me in and scares me at the same time. The idea of him is a flame I stretch my fingers toward, then draw back. Even through the glass, I can feel his power.

There's a knock at the door. The doctor's wife has come with word that we oughtn't dally overmuch in getting down to the hospital. The doctor says Old Mister's time is close.

"We'd best get on," I say and finish Juneau Jane's hair. "Your daddy needs us to tell him it's all right to leave. Say the death psalm over his body. You know it?"

Juneau Jane nods and stands up and straightens her dress.

"Hmmm-hmmmm . . . hmmm-hmmm, hmmm-hmmm," Missy Lavinia carries on, rocking in the corner. I let her keep at it while we get her dressed and ready to go out the door.

"Now, it's time you stop that noise," I say finally. "Your daddy don't need more worries to carry when he goes from this world. No matter what complaints you got with the man, he is still your daddy. Hush up now."

Missy stops her song, and we go to Old Mister's bedside, quiet and respectable. Juneau Jane holds his hand and kneels on the hard floor. Young Missy sits quiet on the stool. The doctor has muslin curtains hung from the rafters and drawn round the bed, so it's only the four of us in that strange, colorless piece of the world. White stones in white lime plaster, white rafters, white sheet against blue-purple arms that lay limp and thin. A face pale as the linens.

Breath sifts in and out of him.

An hour. Then two.

We say the 23rd Psalm, Juneau and me. We tell him it's all right to go.

But he lingers.

I know why. It's the secret that's still inside him. The thing that brings him to haunt my dreams, but that he never speaks. He can't turn loose of it.

Missy starts fidgeting, and it's plain enough, she needs the privy. "We'll come back," I say, and touch

Juneau Jane's shoulder as I take Missy out. Before I close the curtain, I see her lay forward and rest her cheek on her papa's chest. She starts singing a soft hymn to him in French.

A soldier sitting up in a bed at the other end of the room closes his eyes and listens.

I take Missy to do her necessary, which is more work now with her in a proper dress. The day is hot, and by the time we're done, I've worked to a sweat. From a distant, I stand and look at the hospital, and the sun and the hot wind washes over me. I am dry and weary in spirit and body. Dry as that wind and filled with dust.

"Have mercy," I whisper, and move Missy to a rough bench aside a building with a wide porch. I settle in the shade and sit by her, rest my head back and close my eyes, finger Grandmama's beads. The wind fans the live oaks overhead and the cottonwoods in the valley. The river birds sing their songs not far off.

Missy takes up the sound of a wagon axle but just real quiet now, "hmmm-hmmm. . . ."

The tune gets farther and farther off, like she's floating away downwater, or I am. **You better look over and check on her,** I think.

But I don't open my eyes. I'm tired, that's all. Bone tired of traveling, and sleeping on floors, and trying to know what's right to do. My hand falls away from Grandmama's beads, rests in my lap. The air smells of caliche soil, and yucca plants with their strange tall stalks bloomed up in white flowers, and prickly pear cactus with sweet pink fruits, and sagebrush and feathered grasses, stretched out to the far horizon. I float off on it. Float off on it like the big water Grandmama used to tell of. I go all the way to Africa where the grass grows red and brown and gold by the acre and all the blue beads are back together on a string, and they hang on the neck of a queen.

**This place is like Africa.** It's the last thought I have. I laugh soft as I sail away over that grass. **Here I am in Africa.**

A touch on my arm startles me awake. I hadn't been there long, I can tell by the sun.

Elam Salter is standing over me. He's got Missy by the elbow. She's carrying a handful of wildflowers, some pulled up by the roots. Dry soil falls down and glitters in the sunlight. One of Missy's fingernails is bleeding.

"I found her wandering," Elam says from under the trimmed mustache that circles his lips like three sides of a picture frame. He's got a pretty mouth. Wide and serious, with a thick, full bottom lip. His eyes in this light are the brown-gold of polished amber.

Even as I notice all that, my heart jumps up pounding, and my mind spins so fast I can't catch a single thought. Every last tired shred of me comes alive at once, and it's like I been woke up by that swamp panther I once thought he was. Don't know whether to run or stand and stare because I'll likely never again be this close to something so beautiful and so frightful.

"Oh . . ." I hear my own words from far off. "I didn't mean her to."

"It isn't the safest place for her, out past the fort," he tells me, and I can see there's more he won't say about the danger. He guides Missy to the bench. I noticed how he sits her down gentle-like and shifts her hand to her lap, so the flowers won't get ruined. He's a good man.

I stand up, straighten my sore neck, and try to take my courage in hand. "I know what you done for us, and—"

"My work." He stops me before I can go on. "I've done my work. Not as well as I would've liked." He nods toward Missy in a way that says he takes blame for the shape she's in now. "I didn't know of this until after the thing was done. The fellow you followed here, William Gossett, had entangled himself in some way with the Marston Men, and it was for that reason they took his daughters. I'd understood that they meant to hold them at the river landing in Louisiana. I'd left a man there to free them after the **Genesee Star** departed upriver, but when he attempted it, they were nowhere to be found."

"What'd they want from him . . . Old Gossett?" I try to imagine the man I knew tied up in such a thing, except I can't.

"Money, property, or if he was already an ally,

perhaps just to ensure his further and complete cooperation. It's by those methods they've fattened the finances for their cause. They often make use of young folk from well-provisioned families. Some are hostages. Some are volunteers. Some begin as one and become the other once they've caught a case of Honduras Fever. There's temptation in the idea of free land in Central America."

I turn my eyes downward. I think of Missy's troubles, of the baby she's carrying. Heat comes into my face. I stare at the cream-colored dust covering his boots. "That was how Missy Lavinia got tangled up with these people? Thinking to serve her own purposes at first, but then it went wrong?" Should I tell him about Missy's brother? Or does he know already, and he's testing me out? I watch him sidewards, see his thumb and finger smooth his mustache, then stay there pinched over his chin, like he's waiting for me to speak, but I don't.

"Quite likely so. The Marston Men devote themselves to the cause in all manner of thought and deed. This idea of returning to old times and cotton kingdoms—of new land to rule as they see fit—gives them something to believe in, a hope that the days of the grand houses and the slave gangs aren't over. Marston demands absolute loyalty. Wife against husband, father against son, brother against brother, the only importance being that they serve Marston, remain devoted to his purpose. The more bounty they hand over, the more willingly they betray their families, their townsfolk, their neighbors, the higher they rise in the ranks and the more land they are promised in their imagined Honduras colony."

His gaze fastens on me to see how I take that in.

A deep, hard shiver goes through my bones. "Mister William Gossett, he wouldn't be party to something like this. Not if he knew what it was. I'm sure of it." But in the back of my mind, I wonder, was there more to Old Mister's trip to Texas than I knew? Is that why all the books with the sharecrop papers are gone? Did he plan to cheat us out of our contracts and sell his lands and go to Honduras, too?

I shake my head. That can't be. He must've been trying to save Lyle, that's all. "He wasn't a bad man, mostly, but blind when it came to his son. Foolish blind. He'd do anything for that boy. He sent Lyle here to Texas to get him away from a difficulty in Louisiana that ended in a dead man. Then Lyle found trouble here some months ago. That's why Old Mister come all this way. Seeking after his son, and that's the **only** reason."

Elam Salter looks through me like I'm thin as a lace curtain.

"I ain't lying," I say and straighten myself.

We face each other, Elam Salter and me. I'm a tall gal, but I have to turn my head up to him like a child. Some snip of lightning crackles between us. I feel its stings all up and down my skin, like he's touching me, right through the air between us.

"I know you are not, Miss Gossett." His saying

my name that gentlemanly way sets me back a bit. Always been just plain Hannie. "Lyle Gossett had a State of Texas bounty on his head for crimes committed in Comanche, Hill, and Marion Counties. He was reported delivered, dead, six weeks ago to Company A, Texas Rangers, in Comanche County, and the bounty paid."

Of a sudden, I am cold down deep, the chill of a bad spirit passing by.

Lyle is dead. His daddy's been chasing a soul that already belonged to the devil.

"I want no part in this. None of it. Only reason I come here . . . **only** reason I did all I did . . . was . . . was because . . ." Any words I say will sound wrong to a man like Elam Salter. A man who ran from his owner and found his way to freedom when he was no more than a boy. A man who's made hisself somebody that even the white men speak of in a revering way.

And here I am, just Hannie. Hannie Gossett, still called by the name I was given by somebody who **owned** me. Hadn't even picked out a new name for myself, because that might vex Old Missus. Just Hannie, still living in a cropper cabin, scratching a piece of ground to make my means. A mule. A ox. Only a beast of the field and hadn't done a thing about it. Can't read but a few words. Can't write. Come all the way to Texas, looking after white folk, same as in the old times.

Been nothing. Am nothing.

What must a man like Elam Salter think of me?

I clench my hands over the rumpled calico. Push my bottom lip into the top one and try to stand square, at least.

"You've done a brave thing, Miss Gossett." His eyes slide toward Missy, singing to herself there on the bench while she picks them wilted wildflowers clean, petal by petal, and watches the colors fall on the parchment-dry ground. "They'd be dead if not for you."

"Maybe it wasn't my trouble to worry over. Maybe I should've let it happen, that's all."

"You're not the sort." His words melt over my skin like sweet butter. Does he truly think that of me? I try to see, but he's got his face turned toward Missy.

**"For whatsoever he soweth, that shall he also reap,"** he says in his deep voice. "Are you a churchgoing woman, Miss Gossett?"

**"Be not deceived. God is not mocked."** I know the verse. Old Missus used that one all the time to let us know, if she punished us, it was our own fault, not hers. God wanted us to get whipped. "I am a churchgoing woman, Mr. Salter. But you can call me Hannie, if it suits. I reckon at this point, we know each other pretty close up." I think of that moment on the boat, when he grabbed me up in the familiarest way to toss me off. Must've been about then he figured I wasn't a boy.

The corner of his mouth twitches up just a hint, and maybe he's thinking of that, too, but he stays watching Missy.

"I ought to take her back inside, I guess," I tell him. "Doctor says it's to be over with her daddy any time."

Elam nods, but stays where he is. "Do you have a notion of where you'll go when it's done?" He's stroking that mustache again, rubbing his chin.

"Not sure." That's the truth. The only thing I know right now is that I **don't** know. "Got some business to see to in Austin City."

I pull Grandmama's blue beads from under the collar of the dress, tell him about Juneau Jane and me and **The Book of Lost Friends.** I finish up with the Irishman's story about the white girl in the café. "Don't imagine it means a thing. Could be she found them beads, or maybe the story ain't even true—I did hear it from a horse-thief Irishman. But I can't leave, not without knowing for sure. I need to see about that, before I go from Texas. Thought earlier on that I'd stay in this country, keep making my way round with the book, look for my own people, spread the names of Lost Friends, take in more names, ask after folks for other folks and for myself." I don't tell him I hadn't been the one to write in the book and can't read but a little of it. Elam is an up-spoken man. Dignified and proud. Don't want him to see me as less than.

I think again about **The Book of Lost Friends,**

about all the names in it and the promises we made. "Might be, I'll come back to Texas in a year or two, go round with the book then. I know the way, now." I look at Missy, feel her like a full-up field sack strapped over my shoulders. Who in the world will look after her? "Even with all she's done, I can't just leave her to wander, such as she is. Can't leave Juneau Jane with the burden, either. She's still a child and has the grief of losing her papa. And I don't want her cheated from her inheritance. We had hopes to find her daddy's papers and prove what was meant to go to her, but the doctor said Old Gossett was brought here to the fort with nothing."

"I'll write the jailhouse in Mason and see what I can learn of his saddle and gear and ask after someone to see you to Austin for the train east. We're close to Marston and his men now, and they know it. They'll do all they can to keep their cause alive, and they'll want no witnesses left behind who might testify against them, if they're caught and tried. The girls could corroborate the identity of the Lieutenant and perhaps others, and for that matter, you could as well. You'll be better off out of Texas."

"We'd be grateful to you." Wind stirs the leaves overhead, and sun speckles turn his skin dark and light, his eyes soft brown, then gold again. I lose all the sounds of the fort. Everything flies away a minute. "You be careful after them men, Elam Salter. You be mighty careful."

"I can't be shot. That's what they say." He smiles a

bit and lays a hand on my arm. That one touch shoots though me and lands deep in my belly, in some place I didn't know was there. I sway a little, blink, see the shadows swirl and spin. I part my mouth to say something, but my tongue stays pinned. I don't even know what to say.

Does he feel it, too, this wind that circles us in the summer heat?

"Don't fear," he whispers, and then he turns and disappears down the alleyway on the long, even strides of a man who's made his place in the world.

**Don't fear,** I think.

But I do.

## Lost Friends

Dear Editor—I wish to inquire for my father's people. My grandfather is Dick Rideout, grandmother Peggy Rideout. They belonged to Sam Shags, of Maryland, 13 miles from Washington City. They had 16 children—Betty, James, Barbary, Tettee, Rachel, Mary, David, Henderson, Sophia, Amelia, Christian, Ann. My father is Henderson Ripeout [sic]. He was sold, ran off, was caught and sold to a negro trader in 1844, who brought him to New Orleans and sold him in Mississippi. I saw Aunt Sophia in 1866 at which time she was living in Claiborne Co., Miss. My address is Columbia, Miss.

DAVID RIDEOUT

—"Lost Friends" column of the Southwestern
November 25, 1880

## CHAPTER 26

BENNY SILVA—AUGUSTINE, LOUISIANA, 1987

I turn in to the driveway at Goswood Grove. The lawn is freshly mown, indicating that Ben Rideout has been here and done his work earlier today. I slow down to pilot the Bug through the left gate, which hangs open most of the way, swaying a little in the breeze. The right one has fallen closed, as if it's not sure it wants me here. The hinges squeal as it quavers undecided.

I should get out and prop it open, but instead I gun the engine and squeeze past. I'm too ginned up to stop, and I can't quite get past the feeling that, before we're able to accomplish what we've come here to do, someone will show up and try to stop us—Nathan's uncles, a delegation of school board members, Principal Pevoto on a mission to bring me back in line, Redd Fontaine in his police car, conducting surveillance. This town is an old dog with a bad temper. We have rubbed its hair the wrong way and stirred up fleas. If allowed to return to its slumber, it might let me stay, but it's made sure I know that if not, it's ready to bite.

The phone calls haven't slowed down. Fontaine has continued his drive-bys. This morning, four men in a Suburban arrived at the cemetery and tromped around, talking and nodding and pointing toward property lines, including those surrounding my house and the orchard out back.

I'm anticipating a bulldozer and an eviction notice to come next . . . except that the property belongs to Nathan, and he told me he wasn't selling. Is it possible that the land deal has already progressed to the point that he can't stop it? I have no way of knowing. He's spent over twenty-four hours fighting flight delays and airport closures due to a tornado outbreak in the middle of the country. He finally rented a car to get home and hasn't found a minute to stop at a pay phone and call me with an update.

I'm relieved when I see his car, a little blue Honda, in the driveway—at least, I assume it's his rental. I drive past it and park my Bug behind the big house where no one can see it from the road. I'm on my third day of involuntary furlough from school. My kids have been told I've got the flu. I know that because Granny T and the New Century ladies, as well as Sarge, have called to check on me. I've been letting the recorder answer the phone, as I don't know what to say. I **am** sick, but just heartsick.

I hope whatever Nathan's newly discovered information is, it has the power to move mountains, because that's what we need—some sort of Hail Mary pass that saves the game in the final seconds. My students deserve a win, to see their hard work and smarts pay off.

"Well, here we are," I tell the Bug and sit there a moment in solidarity. We've both come a long way since leaving the hallowed halls of the university English department. I'm not the same person anymore. Whatever happens next, this place, this experience, has changed me. But I can't support a system that tells students they are nothing, they'll never **be** anything—that views keeping kids in their desks as the major accomplishment for the day. They deserve the same chance friends and mentors gave me, to see that the life you create for yourself can be entirely different from the one you came from. I have to find a way. I'm not a quitter. Quitters don't build great things. Quitters don't win this kind of war. **You're not defeated until you give up the fight,** I tell myself.

Nathan is sound asleep in the driver's seat of the little Honda with the windows rolled down. He's wearing what I have mentally cataloged as the blue, blue outfit—blue jeans with blue chambray shirt.

His hair is disheveled, but in his sleep, he has the look of a man who has made peace with everything. I know that's not the case. It's incredibly hard for him to be here. The last time he was in this house was the last time he saw his sister alive. But we both understand that this visit can't wait.

"Hey," I say and startle him to the point that his elbow hits the steering wheel and the horn beeps. I slap a hand to my neck and look around nervously, but there's no one else to hear.

"Hey." A lopsided smirk offers chagrin as he turns my way. "Sorry about that," he says, and I'm struck by how much I've missed his voice. He opens the door and unfolds himself from the tiny car, and then I realize how much I've missed **him.**

"You made it." It's tough to keep my emotions in check, but I know I need to. "You look tired."

"I took the long way home." And just like that, he reaches out and pulls me into a hug. Not a shoulder hug, but the real thing, the kind you give to someone you thought of while you were away.

I'm surprised at first. I wasn't expecting . . . well . . . **that.** I was prepared for more of the uncertain off-and-on awkward dance we usually do. **Friends . . . or two people who want something more?** We're never quite sure. But this feels different. I slip my arms under his and hang on.

"Tough few days?" I whisper, and he rests his chin on my head. I listen to his heartbeat, feel the sultry warmth of skin against skin. My gaze lingers on the tangle of wisteria vines and crape myrtle branches hiding the ancient structures of Goswood Grove's once spectacular gardens, concealing whatever secrets they know.

"Tough few days all around, it sounds like," Nathan says finally. "We should go in." But he hangs on a minute longer.

We part slowly, and the next step suddenly seems uncharted. I don't know how to catalog it. One moment, we're as natural as breathing. The next, we're at arm's length—or retreating to our separate safety zones.

He stops halfway across the porch, turns, widens his stance a little like he's about to pick up something heavy. Crossing his arms, he tilts his head and looks at me, one eye squeezing almost shut. "What are we to each other?"

I stand there a moment with my mouth agape before words dribble out in a halting string. "In . . . in . . . what way?"

I'm terrified, that's why I don't give a straight answer. Relationships require truth telling, and that requires risk. An old, insecure part of me says, **You're damaged goods, Benny Silva. Someone like Nathan would never understand. He'll never see you in the same way again.**

"Just like it sounds," he says. "I missed you, Benny, and I promised myself I'd just put it out there this time. Because . . . well . . . you're hard to read."

"**I'm** hard to read?" Nathan has been largely a mystery I've pieced together in fragments. **"Me?"**

He doesn't fall for the turnabout, or he ignores it. "So, Benny Silva, are we . . . friends or are we . . ." The sentence shifts in the wind, unfinished—a fill-in-the-blank question. Those are harder than multiple-choice.

"Friends . . ." I search for the right answer, one not too presumptuous, but accurate. "Going somewhere . . . at our own pace? I hope."

I feel naked standing there. Scared. Vulnerable. And potentially unworthy of his investment in me. I can't make the same mistake I've made before. There are things he needs to know. It's only fair, but this isn't the right moment for it, or the right place.

He braces his hands on his hips, lets his head rock forward, exhales a breath he seems to have been holding. "Okay," he says with a note of approval. His cheek twitches, one corner of his mouth rising. I think he might be blushing a little. "I'll take that."

"Me, too," I agree.

"Then we have an accord." Nathan winks at me and turns and proceeds on to the house, satisfied. "We can talk details later."

I float after him, filled with an anticipation that has nothing to do with today's plans. We're entering a brave new world . . . in more ways than one. I've never been in the front door of Goswood Grove House. In fact, I've never been anywhere but the kitchen, the butler's pantry, the dining room, the front parlor, and the library. Not that temptation hasn't tugged during my visits, but I've been determined to remain respectful of the faith Nathan has shown in me. In other words, not to snoop.

The entry is palatial and startling. I've seen it through the windows, but standing on the threadbare Persian carpet, we're dwarfed by massive paneled walls and arched fresco ceilings. Nathan looks upward, his back stiff, hands resting on his waist. "I hardly ever came in this way," he mutters. I'm not sure if he's talking to me or just filling the silent air. "But I gave you the only key I had to the back door."

"Oh."

"The judge didn't, either. Come in this way much." He laughs a little. "Funny, that's one of the things I remember about him. He liked to use the kitchen door. Steal a little food on the way through. Dicey always kept biscuits or bread or something like that around. And cookies in the jar."

I think of the square art deco glass canisters in the kitchen, picture the large one filled with pooperoos.

"Tea cakes." Nathan alters my mental imagery.

Tea cakes do seem more appropriate for this place. Every inch of her speaks of what she was in her youth. Grand, opulent, an extravagant feast for the eyes. She's an old woman now, this house. One whose bone structure still shows how lovely she once was.

I can't imagine living in a place like this. Nathan looks as if he can't, either. He rubs the back of his neck the way he always does when he considers Goswood Grove, as if every brick, beam, corbel, and stone weigh on him.

"I just don't . . . care about this stuff, you know?" he says, as we move to the bottom of double staircases that spiral in opposite directions like twin sisters. "I never felt a connection the way Robin did. The judge would probably turn over in his grave if he knew I was the one who ended up in charge of it."

"I doubt that." I muse on the stories I've heard about Nathan's grandfather. I think he was, in some ways, a man uncomfortable with his position in this town, that he struggled to navigate the inequities here, the nature of things, even the history of this land and this house. It haunted him, yet he wasn't ready to fight the battle in big ways, and so he compensated in little ways, by doing things for the community, for people who'd lost their way, by buying books from charity auctions and sets of encyclopedias from kids working to pay for college or a car. By taking LaJuna under his wing when she came here with her great-aunt.

"I really believe he'd trust your decisions, Nathan. Personally, I think he'd want to finally acknowledge the history of Goswood and the history of this town."

"You, Benny Silva, are a crusader." He cups a hand along the side of my face, smiles at me. "You remind me of Robin . . . and I don't know about the judge, but Robin would have liked your **Underground** project." He chokes on the words, pushes his lips together, swallows hard, and shakes off emotion almost apologetically as he lets his hand drop to the well-worn bannister. "She would've liked you."

I feel as if she's there in the room with us, the sister he loved so much and grieves so deeply. I've always wanted a sister. "I wish I could have met her."

Another intake of breath, and then he shrugs toward the landing above, inviting me to start upward first. "My mother said, whatever Robin had been working on, that she'd been doing a lot of research, compiling papers but keeping them private. Something to do with the house and things she learned from the judge's files and journals. You didn't find documents like that in the library, did you? Robin's or the judge's?"

"Nothing other than what I've already shown you. Nothing recent, for sure." A note of intrigue plays in my head. I'd give anything to have even one conversation with Robin.

One probably wouldn't be enough.

I see a photo of her finally, upstairs in her room. Not a childhood photo, like the faded studio portraits downstairs in the parlor, but a grown-up one. The driftwood frame sits on the delicate, spindle-legged writing desk, offering an image of a smiling woman with pale blond hair. She's slight and narrow-faced. The deep blue-green orbs of her eyes seem to dominate the photo. They're warm, beautiful eyes. Her brother's eyes.

She's standing on a shrimp boat with Nathan, then a teenager, in the background. They're both laughing as she holds up a hopelessly tangled fishing rod. "The boat was our uncle's." Nathan looks over my shoulder. "On my mom's side. She didn't grow up with money, but man oh man, her dad and her uncles knew how to have a good time. We'd hitch on the shrimp boats once in a while, ride along wherever they were going. Drop a line if we could. Maybe get off here or there and stay a day or two. Paps and his brothers knew everybody and were related to half the population around there."

"Sounds like fun." I picture it again—the shrimp boat, Nathan's other life. His ties down on the coast.

"It was. Mom couldn't stand to be back in the swamp for very long, though. Sometimes people have a thing about where they come from and how they were raised. She married a guy fifteen years older and rich, and she always felt like people on both sides faulted her for it—gold digger and that kind of thing. She didn't know what to do with all that, so she moved away from it. Asheville gave her the art scene, sort of a new identity, you know?"

"Yeah, I do." More than I can possibly say. When I left home, I expunged every bit of my past, or I tried to, at least. Augustine has taught me that the past travels with you. It's whether you run from it or learn from it that makes all the difference.

"It's not as hard as I thought it would be . . . coming in here," Nathan says, but the stiff way he carries himself says otherwise. "I have no idea what we're looking for, though. And to tell you the truth, whatever it is, it could be gone. Will and Manford and their wives and kids let themselves in and appropriated most of what they wanted right after Robin died."

Even though Robin has been gone for two years, our search of her room feels uncomfortably invasive. Her personal belongings are still here. We carefully check drawers, shelves, the closet, a box in the corner, an old leather suitcase. All of it looks as if it has been previously rummaged through, then dumped haphazardly back into place.

We come up with nothing of significance. Credit card bills and medications, letters from friends, holiday notes, blank stationery, a journal with a cute little gold hasp on the front. It's unlocked, the key still tucked among the pages, but when Nathan leafs through, all he finds is Robin's reading list, complete with favorite quotations jotted down, mini summaries of each book, and the dates she started and finished. Sometimes she read several books in a week, everything from classics and Westerns to nonfiction and the **Reader's Digest** condensed editions from the boxes downstairs.

"Your sister was a definite bibliophile," I remark, looking over Nathan's shoulder at the book list.

"She got that from the judge," he replies. Tucked inside the diary, there's also a running tally of billiard games played on the old Brunswick table downstairs in the library, sort of an ongoing tournament between grandfather and granddaughter in the last year of the judge's life. "They had a lot in common."

The desk drawer tips forward as Nathan opens it to put papers back in. A cue ball rolls to the front corner, clatters to the floor, then starts moving, seemingly under its own power. Nathan and I watch it weave over the uneven plank floors, this direction, then that, catching the sun and reflecting fairy lights on the wall before finally disappearing under the bed.

My shoulders shimmy involuntarily.

Nathan crosses the room, lifts the dust ruffle, and looks under the bed. "Nothing but a few books." He toe-nudges them into the open.

The desk drawer resists going back into place. I squat down to eyeball the problem and work the slides back onto the tracks. The triangle-shaped rack and the rest of the billiard balls are wedged in the back end, making the drawer travel unevenly. Years rescuing thrift shop antiques have given me a particular skill with old furniture, and so after a bit of finagling, I have things in their proper order again.

When I turn around, Nathan is sitting on the floor by the cherrywood four-poster bed, his back resting against the dust ruffle, his long legs splayed out. He seems to have sort of collapsed there, lost in the pages of a children's book, **Where the Wild Things Are.**

I open my mouth to ask if that was his, but the answer is evident in his faraway expression. I'm not even in the room with him right now. There's a ghost alongside him, instead. He's reading the book with her. They've done the same thing many times before.

I stand and watch, and for an instant I can see her—the woman in the fishing photo. She's turning the pages. Halfway through, they lay flat. Nathan takes out an envelope and a small stack of photographs, lets the book rest in his lap.

I quietly move closer as he lays the photos on the floor, one by one.

Baby pictures. First day of school photographs, vacations. A family ski photo. Nathan's mother is a tall strawberry blonde in pink insulated overalls. She's supermodel gorgeous. Robin is about ten years old, Nathan a bundled-up toddler. Nathan's father, dressed in expensive gear, holds Nathan in the crook of his elbow. He's smiling, his face devoid of the downturned eyebrows and heavy frown lines so evident in his older brothers, Will and Manford. He looks happy. Unstressed.

Nathan opens the envelope next. I read the enclosed note over his shoulder.

**Nathan,**

**I knew you wouldn't be able to resist this book.**

**Mom had these photos rattling around in her art supply bins. You know how unsentimental she is! I thought I'd better grab them and save them for you. This way, you'll at least know what you looked like once. You were such a cute little pudster, if sometimes annoying. You used to blabber out questions until Mom and**

I wanted to tape your mouth shut. When I asked you why you had so many questions, you looked at me in the most honest way and said, "So I'll know everything, like you do."

Well, little brother—surprise—I don't know everything, but I do know you grew up to be a pretty great guy. You were worth all the trouble. You've got a good head on your shoulders. If you're reading this note, I'm probably leaving you with a few questions I didn't get to answer.

There are things I've been working on this last year since Granddad Gossett died. I always had the feeling there was a secret he was keeping, something he wanted to tell but couldn't bring himself to. Just in case I'm gone and someone else looks through the library before you do . . . you know who I mean . . . I want to make sure you get the information. When you see it, you'll know why. If you don't find my papers in the library downstairs, go to the bank. I've been keeping a copy of most of it in a safe deposit box there. I put your name on the box and paid up the rent, long term, so it'll be waiting there for no one else but you.

You're on your own with this one now, Nat. Sorry about that. You'll have to decide what to do about it all. I hate leaving you with the burden, but you'll sort out the right decisions, whatever they are.

**Like the author of this book (which you made me read to you until I thought I'd go nuts if I had to do it one more time) said before he passed away, "I have nothing now but praise for my life. There are so many beautiful things in this world which I will have to leave when I die, but I'm ready, I'm ready, I'm ready."**

**Find the beautiful things, little brother. Every time you mourn for me, I'll be far away. But when you celebrate, I'll be right there with you, dancing.**

**Take care of Mom, too. She's quirky, but you know how we artists can be. We march to our own music.**

**Love you most,**

**Robin**

There's a key taped inside the back cover of the book. Nathan holds it up and looks at it.

"That's so much like her. That's **just** like her." His words are thick with tenderness as he drops an arm over one knee and lets the card dangle. A long time passes while he stares out the window, watching the wispy white clouds that have blown off the gulf farther south. Finally, he wipes his eyes, and with a rueful laugh, chokes out, "She said not to cry."

I sit on the edge of the mattress and wait until he catches his breath and tucks the photos back into the book, then closes it and stands up. "Is there **anyplace** my sister's papers could be in that library?"

"I don't think so. I've canvassed that room pretty thoroughly over these past weeks."

"Then we're paying a visit to the bank."

He stops in the doorway as we leave, gives the room one last look. Air whistles between the door and the frame as he pulls it closed. A faint rumbling follows—the unmistakable sound of the cue ball finding its way across the floor again. It taps the other side of the door, and I jump.

"It's an old house." A floorboard squeaks when Nathan steps back. The cue ball rattles away from the door.

We start down the stairs, and I catch myself looking back over my shoulder, thinking, **Why would Robin put the pool balls in her desk drawer, anyway?** Granted, they're not needed downstairs. The billiard table was covered when I came, and she had it piled with books.

**The billiard table . . .**

# CHAPTER 27

## HANNIE GOSSETT—TEXAS, 1875

I pray that wherever Elam Salter is, he's as hard to kill as they say. As **he** says.

He can't be shot. Not ever.

I gather the soldiers' stories of him, and build a nest the way a barn cat will in the straw on a cold winter night.

> Had the hat shot off his head twice.
>
> Horse shot out from under him three times.
>
> Brung in the outlaw Dange Higgs,
> single-handed.
>
> Tracked that half-breed Ben John Lester
> into Indian Territory and clean up through

> Kansas. Elam Salter can bird-dog a trail like no other.

The stories carry me through watching Old Mister pass from this world, and then the days of grieving and weeping, and seeing that he is laid to rest, and trying to figure how much Missy understands of what's happened. At the burying, she lays herself down on the grave right beside Juneau Jane and makes a whimpering sound. I watch her dig her fingers in the dirt and hang on.

Those are strange, sad days, and the end of them can't come quick enough.

When it's finally over, we set out along the San Saba River Road, me and Missy and Juneau Jane, in a wagon pulled by army mules, with a driver and three soldiers to ride along. They'll bring a shipment of weapons back from Austin after carrying us there, or that's the plan we've been told.

The three on horseback sit their saddles relaxed, laughing and making chatter together, their rifles and sidearms tied down in the scabbards. No sort of worry or care shows in them. They spit plugs of tobacco, and tease, and bet who can spit the farthest.

The wagon driver rides calm and looks round at the land, not seeming to watch out for anybody coming up on us.

Juneau Jane and I trade our worries in glances to each other. The skin under her eyes is puffy and rubbed red raw. She's cried by the hour, so hard I'm wondering if she'll survive through all this. She turns to the back of the wagon over and over again, to catch one last look at the soil where we laid down her papa. He won't rest easy in that grave, so far from Goswood Grove. Juneau Jane wanted to take him home to bury, but it can't be helped. Even to get back ourselves, we're calling on the mercy of strangers. And for Old Mister's burial, too. Once, the man owned over four thousand acres, and now he rests under a plain wood cross with his name scratched on it. Had to guess, even, at the proper year of his birth. Juneau Jane and I ain't sure, and Missy can't say.

A light rain comes, and we draw the wagon curtains, and just sit and let the wheels wobble on, mile after mile. It's later in the day when I hear the men hail somebody, off distant. The hair on my neck raises, and I climb to my knees and lift the canvas. Juneau Jane moves to follow.

"You stay back and keep Missy there," I tell her, and she does. These past weeks made us more than part cousins. I'm her sister now, I think.

The man comes again like a spirit, as much a part of the land as the brown and gold grasses and prickly pear cactus. He's riding a tall red dun horse, and leading another one that's wearing a Mexican saddle with the rawhide seat stained in dry blood.

My heart quickens up, and I throw back the wagon curtains and look Elam Salter over to make sure that blood ain't his. He sees the question in my eyes as he comes alongside the wagon. "I fared some better than the other man."

"Relieves my mind to see it." I smile wide at him and give hardly a thought to the man who fell dead from that other saddle. If Elam did the killing, it was a man who had took up evil ways.

"I'd hoped to catch you before you set off. My work ran longer than expected." Elam leans an elbow on his saddle horn. He's wet and mud spattered. Dry lather lines the horses' breast collars. Elam slacks the reins, and the poor, tired dun sags its head and fills its lungs with a long breath.

"I wanted you to know, we've cut off the head of the snake," he says, and he looks from me to Juneau Jane and back. "Marston, himself, is jailed in Hico, to be tried for his crimes and hanged. I hope that eases the burden of your loss in some way." He looks at Juneau Jane again and then at Missy. "We'll be after the rest of his lieutenants and higher officers now, but many will lose faith in their cause without Marston, and wander to the frontier or to Mexico. Their leader did not go bravely from his command. We dug him from a corn crib, where he was hiding like a trapped rat. Not a single shot was fired to bring him in."

Juneau Jane sniffles and nods, makes the sign of the cross over her chest, and looks down at her hands in her lap. A tear drips from her cheek and draws a small circle on the front of her dress.

Anger burns in me. The unholy kind. "I'm glad of it. Glad he'll be made to pay. Glad you come back in one piece, too."

His thick mustache lifts with a smile. "As I promised you I would, Miss Gossett. As I promised you I would."

"Hannie," I tell him. "Remember I said you could call me by my name?"

"Indeed I do." He tips his hat, then goes on forward to talk to the men.

That smile stays with me through the day and into evening. I watch him ride away from the wagon, then back, then disappear over the hills. Time to time, I spot him on the horizon. I feel safer, knowing he's there.

It's when we're stopped to camp that the uneasy comes over me again. The animals fret at their pickets, toss heads and twitch ears. Juneau Jane takes the halter of a big gelding and strokes its nose. "They have a sense of something," she says.

I think about Indians and panthers and coyotes and the Mexican gray wolves that howl on the prairies at night. I hold Missy's old reticule close, feel the weight of the derringer tucked inside. It's some comfort, but not much.

Elam Salter comes into our camp, and that's more comfort, yet. "Stay between the rocks and the wagon," he tells us, and then talks quiet with the men on the other side of the wagon. I watch their hands and bodies move, pointing, looking.

One of the soldiers hangs a blanket between two cedar trees for our necessary, and another cooks on a small stove at the wagon.

There's none of Elam's friendly talk or smiles that night.

When we bed down, he's disappeared again. Don't know where he goes or if he sleeps. The dark just grabs him up. I don't hear or see him after that.

"What does he search for?" Juneau Jane asks as we settle in a tent with Missy twixt us. I tie Missy's ankle to mine, case she'd take a mind to get up and wander . . . or I would in my dreams.

Missy's asleep quick as she can get flat on the blanket.

"Don't know what he's after." I think I scent smoke on the wind. Just a hair of it, but then I ain't sure. Our cookstove's been out for hours. "Reckon the night'll pass all right, though. We got five men looking out after us. You and me been in tougher spots." I think of the swamp and not knowing if we'd live to morning light. "We ain't alone, at least."

Juneau Jane nods, but the lantern light through the cloth shines on a brim of tears. "I have left Papa. He is alone."

"He's gone on the other side of the door. He ain't in that body no more," I tell her. "You sleep now." I pull the blanket up, but I don't find rest.

Sleep finally comes like a summer dry river, a trickle that's shallow and splits around rocks and downed branches and tree roots, dividing and dividing, till by morning it's the thin bead of gathered morning dew, dripping lazy off the army tent overhead.

On rising, I think I smell smoke again. But there's barely enough fire in the stove for coffee, and the wind scatters it the other direction.

**It's only your mind, Hannie,** I tell myself, but I make sure we all three get up together and go behind the blanket to see to our necessary. Missy wants to pick snowball flowers there, but I don't let her.

Elam Salter comes in from wherever he's passed the night. He looks like a man who ain't slept. He's keeping watch for something, but he don't ever say what.

We eat pilot biscuits, dunking them in our cups to soften them up for chewing. Missy fusses and spits hers out. "You'll go hungry, then," I tell her. "You need to eat for—" I catch **for the baby** in my throat, and swallow hard.

Juneau Jane meets my eye. This baby won't hide much longer. Missy ought to visit a doctor, but if her mind ain't better soon, any doctor we ask will want to send her away to the asylum.

When we move out, Elam points his dun gelding up and across a rise. I see him there with his spyglass as the sky breaks a full dawn that's like coals from the underside. Red-pink and rose yellow and lined in gold so bright it stays in your eyes when you blink. The sky is wide as the earth, from one end to the other.

Elam and the horse look at home against that fire,

against that wide alone. Our wagon circles the hill and wobbles down into a rough draw, and Elam disappears bit by bit.

I keep watch out one side of the wagon, then the other, trying to hold on to the sight of him, but he's soon gone and we don't see him again, rest of the morning.

By noon, I take the little derringer out of Missy's reticule, check it, then set it in reach. Still not sure if it'd fire at all, but I feel better having it there.

Juneau Jane slides a glance over the gun, then at me.

"I was looking at it," I say. "That's all."

We pass a wagon or two on the road time to time through the day. Farmers and freighters. A mail wagon. Horsebackers and, near the towns, people on foot going to their farms and back. Here and there, riders take a wide path round us. I wonder what kind of folks those are that don't care to be seen up close by the soldiers.

At night we camp, and the men tell us to stay near, so we do. Come morning, we break camp and roll off again. Do the same thing the next day and the next and then again. Sometimes Elam joins our camps or rides alongside the wagon, but mostly he ranges. When he does come in, he's watchful and quiet. I know he's found signs of something out there.

The days go by as we push hard from first light to last, while the weather's fair.

A storm comes finally, and we pull the wagon

curtains down tight. The horses and mules plod along in the rain and the mud till finally we make our way through it, and it stops quick as it started. I look out for Elam, but don't see him. Hadn't all morning and that vexes me.

We meet a man on the road who don't speak to the soldiers, but stands his saddle horse just barely aside. Once we're past, he sidles his mount forward to get a peek through the rear gap of the wagon bonnet, see if there's anything in here he wants. The bold way of him leaves me bad skittish, and I look at the little derringer again. The light shines on its carved silver roses, and Missy reaches for it, and I swat her hand away.

"Don't you touch that," I scold. "It ain't for you to have."

She squeaks and scrambles out of reach and stares at me narrow eyed. I tuck that pistol down under me where she can't get it.

Near middle of the day, we come on a water crossing.

The sky has started to rumble again, so we go ahead to make the ford instead of stopping to rest the horses and mules first. The current is fast, but ain't deep.

"Keep them moving right on up at the slope!" the sergeant yells, circling a fist above his head. "We'll stop on the other side and rest and water the stock then."

The sergeant leads, then the driver whips up the

team, and the soldiers come along either side to make sure the mules don't stop and let the wagon drift. The streambed is rocky, so the wagon box rises and sinks, side to side. It falls hard into the deep spots. Missy hits her head and cries out.

I move all us closer to the back of the wagon, where we can get out if it swamps. This ain't supposed to be a hard crossing, but it is.

Leaning out the keyhole gap over the tailgate, I see Elam. He keeps well back up the slope, but he's there.

The mules get belly deep, and little seeps of water come through the wagon bed.

It's then I hear a sharp crack like a wheel or axle broke.

The canvas shudders above our heads. I turn to look over my shoulder, see a round hole and sunlight. Another crack echoes out. Another hole in the canvas.

"Bushwhack!" one of the troopers yells. The mules jerk forward. The driver goes to the whip.

My fingers slip on the tailgate and I tip forward, fall halfway out the back of the wagon. The tailgate pushes the breath out of me, and water rushes just under my chin. A hand grabs my dress. It's a big, strong hand, and I know it's Missy. Juneau Jane scrambles to get me, too, and they haul me up, and we all tumble toward the wagon bed. It's when I'm falling that I see Elam Salter and his big dun horse go straight over backward. I don't see them land. I hear a horse scream, hear the whine of a bullet, then a soldier's groan, a splash in the water. Hooves clatter away and up the bank. The soldiers return fire at whoever's come on us.

The wagon's got no way out but forward over the rocks, and the mules lurch through the water, the wagon rocking wild like a child's toy as they scrabble up the bank to dry land. I gather Juneau Jane and Missy, hold them down flat and push my head twixt them. Splinters of wood and dust and canvas rain down.

I say my prayers, make my peace. Might be after all that's happened, this is how it ends. Not in the swamp from a wildcat, not at the bottom of a river or on a freight wagon in the wild country, but here in this creek, waylaid for a reason I don't know.

I lift my head enough to search with my eyes, to find Old Mister's pistol.

**Can't let them take us alive if this is Indians or road agents,** is my only thought. Heard too many stories since we been in Texas, tales of what can be done to womenfolk. Seen it, too, with Missy and Juneau Jane. **Lord, give me the strength to do what's needed,** I pray. But if I find that pistol, it's got only two shots, and there's three of us.

**Give me the strength, and the means.**

Everything's shifted and turned upside down, and the pistol is no place I can see.

Of a sudden, the air goes quiet. The gun thunder and screams stop like they started. Powder smoke hangs thick and silent and sour. The only noise is the slow groaning of a horse and the terrible death rattle of blood-smothered breath.

"Ssshhh," I whisper to Missy and Juneau Jane. **Maybe they'll think the wagon's empty.** The thought's gone quick as it comes. I know better.

"Come out!" a voice orders. "Some of these soldier boys might live to fight another day, you come on out peaceful."

"Your choice," another man says. It's low and plain, and my ear knows it in a way that turns me cold inside, except I can't put a place to it. Where've I heard that voice before? "You want four dead soldier boys, plus a dead deputy marshal on your conscience? Ends the same, either way."

"Don't—" one of the soldiers hollers. There's a crack like a gourd getting split, and he goes quiet.

Juneau Jane and me look back and forth to each other. Her eyes are wide and white-edged. Her mouth trembles, but she nods. Beside me, Missy's already getting up, I guess because the man said to. She don't understand what's happening.

I feel for the pistol again. Feel for it everyplace. "Coming out!" I holler. "Might be we're shot already." I'm scrubbing the floor with my hands. **The pistol . . .**

**The pistol . . .**

"Out **now**!" the man hollers. A shot fires off and tears through the canvas not a foot from our heads. The wagon jerks forward, then stops. Either somebody's holding the mules or one's dead in the harness.

Missy scrabbles over the gate.

"Wait," I say, but there's no stopping her. No finding the derringer, either. Don't know what'll happen now. What kind of men are these, and why do they want us?

Missy's on her feet and moving away from the wagon by the time Juneau Jane and me get out. My mind slows, takes notice of each thing—the soldiers on their bellies, one bleeding from the leg. Blood drips from the head of the wagon driver. His eyes open and close, and open again. He tries to wake, to save hisself or us, but what can he do?

The sergeant lifts his head. "You're interfering with a detail of the United States Cavalry in—" A pistol butt comes down hard.

Missy moans like it was her that got struck.

I glance at the one holding the pistol. He ain't much more than a boy, might be thirteen or fourteen.

It's then I look past the boy and see the man come out from the brush. A rifle rests comfortable over his shoulder. He moves in a slow, easy stride, satisfied as a cat that's got its next meal cornered. A slow smile spreads under his hat brim. When he tips it up, there's the patch on his eye, and the melted scars on one side of his face, and I know why his voice caught me. Might be this is the day he finishes the job he started at the river landing.

Missy growls in her throat like a animal, gnashes her teeth, and chomps at the air.

The man tosses his head back, laughing. "Still a

biter, I see. I thought maybe we'd worked that out of you before we parted ways."

That voice of his. I sift memories like flour, but they fly away, carried off by the storm winds. Did we know him before? Was he somebody Old Mister knew?

Missy growls louder. I reach up and grab her arm, but she strains away from me. I try again to place the man. If I can call his name, maybe it'd catch him by surprise, throw him off long enough the troopers could get at the boy that's closest, grab his gun.

I hear horses splash through the water and scrabble up the bank behind us. But I keep my eyes on the man with the rifle. He's the one to worry about. The boy with him looks crazy and blood hungry, but it's this man who has charge of it all.

"And you." He turns to Juneau Jane. "It is a shame to dispatch a perfectly good yellow girl. Especially a fetching one who has . . . a certain sort of value. Perhaps it is a fortuitous turn of events that you've managed to survive, after all. Perhaps I'll keep you. A final recompense for all the loss I've suffered at your father's hands." He holds up a left glove with missing fingers sagging down, then he passes across the eye that's gone.

This man . . . this man believes Old Mister's to blame for his disfigurings? Why?

I let go of Missy, scoop Juneau Jane round behind me. "You leave this child be," I tell him. "She ain't done nothin' to you."

He cocks his head to see me better, looks at me for

a long time through the one good eye. "And what is this? The little boy driver Moses told me he'd done away with? But none of us are what we seem to be, are we?" He laughs, and there's a familiar sound to it.

He steps in closer. "I might just keep you, too. A good set of slave irons, and you'll be no trouble. Your kind can always be broken. The infernal Negro. No better than a mule. No smarter. All can be broken to harness . . . and to other uses." He studies me in pure meanness, but that's familiar, too. "I think I knew your mammy," he says and smiles. "I think I knew her quite well."

He looks away toward the men coming up from the river. My mind tumbles back, and back, and back. I see past the scars and the patch on his eye, take in the shape of his nose, the set of his sharp, pointed chin. I grab the memory, see him crouched beside the wagon where we're curled in the cold with Mama. His hands catch her, drag her out, her arm still chained to the wheel spokes. The sounds of her suffering bleed into dark, but I don't see. "You keep down under the blanket, babies," she chokes out. "You just stay there." I push the blanket hard against my ears, try not to hear.

I cling to my brothers and sisters, night after night, eight, then seven, then six . . . three, two, one, and finally just my cousin, little Mary Angel. And then only me, curled in a ball underneath that ragged blanket, trying to hide.

From this man, Jep Loach. Older, scarred and melted so that I didn't know his face. Right here is the man who took my people away. The man Old Mister had tracked down all them years ago and had dragged off to the Confederate army. Not killed on a battlefield someplace back then. Right here standing.

Once I know that much, I know I'll stop him this time, or die in the trying. Jep Loach can't steal one more thing from me. I can't stand for it. I can't live past it.

"You take me instead of her," I say. I'll be stronger without Missy and Juneau Jane to look after. "Just me alone." I'll find a way to do what needs to be done to this man. "You take me and leave these two girls and these soldier men be. I'm a good woman. Good as my mama was." The words rise up my throat and burn. I taste hardtack and coffee, soured now. I swallow it down, and add, "Strong as my mama was, too."

"None of you are in a position to bargain," Jep Loach says, and laughs.

The other men, the two behind us, laugh along as they circle on opposite sides. I know the one to the left, soon's he comes into view, but I can't make my eyes believe it even after all I heard about him throwing in with bad men. Lyle Gossett. Back from the dead, too. Not turned in for a bounty as Elam Salter thought, but here with his uncle, two men cut of the same cloth. The black cloth of Old Missus's people.

Lyle and the other rider, a skinny boy on a spotted horse, stop behind Jep Loach, turn their mounts to face us.

Missy growls louder, bites the air and bobs her chin and hisses like a cat.

"Shut . . . shut her up," the boy on the paint horse says. "She's givin' me the botheration. Got a demon. She's tryin' to . . . to witch us or somethin'. Let's just shoot 'em and go on."

Lyle lifts his rifle. Raises it up and points it at his own sister. Kin against kin. "She's gone in the head, anyhow." His words come cold and flat, but there's pleasure in his face when he rests his thumb on the hammer and pulls it back. "Good time to put her out of her misery."

Missy's neck tucks, her chin swaying against the collar of her dress. Her eyes stay pinned to Lyle, bright blue circles rolled up half under the lids, white underneath.

"She's pregnant!" I holler, and try to pull Missy back, but she rips herself out of my hand. "She carryin' a child!"

"Do it!" the other boy hollers. "She's witchin' us! Do it!"

"Stand down, Corporal," Jep Loach yells. He looks from one boy to the other. "Whose command is this?"

"Yours, Lieutenant," Lyle answers, like they're soldiers in a war. Soldiers for Marston. Just like Elam talked about.

"Do you serve the cause?"

"Yes, sir, Lieutenant," all three of the boy soldiers say.

"Then you **will** obey your superiors. I give the orders, here."

"Marston's been caught by deputy federal marshals." One of the cavalrymen on the ground tries to speak up. "Caught and jail—"

Jep Loach puts a bullet through the man's hand, then takes three quick steps and stomps a boot on his head, shoving him face-first into the mud. He can't breathe like that. He tries to fight, but it's no use.

Lyle laughs. "He ain't backtalkin' now, is he?"

"Sir?" the boy on the paint says, his jaw slackening. He backs the horse a step, shaking his head, his face doughy pale. "What . . . what's he sayin' about Gen'ral Marston? He . . . he been caught?"

"Lies!" Jep Loach swivels his way, crushes the cavalryman's head into the soil. "The **cause**! The cause is bigger than any one man. Insubordination is punishable by death." He draws his pistol and swings round, but the boy is a runnin' mark now, spurring for the brush, then gone, bullets following after.

The soldier on the ground groans, getting his face up and sucking a breath while Jep Loach paces away and back, wagging his pistol and shouldering the rifle. His skin goes fire red against the wax melt of scars. He talks to hisself as he paces. "It's handy. Handy, that's what it is. All of my uncle's heirs, here in one place. My poor auntie will need my help with

Goswood Grove, of course. Until the grief and her ill health overcome her, which won't take long. . . ."

"Uncle Jep?" Lyle ain't laughing now. He chokes on his own voice. Gathering the reins, he looks toward the brush, but he's barely put the spurs to his horse before Jep Loach lifts the rifle, and a shot meets its mark, and young Lyle tumbles hard toward the ground.

The air explodes, bullets whining past, kicking up dirt and knocking branches off trees. Juneau Jane pulls me backward onto the ground. I hear yelling, groans. Cavalrymen gain their feet. Bullets hit flesh. A scream. A groan. A howl like a animal. Powder smoke chokes the air.

It's quiet then. Quiet as the dawn, just a moment or two. I cough on the sulfur, listen, but lie still. "Don't move," I whisper into Juneau Jane's hair.

We stay there till the soldiers get up off the ground. Jep Loach is sprawled out dead, shot through the chest, and Lyle lies where he fell from the horse. There in a spill of blue cotton is Missy. Not moving. Blood seeps over the cloth like a rose blooming against a patch of sky. The wagon driver drags hisself to us and rolls her over to check her, but she's gone.

The old derringer hangs in her hand. The soldier slips it away, careful.

"Missy," I whisper, and Juneau Jane and me go to her. I hold her head and brush the wispy mud-caked hair from her blue eyes. I think of her as a child, and a girl. I try to think of good things. "Missy, what'd you do?"

I tell myself it was her shot that killed Jep Loach. Hers that did him in. I don't ask the soldiers if the derringer pistol got fired or not. Don't want to know. I need to believe it was Missy that did it, and that she did it for us.

I close her eyes, take the headscarf from my hair, and lay it over her face.

Juneau Jane makes the cross and says a prayer in French as she holds the hand of her sister. All that's left of Mister William Gossett lies dead here, bleeding out into this Texas soil.

All but Juneau Jane.

I stand outside the café in Austin City a long while. Can't go in, not even to the little yard, where the tables sit in open air under the spread of long-armed oaks. Branches twine theirselves overhead like the timbers in a roof. They share roots, these live oak groves. They're all one tree under the soil. Like a family, made to be together, to feed and shelter one another.

I watch the colored folk come and go from tables, serving up plates of food, filling cups and glasses with water and lemonade and tea, and carrying off dirty dishes. I study each worker from where I stand in the tree shade, try to decide, **Do any look like me? Do I know them?**

Three days, I been waiting to come here. Three

days since we limped into Austin with four wounded soldiers and what's left of Elam Salter in the wagon. It's still true that there ain't a bullet able to hit him, but the horse crushed him pretty good when it fell. I been there at his bedside by the hour. Only left it now with Juneau Jane to watch after him awhile. Nothing more to do now but wait. He's a strong man, but death has opened the door. It's for him to decide if he'll step through it soon, or at another time long in the future.

Some days, I tell myself I should let him cross over and be at peace. There's so much pain and fight ahead of him if he clings to this life. But I hope he means to stay. I've held his hand and wet his skin with my tears and told him that over and over.

Am I right to beg him to do that for me? I could go back to Goswood Grove. Home to Jason and John and Tati. Back to the sharecrop farm. Bury **The Book of Lost Friends** deep in the earth and forget everything that's happened. Forget how Elam lies broken. If he lives, he'll never be the same, the doctor says. Never walk again. Never ride.

This Texas is a bad place. A mean place.

But here I stand, breathing its air another day, watching this café I walked halfway across town to find, and thinking, **Could this traveler's hotel be the one?** If it is, was all this worth the doing? All this spilled blood and misery? Maybe even the loss of a brave man's life?

I study on a walnut-brown girl who carries lemonade

in a glass pitcher, pours it for two white ladies in their summer bonnets. I watch a light-skinned colored man carry a platter, a half-grown boy bring out a rag to wipe up a spill on the floor. **Do they look like me? Would I know my people by sight after all these years?**

I remember the names, where they left us, who carried them away. **But did I lose their faces? Their eyes? Their noses? Their voices?**

I watch awhile longer.

**Silly thing,** I tell myself over and again, knowing it's likely the Irishman horse thief made it all up, that story.

**A traveler's hotel and restaurant down Austin way, just along Waller Creek. Three blue beads on a string. Tied round the neck of a little white girl . . .**

Never even true, I'll bet.

I walk away, but only far enough to see that a stream is near. Looking down into its waters, I think, **Well, here's this.** I ask a old man passing by with a child in hand, "This Waller Creek?"

"Reckon," he answers and shuffles on.

I take myself back to the café again, walk round the big lime-plastered building that's shaped like a tall, narrow house, with rooms for travelers to stay by the night. Standing on my toes, I peek through the open windows, look at more colored people working. Nobody I know, far as I can tell.

It's then I see the little white girl at the well out back. She's skinny and small, wiry. Eight years old, maybe ten, more hair than anything else to her. It falls from a yellow headscarf, tumbles down her back in red-brown waves. She's strong, though, hauling a heavy bucket in both hands, water splashing down her leg, wetting the apron over her gray dress.

I'll ask her, at least: **There anybody here that goes by the name of Gossett? Or did back before the freedom, even? You ever see anybody with three blue beads like these? A colored woman? A girl? A boy?**

I finger the string at my neck, move to come into the girl's path and think to be careful how I say the words, so it won't scare her off. But when she stops, looks up at me, her gray eyes surprised in a face that's sweet like a china doll's, I can't even speak. There at her neck, tied on a red ribbon, hang three blue beads.

**The Irishman,** I think to myself. **He told it true.**

I sink down to the dirt. Fall hard, for my legs go weak, but I barely feel the ground. I feel nothing, hear nothing. I hold up my beads, try to speak, but my tongue has clamped itself still. I can't make the words. **Child, where'd you come by them beads?**

Seems forever, we're froze that way, the girl and me, just looking and trying to reason it out.

A sparrow flies down from the tree. Only one little brown sparrow. It lands on the ground to drink of the water dripping from the bucket. The girl drops her burden, and water flows in rivers, quenching the dry soil. The sparrow dunks its head under and shakes the water over its feathers.

The girl turns and runs, scampers fast up the stone walk and through the open back door of the building. "Mama!" I hear her yell. "Maaa-ma!"

I climb to my feet, try to decide, **Should I run?** The girl is white, after all, and I gave her a fright, just now. Should I try explaining? **I didn't mean her any harm. I just wondered, where'd she come by the three blue beads?**

It's then I see her in the door, a tall copper-colored woman standing with a wood kitchen spoon still in her hand. At first I think it's Aunt Jenny Angel, but she's too young to be. She's only Juneau Jane's age, not a girl, not quite a woman. She sends the white child inside, squints through the sun at me as she starts down the steps. Round her neck hangs a cord and three blue beads.

I remember how she looked the day them beads were first tied there, the last day I knew her, when she was only three years old at the trader's yard. I see her face before the man picked her up and carried her away.

"Mary . . ." I whisper and then cry out across a space that of a sudden seems both too long and too short. My body goes weak. "Mary Angel?"

A shadow stands in the door then, and the shadow takes on sun as it comes out. There is the face I've kept in my mind all these years. I know it, even though the hair is gray round it, and the body stooped over a bit.

The little red-haired girl holds to her skirt, and I

see how they look alike. This is my **mama's** child. My mama's child by a white man, born sometime after we were lost to each other all them years ago. It shows in her eyes, turned up on the corners like Juneau Jane's.

Like **mine.**

"I'm Hannie!" I shout across the courtyard, and I hold out Grandmama's three blue beads. "I'm Hannie! I'm Hannie! I'm Hannie!"

I don't even know at first, but I'm running. I'm running on legs I can't feel, across ground I don't see. I run, or I fly like the sparrow.

I don't stop until I come into the arms of my people.

## Lost Friends

OCEAN SPRINGS, MISS.
Dr. A. E. P. Albert:

Dear Brother: The SOUTHWESTERN has been the means of the recovery of my sister, Mrs. Polly Woodfork and eight children. I owe my joy to God and the SOUTHWESTERN, and wish the editor success in getting 1000 cash subscribers in the next thirty days. I will do all in my power to get all the subscribers I can. God bless Dr. Albert and crown him with success.

MRS. TEMPY BURTON

—"Lost Friends," column of
the Southwestern
August 13, 1891

# CHAPTER 28

## BENNY SILVA—AUGUSTINE, LOUISIANA, 1987

I take the stairs in giant leaps, grab the turn in the bannister at the end, and run frantically down the corridor.

"Benny, wha . . ." Nathan thunders after me. We collide at the library door. "What's going on?" he wants to know.

"The billiard table, Nathan," I gasp. "The table. It had a dust cover on it the first time I came here, and there were paperbacks stacked on top. We've been piling books for the city library and school there ever since. I never looked underneath. What if Robin didn't want anyone to have a **reason** to uncover the table, so she hid the balls and cues, and stacked old paperbacks on top? What if that's where she was keeping her work? She knew nobody could sneak in here and walk off with a billiard table. You'd have to bring an entire moving crew to relocate that thing."

We hurry to the old Brunswick table, grab stacks of legal thrillers and gunslinger Westerns, and pile them around the ornate, maple inlay legs with an uncharacteristic lack of care.

Papers rattle as we lift the stiff vinyl cover. We toss it aside, wafting up dust that flies in tornadic swirls, then settles on the foam and vinyl inserts that have been carefully fitted within the well of the table, leveling up the surface.

It's beneath them, meticulously laid out on a length of clean, white linen, that we find Robin's work, a quilt of sorts, an enormous live oak tree created in a mixed media of silk fabrics, embroidery floss, felt leaves, paints or dyes, and photographs slipped into padded fabric frames with clear plastic covers. At first it looks like a work of art, but it's also a careful documentation of history. The story of Goswood Grove and many of the people who have inhabited this land since the early 1800s. Deaths and births, including those that took place within the bonds of marriage and beyond them. A nine-generation Gossett family tree. A story both black and white.

A beige felt cutout of a house denotes how the property ownership has passed down through the generations. The people are represented by leaves, each labeled with a name, year of birth, and year of death, followed by a letter that is explained through a map key in the bottom right corner of the canvas.

**C** = citizen
**E** = enslaved
**I** = indentured
**L** = **libre**
**A** = **affranchi**

I know the last two terms from our **Underground** research. **Affranchi,** a French word for those emancipated from slavery by their owners, and **libre,** those born as free persons of color—tradesmen and landowners, many highly prosperous, some slave owners themselves. My students have struggled to understand how people who suffered the effects of injustice could themselves perpetrate it on others and profit from it, yet it happened. It's part of our historical reality.

Reproductions of newspaper articles, old photos, and documents remain pinned to the fabric here and there, awaiting the addition of more pockets, I suppose. Robin was thorough in her research.

"My sister . . ." Nathan mutters. "This is . . ."

"Your family's story. All of it. The truth." I recognize so many connections from my students' work. Tracing the lines upward, I move past branches that dwindle and disappear, fading like estuaries into the ocean of time. Death. Disease. War. Infertility. The end of this family line and that one.

Other branches continue, twisting through the decades. I see Granny T and Aunt Dicey. Their lineage travels back to both the black and the white Gossetts. To the grandmother they have in common, Hannie, born 1857, enslaved.

"The New Century ladies," I say, and point to Hannie's leaf. "This is the grandmother that Granny T told my class about, the one who started the restaurant. Hannie was born here at Goswood Grove, enslaved. She's also the grandmother of the woman who used to live in the graveyard house, Miss Retta."

I'm fascinated, astounded. I let my hand travel outward, onto blank sections of Robin's canvas. "A few of my kids would be right around here somewhere, LaJuna, Tobias—and Sarge, too. They'd all be farther along on this branch."

I feel the tingle of history coming to life as I trace backward through the generations again. "Hannie's mother is biracial, a half sister to the Gossetts living in the Grand House at the time. This generation, Lyle, Lavinia, Juneau Jane, and Hannie, are brother, sister, half sister, and a cousin in some form or fashion. Lyle and Lavinia die fairly young, and . . . that leaves the daughter of the second wife to . . . whoa . . ."

Nathan looks up from his study of the family tree, meets my eye curiously, then steps in beside me to take a closer look.

I tap a finger to one leaf, then another. "This woman, the mother of Juneau Jane, is **not** William

Gossett's second wife; she's a mistress, a free woman of color. Her daughter, Juneau Jane LaPlanche, is born **while** William Gossett is married to Maude Loach-Gossett. He's living here in this house as the owner of the plantation. He already has a son with Maude, and then he fathers two daughters less than two years apart, one with his wife and one with his mistress. Lavinia and Juneau Jane."

I know such things went on, that an entire social system existed in parts of New Orleans and other places, through which wealthy men kept mistresses, raised what were casually referred to as **left-hand families,** sent mixed-race sons and daughters off for education abroad or kept them in convent boarding schools, or provided tradesmen's education for them. Still, I can imagine the human drama that must have simmered below the surface of such arrangements. Jealousy. Resentment. Bitterness. Competition.

Nathan glances over but doesn't answer. He's tracing something up from the roots of the tree, toward the branches, the path of his fingertip connecting the tiny house-shaped symbols that track ownership of Goswood Grove.

"Here's the thing," he says, and stops on the leaf that represents William Gossett's younger daughter, the one born to the mistress. "I can't figure out how it is that Gossetts still own this house today. Because here, the last Gossett son, Lyle, dies. The Grand House and land pass to Juneau Jane LaPlanche, who, according to Robin's tree, never has children. Even if she did, their name wouldn't have been Gossett."

"Unless this is just where the research stopped. Maybe Robin never got any further. She was obviously still working on the project. It seems almost like . . . an obsession." I imagine Nathan's sister poring over these documents, this quilt of the family history she was creating. What did she plan to do with it?

Nathan seems equally perplexed. "That there are two strains of the family is sort of a secret that everyone knows about, to be honest." He straightens away from the table, frowning. "I'm sure it's something the rest of the family, and probably a lot of the people in town, would prefer not be brought up again, but no one would be shocked . . . except for, maybe, this part." He taps the tiny white felt house that indicates the property's passage into the hands of Juneau Jane. Stretching over me, he unpins an envelope nearby. **Hannie** is written on it in Robin's neat, even script.

A tiny felt representation of Goswood Grove House drops from underneath the pin and lands beside Hannie's felt leaf. The xeroxed 1887 newspaper article inside Hannie's envelope tells us why it was there.

# SHAM INHERITRESS DEFEATED!

## Goswood Property Restored to Rightful Owners

Following more than one dozen years of hard fought battles to preserve its lineage and heritage, the defenders of old Goswood Grove Plantation have been vindicated for all time in a final decision of the Louisiana Supreme Court, which may not now nor evermore be challenged or appealed. The pretend heiress, a colored Creole woman of dubious and unsubstantiated lineage, who in court papers most audaciously referred to herself as Juneau Jane Gossett, has been dispossessed of the property by force.

The rightful inheritors, in-line relatives of the late William P. Gossett, and legally bearing the Gossett name, now make haste to occupy the home and lands and to protect and prosper the aforementioned. "We, of course, intend to return the grand old place to its former glory, and are grateful to the courts for this unequivocal dispensation of justice," spoke Carlisle Gossett, a resident of Richmond, Virginia, first cousin to the late William P. Gossett, and the henceforth owner of the old Goswood property.

The story goes on to describe twelve years of legal attempts to strip Juneau Jane of her inheritance, first by William Gossett's widow, Maude Loach-Gossett, who refused to accept the small settlement left to her in William's will, and then by more distant relatives bearing the Gossett name. Various former slaves and sharecroppers came forth to testify on Juneau Jane's behalf and to validate her parentage. A lawyer from New Orleans tirelessly argued her case, but in the end it was of little use. Cousins of William Gossett stole her inheritance, and Juneau Jane ended up with forty acres of bottomland bordering the Augustine cemetery.

The land I'm living on now.

Her eventual dispensation of that land is given in her own words, in a copy of a will handwritten in 1912. Robin stapled it to the back of the article. Juneau's house and deeded land are left to Hannie, **"who has been as close as a sister to me and is the person who has shown me, always, how to be brave."** Any further inheritance that might eventually be recovered in her name is left to benefit children of the community, **"whom I hope I have served faithfully as a teacher and a friend."**

The final sheet of Robin's attached research is a newspaper article about the 1901 opening of the Augustine Colored Carnegie Library. I recognize the photo of the library's New Century Club women. Decked out in their finest hats and dresses—Sunday clothes around the turn of the century when the photo was taken—they're posed on the steps of the beautiful new building for the ribbon cutting. Granny T brought the original print of that photo to my class the first day she told us the story. She'd unearthed it from the storage boxes where the library's history was tucked away at the end of segregation, when libraries were no longer restricted by race.

In this newspaper copy, Robin has identified two of the club members, noting **Hannie** and **Juneau Jane,** above their images. When I trail down to a smaller photo positioned among the text, I recognize the two women standing alongside the bronze statue of a saint, as it awaits placement on its nearby pedestal.

I also recognize the saint.

***The library's first book,*** the bold print says on the caption.

I rest my chin on Nathan's shoulder and read on,

> **Within this fine marble pedestal, the members of the library's formation committee have placed a Century Chest that was moved from the original Colored Library behind the church, to the library's fine new Carnegie building. The items within the chest, contributed by library founders in 1888, were not to be seen for one hundred years from that time. Mrs. Hannie Gossett Salter, recently moved from Texas, here sees to the placement of a statue donated in memory of her late husband, the much-revered Deputy**

**U.S. Marshal Elam Salter, with whom she traveled the country as he spoke of the life of a frontier lawman after an injury forced his retirement from field duty. Donation of the statue is courtesy of Texas and Louisiana cattleman Augustus McKlatchy, a lifelong friend of the Salter family and patron supporter of this new library building and many others.**

**Within the Century Chest, Mrs. Salter places** The Book of Lost Friends, **which was used to inform distant congregations of the "Lost Friends" column of the** Southwestern Christian Advocate **newspaper. Through the newspaper and the notations in Mrs. Salter's book, countless families and lost loves were reunited long after separation by the scourge of slavery and war. "Having found many members of my own family," Mrs. Salter remarked, "this was an impassioned service I could provide for others. The greatest hardship to the heart is to endlessly wonder about your people."**

**Upon the cessation of ceremonies today, the marble base will be sealed, containing the Century Chest within, to remain so until the future year of 1988, that the importance of this library and the stories of its people be remembered by generations yet unborn.**

**Awaiting placement atop the sealed pedestal, the donated statue stands both benevolent and ever watchful.**

**St. Anthony of Padua, the patron saint of the lost.**

## EPILOGUE

### BENNY SILVA—1988
### LOUISIANA STATE CAPITOL GROUNDS, BATON ROUGE

A single ladybug lands featherlight on my finger, clings like a living gemstone. A ruby with polka dots and legs. Before a slight breeze beckons my visitor away, an old children's rhyme sifts through my mind.

**Ladybug, ladybug, fly away home,**
**Your house is on fire, and your children**
**are gone.**

The words leave a murky shadow inside me as I touch LaJuna's shoulder. She's breaking a sweat under the blue-and-gold calico dress. The open-air classroom we've set up today as part of a festival on the Louisiana State Capitol grounds is the biggest undertaking yet in our year-long living history project. The opening of the time capsule has provided us with opportunities we could never have dreamed of otherwise. While our pageants have not yet taken us to the cemetery in Augustine, Louisiana—and may never—we've told our **Tales from the Underground** at museums and on university campuses, at library festivals and in schools across three states.

The hand-stitched neckline of LaJuna's costume hangs unevenly over her smooth amber-brown skin, the garment a little too large for the girl inside it. A single puffy scar protrudes from the loosely buttoned cuff. I wonder about the cause of it, but resist allowing my mind to speculate.

**What would be the point?** I ask myself.

**We all have scars.**

It's when you're honest about them that you find the people who will love you in spite of your nicks and dents. Perhaps even because of them.

The people who don't? Those people aren't the ones for you.

I pause and look around our gathering place under the trees, take in the various Carnegie ladies, as well as my students' little brothers and sisters, Aunt Sarge, and several parent volunteers, all dressed in period costumes to add authenticity to our project today, to stand in respect and solidarity with those long-ago survivors who are not here to speak their truth. While we've told our **Underground** stories many times, this is our first attempt at a recital of the Lost Friends ads. We've tried to reimagine how they may have been written over a century ago in churches, on front porches, at kitchen tables, in improvised classrooms where those who had been denied literacy came to learn. In towns and cities all over the country, letters were composed for publication in newspapers like the **Southwestern,** sent out with the hope that loved ones stolen away years, decades, a lifetime before, might be found.

We have the Century Chest and **The Book of Lost Friends** to thank for giving us rock-star status here at the state capitol. It's enough of a story to have beckoned the TV cameras our way. They're really here to cover a contentious special election, but they want to film us, too. The media attention has produced an audience of dignitaries and politicians who want to be **seen** supporting our project.

And that has pushed the kids into meltdown mode. They're terrified—even LaJuna, who is normally a rock.

While the others fumble with nib pens and inkwells, pretending to compose letters to the "Lost

Friends" column, or hunch over their papers, mouthing the words of the ads they're about to recite out loud, LaJuna is just staring off into the trees.

"Fully prepared?" I ask, angling a glance at her work, because I have a feeling she's not. "You've practiced reading it aloud?"

Beside us, Lil' Ray bends over his desk, distracting himself with a pearl-handled nib pen from the collection I've amassed over the years at estate sales and flea markets. He's given up on pretending to write the "Lost Friends" letter he'll soon recite for the audience.

If LaJuna doesn't come through, I have the sinking sense that we're headed for a train wreck. She should be fully confident, as she knows the ad she'll be reading very well. We discovered it, neatly cut out and pasted inside the cover of **The Book of Lost Friends,** along with the date it was printed in the **Southwestern.** On either side of the ad, in carefully written letters, are the names of Hannie's eight lost siblings, her mother, her aunt and three cousins, and when they were found again.

**Mittie**—my dearest Mama, a restaurant cook—1875

**Hardy**

**Het**—eldest and dear sister also with her children and husband—1887

**Pratt**—older dear brother, a timber train worker, with wife and child—1889

**Epheme**—beloved sister and always my special best, a teacher—1895

**Addie**

**Easter**

**Ike**—littlest brother, a fine and educated young man tradesman—1877

**Baby Rose**

**Aunt Jenny**—dear aunt and also her second husband, a preacher—1877

**Azelle**—cousin and child of Aunt Jenny, a washer woman with daughters—1881

**Louisa**

**Martha**

**Mary**—dear one and cousin, a restaurant cook—1875

It's a story of the joy of reunion and the pain of absence, of perseverance and grit.

I see that same grit in LaJuna, passed down through the generations from her five times great-grandmother, Hannie, though at times LaJuna doubts that it's there.

"I can't do it." She sags, defeated in her own mind. "Not . . . not with **these** people looking on." Her young face casts miserably toward the bystanders, moneyed men in well-fitting suits and women in expensive dresses, petulantly waving off the afternoon heat with printed handbills and paper fans left over from the morning's fiery political speeches. Just beyond them, a cameraman stands perched on a picnic table. Another crew member has stationed himself near the front of our classroom, poised with a microphone on a pole.

"You never know what you can do until you try." I pat her arm, give it a squeeze, trying to brace her up. There's so much I'd like to say: **Don't sell yourself short. You're fine. You're good enough. You're** more **than good enough. You're amazing. Can't you see it?**

It might be a long journey for her, I know. I've been there. But it's possible to come out the other end better, stronger. Eventually you have to stop letting people define you and start defining yourself.

It's a lesson I'm both teaching and learning. **Name yourself. Claim yourself.** Classroom Constitution, Article Twelve.

"I **can't,**" she moans, clutching her stomach.

I bundle my cumbersome load of skirts and petticoats to keep them from the dust, then lower myself to catch her gaze. "Where will they hear the story if not from you—the story of being stolen away from family? Of writing an advertisement seeking any word of loved ones, and hoping to save up the fifty cents to have it printed in the **Southwestern** paper, so that it might travel through all the nearby states and territories? How will they understand the desperate need to finally know, **Are my people out there, somewhere?**"

Her thin shoulders lift, then wilt under the pressure. "These folks ain't here because they care what I've got to say. It won't change anything."

"Perhaps it will." Sometimes I wonder if I'm promising more than the world will ever be willing to deliver—if my mother might have been right about all my rainbow and unicorn ideas. What if I'm setting these kids up for an eventual blindsiding punch, especially LaJuna? This girl and I have spent hours and hours sorting books, moving books, dealing in the sale of antique books that turned out to be valuable, plotting and planning what sort of materials will be purchased for the Augustine Carnegie Library with the money that's coming in. Eventually, it will provide local kids with the sort of state-of-the-art advantages students at Lakeland Prep have. And when the library's new freestanding sign is erected, its original patron saint will be returned to his proper pedestal to watch over the place into the coming century and beyond. That old library now has a long life ahead of it. It's Nathan's intention that Robin's estate be moved into a foundation that will support not only the library but also the preservation of Goswood Grove and its conversion into a genealogy and history center.

But can all of that, can **any** of that, change the

world these television cameras, these politicians, all these onlookers will go back to when they leave this space under the trees? Can a library and a history center really accomplish anything?

"The most important endeavors require a risk," I tell her. It's the hardest piece of reality to accept. Striking off into the unknown is terrifying, but if we don't begin the journey, we'll never know where it could lead.

The realization grips my throat momentarily, holds me silent, makes me wonder, **Will I ever have the courage to face** my **unknown, to take the risk?** I straighten upward and smooth my gathered skirts, look past the classroom, see Nathan on the fringes of the crowd with the library's new video camera on his shoulder. He gives me a thumbs-up and adds the sort of smile that says, **I know you, Benny Silva. I know all that's true about you, and I believe you're capable of anything.**

I have to try to be for these kids what Nathan has been for me. Someone who has more faith in me than I sometimes have in myself. Today is about my students. And about the Lost Friends.

"At the very least, we must tell our stories, mustn't we? Speak the names?" I slip into my 1800s teacher voice, because suddenly there's a microphone on a pole hovering dangerously near. "You know, there is an old proverb that says, 'We die once when the last breath leaves our bodies. We die a second time when the last person speaks our name.' The first death is beyond our control, but the second one we can strive to prevent."

"If you say so," LaJuna acquiesces, and I cringe, hoping the microphone didn't pick that up. "But I best do it right off, so I don't lose my nerve. Can I go on and give my reading before the rest?"

I am beyond relieved. "If you start, I'm certain the others will know to follow." **I hope.**

I grit my teeth and cross my fingers in the pockets of my plain dotted Swiss schoolmarm dress and hope this comes off the way we planned it, and that these stories make a difference in the minds and hearts of the people who hear them. Nearby, **The Book of Lost Friends** sits in the display case along with notes and needlework and other mementos from the Century Chest. I think of the Lost Friends, all those people who had the courage to search, to hope, to seek after their lost loves. To take the risk of writing letters, knowing their worst fears might come to pass. The letter might never be answered.

I'll take that risk as well, one day when the time is right. I'll look for the baby girl I held for less than a half-hour before a nurse whisked her from my arms, replacing her with a cold, hard-edged square of plastic. A clipboard, bearing papers I was expected to sign.

Everything in me wanted to set the documents aside, tear them up, make them go away. I yearned to call after the squeaky echo of the nurse's clean white shoes, **Bring her back! I want to see her more, longer, again, memorize her face, her smell, her eyes.**

**I want to keep her.**

But I did what was expected. The only thing that was allowed. The only option I was given. I signed the papers and set them on the nightstand, and cried into my pillow, alone.

**It's for the best,** I told myself, repeating my mother's words, the counselor's words, the nurses' words. Even my father's words when I tried going to him for help.

They are the same words I still recite to myself, wrapping them around my body as a comfort on each birthday, each Christmas, every special occasion of every passing year. Twelve of them now. She'd be twelve.

I like to believe that I spared her the guilt and public condemnation that fell crushingly on a fifteen-year-old girl, pregnant by an older man, a neighbor who already had a family of his own. The kind of man who'd take advantage of a fatherless child's naïve need to feel worthy and wanted. I like to think I spared that tiny baby girl the shame I carried with me, the disdainful looks other people cast my way, the horrible names my mother called me.

I hope I gave my daughter to wonderful parents who never for a moment let her feel unloved. If I ever see her again, I'll tell her that she was **never** unloved, not for a moment. Someone else loved her from her first breath, wanted her, thought of her, hoped for her.

**I remember you. I've always remembered you.**

On that day of reunion, whenever it comes, those are the first words I will say to my own Lost Friend.

## Author's Note

Each time a new book enters the world, it seems as though the most oft-asked question is, **How did this story come to be? What inspired it?** I'm not sure what this process is like for other writers, but for me there is always a spark, and it is always random. If I went looking for the spark, I'd probably fail to find it.

I never know when it will come my way or what it will be, but I feel it instantly when it happens. Something **consuming** takes over, and a day that was ordinary . . . suddenly isn't anymore. I'm being swept along on a journey, like it or not. I know the journey will be long and I don't know where it will lead, but I know I have to surrender to it.

The spark that became Hannie's and Benny's story came to me in the most modern of ways—via an email from a book lover who'd just spent time with the Foss family while reading **Before We Were Yours.** She thought there was another, similar, piece of history I should know about. As a volunteer with the Historic New Orleans Collection, she'd been entering database information gleaned from advertisements well over a century old. The goal of the project was to preserve the history of the "Lost Friends" column, and to make it accessible to genealogical and historical researchers via the Internet. But the data entry volunteer saw more than just research material. "There is a story in each one of these ads," she wrote in her note to me. "Their constant love of family and their continued search for loved ones, some they had not seen in over 40+ years." She quoted a line that had struck her as she'd closed the cover of **Before We Were Yours:**

> In your last pages: "For the hundreds who vanished and the thousands who didn't. May your stories not be forgotten."

She directed me to the Lost Friends database, where I tumbled down a rabbit hole of lives long gone, stories and emotions and yearning encapsulated in the faded, smudged type of old-time printing presses. Names that survived perhaps nowhere beyond these desperate pleas of formerly enslaved people, once written in makeshift classrooms, at kitchen tables, and in church halls . . . then sent forth on steam trains and mail wagons, on riverboats and in the saddlebags of rural mail carriers destined for the remote outposts of a growing country. Far and wide, the missives journeyed, carried on wings of hope.

In their heyday, the Lost Friends ads, published in the **Southwestern Christian Advocate,** a Methodist newspaper, went out to nearly five hundred preachers, eight hundred post offices, and more than four thousand subscription holders. The column header requested that pastors read the contents from their pulpits to spread the word of those seeking the missing. It also implored those whose searches had ended in success to report back to the newspaper, that the news might be used to encourage others. The Lost Friends advertisements were the equivalent of an ingenious nineteenth-century social media platform, a means of reaching the hinterlands of a divided, troubled, and fractious country still struggling to find itself in the aftermath of war.

I knew that very day, as I took in dozens of the Lost Friends ads, meeting family after family, searcher after searcher, that I had to write the story of a family torn apart by greed, chaos, cruelty, despairing of ever again seeing one another. I knew that the Lost Friends ads would provide hope where hope had long ago been surrendered.

Hannie began speaking to me after I read this ad:

## Lost Friends

We make no charge for publishing these letters from subscribers. All others will be charged fifty cents. Pastors will please read the requests published below from their pulpits, and report any case where friends are brought together by means of letters in the SOUTHWESTERN.

Mr Editor—I wish to inquire for my people. My stepfather was named George, and my mother's name was Chania. I am the oldest of ten children, and am named Caroline. The others were Ann, Mary, Lucinda, George Washington, Right Wesley, Martha, Louisa, Samuel Houston, Prince Albert, in order of age, and were all my mother had when separated. Our first owner was Jeptha Wooten, who carried us all from Mississippi to Texas, where he died. We were stolen from Texas by Green Wooten, a nephew of Jeptha, who brought us back to Mississippi, on Pearl River, where he sold us to a lawyer named Bakers Baken, who seems not to have paid for us. My stepfather and oldest brother were stolen and carried off by him to Natchez, Miss., and there sold. The remainder of us were taken from him and put, for safe keeping, in the Holmesville, Pike county Miss., jail, after which we were put in the hands of another lawyer, John Lambkins, who sold us all. My mother and three children were sold to Bill Files, in Pike county, Miss; my sister Ann to one Coleman, in same county; she was foolish and dumb. My sister Mary to a man named Amacker, who lived in the vicinity of Gainesville, Miss. Lucinda was sold into Louisiana. Right Wesley was sold at the same time, but to whom or where to, I do not know. Martha was also sold to somewhere in the settlement near my mother, but I don't know to whom. I was sold to Bill Flowers, being quite a young woman. I am now 60 years of age and have one son, Orange Henry Flowers, preacher in the Mississippi Conference, located in Pearlington, Hancock county, Miss., on the Bay St. Louis charge. Any information will be acceptable and thankfully received. Write to Caroline Flowers, in care of Rev. O. H. Flowers, Pearlington, Hancock county, Miss.

I knew that Hannie's situation would, in some ways, be directed by the life of Caroline Flowers, who wrote this ad, but that Hannie's search would lead her to strike off on a quest. Her journey would be life-altering, an odyssey, of sorts. It would change her forever, redirecting her future. For the purposes of Hannie's age and the particularly lawless, perilous postwar era in Texas, I reimagined history a bit, setting the story in 1875, ten years after the ending of the war. While separated families had been placing ads in various newspapers since the close of the war, distribution of the "Lost Friends" column actually sprang to life in 1877 and continued through the early part of the twentieth century.

I hope you felt the connection to Hannie's and Benny's stories as much as I felt the connection to them while writing about them. They are, in my view, the sort of remarkable women who built the legacies we enjoy today. Teachers, mothers, business owners, activists, pioneer farm wives, community leaders who believed, in some large or small way, that they could improve the world for present and future generations. Then they took the risks required to make it happen.

May we all do the same in whatever way we can, in all the places we find ourselves.

And may this book do its part, whatever that part might be.

## Notes from the Author About Dialect and Historical Terminology

In a fractured world, sensitivities related to race, economic class, and geographical dialects have justly increased. Modern ears don't skip casually over words that would have been commonplace a half century ago, or variations in dialect that remain the norm in other parts of the country today. Hopefully that means we're more aware—but it also puts us in danger of sanitizing what **is** and what **was.** As a storyteller, I have tried to respect authentic voices and authentic representations of historical eras.

Wherever possible, I've attempted to be faithful to the various dialects of Louisiana and Texas, the narratives left behind by men and women who lived during the historical time period of the story, and the racial and ethnic terminology Hannie would have experienced in her day.

History has much to teach us. That was one of the reasons for the inclusion of the real-life Lost Friends ads in this book. They are the true voices of actual people who lived, and struggled, and who left these small pieces of themselves for posterity. Their history has taught me more than I can ever say, and for those hard-won lessons, I remain eternally grateful.

## Acknowledgments

No story is a solo creation—the scenes sketched, colors added, highlights and shadows dabbed on in solitude. These literary creations start as casual doodles, and they invariably grow outward from there. They become a community project of sorts, a mural with many and diverse contributors who have only one thing in common—they were kind enough to stop by and fill in a blank section or two. **The Book of Lost Friends** is no exception, and I'd be remiss if I didn't write the names of a few kind souls on the wall before I go.

To begin with, I'm grateful to the hardworking people behind the Historic New Orleans Collection for creating the invaluable Lost Friends database. You have ensured that the history of a place, an era, and thousands of families is not only preserved but available to the public, researchers, and countless descendants searching for family roots. In particular, thank you to Jessica Dorman, Erin Greenwald, Melissa Carrier, and Andy Forester for your devotion to HNOC, the Lost Friends, and to history itself. To Diane Plauché, what can I say? If you hadn't brought the Lost Friends to my doorstep, I would never have met them, and Hannie and Benny wouldn't exist. Thank you for introducing me, for sharing your volunteer work digitizing the ads for the database, and for telling me your family's story. I will always be grateful to you and Andy for the hours spent together, listening to stories, soaking in the history, studying old documents, talking with Jess and her folks, and walking the quiet cemetery grounds, reading the time-worn markers and wondering what might not be marked. The most surprising thing about these literary journeys is that they bring about new friendships in the real world. I'm honored to count you among them.

To the many other kind folks who offered up their time and knowledge during my travels in Louisiana, thank you for generously sharing your home state. How could a wandering writer expect anything less from a place so well known for its hospitality? In particular, my gratitude goes out to the hosts, tour guides, and curators at Whitney Plantation and to the friendly staff at Cane River Creole National Historical Park. Thank you, park ranger Matt Housch, for taking me under wing, giving me a fantastic personalized tour, answering all of my questions, and even confirming the existence of hidden access hatches in the floor of the plantation house.

As always, I (and this story) owe so much to an incredible group of family, first readers, and old friends who helped to bring **The Book of Lost Friends** into being. To author pal Judy Christie, thank you for sitting on the porch swing with me during the initial "doodle" stages of this book, kicking around ideas, and then for generously reading draft after draft, adding not only your Louisiana expertise but needed doses of encouragement, love, and an occasional lunch of the intrepid Paul Christie's chicken soup or chili. To my mother, Aunt Sandy, Duane Davis, Mary Davis, Allan Lazarus, Janice Rowley, and incredible author assistant Kim Floyd, thank you for being the best beta reading team ever, for helping to refine the story, and for cheering Hannie and Benny on to the finish line. Without you, I don't know where they would be.

On the print and paper side of things, I can't say thank you enough to my brilliant agent, Elisabeth Weed, who believed in this story from the first mention of the idea and encouraged me to write it. You are the best! To editor Susanna Porter, thank you for always being behind this book and for sifting through its many iterations. What book would be complete without the perfect publishing team? Thank you to Kara Welsh, Kim Hovey, Jennifer Hershey, Scott Shannon, Susan Corcoran, Melanie DeNardo, Rachel Parker, Debbie Aroff, Colleen Nuccio, and Emily Hartley for being the engine behind this book, for cheering each new publishing milestone with me, and for being just all-out fun people to work with. I can't imagine more joyful journeys than the ones we've shared. I'm grateful also to the teams in production, marketing, publicity, and sales, and to Andrea Lau for the interior page design, as well as Scott Biel and Paolo Pepe for the book's gorgeous cover concept. If not for you, these stories would never find their way to bookshelves, nightstands, and the hands of readers.

Speaking of readers, I'm eternally grateful to all the booksellers, librarians, and communities who have hosted book talks and signings, sent notes, recommended my books to readers, hosted book clubs, and welcomed me to your stores and hometowns. Lastly (but most important), a huge load of gratitude goes out to so many reader friends, whether around the corner or on the other side of the world. Thank you for giving my books such loving homes. Thank you for sharing them with friends and family, for handing them to strangers in airports and suggesting them to book clubs. You are the ones who turn story into community. And for that, I remain in your debt.

Today, tomorrow, and always.

**—Lisa**

# Bibliography

## WEB AND LIVE SOURCES


"Lost Friends Exhibition." https://www.hnoc.org/database/lost-friends/. Historic New Orleans Collection. Web. 2019.

"Piecing Together Stories of Families Lost in Slavery." https://www.npr.org/2012/07/16/156843097/piecing-together-stories-of-families-lost-in-slavery. National Public Radio. Web. July 16, 2012.

"Purchased Lives Panel Exhibition." https://www.hnoc.org/exhibitions/purchased-lives-panel-exhibition. Historic New Orleans Collection. Web. n.d.

**PRINT SOURCES**

Federal Writers' Project. **North Carolina Slave Narratives: Slave Narratives from the Federal Writers' Project, 1936–1938.** Bedford, Mass.: Applewood Books, 2006.

Federal Writers' Project. **Texas Slave Narratives and Photographs: A Folk History of Slavery in the United States from Interviews with Former Slaves, Illustrated with Photographs.** San Antonio: Historic Publishing, 2017.

Howell, Kenneth W. **Still the Arena of Civil War: Violence and Turmoil in Reconstruction Texas, 1865–1874.** Denton: University of North Texas Press, 2012.

Jacobs, Harriet. **Incidents in the Life of a Slave Girl: Written by Herself.** Edited by Marie Child. Cambridge, Mass.: Harvard University Press, 2000. First published in 1861.

Katz, William Loren. **The Black West: A Documentary and Pictorial History of the African American Role in the Westward Expansion of the United States.** New York: Broadway, 2005.

Minges, Patrick, editor. **Black Indian Slave Narratives.** Real Voices, Real History. Winston-Salem, N.C.: Blair, 2004.

Mitchell, Joe, and Federal Writers' Project. **Former Female Slave Narratives & Interviews: From Ex-Slaves in the States of Arkansas, Florida, Louisiana, Tennessee, Texas, and Virginia.** San Antonio: Historic Publishing, 2017.

Northup, Solomon. **Twelve Years a Slave.** New York: Penguin, 2016. First published in 1853.

Smallwood, James M., Barry A. Crouch, and Larry Peacock. **Murder and Mayhem: The War of Reconstruction in Texas.** Sam Rayburn Series on Rural Life. College Station: Texas A&M University Press, 2003

Sullivan, Jerry M. **Fort McKavett: A Texas Frontier Post.** Learn About Texas. Austin: Texas Parks and Wildlife Department, 1993.

Washington, Booker T. **Up from Slavery.** Edited by William L. Andrews. Oxford: Oxford University Press, 1995. First published in 1901.

Williams, Heather Andrea. **Help Me to Find My People: The African American Search for Family Lost in Slavery.** The John Hope Franklin Series in African American History and Culture. Chapel Hill: University of North Carolina Press, 2012.

## ABOUT THE AUTHOR

Lisa Wingate is the author of the #1 **New York Times** bestseller **Before We Were Yours.** She is the author of over thirty novels and a nonfiction book, **Before and After,** co-authored with Judy Christie. Her award-winning works have been selected for state and community One Book reads throughout the country, have been published in more than forty languages, and have appeared on bestseller lists worldwide. The group Americans for More Civility, a kindness watchdog organization, selected Wingate and six others as recipients of the National Civics Award, which celebrates public figures who work to promote greater kindness and civility in American life. She lives with her husband in North Texas. More information about her novels can be found at lisawingate.com, where you can also sign up for her e-newsletter and follow her on social media.

Facebook.com/LisaWingateAuthorPage
Twitter: @LisaWingate
Instagram: @author_lisa_wingate